"So, I DON'T HAVE A DEMON and the Accuser is after me. Does that mean something? Am I, like, the chosen one?"

"Oh, absolutely. When you were born the angels sang. You humans are obsessed with that concept. You haven't been chosen for anything, Megan. You're simply an anomaly and we're still trying to resolve it without any problems. We're not sending you off to Mordor just yet."

"You read *Lord of the Rings*?"

"All demons read *Lord of the Rings*. It's the perfect example of what not to do. Armies of mutant bad guys, shrieking entities on bloodied horses . . . Sauron could have done much better for himself if he'd spent more time persuading and letting nature take its course, less time posturing and trying to look scary."

"Is that what you do?" She knew he was trying to change the subject, but couldn't resist.

"Of course. It's all about leading people down the path to darkness while making them think it's their own idea." He checked his watch. "We should go."

She let him help her up and watched while he extinguished the fire. "Thanks," she said. "For helping me shield, and bringing me here. It was . . . thanks."

"Always happy to help."

"My hero."

His fingertips brushed her cheek, so softly she would have doubted the touch if she hadn't seen his hand move. "I'm not interested in being a hero," he said.

PERSONAL DEMONS

Stacia Kane

JUNO

All poetry quoted in *Personal Demons* is in the public domain:

"When thou sigh'st, thou sigh'st not wind,
But sigh'st my soul away."
—"Song" by John Donne (1633).

"For Godsake hold thy tongue, and let me love."
—"The Canonization" by John Donne (1633).

"She is neither white nor brown, but as the heavens fair; There
is none hath her form divine In the earth or in the air."
—"As Ye Came From the Holy Land" by Anonymous, [(16th
Century) sometimes attributed to Sir Walter Raleigh].

". . . the liquefaction of her clothes . . ."
—"Upon Julia's Clothes" by Robert Herrick (1648).

To my family.

Chapter One

"Welcome back to *Personal Demons*," Megan said into the microphone. "Our next caller is Regina. Hi, Regina, how can I slay your personal demons?"

The words tasted like shame. She and Richard had fought over that line, just as they'd fought over the massive publicity campaign he and the station had orchestrated for the show.

Richard signed the paychecks, so Richard won. Never let it be said that good taste and actually helping people outweighed silly gimmicks in the media world.

"Regina? Are you there?"

"I'm scared." The rush of images accompanying the small, almost childish, voice raised goosebumps on Megan's skin and drove all thoughts of Richard and tacky taglines from her mind. *The pale, pointed face of a woman, limp blond hair tucked behind her ears. Blood poured over the vision, red and viscous. Gnarled six-toed feet stepped in the blood leaving strange misshapen impressions that fissured the vision like a shattering mirror.*

Megan gasped, rocking back in her chair. What the hell was that? She instinctively raised her psychic shields, only to immediately drop them. Regina was her patient now, just like any other. She deserved everything Megan could give to help her.

Bill and Richard gestured at her from the booth, their faces reddening. Dead air was a mortal sin in radio and both her engineer and her boss looked ready to inflict eternal punishment.

"Sorry, sorry. We had a minor technical problem. You said you're scared?"

"Yes." Regina sniffled. "I can't do it anymore. I can't take it anymore."

Now that the initial terrifying flash had passed, Megan received more mundane pictures. A car, a bland pale green office cubicle looking like every other bland pale green office cubicle. An attractive man, smiling down at her—at Regina. A boyfriend, maybe?

Megan forced her muscles to relax. "Why don't you tell me what's happening."

"It's the voices. They talk to me all the time. When I'm awake, when I'm asleep . . . I hear them."

"Voices?"

"Evil voices. They tell me to . . . to hurt myself. To hurt other people. And I don't do it, but I think I might. I have to make them stop."

"Have you spoken to anyone—"

Regina's sobs shuddered through the phone line, cutting off the question. "They won't go away, they won't leave me alone, and they say horrible things, and they want me to do horrible things, and I think if I were dead I wouldn't hear them anymore. I don't want to die, but I can't listen to them anymore either!"

To Megan, Regina didn't feel organically disturbed, but mentally sound people did not hear voices. And none of this accounted for that scaly, misshapen foot she'd seen or the cold panic it inspired.

"Regina, suicide is never the answer. Listen to me. You can be helped. We can find out why this is happening to you, and we can make those voices go away. Okay? You can be happy again. You're a good person and you deserve to be happy."

"I don't know if I deserve happiness. I don't think I do. They told me I'm not . . . they told me they're with me because I'm bad."

"You're not bad." Megan sat up straighter in her chair and leaned forward, staring at the microphone as if Regina could somehow see her through it. "Not at all. Your friends, your family, the people you work with don't think you're bad, do they?" The face of the man in the office flashed again. "Is there anyone you can trust, who you can talk to?"

Regina blew her nose—not, most decidedly, a pleasant on-air sound—then squeaked, "Maybe."

"Then here's what I want you to do. I want you to think of those people, okay? Think about them, and think about your parents, and all the people who care about you. When you hear those voices telling you to hurt yourself, you think about them. My engineer, Bill, is going to give you a different phone number to call. The people who answer are going to help you, too. You don't have to be scared anymore."

"Thank you," Regina said.

"Good," Megan replied, relieved. "Our time is up for this evening, but I want you to call me back next week and tell me how you're doing, Regina. Will you do that?"

"Yes. I'll call you. Thank you. Thank you so much."

"You're welcome. You take care of yourself and call me next week." Megan signaled Bill to transfer Regina back. He already had the list in his hands, ready to give her the suicide hotline number. At least Regina had genuinely wanted help, unlike most of Megan's other inaugural show callers. Three lonely hearts, one rebellious teen, a man who thought Elvis lived next door, and one pervert had not made for a stellar beginning.

Thirty seconds to the blessed moment Megan could go home and not come back for another week. "There is always a reason to live, no matter how you might feel right now. There are always people who care about you, people willing to listen and try to help you. If you think you don't have anyone, you're wrong, because you can call me, here on this show. I care and I'll listen. We're out of time for tonight, but I'll be back next week."

Once more the music filled the studio. Bill gave her the thumbs up, but Richard leaned over him and pushed a button. "That was great." Megan smiled, but he continued, "But you didn't use the phrase. Don't ever go to break or end the show without using the phrase. It's the most important thing you'll do on the air."

HE CONTINUED HARPING about it all the way through the almost-empty station and into the parking garage. "Your show is a vehicle for advertisers, Megan. You understand that, right?" He didn't even glance at her, which was probably a good thing as she was having difficulty keeping her face blank. "You must identify the show and the station. You must use your tagline. We put a lot of thought into—"

"I understand." Opening herself to so many people, so many problems, over the course of two hours drained her more than she had expected. All she wanted to do was go home, have a glass of wine and a snack, and take a long, hot bath. None of which she could do until she escaped Richard and his evidently unending lecture.

"I'm still new at this, Richard, but I realize the audience needs to be reminded of brand identity, especially when they may have been distracted by something as insignificant as suicide. It won't happen again."

"I hope not," he said, completely missing the sarcasm. In Richard's world, everyone was a consumer. The only help they needed was to be steered toward the right brands.

They walked through the parking garage, their heels echoing on the gritty concrete. Megan shivered. She hated parking garages, with their stale, oil-smelling air. A minor phobia, but one that still bothered her. Even Richard's echoing monologue seemed preferable to silence here.

"I have an interview set up for you," he said. She'd been wrong. It was better when he didn't speak. "Tomorrow evening, a dinner. Seven at Café Neus. It's a reporter for *Hot Spot*."

For what felt like the millionth time in the last few weeks, she cursed her decision to take the show. The only reason she accepted was because Richard would have hired Don Tremblay—the male Nurse Ratched of local counselors—if she'd turned it down. Now she wondered if it mattered. Would any of her callers have minded? Maybe the heavy breather; calling a guy might not be fulfill his particular "needs" . . . and Regina.

"Richard, I don't want to be in that tabloid."

"You say 'tabloid', we at the station say 'invaluable source'. Do you have any idea how many subscribers they have?"

They reached Megan's car, sitting all by itself under one dim fluorescent light. "No, but I bet you're going to tell me."

"Over fifty thousand. Fifty thousand subscribers, and that doesn't include off-the-shelf readers or people in waiting rooms. They're a big deal, and they want to do a big story."

"One interview isn't a big story. I don't think *GQ* or *Vogue* do just one brief dinner interview and turn it into—oh, no." Clutching her purse in front of her like a shield, she said, "You didn't sign me up for that 'Week in the Life' thing, did you?"

"It's good publicity. Besides, they'll plug the Femmel Foundation by writing about the charity ball. You do want to do your part for charity, don't you?"

"It's an imposition."

"It's your job."

Megan glared at him. "Fine."

Richard waited while she got into the car and settled into the driver's seat. Just before he closed the door for her, he said, "Wear something sexy. They might take pictures, too."

By the time she thought of a nasty enough reply, he was too far away to hear it.

SOMEONE WAITED ON HER PORCH.

Megan froze in the middle of the walkway, her fast-food bag still clutched in her hand, and lowered her shields. Better to have some idea what was in store. Her free hand twisted the little cap on her pepper spray keychain. If he planned to slit her throat and run, at least she'd have a fighting chance.

Nothing.

She opened the shields more. Surely something would come through. She almost always managed to get some glimpse of the other person's character or motives.

Still nothing. Perhaps she was more drained than she thought.

The figure in the shadows moved. "Hello, Dr. Chase." A man's voice, smooth as glass against silk. "I enjoyed your show very much."

Megan took a cautious step forward. This was her home. It was just past 9:30 P.M. on a bright September night, and she would stand her ground.

"Thank you," she said. "And who are you, please?"

The man stepped off her porch. Moonlight made the sharp, aristocratic bones of his face stand out like bas-relief under a shock of thick dark hair. He was tall—of course, to someone as short as Megan most people were tall, but she thought he was a few inches over six feet. She'd remember that if the police asked her about it in the emergency room later.

He could send her there without breaking a sweat, too. Broad shoulders encased in a suit even she could tell was tailor-made hinted at a muscular body. He looked like a successful businessman.

Successful businessmen could be rapists too.

"My name is Greyson Dante," he said, reaching into the interior pocket of his suit coat and pulling out a card so white it glowed. He held it out to her. She didn't step forward.

"And what are you doing here?"

He lowered his hand to his side without a trace of embarrassment. Was he a lawyer? She'd never met anyone who enjoyed being rebuffed as much as attorneys seemed to. "I came to speak to you about your show. I have a client who is very interested in your concept."

"If it's about the show, your client should call the station."

"It's not an offer for the station. It's for you, personally."

She sighed. "Then he or she should call me at my office, not send a lawyer to lie in wait at my home."

"Did I say I was a lawyer?"

"No."

He waited for her to continue, smiling when she remained silent. The more she looked at his face the more she wanted to look, and she couldn't imagine she was alone among women in that reaction.

And she bet he knew it. She concentrated very hard on seeming unimpressed.

"Listen, Mr . . . ?"

"Dante." His voice was a perfect blank. It wasn't just a bland accent, it was accentless, as if he'd spent years removing any identifying trace from his speech.

"Yes. This is all very pleasant, but it's late and I'm hungry and tired. You can leave a message at my office tomorrow if there's something you need to discuss. I may even have time to call you back."

He kept smiling. Megan reached out to him with her mind. Maybe he simply wasn't much of a transmitter. Some people weren't. If she could have a little feel-around inside his head, though, she might get a better idea of what he wanted.

It was no use. Not only could she not get into his head, but the grin on his face made her think he knew—or at least suspected—what she was doing. Which wasn't possible. Was it?

"Dr. Chase." She could almost see him switch gears from "slick and sophisticated" to "your good friend who wants to help you" mode. "I don't think I'm making myself very clear. My client wants only to aid you and possibly come to a mutually beneficial arrangement. If you would just give me ten minutes of your time, I could explain—"

"I'm sorry, but I have a lot to do this evening. I don't have time to sit here and talk."

"We're standing."

"I don't have time to sit or stand with you." She crossed her arms over her chest. The paper bag full of fries flopped against her stomach.

He studied her for a minute, his head tilted to one side. "I'll be in touch," he said. "Meanwhile, I'd appreciate it if you could do me a favor."

"You want me to do you a favor?"

He nodded.

"What?"

"Don't accept any new offers until you've heard what my client has to say."

"Fine." What difference did it make? Wasn't as if any offers of any kind were likely to come her way soon. Besides, if listening would get him to leave, then she'd listen.

"Thank you." He turned to go, then stopped and held out his hand. "My card."

He didn't move as she took it from him. The heavy, thick card stock whispered against her skin as her finger slipped over the raised lettering.

Megan watched him go, crossing the street and stopping next to a sleek black Jaguar, which unlocked with a discreet click. "Oh, and Dr. Chase?"

"Yes?"

He opened his mouth, closed it, then opened it again. Megan was ready to give up and go inside when he finally spoke.

"Be careful."

Chapter Two

"Kevin?"

The man sitting on the tan leather couch looked up. "Dr. Chase?"

She nodded and extended her hand. "Call me Megan."

Kevin was a pleasant-looking man, with light brown hair cut short and a round, innocent face. Average height, average build, just one of the many people one sees on the streets every day and doesn't remember two minutes later.

So Megan didn't understand why she started feeling sick as soon as her skin touched his.

"Thanks for seeing me on such short notice, Dr. Chase—I mean, Megan." Kevin let go of her hand. Megan gasped as the nausea eased off. It didn't disappear, it stayed lurking in her stomach and making her mouth water, but it did ease. "I just . . . . I had to talk to someone."

Megan swallowed and forced a smile. "That's why I'm here. What would you like to talk about?" She made her way to her chair and sat down harder than she planned.

Kevin had quite a few troubles to talk about. He was lonely, he was depressed, he had low self-esteem and worked in a dead-end job at a bank. Kevin was afraid of heights and small spaces, snakes and spiders and bugs.

In all, Kevin was basically just like everyone else whose life hadn't turned out exactly as they'd hoped or expected it would.

Megan tried not to let her mind wander, but she couldn't seem to focus. Her memory of Regina's pale face and the deformed feet and the twisting tension in her stomach when Kevin touched her hand all pointed to a problem she'd never faced before, not like this.

Anyone with psychic abilities dealt with their share of what Megan called "the shivers." Some people just didn't "feel" right. Maybe they liked kicking puppies, or swindling old ladies, or occasionally something even more violent and horrible. She'd met such people, of course. But Kevin made her feel like she was the problem, as if whatever threat existed came from deep inside herself.

"How long did you attend—" she checked the file and forced herself not to roll her eyes—"Fearbusters?"

"Six months," Kevin said. "And it's a good program and everything, but lately . . . I'd rather see how I do on my own, you know?"

"Of course." She glanced at the clock. Twenty minutes left in this session. "Is there something in particular you'd like to focus on today in the time we have left?"

"I had a nightmare last night," he said. "A bad one." For the first time she noticed something other than sadness and loneliness in his eyes. Fear lurked in the depths like a wasp in a flower bouquet.

"Tell me about it."

Kevin lay back on the soft leather couch, resting his head on the armrest, and closed his eyes. He smiled faintly, clearly enjoying this part of the session. It was a relief to talk to someone who listened.

Megan tensed. At this point in a session she started tuning in, seeing what the patient saw, noticing what they mentioned or omitted and asking careful questions to find out why.

She had to steel her nerves to do it for Kevin.

She saw the room he walked across as he described it to her, and sighed with relief. No nausea, no fear.

The cavernous room seemed to stretch into nothingness, with a ceiling so high only the fuzzy variations of color let her know something decorated it. The walls weren't walls at all, but cupboards, with hundreds of doors in them, each two or three feet tall. It was like being in an enormous library card catalog, but lights came from under the small closed doors.

"Was it an empty room, Kevin? Or was there furniture? Doors to other rooms?"

"There were doors. A lot of doors."

"What's behind them?"

In the dream memory Kevin paused and looked at the thin line of light on the floor. "I don't know. Weapons?"

Megan noted that answer on her pad. "Did you think you needed a weapon, Kevin?"

"I didn't think," he said. "I just tried to get to the end of the room. There was something waiting for me there, something that wanted me to see it."

"What was it?"

"I didn't know. I just knew I needed to get there."

Another note. "What happened when you did?"

At the end of the room another door loomed, larger than the others, with ornate carvings in the dark wood. She felt sweat rolling down her face—Kevin's face. Was there a fire behind the door? Fire was a pretty common fear.

Kevin's voice changed now, growing higher and faint. Whatever hid beyond that door must not be pleasant. She braced herself as he reached for it. His hand closed over the ornate brass knob. Flesh sizzled.

Kevin screamed. Something slammed into Megan with enough force to knock her out of her chair. She cried out, her head hitting the floor with a painful thud. The door still loomed in front of her, even as she saw Kevin jerking and convulsing on the couch, his mouth open, his eyes wide. Desperately Megan tried to put her shields back up, to break her connection with Kevin's dream, but she could not. Something had grabbed hold of her mind and refused to let go.

She tried to cry out for Lucy the receptionist, for anyone, but no sound escaped her constricted throat. She reached up, her fingers scrabbling for what felt like a cord squeezing her neck, but she scratched at empty air.

Kevin fell off the couch, smashing into the glass-top table in the middle of the floor. His body still twisted and writhed, horrible gagging noises coming from his open mouth.

Megan's vision started going black around the edges, black as the dream door that screeched on huge brass hinges . . .

Just before she saw what lurked behind it, the door to her office burst open. Lucy's terrified face was the last thing Megan saw before darkness overtook her.

"I'M FINE." Megan sat up on the bed and swung her legs over the side. "I just want to go home."

"The doctor hasn't released you," the nurse replied, in the weary tones of a woman used to being ignored and treated badly by the people she tried to help.

"Can you call her for me, please? I'm fine." It was a lie. She was not fine, but the hospital couldn't do anything for her.

Twice in two days now she'd had an unusual reaction when tuning in to someone. Three times, if you included her inability to read anything from the lawyer on her doorstep. Was it possible for psychic abilities to suddenly become uncontrollable? Or was it a coincidence, some odd alignment of the planets? Maybe Kevin was epileptic or had an organic brain dysfunction?

She had no way to find out, no one she could ask. In her youth Megan had looked for a mentor, someone else who could do what she did. Once she'd realized her parents couldn't help, she'd tried making appointments with Tarot readers and psychics. None of them were able to do anything for her, with the exception of the Tarot reader who'd advised her to let go of her anger. Megan liked her anger and ignored the advice.

Through trial and error, not to mention desperation, she'd found a way to shield herself, but she'd never advanced beyond that.

The nurse looked her up and down. "Are you the kind of person who ignores doctor's orders?"

Megan smiled. "No. I'm not an idiot."

"You don't look like an idiot," the nurse said, returning the smile. "I'll get her." She turned and headed for the busy nurse's station in the middle of the Emergency Care area, her jogging shoes making little squeaks on the polished tile floor. Megan bit her fingernails and waited.

"You know, we have a snack machine," the doctor said, entering Megan's little curtained cubicle. "In case those nails don't fill you up."

Megan blushed. "Nervous habit. Oral fixation."

"Mmm-hmm. You're a counselor, right? PhD?" The doctor—Janet Hunter, according to her ID badge—cocked an eyebrow and grinned.

"Physician, heal thyself?"

"Something like that. I suppose it could be worse. You could smoke."

"No smoking. Just clean, non-lethal nasty habits."

"Great. Lisa tells me you're feeling fine, and I don't see any reason to keep you here, but try to take it easy for the next few days, okay? And call your regular doctor if you have any dizziness or pain that can't be treated with a couple of Tylenol."

Megan nodded.

"Dr. Chase?"

A man in a plaid shirt and a pair of brown corduroy jeans that had seen better days stood in the entryway to Megan's room. Large glasses dominated his smiling face. "I'm sorry to interrupt," he said. "I wanted to catch you before they discharge you."

"I'm done with her, Art. Signing her discharge now, you're just in time."

"Excellent." The man stepped further into the room while Megan thanked Dr. Hunter. "I'm Arthur Bellingham." He held out his hand. Megan shook it. It was warm and limp. "I'm head of the Fearbusters program here at the hospital."

"Right," Megan looked at him with new interest. "Kevin's therapist."

"Yes, Kevin's therapist." Something about the way he said it made Megan itch to tune into him, but she refrained. She wasn't about to take a chance of something else going wrong when she was so close to freedom from the hospital. "That's why I wanted to talk to you. What happened to Kevin?"

"It looked like a seizure, but you'd have to ask Dr. Hunter if it was."

"I will," Bellingham replied. "I'm glad neither of you were seriously injured."

"Me too." What did he want? He was clearly building up to something, and Megan wished he would just come out with it so she could leave.

"I suppose things could have gone very badly if your receptionist hadn't come and found you."

How did he know that? Had he been peeking at her triage forms? Not worth arguing about. It wasn't like there was any information there he couldn't get elsewhere anyway. "I suppose," she said. "I'd rather not think about it."

"Oh, come now, Dr. Chase. We're psychologists. It's our job to face fear."

"It's our job to help our patients face their fears."

"You say potato. Actually, it's just that kind of thing I was hoping to discuss with you. Fears, I mean, not potatoes!" He chuckled at his own joke.

Megan smiled with her mouth closed. "What about them?"

"Well." He thrust his hands into his pockets and leaned against the EKG monitor, only to stumble and nearly fall when the monitor on its wheeled cart rolled away. Megan tightened her lips to keep from laughing as he pulled it back into place. He looked back at her, with the guilty expression of a child who expected to be beaten for his clumsiness.

"Stupid wheels," Megan said. "Whose idea were they, anyway?"

He gave a nervous little giggle. "Yes. Right. Anyway, I wanted to talk to you about Fearbusters."

"The program Kevin was in?"

"The program Kevin *is* in. He hasn't officially left."

"Most therapy clients don't officially leave, do they, Mr. Bellingham? I mean, there's no graduation ceremony for feeling better. They just stop making appointments."

Bellingham shrugged, but the lines of his face tensed. "Fearbusters is . . . different. Special. We do have a ceremony of sorts, and our clients sign up for a set period of time. If they feel better before that time is up, they help mentor those who aren't as strong yet. It's a wonderful program."

It may be wonderful, but it also sounded unethical. "And they pay for the sessions where they're acting as mentors?"

He nodded. "We reduce the fee, but our theory—and our clients agree—is that they're still learning new coping mechanisms while helping others to cope. Often they decide to stay, even after they've had their Leaving Ceremony."

"I see."

He narrowed his eyes. "If they really want to leave, they can. They just have to tell us. But in the two years we've been running the program, only one person has."

"Impressive."

"Thank you. Let me cut to the chase, Dr. Chase." He smiled. Megan smiled back, just as if she hadn't heard that joke a million times. "I'd love to have you on board. I heard you on the radio last night, dealing with the woman who heard voices. You were great. Most of our clients have issues like hers, hence our name. I think you'd be a great asset to our team."

Was there a person in the city who hadn't been listening? In her worst nightmares she'd never imagined Richard's stupid publicity campaign being this effective.

"I'm flattered," she began. "But with my own practice and the show, I'm working six days a week. I just don't see how I can fit it in."

"Maybe you could come down one evening and sit in on a session? We meet here at seven every weeknight, Conference Room B in the Outpatient Center. We'd love to have you."

"I'll try."

Bellingham brightened. "Great. Here's my card." The card was much flimsier than the one her mysterious visitor had presented her last night. "Please call me anytime if you have the chance to come in."

"I will." Megan hopped off the bed and landed with a thud on her feet. The bed was a little higher than she'd thought. She grabbed her purse. "It was nice meeting you, Mr. Bellingham."

"Call me Art." He gave her another limp handshake. It was like holding hands with an uncooked chicken cutlet. Megan suppressed a shudder. "Megan," she said.

"Megan, then. I hope you'll call."

She waited until he was gone to wipe her hand on her skirt.

Chapter Three

Café Neus was part of the "new millennium" rebuilding project the city counselors had gone into paroxysms of glee over a few years back. Megan hated it. All the old buildings that used to give downtown character were gone, replaced by gleaming storefronts and chi-chi restaurants that looked like a strong wind would blow them over.

But she had to admit, it certainly had made the area more popular. Megan hunted for fifteen minutes before finding a place to park her little Focus, seven blocks from her destination. By the time she entered the cool, leafy interior of the restaurant she was grumpy, her feet hurt, and she wished she could go back in time and slap herself for agreeing to do the stupid radio show at all.

Don Tremblay wasn't so bad, was he? So what if he loathed Megan as much as she disliked him, especially after she'd lost her temper a year before at a conference they'd both attended and told him she'd recommend Hannibal Lecter as a therapist before she'd recommend him? So what if he'd told at least one client to grow up and stop whining so much, then charged the client double for the session saying it was because he hated her? Could she herself honestly say she'd never been tempted to do the same? It was hypocritical of her to judge poor Don, who'd

been a therapist for years, poor Don whose wife had left
him three years ago, poor Don, who was . . . heading right
for her.

"Megan." He smiled his artificial smile and grabbed
her hand in both of his. She focused all her energy into
her shields as he trapped her between the fake bamboo
hostess stand and his pudgy body and forced his wet lips
to her cheek. "It's nice to see you. I heard your show.
What a sweet little effort."

"Sweet little effort?"

"Of course." He clasped his hands together in front of
his chest and grinned at her. The effect was not what she
thought he intended. He looked like a mad scientist about
to cut up some dead bodies and make amusing shapes
with their cold innards. "When Richard Randall told
me you'd agreed to do it, I thought you were both a little
crazy, but after listening . . ." He picked up her hand again
and kissed it. "*Magnifique*. A word of warning, though.
There are some in our illustrious profession who may not
take kindly to your sudden fame."

Like you, she thought, but did not say. Tremblay's eyes
were cold and watchful, and he was not afraid to make a
scene. She didn't want to make things worse, especially
when there was a reporter somewhere in the room ready
to write about her. FAME-HUNGRY COUNSELOR STABBED
BACKS FOR RADIO SHOW was not a headline she cared to
read. At least, not on a story about herself.

"Thanks for the warning. I'll keep that in mind."

"I'm always happy to help a young lady unschooled
in making the right impressions." Good old Don, always
ready to patronize. "In fact, seeing as how you're dining
alone again, perhaps you'd care to join me and my
friends?"

"I'm sorry, I can't. I'm meeting someone."

"Blind date? It's hard for a girl like you to meet people these days, isn't it?"

Some people made her want to gouge out their eyes with a grapefruit spoon. Don was one of them. With effort, she refrained. "Yes, my enormous sexual appetite tends to scare men away. Now if you'll excuse me, I need to find my dinner date."

She left him standing next to the gaping hostess.

"Here's how it works." Brian Stone, reporter for *Hot Spot,* rummaged around in his large backpack and set a mini-recorder on the table between them. His eyes sparkled. Megan envied his enjoyment of his job. "I ask questions, you answer. It's simple, but the tricky part is not sounding self-conscious. I want this to be a good article. I'm not planning a hatchet job, don't worry. If we do it right, it turns into a conversation and we both forget the recorder. We're going to be together all week, so it's best if we get the uncomfortable part out of the way fast, okay, Dr. Chase?"

He had an easy, quick way of talking as he gave this little speech. His light brown hair was short and tidy, his smile wide and welcoming. Everything about him was designed to be reassuring and encourage confidences. Megan refused to be won over.

"I'll certainly give it a try."

"But you don't want to."

"What?"

"You don't want to be interviewed, I can tell. It's okay. I mean . . . it's not okay, because it makes my job harder . . . but I understand you feeling that way. A lot of people do."

"But you push them anyway."

"Don't you?" His blue eyes looked directly into hers, pinning her to her chair. She looked away.

"I don't think of it that way. They pay me to ask questions, to find out what's at the heart of their problems. Sometimes to do that you have to force people to confront things they'd rather not face."

"Is that your theory, then? That your job is forcing your patients to look into all the nasty corners of their minds?"

"They are not necessarily 'nasty corners' and I don't 'force' anyone, Mr. Stone. Nor do I think confronting the truth in order to deal with problems is theory. It's the truth. If you go to the doctor with pains in your stomach, but refuse to allow an examination, you've wasted a trip to the doctor. Same with a counselor."

She hadn't expected the interview to be fun, but she hadn't expected to react with gut-clenching rage, either. Her Coke sat on the table next to her as yet untouched salad. She wished she'd ordered something stronger.

"It's not the same, though, is it? What you don't tell a real doctor can kill you. What you—"

"Hold it right there, Mr. Stone. I may not be a medical doctor, but I earned a doctorate in Counseling Psychology. I'm a highly qualified, licensed counselor, I'm not doing this as a lark."

"I know."

"Furthermore, I—what? What do you mean, you know?"

Stone smiled. "Of course I know your qualifications. You have an excellent reputation, and it's certainly not everyone who can earn a Master's and a Doctorate in eight years. But I've gotten you to loosen up a bit. You're ready to talk now, right? More than you were earlier? And to call me Brian?"

"The only thing I'm ready to do now is dump my salad on your head."

"Please don't. It takes forever to get the dressing out."

In spite of herself, she laughed. "Okay, Brian. I admit I'm not as nervous as I was. That doesn't mean I approve of your methods."

"I can only do my best," he said, taking a bite of his own salad. "You should eat."

"Desperate to take a photo of me with spinach in my teeth?"

"No, but I will if you aren't nice to me."

Megan smiled in acknowledgment and took a sip of her Coke, scanning the restaurant over the top of her glass. Her gaze stopped on two tables at the back. At one sat Don Tremblay with Jeff Howard—one of the partners in her co-practice who'd been vocally opposed to her joining—and a woman she didn't recognize. So Tremblay was friendly with Howard. She'd never known that, but it certainly made sense.

The other table was more worrisome. As the giggling waitress stepped away from it, Greyson Dante held up his wineglass in her direction. She ignored him.

"So," Brian said, after thanking the waitress for his entree, "I'd like to be in your office by ten every morning. That way our photographer can get some good shots, and I can interview some of your patients."

"You can't interview my patients. They have a right to confidentiality."

Brian shrugged. "Some of them will probably want to keep that privacy intact but still speak anonymously. But I'm sure a few of them would love to have their picture in our magazine, so everyone knows they get to see Dr. Demon Slayer on a regular basis."

Megan almost choked on her steak. "The who?"

"The demon slayer. That's what the station specified we were to call you. Part of the theme of the show."

"Oh, god." Megan buried her face in her hands. The dull throbbing ache in her head promised to get worse as this hell continued.

"I was thinking we could get a picture of you holding a pitchfork or something. Maybe a big wooden cross? Sound good?"

She stared at him. He lifted his hands and leaned back in his seat, as if he was afraid she might start spitting on him. "Hey, only joking."

"Very funny."

"Oh, I do love jokes." Greyson Dante stood by her side.

"Hello, Mr. Dante. I'm afraid this is a private conversation, so you will, of course, be going now."

His grin widened. Was there no way to insult the man? "Why, Dr. Chase, if I didn't know better I'd think you didn't want to see me."

"What makes you think you know better?"

"I always do."

Brian looked from one of them to the other. "Don't you want to introduce me to your friend, Megan?"

Dante still stood there smiling, his wineglass in one hand, looking like Cary Grant on a luxurious cruise. She hadn't been wrong in her first moonlight impression; he really was handsome, with dark hair and eyes and smooth, lightly tanned skin. She'd always liked dark-haired men, probably to contrast with her own blond paleness. Megan often thought she looked like a ghost. A dark man seemed to anchor her to earth, somehow, or perhaps it was just her obsessive childhood crush on Burt Reynolds.

Before she could disavow friendship with Dante and say *no*, Mr. Tall Dark Handsome and Annoying was shaking hands with the reporter.

"Dante. Greyson Dante."

Brian smiled. "Mr. Dante, then. Sit down. I'd love to talk to some of Megan's friends. Get some more personal information, you know?"

"I'd be glad to share what I know." Greyson grabbed an empty chair from a nearby table—without asking the table's occupants, Megan noticed—and pulled it to theirs.

"Which isn't much," she said under her breath.

Brian glanced at her. "What?"

Dante grinned. Megan wanted to stab him in the hand with her fork. Of course he was grinning. She couldn't say anything to him. She couldn't yell, or claim he was a crazy stranger, or be nasty to him. Brian was a reporter, a man with the power to make or break her reputation. Radio Counselor Can't Remember Names of Casual One-Night Stands . . . Power-Mad Radio Host Turns Her Back On Friends Now That She's a Success . . . Fame Drives Radio Counselor Insane . . .

"And how do you two know each other?" Brian was either trying to figure out what was wrong between them or, innocently unaware, was just trying to make conversation. Megan hoped it was the latter. She opened her mouth to speak, but Greyson got there first.

"I'm a counselor, too. From out of state. We met at a conference last year."

Megan would have bet her car that the closest Greyson ever came to counseling was recommending it for his clients in the hopes they would get larger damages in court.

If he was a lawyer. Which she had to admit she wasn't certain about. It was just a feeling she had, but without being able to read him she couldn't be sure.

"Our methods are very different," Megan started, but Dante cut her off.

"But we both love helping people. I think 'help' is Dr. Chase's favorite word."

"And what's yours? 'Malpractice'?"

"Oh, no." He folded his hands on the table and leaned forward. "*Sin* is my favorite word, Dr. Chase. Sin."

His eyes caught hers, held. She leaned forward before she realized she was doing it, and sat back so quickly she knocked her knife onto the floor.

Dante tsked and picked it up, nodding to his pet waitress, who leapt to their table as if they were the only customers in the restaurant. Megan calmed herself and started studying the room, trying to avoid even looking at him.

Perhaps it was fallout from earlier, but the steak that had looked appetizing now made her throat close, and she made no move to use her new knife. She thought if someone made a loud noise she would jump right out of her skin, and it wasn't just the tension of the last day or so catching up with her.

The men continued chatting, unaware of her lapse into silence. "Oh, Megan is highly respected," Dante said. "She's a real counselor's counselor."

A *counselor's counselor*? Where was he getting that shit?

Trying to soothe her churning stomach, Megan reached for her Coke and took a long swallow.

Something hovered in the air over the right shoulder of the woman at the next table.

The shadowy form lacked definition but as Megan watched she caught a flash of what looked like dark green before the color disappeared. The shadow stayed, rippling at the edges but hovering in place.

The woman didn't notice, but Megan stared transfixed. Blurry edges of darkness reached out and passed over the woman's face, then slipped back into the semi-solid mass.

The image made her gorge rise, but she kept staring, unable to move or blink. If she looked away, would it disappear? Or would it move, leaping to one of the other diners, as if trying to gain entry to someone's body? It felt so wrong, so . . . evil. Her skin prickled and itched.

While the woman laughed and ate her food, the blurry form twisted and darted around, staying in the same space but writhing as if trying to burst through some kind of membrane.

Megan's stomach gave up the battle. She leapt from her chair, knocking it over in the process, and ran for the ladies' room. She barely made it in time.

"I'LL WALK YOU to your car, if you won't let me call a cab." Dante faked concern pretty well.

"I'd rather walk." She was tempted to tell him she didn't need his company, but it was after dark in the city and she wasn't stupid. Why walk alone when she could have a man she trusted—okay, a man she was fairly certain wouldn't attack her—to walk with her?

"What exactly do you want, Mr. Dante?"

"Call me Grey." His footsteps fell in time with hers as they passed groups of revelers still out, most of whom looked like professional partiers. Megan, with her pallid face and businesslike suit, felt out of place, a grandma trying to hang out with teenagers. Which was ridiculous. At thirty-one she was still in the age range the stores and clubs catered to, but she didn't think she could ever go to them. It simply wasn't her scene, aside from how difficult it was to keep her shields tightly closed after spending hours in a hot room and having a few drinks.

"Megan?"

"What?"

"What happened back there in the restaurant?"

"What do you mean?"

"Before you ran off, you were staring at a woman behind me. I got the feeling something about her disturbed you."

Megan forced herself not to gag. She didn't even want to think about what she'd seen, that squirming mass, the sense of malevolence radiating from it. She certainly wouldn't discuss it with Greyson.

"I wasn't feeling well, that's all. I've been feeling off all day."

"Before you went to the hospital?"

"Yes, I—" She stopped short and swung to face him. "How the hell do you know that? Are you following me? Who the hell are you, anyway?"

Greyson raised his hands and stepped back. "Hey, hold on. It's not necessarily—"

"Don't tell me what it necessarily is or isn't. You tell me how you know all this about me. Who are you, Mr. Dante, and what do you want from me?"

If she'd hoped to disarm him, it didn't work. His face went carefully blank and he put his hands back in his pockets. "I just want you to listen to my—client's offer. That's all."

"Why are you following me? And you're either a moron, or you've been going out of your way to let me know you're following me. Why? What are you up to?"

"I want to help you."

"Help me what?"

"Sudden fame can be very difficult. You could attract some . . . unwanted elements."

"Stop lying to me!"

"I'm not lying. Stalkers—"

"Stalkers? Like, for example, *you*?"

"I'm not a stalker."

"Oh? Let's see. What does a stalker do? Follows someone around, tries to insinuate his or her way into the target's life, maybe drops some vague hints and threats along the way? Sound familiar? Are you going to start telling the press you're my secret husband next?"

His face darkened. "Megan, if you would just listen—"

"Fuck you." She turned and started walking away. "Leave me alone, Mr. Dante," she called over her shoulder. "You might be a lawyer, but that doesn't mean I can't still have you arrested."

"I never said I was a lawyer," he called after her.

Don't take the bait, don't take the bait, don't take the bait . . .

She turned around when she reached the end of the block. He was gone.

A BIG RED BLINKING "2" on her answering machine welcomed her home. Someone wanted to sell her aluminum siding, she guessed, and perhaps the other call would be a hang-up for variety. She'd been getting a few of those lately.

Hearing Brian Stone's voice checking her well-being made her smile. Brian wasn't as bad as she'd thought. At least he didn't wear a fedora with a PRESS card tucked in the band or talk out the side of his mouth or try to bribe people for information about her. At least she assumed he wouldn't.

The second message erased the smile. Kevin Walford's voice quavered out of the machine. "Um, Dr. Chase, I hope it's okay for me to call you at home, I mean, I'm sorry if it bothers you, but I wanted to thank you for earlier? For taking me to the hospital and all? I was hoping you could meet me there tomorrow, well, I was hoping maybe you'd meet me at Fearbusters, and Mr. Art said he'd talked to you about coming there anyway, and we thought maybe you would come down tomorrow because I wanted to thank you in person." He finally took a breath. "So, um, call me if you can, or call Mr. Art, okay? And thank you." He finished by reciting his phone number three times.

"Mr. Art" must be Art Bellingham. Why did that man want her to meet his group so badly? For a second she imagined he wanted her to lend her newfound fame to the program, but she managed to stop herself before the thought fully formed. It was only a little Sunday-night radio show in a mediocre radio market. So why was it suddenly so important for her to get to Fearbusters?

She'd left Bellingham's card on a little bronze tray on a table near the front door with her mail. The cheap paper stock felt slick and flimsy in her fingers, which reminded her of Dante's elegant, obviously expensive card. She fished that one out too.

Two men, each with some hidden agenda, each of whom seemed to want her to do something for them.

Either she was suddenly the most popular girl in town, or something was going on. Tomorrow she'd start finding out exactly what.

Chapter Four

The Outpatient Center was tucked behind the main hospital building and accessed by a tidy little path through landscaped lawns. Even the small, brightly illuminated parking lot had the incredibly clean and even look of a child's playset, the ones with gas stations and helicopter pads right next to each other on a smooth plastic street.

Megan parked and crossed the lot, shivering in the early autumn breeze. They were due for a cold snap, the first of the season, and she wished she'd brought a jacket. As it was she was dressed down, in jeans and a long-sleeved T-shirt, with her favorite tennis shoes. She did not want to look like she was here for professional reasons. Neat, adult, and competent, yes. Ready to join the group and start working with clients, no.

Not that she couldn't use the work. The partners she worked with had certainly made their feelings clear, in a meeting that morning. Megan's show and its attendant publicity damaged their practices. Any further problems and she'd be out. For now, in order to protect their patients from further invasions of privacy, she was to hire her own receptionist and arrange additional soundproofing for the offices. They'd hired a locum to take her patients until she complied. She was officially on leave.

The doors were locked and the receptionist's desk was empty. Megan hit the after-hours buzzer.

"Yes?"

"I'm Megan Chase," she said into the tiny grill of the microphone. "I'm here to see—"

"Megan!" It was Art. "I'm glad you could come."

The lock gave a low hum and a click. Megan opened the door and entered the building.

The spacious lobby smelled like hospital, which was to be expected, but on top of it was a different scent, one that made Megan think of dorm rooms and New Age shops before she realized it was incense. Incense? It wasn't anywhere near as pleasant as the smell of the restaurant where Brian had taken her to dinner earlier. Of course, the fragrance had been one of the only good things about that meal. Brian wasn't a bad guy, but the questions about her background and childhood made her uncomfortable. She'd moved to the city to get away from all of that. Even giving him a carefully censored version hadn't helped. Silently she crossed the tile floor, past the shabby, lonely-looking blue chairs of the waiting area.

"Hi there!" The lone fluorescent fixture in the hallway gave Art Bellingham a pale greenish cast and glinted off his glasses, hiding his eyes. The unnatural light did nothing to improve the multiple hues of Art's cheap tie or the fit of his too-short, too-tight slacks.

"Hi."

"I was hoping you would take me up on my offer," he enthused, pumping her hand.

"I'm not—" she started, but Kevin entered the hall and she broke off.

"Dr. Chase," he said, walking towards her with his hand offered. His eagerness trapped her.

The two men led her into the meeting room. This was the source of the incense—four or five sticks burned in various places. The furniture hugged the walls, leaving a space in the center of the floor which was covered with blue gymnastics mats.

Art followed her gaze. "We sit on the floor, generally. That way if anyone wants to lie down or be held, it's easier."

Megan nodded. "And the chairs?" There were two comfortable-looking armchairs, each placed at opposite ends of the mats.

Art smiled. "One for me and, tonight, one for you."

"I see." Megan didn't like this set-up at all. It wasn't the idea of clients sitting on the floor, it was the idea that, for whatever reason, Art didn't think he should be on the floor with them.

Perhaps her plan to ask Art pointblank what he wanted should be forgotten. She generally tried not to read people unless she felt she might be in some kind of danger, but she opened herself a little bit, feeling for his mind with her own. It never took her long to get what she needed, but she was always cautious.

Sometimes people knew, like she'd suspected Dante had two nights before. They didn't *know*, but they sensed something. Better to be careful. She'd learned that lesson as a child, when she'd gained an unwanted reputation as "the creepy girl" because she hadn't been able to control her abilities.

Art didn't seem to notice. He kept talking, explaining the group's philosophy, but she stopped listening.

Something went through her mind, disappearing before she could make sense of it. It was so cold, so . . . empty. Blackness filled her vision, and for a moment she couldn't breathe. Her stomach lurched. All the while the cold seeped into her, filling her mind, her body.

Megan.

The voice came from everywhere, from inside her head, low-pitched and unctuous. She bit her lip to keep from crying out while Art continued speaking to her, his thin face glowing with pride.

She cut him off with a gasp as the darkness left. The lights brightened as if someone had removed a filter. The feeling of sickness disappeared, leaving her wondering if it had been real, or if she'd imagined it.

"Megan? Are you okay?"

She swallowed a mouthful of saliva and tried to smile. The muscles in her face protested so much she expected an audible creak. "I'm fine," she said. "Just—impressed."

"You haven't heard the best part yet." Art took her hand and led her to a chair. She sat. She didn't have the strength to do what she wanted to do—turn and run away as fast as she could—and, she suspected, even that wouldn't dissuade Art from pursuing her.

Of course, she could be seriously disturbed. Nothing said counselors never had problems. Her powers could be fizzling out. She could be seeing the darkness of her own soul. Certainly that had happened before. That was why she became a counselor to start with—because of what happened when she was fifteen.

It made a more likely explanation than the idea that Art was some evil creature bent on eating her soul. The man couldn't even afford decent slacks.

"What's the best part?" she asked.

"Our clients!" Art said with the same twittering high-pitched laugh she'd heard the day before. He sounded like a little old lady. "They're such a special group of people, and if I'm not mistaken—" the buzzer for the door sounded "—that's them now. Stay here with Kevin, I'll go let them in."

Kevin smiled. "I hope you didn't mind me calling you at home. Mr. Art gave me the number."

She nodded. "I assumed." Assumed he'd taken it from her hospital file, the creep. "It's okay, Kevin."

"I won't do it again," he said, twisting his hands at waist level. "I promise."

"Kevin, don't worry," she said. "How are you feeling?"

"Much better," he said, "now that Mr. Art isn't—" Raised voices sounded in the hallways, a woman's footsteps echoing beneath them.

"Isn't what, Kevin?" Megan leaned forward. "Now that Mr. Art isn't what?"

But Kevin only shook his head. "Never mind. It's not important."

The rest of the Fearbusters group entered the room, moving together but oddly apart. They talked to each other, even smiled, but what Megan felt in the air was disconnection. These people were terribly wrapped up in themselves, huddling into their bodies like threatened mollusks pulling into their shells. They didn't relate to each other at all.

Perhaps she'd judged Art too harshly. Maybe with a group like this the best thing to do was get them together on the floor and try to make them touch each other, pull each other out of themselves.

She'd have to see.

One by one, they introduced themselves, with varying degrees of welcome and suspicion. There was Bob, a glowering giant of a man who must have been at least six and a half feet tall, with thick black hair cut in a military buzz. Hanna gazed at Megan from under long light-brown bangs and through owlish pink glasses. Her entire body was encased in shades of drab, topped with a dress that looked like something a Laura Ingalls Wilder character had discarded.

Joe, chubby and smiling, radiated a nervousness Megan felt even with her shields up. Last was Grant, barely out of his teens, with dyed black hair, a pierced eyebrow, and black-enameled fingernails.

Art closed the door behind them and turned off the overhead lights. Megan hadn't noticed the candles earlier, but they glowed on the windowsills and tables by the walls, giving the room a low, intimate ambience. Some of the clients' tensions eased as they settled themselves onto the mats, but to Megan the whole set-up felt more like a séance than therapy.

"Okay," Art said, clasping his hands and sitting in the chair on the other side of the mats. "You've all introduced yourselves to Dr. Megan Chase." He nodded across their heads indicating Megan. "Megan has her own practice for individual counseling, but she's accepted my offer to come and help us out at Fearbusters."

"I didn't—" Megan started, but stopped. These people were paying for a session. She wouldn't waste their time arguing with Art.

"Now, yesterday we discussed some of the feelings we get before we're afraid, right?" Art's voice lowered. "What we see or hear right before we notice the fear."

The group murmured assent. Kevin's hands were clenched tight.

"Let's talk about that," Art said. "Hanna, what do you see, hear or feel before you notice you're afraid?"

Hanna's voice wavered. "I hear a voice. It whispers in my ear. It tells me something bad is going to happen."

"Doesn't it only *feel* like it's whispering in your ear?"

"No."

"It's just a voice in your head, Hanna."

"No!"

Megan leaned forward, trying to understand why Art was arguing with the poor girl and why she was fighting back. "It's a whisper in my ear. Sometimes I feel its breath."

"I hear them, too," Grant said. "Just like that."

"No, you don't," snapped Joe. Megan had been right about his nerves and dislike of the group. "You say whatever Hanna says, you always do."

"I don't!" Grant said.

"Okay, guys," Art said. "Let's not argue. Let's get back to Hanna. It's her turn. Hanna, what does the voice tell you?"

Megan's discomfort grew as Hanna continued speaking.

"It tells me I'm a terrible person. Or that other people are terrible and I should hurt them. Like the other day at work it told me to erase one of my boss's files when he wasn't looking."

Bob laughed. "That's your own subconscious anger."

"Bob," Art said. He sounded . . . pleased. Like this was what he wanted to hear. "Remember who the therapist is here. You're not a mentor yet."

"I want to hear more from Hanna," Grant said. At least, Megan thought it was Grant. It was difficult to know exactly who was talking. Her eyes didn't seem to be adjusting to the light anymore. In fact, the room seemed to be getting darker, even though she could still see the candles burning.

"That's all," Hanna said. "I'm cursed. I hear the voice, and it's like I have to believe it and do what it says or it won't stop talking. It won't leave me alone."

Chapter Five

Regina's voice echoed in Megan's head. *"They won't go away, they won't go away . . ."*

"Hanna," Megan said, not knowing or caring if she was committing a sin by interrupting the session, "do you hear the voice when other people are around?"

If Hanna was surprised, her voice didn't reflect it. "No. Just when I'm alone. And not here. Never here, in this building."

"That's because you know this is a place of healing," Art said. "Your subconscious voice does not speak to you here because you know this is where you get better."

Megan wished he would shut up. If there was some kind of connection between Regina and what Hanna was experiencing—and what Grant apparently felt too—she might see it if she tuned in to Hanna. This was no time to be afraid. This was her job.

She exhaled and reached out with her mind, finding the shape on the floor that was Hanna and feeling it, touching it. Steeling herself for whatever grisly images might come, she probed inside.

A little house, decorated with old-fashioned furniture, down home ginghams, and country quaintness. Three cats snuggled on the flowered couch next to Megan—next to Hanna—and watched what looked like a Lifetime movie.

Other than that, nothing.

Megan tried harder. Now she saw an office interior. People liked Hanna, although they found her a little dull. She was reliable and friendly. Her boss depended on her. It was all very nice, but there was still no grinning face, no blood, no horrible feet. Nothing she saw made Megan think Hanna and Regina were suffering the same problem.

Then why were their stories so similar? Most people had similar anxieties, but Megan had never heard of two people who didn't read as organically disturbed having the exact same kind of delusions.

She read Grant next. His home life was nowhere near as happy as Hanna's, but just as lonely. Adults—Megan assumed they were his parents—flitted around like moths around a flame, but ignored him. They were there, but they didn't pay attention. His sister smelled of alcohol and laughed when Grant said something about it. The kids at school ignored him, too. It didn't paint a pretty or happy picture, but there was nothing to be scared of in the way Megan had been scared by Regina.

Another voice spoke. Bob. "My voice tells me to burn things."

"Mine tells me to kill people," Joe retorted.

Ah. The group members were playing off each other, trying to one-up each others' illnesses or disturbances. In the hands of a good therapist such things did not happen. Art was not a good therapist. The whole thing distressed and disheartened her.

The conversation continued, but Megan tuned it out. No wonder Kevin had tried to leave. This was dangerous, a mockery of what therapy was supposed to be, and Art Bellingham was enjoying it. She heard it in his voice, the sort of rich happiness that comes from a job well done.

Whatever cheap thrills he got by playing Svengali were going to end, though. Tomorrow she would start making calls to the proper people. This could not be allowed to continue.

The room was almost completely dark. Megan couldn't understand why the candles were no longer providing light or why the temperature seemed to be dropping. The exercise mat whispered softly as the people on it moved, presumably crowding closer together—whether for comfort or warmth she did not know. The energy in the room was changing, becoming more alive. Voices merged together into something like a chant, but Megan couldn't understand what they were saying.

Their energy melded too. Their emotions swirled around her, combining into one, separating again.

She floated in the darkness, her arms outstretched, facing upwards. Far below her were the voices and the sadness, the fear. She felt it, but it felt . . . good. Right, somehow. It clung to her skin like syrup and she licked it off, savoring the piquancy. Why do this job if you couldn't gain something from taking the fear into yourself ?

The vision shifted abruptly. She stood in the kitchen of her childhood home, holding her schoolbooks. She was sixteen years old, just come home from school to an empty house. What could be more exciting?

Megan threw the books down and headed upstairs to her room. The Ouija board waited under her bed. Ever since she'd realized she knew things about other people, that she could somehow see into their heads, she'd wanted to try this. Maybe she could talk to ghosts. Maybe they could make Todd Gentry fall in love with her, or force that bitch Tara Coleman to leave her alone.

She pulled the box out from under her bed. The conscious, adult Megan tried to fight, tried to scream. This would lead to no good, she knew it, she felt it . . . Megan screamed in her head, screamed as loudly as she could.

The lights went on. Megan blinked as her eyes started watering from the sudden illumination. On the floor beside her chair, some of the others squinted or rubbed their eyes; some yawned and stretched. The session was over.

What the hell had happened?

Everyone headed for a small table by the door, covered with paper cups and bottles of juice, cookies, and other snacks. Art smiled at Megan.

"We always have something to eat afterwards," he said. "After working this hard, we need something to keep our strength up, right guys?"

The others murmured noises of assent, but they were too busy eating and drinking to speak. They'd fallen on the food like a pack of hungry baby wolves.

Art handed her a cup of warm Coke and a cookie before pulling her into a corner. His hand clung to her sleeve like a horrible insect she couldn't brush off. "What did you think? Interesting?"

"Um, yes." The Coke was flat, too. "Definitely interesting." When could she leave? Would it be rude to leave now?

Art watched her. Again the light caught his glasses and obscured his eyes. She was beginning to think he did it on purpose. "How did you like the affirmations at the end? I wrote them myself."

Affirmations? Oh . . . the chanting. She hoped. "Great. You'll have to give me a copy."

Art wagged his finger at her. "Oh, no. If you want access to them you have to come work with us again."

"Gee, Art, I'd love to," she lied, "but as I said before I'm just *too* busy these days. It sure is a great program, though." As unobtrusively as possible, she glanced at the clock. It was quarter to nine. She'd called Dante and told him to meet her outside at nine, but she thought she would scream if she had to talk to Art for fifteen more minutes.

"Maybe you could mention us on your show. We can always use more clients, you know."

"Sorry, I'm not allowed to advertise."

"Of course. I understand." His expression clearly showed he did not. "Maybe you could see what you can do, though?"

"I sure will," she said, knowing that he knew she wouldn't. They smiled falsely at each other while Megan scrunched her toes up in her shoes in an effort to calm her restlessness.

She took her leave from the group a few minutes later, practically running out the door in her haste to get away from Arthur's stare. She still didn't know what had happened. Had she fallen asleep in the spicy-smelling darkness? It wouldn't surprise her, considering she'd had a rough night and a rougher morning. The demands of the partners still hovered over her like the blade of a guillotine. Tomorrow she'd have to start looking for a new receptionist, start finding a company to do the soundproofing—all out of her own pockets, which were not that deep, despite the boost the radio show gave her finances—and figure out a way to explain to Richard Randall at the station that his publicity was putting her practice in jeopardy. Not that he would care, but maybe she could make him care.

All while trying to look like a competent, together professional for Brian Stone.

The locked front door rattled when she pushed it but did not open. She searched for the buzzer by the door but couldn't find it. The area behind the empty receptionist's desk was blocked off by a wall, a little over waist-high. It, too, was locked. Shit. Was she going to have to go back and ask Art to let her out?

Sighing, she turned towards the hall. Off to her right was a glowing "Exit" sign, but Megan suspected it was a fire exit. She certainly wasn't going to set off an alarm just because she didn't want to see Art Bellingham again.

Holding her car keys loosely in her hand, she walked back across the lobby, an act that seemed to take a lot longer than it should have. The murky silence of the building confused her, considering there was still a group of people in it. She would have expected to hear them talking as they got ready to leave, but she didn't.

Something clattered to the tile in the corner of the room. With a tiny, nervous cry, Megan turned towards the noise, but before she could find its cause the lights went out.

Not even a shaft of moonlight came in through the windows. It was as if something had covered them or they'd disappeared. The exit sign had gone off. The lobby was dark and silent as a tomb.

Megan's skin prickled. Someone else was in the room.

First there was only a tiny movement, a rustling noise, like the whisper of grass in the wind. Megan swallowed. She hoped it was one of the Fearbusters people, but she hadn't heard their door open, and there were still no voices. Only the unshakable certainty she was not alone in the stygian blackness of the cavernous room.

Another sound, like a drop of water hitting a pool. *Plop*. Her eyes hurt from her refusal to blink. The darkness pressed against them, dry and hot.

Faint rustling answered her next tentative step forward. Something skittered across the floor: tiny fast little footsteps rattling like marbles. The noise sounded like it came from her right, but she couldn't be sure.

"You're not scaring me." She couldn't seem to catch her breath. The darkness crawled over her skin, setting off tiny alarms in her head, making her muscles ache. She lowered her purse and wrapped the strap around her wrist, ready to swing but certain she didn't have a chance at hitting whoever . . . whatever it was. For some reason she didn't think the presence in the dark was human. By the time she knew the thing's location it would be too late.

Someone giggled, a high-pitched gurgling twitter. The sound sent shivers up her spine. Her heart beat so fast she thought it might explode. She hadn't been this scared since . . . well, since she was sixteen.

Realization hit her and she almost laughed. This was an after-effect of her odd dream. This wasn't the first time it had happened. She'd always assumed it was because of her abilities, that somehow her subconscious stayed alert for longer. Given that she'd just revisited that long-ago winter, it was no wonder this was happening now. The sweat on her brow started to dry and she once again felt the coolness of the temperature-controlled room. She must be more tired than she'd thought, to panic like that. What did she think, that some sort of evil creature stalked her in the hospital?

She strode back in what she thought was the direction of the hall, with her left arm outstretched. Soon she would touch a wall and follow it back to the Fearbusters room.

Something cold grabbed her hand, something hard and scaly and wet. "Megan," said a voice, the same slithery voice she'd heard giggle a moment before. The speaker was right next to her ear.

Megan screamed. She swung her purse but only hit her own left hip. She didn't even feel the impact. She tried to pull away but the thing that held her refused to let go, squeezing her hand so hard she thought she could feel the bones rubbing together. She heard a high wordless wail and realized, as her throat began to hurt, the cry was her own.

Then—as suddenly as it had grabbed her—the hand let her go.

The lights came back on.

She was alone.

"MEGAN?"

Still shaking, Megan turned. Art walked towards her. "I thought I heard you scream. Is everything okay?"

Megan nodded and forced herself to speak. "I thought I saw a rat."

"Oh, no, how terrible." Art glanced around the lobby. "Where?"

"It was probably nothing. I'm afraid I'm a little tired." The last thing she wanted was for him to insist on looking for it. "Could you just let me out, please?"

"Of course." He leaned over the receptionist's desk. The buzzer sounded and the door clicked. "I should have told you where the switch was."

"That's okay. Thanks, Art." Nothing had ever looked better than the smooth-mown lawn outside the building. Megan practically ran for it. Her body still buzzed with adrenaline, her mind twisted in confused circles.

"We'll see you again," he called after her. She didn't bother to answer.

MEGAN KNEW CITY POLLUTION choked the air outside, but the breeze dried the cold sweat on her skin and the faint odor of exhaust smelled like freedom. The parking lot was still brightly lit; the cars still in their neat rows like children bunked up for the night. She headed straight for her car, seeking the safety of its steel body. Dante was nowhere to be seen and, at that moment, she didn't care. She hoped he wouldn't show up. All she wanted was to go home and curl up in her bed with a good romance novel and a bag of potato chips.

Headlights flashed to her left. The car's engine was so quiet she hadn't noticed it. She glanced toward the flash—a Jaguar . . . Dante's Jag.

"Get in." Dante's voice. He was standing on the driver's side, leaning on the top of the low-slung car.

"I'm not getting in your car with you."

"You called me and asked me to meet you here."

"Yes, to meet me here and talk, not to go driving around the city with you."

He glanced at the Outpatient Center, then looked at Megan again. "Come on. If I was going to attack you I would have done so already, don't you think? Just get in."

She still didn't feel good about it, considering she hadn't been able to read him, but he did have a point. Twice now she'd been alone in dark places with him and he hadn't even touched her casually.

The wind lifted her hair from her shoulders as she crossed the parking lot. It felt good, as did the cold leather-scented interior of the car. Dante didn't bother to open the door for her, but he did wait—barely—until she'd settled herself down and fastened her seatbelt before he stomped on the gas and roared out of the parking lot and onto the road by the main hospital building.

"You don't have to go so fast."

"Says who?" His lips tightened.

"You don't have to take that attitude with me, either. You didn't have to come meet me."

"I tried to get out of it, if you'll recall." He turned right off the hospital grounds.

"I thought you wanted to help me. To keep me safe from all those stalkers following me around? Yesterday you were my hero, today you don't even want to talk to me. Not that I care. I just find it odd."

"I changed my mind."

"Why did you come, then? Why not stand me up? Do you want to talk or not?"

He sighed. "No. Well, I did, but now I don't. You lied to me."

"I did no such—"

"You did. The other night you promised you wouldn't accept any other offers. Then you agreed to go work for Arthur Bellingham and his little gang of deviants. Sounds like a lie to me."

"I didn't *agree* to work *for* him. I just agreed to go to a session. One of my patients asked me to."

"Does Bellingham know that? I bet he told them all you'd be working for him, didn't he?"

"No, he—" She stopped. He had said that, hadn't he? She shook her head. "It doesn't matter what he thinks. I don't work there, I'm not going to work there. In fact, I'd be much happier if I never set foot in the place again."

"Creepy? Upsetting?"

"Actually, yeah, it—that's none of your business."

"It is. You promised me first."

"Oh my god, what are you, a Klingon? So I went there. So I accepted an offer and I said I wouldn't. So what? What are you going to do, cut out my tongue?"

"Unfortunately, no. I'm not allowed."

"Excuse me?" Megan reached for the door handle as unobtrusively as she could. She could probably jump out at the next stoplight. Dante seemed to have the devil's own luck with the lights, though—they were all turning green as soon as the car got within braking distance.

"I'm not allowed to hurt you. In any way. I'd be punished if I did."

"Punished?" Her fingers tightened on the door handle.

The headlights from cars going in the opposite direction washed over his face, casting it into light and then shadow, shadow then light. "It's some stupid new public relations push. We aren't allowed to physically hurt people anymore. Bad for our image, or something. Can you imagine?"

"What are you talking about? Whose image?"

"Demons."

"Excuse me?"

"Demons." He made another right turn. They were already in her neighborhood.

Megan thought carefully about how to phrase her next sentence. "You're telling me you believe you're a demon."

"I don't believe anything," he said. "And I'm not one of your patients. Don't speak to me as if I am."

"You might want to consider getting some psychiatric help, if you think you're a demon."

"I don't think I am, I know I am. And you need to know it, too."

This should be good. "Why?"

"Because a considerable number of us are after you."

Chapter Six

Megan didn't know if she should laugh or start crying. The man was obviously not well. But was his illness dangerous to her?

"I see," she finally said. "There are demons out there after me. Hmmm. I haven't seen any, but I'll keep my eyes open from now on, okay?"

He pulled into her driveway and cut the engine. "You arrogant woman. You're a psychic and you refuse to believe there might be supernatural beings living on earth?"

Megan stiffened. "Psychic?"

"Cut the shit, Megan. You know it and I know it, just like I know you tried to read me the other night, just like I know you read your patients all the time."

She cleared her throat. Her eyes stung. "Why do you care?"

Dante shifted in his seat. Megan, her eyes focused on the door of the glove compartment, only caught the movement out of the corner of her eye. "Looks like this will have to wait," he said. "You have company."

Brian Stone stood near the front of the car, peering through the windshield with his arms folded. His lips were set in tight, thin lines.

Megan picked up her purse. "This is not over."

"Not by a long shot." He sounded as glum as she did. Brian would probably think they were having some kind of lovers' spat. RADIO COUNSELOR CANNOT HANDLE STRESS OF ROMANTIC RELATIONSHIPS.

Megan and Dante got out of the car like condemned prisoners who'd just finished their last meal.

"Hi, Brian." She tried to sound cheerful and relaxed, but she suspected he wasn't fooled. Or maybe he was just too angry to care.

"Can I talk to you for a minute?"

A negative reply was on the tip of her tongue, but she changed her mind and shrugged. He might as well. "Come in."

The three of them trooped up the steps to the porch, where the men waited and did that peculiar looking-at-the-sky thing like strangers in line at the ATM while she unlocked her door.

She'd barely even turned on the lights when Brian grabbed her arm and steered her into the blue-gray kitchen. Dante walked past them, presumably into the living room but Megan didn't trust him to stay there. Her bedroom was right off of it. It wouldn't have surprised her one bit to find him nosing around in her drawers.

Brian glanced over his shoulder to make sure Dante wasn't lurking behind him. "Why didn't you tell me, Megan?"

"What do you mean?"

"I know you aren't crazy about this whole interview thing. But I'm a good journalist, and something like this was sure to come out. You should have told me."

"Told you what?" Her eyes shifted towards the living room.

Brian followed her gaze, then looked back at her. "I got a email this evening, from an address I didn't recognize.

Normally I'd delete it as spam, but the subject line was your name, so I opened it."

"And?"

He reached into his back pocket and pulled out two folded sheets of paper. Opening them, he handed her one.

> *Dear Mr. Stone,*
> *I know you are writting about Megan Chase.*
> *Megan is a murderor. She don't deserve your story.*
> *A Concerned Friend*

"Oh my god." The words left her lips before she realized it. She leaned against the countertop. The marble lip made a cool stripe across her back and soothed her. It felt real. Nothing else did.

She cleared her throat and started to hand the paper back to him. "Some crazy, I guess."

He didn't reply. Instead he handed her the other sheet.

She took it with unsteady hands. It was a scan of a photocopy, she guessed from the slightly out-of-focus look of the page, but it was clear enough to read the headline: Teen Will Not Face Charges.

Megan closed her eyes.

"Read the article."

"I don't need to read it," she said. "You know I don't."

"Why didn't you tell me about this?"

The TV went on in the other room. Dante was channel-surfing. Each time the sound changed she cringed. Brian loomed over her in front, Dante made himself right at home in her living room. Even her house wasn't private.

Her life certainly didn't seem to be.

"I try not to think of it. It was a long time ago, I was innocent and the story never made the bigger papers. I thought it was forgotten."

She'd thought she'd left it behind. Left it in Grant Falls along with everything else. That's why she hadn't said anything. She wanted to kick herself. How arrogant she'd been, to think she could move on.

"We talked about your childhood," Brian said. "About small-town life, remember? Just today, in fact. But you kept this hidden." He put the papers back in his pocket. "Don't you see the position you put me in by hiding this from me?"

"You're writing a puff piece. Why do you need to know that when I was sixteen I was a suspect in the murder of a local homeless man? A murder I did *not* commit?"

"Not just a murder, Megan, a violent, ritualistic murder, and I need to know because my editor got a copy of this, too, and wanted to know why I hadn't discovered it on my own. There was nothing about this in the papers in Redwoods City. Which makes sense, since it turns out you lied about where you grew up." His anger throbbed around her. "I'm used to reticence. I can even understand why you didn't mention this. But I would have found out anyway, you know. Like I said, I'm a good journalist."

She crossed her arms over her chest. "What are you going to do about it?"

"I'm going to do what I have to do." Tears sprang to her eyes, but he wasn't done talking. "If you'll help me, if you'll be open and honest about this, I can turn it into nothing—a brief mention in an otherwise glowing article. If not—if you keep lying and hiding things from me, and ditching me so you can go on dates like you did tonight—"

"I wasn't on a date. Dante picked me up. My—car wouldn't start. I called him." What the hell was his problem with her anyway? So she'd lied about her past. She couldn't imagine she was the first of his interviewees ever to do so. Did every local socialite tell the truth about her age and upbringing?

Something deeper hid behind Brian's anger, but the thought of reading him and finding out what it was filled her with exhaustion. Tomorrow she'd do it. Tomorrow she'd take care of all of this.

"Sure." He didn't meet her gaze. "Anyway. Tomorrow we have a lot of talking to do. Just promise you'll tell the truth."

Megan bit back a sharp reply and nodded. "I promise."

"Great." He reached out and took her arm, his hand cold through the fabric of her shirt. "I like you, Megan. But I'm not going to pretend a story doesn't exist if there is a story. So play fair with me and stop trying to make me look like an idiot."

"I wasn't." Now that the conversation she dreaded had been put off for at least a day, Megan didn't want to stand in the kitchen anymore. She wanted to go sit down. Preferably with both men gone and a nice large drink in her hand.

"Sure you weren't."

"Hey, Brian? Don't talk to me like that. I didn't want to do this stupid story to begin with. The only reason I am doing it is because my boss is making me. I'm not here to help you or make sure you get a good story, I'm here because I have to be."

He didn't move. The TV in the other room was still blaring and Megan wanted to go in and see what Dante was up to. If she didn't hurry up he'd probably order pay-per-view pornography or something. She wouldn't put anything past him. He was trying to convince her he was a demon. She doubted costing her a few bucks for *Sex Planet Five* would worry him.

"Megan? I'm making cocktails." Speak—or think—of the devil. Dante's voice floated into the kitchen, breaking into the glaring silence. He must have found her liquor cabinet. "I need some ice."

She looked at Brian. "Are we done?"

He dropped her arm. "Yeah. Except I guess your friend is making us drinks."

Actually, she thought, he was probably making drinks for himself and her, but she didn't say anything. She couldn't exactly kick the reporter out of her house, not if she hoped to keep that damn article secret. Of all the nights. She hadn't thought she wanted to be alone with a man who claimed to be a demon, but she now realized she did. Being alone with Dante was the only way she was going to get the entire—probably ludicrous—story of what he thought was going on.

"Why don't you stay? We'll declare a truce."

"Ice, please?" Glasses clinked in the other room.

Megan yanked the freezer door open and pulled out a tray of ice cubes and took it to the living room. Brian trailed behind.

"I see you made yourself comfortable," she said to Dante. His jacket was off and draped over the arm of her favorite chair; his sleeves were rolled up and top shirt button undone. He stood in front of the television with the remote in his hand.

"Was I not supposed to?" He took the ice tray from her. She noticed he'd already dug out a selection of bottles. "This is a nice liquor cabinet," he said. "You're not a teetotaller, are you?"

She glared at him and snatched the tray back, twisting it to free the cubes. "What do you drink, Brian?"

"Gin and tonic, if you have it."

She plopped ice cubes into the scotch Dante had poured for himself and then assembled gin and tonics for Brian and herself. She tried to draw it out, hoping that one or both of them might disappear while she wasn't looking, but when she turned back they were both still there, watching her. She handed them the glasses.

"What was this group you were at tonight?" Brian put a chatty conversational tone to the question that made Megan feel more like an interviewee than she ever had. She debated what to tell him.

"It's a group called Fearbusters," she said. "At the hospital."

"And you're working there?"

Dante raised his eyebrows. She ignored him.

"No, I'm not," she said. "I was asked to go sit in on a session, so I did, but I'd appreciate it if you wouldn't write about that. I'm not associated with the group and I'm afraid it might seem an endorsement."

"You wouldn't endorse it, then?"

"I didn't say that." Not for the first time, she felt like a bug under a magnifying glass in the face of his rapid-fire questions. He didn't seem to want to give her time to think, just looking for whatever answer popped into her head. Certainly an effective technique, if an irritating one.

"You didn't have to," Dante murmured.

"I'm not allowed to endorse any groups," Megan said. "Part of my contract at the station."

"But would you endorse them, if you could?"

"Why do you ask?"

He shrugged. "Just curious."

"Why don't we all sit down?" Dante suggested. He settled himself onto the couch, smiling. Was he helping her? But then, if he had some kind of problem with Fearbusters, he wouldn't want to take the chance of her saying something nice. He never had said what he did for a living, unless somehow "demon" had become a valid profession while she wasn't paying attention. Maybe he was the attorney for some other group, one that was suing Fearbusters—no, that was nonsensical.

"What exactly do you do, Dante?" The question was out of her mouth before she even thought about it.

Both men stared at her. Shit. She'd totally forgotten that Dante was supposed to be another counselor from a different city.

"Very funny," Dante said. He turned to Brian, who sat on the other end of the couch. "I think that's Megan's charming way of suggesting you bother me for my opinions about group therapy. I'm happy to give them, if you like."

Brian smiled politely while Megan's heart started beating again. If Brian caught her in another lie just then he'd probably make her out to be a serial killer in his article. "No, thank you. Perhaps another time."

"You let me know." Dante got up to pour himself another scotch. "I have lots of opinions on things."

"You certainly do," Megan said. "Lots of ideas, too."

Dante turned to her and grinned, lifting his right hand into the air. He waved it. A small flame appeared at the tip of his index finger. As she watched, transfixed, the flame grew and spread down his hand, then disappeared. She glanced at Brian. He was watching her.

"Are you okay?"

"Fine." She took a large swallow of her drink. It had to be a trick. Some kind of magic trick. Nobody could set their hands on fire. Nobody could make flames appear from nothing.

Somehow, though, the image of Greyson Dante pulling rabbits out of hats on some cheap, hollow-sounding stage in a dive bar by the airport didn't ring true.

Brian rolled his glass between his palms. "Are you going to that big charity thing the station is doing on Friday?"

"Yes."

"Maybe we can go together?"

"Sure."

Dante sat down. "The Femmel Foundation? I'm going to that, too."

Megan raised her eyebrows. "You support charities?"

"I support all kinds of things, my dear," he said. "I guess I'll see you two there."

"What a delight." Megan finished her drink and got up for another. This evening was never going to end.

"AT LAST," DANTE SAID. "We are alone." He lounged on the couch, one stockinged foot resting on the edge of her glass-topped coffee table. She stared at it. He did not move.

"Yes." Was she too drunk to be nervous or too nervous to be drunk? "Just me and the demon man."

He looked wounded. "I'm not a demon-man. I'm full-blood demon."

"You don't look like a demon."

"How do *you* know?"

She blinked. "I need another drink."

"I think you've had enough."

"How do *you* know?"

"Because you don't look scared, nervous, or even particularly angry at me, and because you're not calling me crazy."

"I'm a counseling psychologist. We don't call people crazy."

"Okay, you're not calling me delusional." He sat up, taking his foot off the table and leaning forward with his elbows on his thighs, his hands dangling between his knees.

"How did you do that?" She wasn't asking how he'd taken his foot off the table.

"I already told you."

"Demons can set themselves on fire?"

"Some of us, yes. It depends on what kind of demon you are."

"What kind are you?"

"*Vregonis*. Fire demon." He snapped his fingers and another small flame appeared. He cupped it in the palm of his hand, then tilted his arm. The flame crawled back around to the top of his hand. As Megan watched, it crept up his forearm to almost touch the edge of his rolled-up sleeve, then back down.

Megan was impressed but determined not to show it. "That could just be a party trick."

"Like separating two metal rings?" He grinned. In spite of herself, Megan smiled back.

"I was thinking of you pulling a rabbit out of your hat."

"There are some demons that can. Although you generally wouldn't want to see what they do with the rabbits afterwards."

Megan shook her head. "Let's not get sidetracked here," she said. "You say you're a demon. I say they don't exist. Where's your proof?"

He raised his eyebrows and looked at the little fireball still burning merrily in his hand.

"Yeah, but that could still be a trick. For all I know, you've hypnotized me."

He shook his head. "You'd know if I had, I think. It's almost impossible to hypnotize a psychic. Haven't you noticed?"

A bell rang in Megan's head. Something about what happened at Fearbusters earlier, but she couldn't quite pin the memory down . . . she rubbed her forehead with her fingertips.

"What's wrong?"

"Nothing." She'd think about it later, when her mind was a little clearer. "Okay, you can't hypnotize me, but—"

"I didn't say I couldn't, just that it's very difficult." He closed his hand and put out the little flame. "But I'm very good."

There was too much innuendo in that line to ignore, but she would try. "You didn't hypnotize me, but how do I know you're telling the truth?"

He stood up, unfolding his tall, lean body. "All right." His hands went to the buttons of his shirt, and he started undoing them. "Let's get this over with."

"Excuse me." Her throat was dry. "I don't think—"

"Hush." He finished unbuttoning the shirt and opened it, peeling it back off his shoulders to expose his muscular chest and flat stomach. Demon or man, jerk or savior, Greyson Dante looked awfully good without a shirt on and she was acutely aware that the bedroom was only a few feet away.

He finished removing the shirt, tossed it onto the couch, and turned around.

Megan gasped. A black line of tiny, dull spikes started an inch or so below his neck and ran down the center of his broad, strong back, stopping just above the line of his belt.

"Are those . . . what are those?"

"They're called *sgaegas* in the demon tongue. It loosely translates to 'spinelets'."

Megan stood up. "May I touch them?"

She did not want to touch him. Not when something in the atmosphere of the room had changed, something small but still big enough to make it hard to breathe. She didn't want to *not* touch, either. For all she knew the spinelets could be made of black rubber, glued on in an effort to fool her.

His upper body twisted as he turned to look at her, giving her a quarter view of his trim waist. "Yes." His dark eyes were unreadable.

It only took a couple of steps to reach him. Heat radiated from his bare skin when her hand got close. She hesitated, letting him warm her palm. No matter how clinical she tried to be, she could not deny that touching his back made her nervous. Unsettled. She was alone and tipsy in her living room with a strange—and handsome—shirtless man, who may or may not also have been a little the worse for drink. It wasn't the safest situation she'd ever encountered.

Dante cleared his throat. "It's okay. I know you have to be sure."

Megan bit her lip and laid her fingertip on one of the little spikes. It was as dull as it looked. Without realizing it, she'd been expecting the spikes to feel slimy, alien. They did not. They felt like skin, no different from hers than anyone else's.

Goosebumps appeared on his back. She ignored them. Ignored, too, the way her heartbeat quickened as she ran her fingertip all the way up his spine and back down. She repeated the motion with her palm. His skin was soft. The firm muscles beneath it seemed to ripple as she touched them. Heat gathered between her legs.

Drawing in a long, shaky breath, Megan forced herself back to earth. This was not a seduction. The very idea was laughable—to her, at least. She had no doubt Greyson would be willing. She suspected Greyson would somehow manage to put off the apocalypse if doing so would get him laid.

Just lightly touching the things didn't prove they were real. She swallowed. "I'm going to really test now."

He nodded, but did not speak or turn to look at her. She took another deep breath and took the tip of a spike between her thumb and forefinger. She twisted it as hard as she could. The skin bunched, but clearly the spike was beneath it.

Dante's muscles twitched. "Ow."

"Sorry."

She tried a different one, then another, twisting, pushing, pulling. Dante twitched each time but said nothing.

Finally she lowered her hand and stepped back. Her palm tingled.

He turned around. "Anything else?" His handsome face was a little flushed.

Megan crossed her arms over her chest and avoided his gaze. "I don't know. Do you have horns, or a tail, or a forked tongue?"

"No, no, and not really."

"Not really?"

He stuck out his tongue. She watched, fascinated, as the smooth pink tip of it split, leaving a tiny indent in the center.

"Oh." She wasn't even going to come close to mentioning what that made her think of. "And is—is that all?"

"You sound disappointed." He turned around to pick up his shirt and put it back on. Megan blinked as his chest disappeared from view. "Would it help if I told you I was born with webbed feet?"

"No."

"Well, I was. Plastic surgery is a godsend."

"Are you allowed to say that?"

"Allowed to say what?" He finished buttoning his shirt and picked up his glass from the table. A thin layer of scotch still covered the bottom. He gulped it down and poured himself another.

"God."

"Why wouldn't I be? Oh . . . right. It's very complex and would take a long time to explain, but basically, the Christian god has very little to do with demons. It's not a rivalry, there's no competition for souls—well, not exactly, but I'm sure we'll get to that—and he has no power over us. There's quite a lot more to it all than the battle of Good versus Evil or whatever you want to call it."

"There is a god?"

"Of course there is. There are all kinds of gods. There's a god of shallow ponds, there's a god of walking under ladders. But how relevant those gods are to you is your choice. It stopped being a requirement for the various afterlifes a long time ago." He paused. "Except the Norsemen. They're still very picky about Valhalla."

"What does all this have to do with me?" Her hand trembled as she poured another drink.

"Haven't you figured it out? I thought you were smarter than that."

She had. She just didn't want to admit it. "The radio show," she said. "The demon slayer thing. They think it's real." She glanced at Dante.

He nodded. "They think it's real. And they want to get you first."

Chapter Seven

"How much time do I have?"

She hadn't intended to ask, but the question fell out of her mouth just the same.

Greyson shook his head. "I don't know. A lot of demons are involved in this. They don't like you right now and they're not forgiving enemies."

"But you're not scared?" How dumb was she? The man was a demon—or the demon was a demon, could she still refer to him as a man?—and she was trusting him. She sat in her living room alone with someone who could be the demon equivalent of a hired assassin. He had originally mentioned clients, hadn't he?

"I'm not scared," he said. "I was, shall we say, nervous at first. I came to see you. It was obvious you didn't know what I was. Even after you saw the demon in the restaurant last night you didn't know what you'd seen."

"The de—that thing, that thing on the woman's . . . it was a demon? You saw it?"

"Of course I saw it. It was showing itself. Only you humans don't see them when they do that, no matter how powerful your psychic abilities may be." He took another sip from his glass. Now that they were both back in their chairs and fully clothed, some of the tension in the room had eased. Or maybe it was just that being told she was in danger of being killed by demons tended to put a damper on a girl's sex drive.

"But you didn't say anything."

"What was I supposed to say? 'Oh, you saw a demon, don't worry because I'm sure you'll be fine'? I wasn't going to say anything at all and try to just take care of it myself, but then you had to go and accept that offer."

Was he going to harp on that forever? "What the hell is the big damn deal about accepting offers?"

He leaned forward in his chair. "It's demon rules of engagement. You made a promise to me, which should have been binding. You broke it. You accepted an offer, but now you're going to refuse to follow through. Another broken promise."

Megan stood up. This was ridiculous. This was beyond ridiculous. She started pacing, pausing only to turn off the television, which had been on with the sound off the entire evening. Not evening anymore. She glanced at the clock. It was just after midnight. "I didn't accept Art's offer. He wanted me to come work for him. I said no. And what does he have to do with all of this anyway?"

"You didn't say no, you said maybe. Then you showed up there tonight and asked questions in a professional capacity. Even worse, when he told his clients you were there to work, you didn't argue."

"I didn't ask any—" Oh, no. She had. She'd asked Hanna about her voices. She'd treated one of the group's clients in the group setting. She didn't need Greyson to tell her what that might mean. If she was understanding him properly, it was the appearance, the actions, that mattered. The intent or equivocation was unimportant.

"How did you know that?"

"Word gets around."

"And now they all know."

He nodded. "You asked questions, which means in Art's eyes, in the demon world's eyes, you're working for Art. But first you made a promise to me, which I duly reported to my . . . superiors. That made them angry. They think you're his weapon now."

She stopped pacing. It wasn't helping anyway. "Weapon?"

"You call yourself a demon slayer. You're a psychic. That's powerful. It means something to us. It especially means something to the personal demons, because it's their game you're interfering with. Now it looks like you've taken sides and joined the fun. What are they supposed to think?"

She must be dreaming. That's what this was, a dream, a horrible nightmare that she would wake up from any minute and it would be morning . . . She let herself imagine it for another minute before she had to give up. This was no dream.

"The personal . . ." She shook her head. Every word she spoke or heard dragged her deeper into this and she didn't want to go any further down the slope tonight. Or any night, for that matter. "Maybe you could tell them? Just tell them I'm not a demon slayer or anything, and they'll leave me alone."

He shook his head. "That might have worked before," he said. "But now they think you're playing sides. Demons don't leave you alone. You may have noticed we're rather a persistent bunch. There's no 'out' with demons. You're in. You have to win or you have to die."

SHE HADN'T WANTED to talk anymore. She wanted out. Out out out. She was too drunk and tired to think of anything else.

There had to be some way to accomplish that, other than death or battle. She didn't know if she believed Greyson's story about her options or not. On the one hand, it sounded reasonable. On the other, she still didn't know exactly what his purpose in being here was. Was he protecting her or what? Was he just waiting for his chance to kill her and get whatever glory she presumed would come to the demon who killed her? Did he just want to see if he could get her into bed?

She was inclined to believe the last, especially after he'd spent ten minutes trying to convince her he should spend the night with her. All the offers to sleep on the couch in the world meant nothing when a man had that look in his eyes.

Not that she thought his desire had anything to do with her personally. Dante was a user and she was a challenge, it was that simple. If she ever did sleep with him—which she wouldn't—he'd never call her again.

Maybe that was the way to get rid of him. Sleep with him, tell him she expected him to marry her, watch him inform the demon council or organization or whatever that she wasn't a threat and they should all stay very far away.

Focusing on the amusing aspects of that image and not the sensual ones, she climbed into bed with a bag of tortilla chips, a glass of water, and a book. She wasn't especially hungry or thirsty, but *Hot Spot* had scheduled a photo shoot for the next day and it would be best if she wasn't too hung over. It would be nice to have some professional photos of herself, with her make-up and hair done.

The book was no help. For once she couldn't lose herself in the adventures of Lord Gruffydd and his reluctant bride. There were too many worries to be dealt with.

She checked the phone next to her bed and set Dante's card next to it. He'd insisted on scribbling his home— where would a demon live, anyway?—and cell numbers on it. Much as she wasn't sure what to do about him, she had to admit she was glad she had them. Just in case.

Maybe the chips and water were a bad idea. Maybe she should have just kept drinking until she passed out. At least then she wouldn't be turning off the light and trying to fall asleep with images of Greyson Dante's naked back in her mind, as clear as a photograph.

Damn demon.

MEGAN WASN'T SURE what woke her, dragging her from a sound sleep and flinging her into a state of hyperconsciousness. She reached for the lamp next to the bed, only to stop before she touched it.

Something was outside the large picture window on the wall to her right, something human-shaped. It stood framed by the window, the moonlight behind it casting a fuzzy shadow on the sheer curtains of her bedroom. She wasn't seeing a profile, either. Whatever it was, it was looking into the room.

Looking at her.

Slowly, she pulled her arm back under the covers, gripping the edge of the comforter with both hands. Her heart threatened to pound right out of her chest.

Part of her wanted to huddle under the covers and pretend nothing was wrong. Just like she'd done as a child. Hiding while her parents talked about her, argued about her, while her brother started bringing home more and more unsavory friends to fill the house with pot smoke and loud music.

Mentally she chastised herself. You're a grown woman, Megan. Get out of that bed! Fight, damn it! GET UP!

Over the rasping of her breath came a tiny scraping sound. *Skritch. Skriiiitch.* Fingernails scratching at the glass, at the lock. He was trying to get in. He was trying to break into her bedroom.

A scream fought to escape from her throat. She bit it back. Sweat broke out on her forehead.

Something clattered in the kitchen. Had she locked the door after Dante left. She had, hadn't she? It didn't matter, did it, because someone was trying to break into her bedroom and someone was in her kitchen and *oh my God I'm going to die if I stay in this bed—*

She took a deep breath and tried to center herself mentally. She could do this. She had to do this.

One . . . two . . . THREE!

She leapt out of bed, almost tripping on the bedcovers, and grabbed the phone and Dante's card as she ran into the bathroom, yanking the door shut behind her and turning the lock. Fighting back sobs, she scrambled into the tub, flipped the bolts on the window and flung it open. The ground a few feet below was soft dirt. Nothing had ever looked more inviting as that dirt, or her cool moonlit yard beyond it.

She grabbed the phone and business card and set them on the sill, then shifted her weight so she balanced on the thin inner edge of the tub on her toes, with her bottom pressed to the narrow windowsill.

Her neighbors' house was about forty yards away. Why had she moved to this goddamned secluded neighborhood?

Glass smashed in the house. She jumped, slipping back into the tub. The phone fell from the windowsill onto the soft earth outside. No big deal. She'd pick it up when she hit the ground. She didn't need it anyway. They would have a phone at her neighbors' house, it was safe there, she would be safe there.

Tears poured down her face. Adrenaline pumped through her body. She had no idea where her intruders were. The glass could have been the window or the coffee table or anything.

Something moved in the bushes in her yard. A head appeared, then shoulders. A man lurked there. She didn't need to read him to know something about him wasn't right. Blackness seeped from him like a dank fog.

Noises came from her bedroom. Even over the beating of her heart she heard it, the sound of the closet being opened, of the lamp breaking.

The phone was on the ground. The man in her yard was looking right at her. She did not know if she could get through the window and grab the phone in time. If she didn't get the phone she would die here. The people— or demons, go ahead, call them demons—would know where she was. They would check the bathroom door in a minute and find it locked. Would they shoot the lock? Would they shoot her? Did demons use guns to kill? She hoped they did. She would rather be shot, die quickly, than be . . . ripped apart or eaten alive or any of the other nasty ends Greyson had alluded to. Was she the rabbit who would be pulled out of a hat tonight?

The man emerged fully from the bushes. He moved so slowly, jerkily. The moonlight fell on his face. Megan choked on the terrified sob in her throat.

The bathroom doorknob rattled. The man in the yard, half his face missing, rotted, started towards her, his feet dragging through the stiff dying grass. *His face was rotted.* Bones and teeth were visible through the shreds of greenish skin. It had to be some kind of demon, had to be, because the word her brain came up with, the word *zombie,* was not possible. Demons might exist. Her exhausted brain rebelled at the thought of zombies.

She might be able to outrun him. She might not. She did not want to be eaten by some horrible, decayed thing, to have her last vision on earth be that terrible grinning face.

Another figure appeared in the yard, a woman, walking towards Megan with the same jerky gait. Then another. How many more were out there?

A knife—or, oh god, fingernails, long hard fingernails—scraped the door. Someone moaned.

Crying, she climbed through the window and lowered herself to the ground. The man heading towards her sped up, limping across the yard in a way that reminded her horribly of the way she and her girlfriends used to play horses when they were younger—*clopclop, clopclop*, a sort of bastard skip that nonetheless carried him faster than she'd hoped. The other creatures in the yard did the same, destroying her hopes of escape to the neighbors' house.

The earth was cool under her feet and smelled safe. She longed to bury herself in it.

No, she did not! Buried meant buried, dead. She was not going to die.

The thing headed for her wailed, a horrible dead cry. The others echoed it, their voices tearing the silence of the night to shreds. Megan screamed too. She picked up the phone and threw it into the bathroom. Indoors she might have a fighting chance.

She grabbed the windowsill and lifted herself, her arms shaking, her feet scrabbling and scraping against the stucco wall. In her hyperaware state, the sound of grass shuffling and sighing beneath the feet of the outside creatures reverberated through her head.

Her toes stung. They slipped against the wall, wet with her blood.

Finally she managed to hook one arm over the sill and into the bathroom. The door shook as the beasts pounded on it. It needed to hold long enough for her to think, long enough to call Dante. Long enough for him to get there or send some hellbeasts or whatever he would do . . .

She got her entire upper body into the bathroom and was in the middle of her final heave before the thing . . . the demon . . . the zombie . . . the whatever it was, grabbed her ankle. Ice-cold fingers pulled harder than she'd ever imagine anything could pull. Megan screamed. She kept screaming even as she fought, as it pulled her partway back out of the window. Teeth sank into her calf. She kicked with her other foot as hard as she could, her body shaking. She kept kicking after she felt something cave, as something slick and cold and wet coated her foot and the teeth and hands holding her let her go.

The bathroom door shook and bowed inward every time the creatures hit it. Megan grabbed the phone in shaking, hurting fingers. She could barely press the buttons.

She called Dante. Holding the phone to her ear with her left hand, she hunted for a weapon with her right. Bottles and jars crashed to the tile floor as she scrabbled along the countertop for something, anything to use. The only razor she owned was a safety razor and it wasn't a very good one. She was a waxer. Once in a movie she'd seen a woman beat a man over the head with a toilet tank lid, but she only had one free hand at the moment. She grabbed a book of matches she'd used for a candlelight bath one night.

In the cabinet under the sink she had an ancient aerosol can of hairspray, a bottle of bleach, a toilet brush, scrubbing cleanser, and a plunger. Her sweat-slick fingers slipped on the metal of the cans as she reached for the plunger's solid wood handle.

The phone stopped ringing in her ear. Dante sounded wide awake. "Megan."

A shout echoed in the room. Megan swung around. The man and woman were just outside, their faces in shadow from the moonlight shining on the backs of their heads. It gave them an oddly haloed look as they yowled, reaching in through the small window. Reaching for her.

Megan screamed. "They're in the house, Dante, they're in the—"

The door broke. The phone fell from her hands. She lunged for the plunger, wielding it like a baseball bat, and swung.

She hit the one closest to her across the forehead. The noise in the room was deafening. Her screams, the screams of the things outside and inside reverberated through the tiny tiled room. Nothing existed in the world but noise and confusion and the revolting smell, the stink of decay and filth.

The thing fell. Megan pulled back the plunger to hit the other. The handle was broken. She sobbed and fumbled for the hairspray.

Her fingers closed over it just as cold hands clutched her head, pulling her entire body to the right. She shrieked and swung the can up towards it with both hands. The can vibrated in her hands when the blow connected.

It let go of her, but the first was already moving again. Megan grabbed the matches. She put the can between her thighs and yanked one match from the pack, her hands shaking as she pressed the head of the match against the sandpaper strip with her thumb.

Nothing happened. One of the creatures reached for her again. The match lit.

With her left hand Megan picked up the can and sprayed, dropping the book of matches onto the floor.

Her aim was off but when she lifted the match the flame caught. She felt the heat but no pain as a ball of flame poured from the can, igniting the thing closest to her, driving it back against the wall. It fell in a heap to the floor.

The spray kept flaming. She turned it on the other creature, ignoring the cacophony of howls that filled the room, seeing only the flames rising from the two bodies. Hot, horrible triumph filled her as they shrieked and writhed.

One of them got up, still intent on capturing her. Flames spread as its ragged clothes caught fire. Megan stepped into the tub, only to feel hands in her hair. She threw herself forward, hitting her shoulder on the wall. A flaming hand reached for her. She swatted at it, burning her fingers, terrified of catching fire. With her left hand she fumbled for the shower spigot. The water was cold, but she barely felt it as it plastered her hair to her head, made her T-shirt stick to her skin.

One of the creatures was down, a ball of flame on the pale gray-and-tan tile floor of her bathroom. Its writhing slowed as she watched. She might risk extinguishing the flames on the other one with the water, but she didn't want to burn to death. She wore only an old cotton T-shirt, highly flammable.

Megan wrenched the detachable shower head from its metal cradle and beat the creature with it. Water flew into her eyes and up her nose, into her raw and burning throat. She could barely see, barely breathe. Her feet slipped beneath her but somehow she kept her balance, bracing her feet against the sloping sides of the tub.

She turned the water off, her shoulders aching as she kept beating the creature. Its charred hands flailed in the air, reaching for her, not taking its focus away from her even as its nose broke under the nozzle. Fingers dug into her flesh. White-hot pain riddled her body, adding to the adrenaline and terror already forcing her to keep going, keep fighting. She continued to beat the thing, her mind free of all conscious thought except to kill, kill, kill. Kill it, beat it, live, win.

Her screams seemed to come from her entire body. Her arms moved on their own accord, lifting the makeshift weapon, bringing it back down.

The thing's skull caved under the nozzle, now slick with black slime and water. Her fingers ached from holding it.

Finally the thing fell, half into the tub. The two things outside still poked shriveled arms through the bathroom window, but they couldn't reach her. Megan forced herself not to look at them, not to go near them. She stood, soaking wet in the tub, her body shaking and covered with blood, her legs trembling with the effort of standing.

Dante called her name.

Sirens sounded in the distance.

Chapter Eight

"**O**fficer, she's already told you what happened," Dante said. "Miss Chase is very grateful you arrived, but she's also been injured. I'd like to get her to the hospital as quickly as possible."

Megan said nothing and huddled further into the blanket draped around her. Beneath, her shirt still stuck to her cold, wet body. Her muscles ached from shaking.

The policeman—Officer Barrow, his name tag said—peered at her. "You sure you don't want us to call an ambulance, ma'am?"

Megan nodded.

Officer Barrow tucked his notepad back into his breast pocket. "We've got people out looking for them, but I wouldn't count on us finding them, to be honest. They probably had a car parked somewhere and took off."

The police wouldn't find the broken, charred bodies. Somehow Greyson managed to get them out to her garden shed and give her bathroom a perfunctory hose-down with the damaged shower head before the police arrived. She had no idea what kind of mind control or psychic push he might be using on them to make that good enough to fool them. She didn't think she wanted to know.

"'S the way it usually works. You sure you never seen them before? You haven't been getting any threatening letters or anything?"

Megan shook her head.

"A woman alone in a secluded house like this can be pretty vulnerable." Officer Barrow glanced at Dante, who wore only a pair of black silk pajama bottoms and a loose black T-shirt. The tiny spikes of his spine poked at the cloth, but none of the officers seemed to see them. "You might want to have your—attorney—stay here for a while. Just a word of advice."

"We'll find someone to stay with her," Dante said, offering his hand. It was a dismissal, and the officer knew it. "Thanks, Officer Barrow. Let us know if anything turns up."

Officer Barrow nodded, gave Megan one last look, and left. The other cops, who'd been standing in the entrance hall drinking coffee and chatting, followed. Greyson closed the door behind them and rested his forehead against it. "Get dressed."

"Where are we going?"

He turned around. His dark eyes looked black in the pallor of his skin. "Are you serious?"

"Yes."

"We're going to the hospital. Get dressed."

"I cleaned the bite. I cleaned all my . . ." she swallowed. "Wounds."

"The hell with Bactine and Neosporin. You need a damn tetanus shot." Drawers opened and closed.

"I'm—"

He reappeared in the doorway with a bundle of clothes in his arms. "Put them on, now. You were bitten by a zombie. They're filthy things. You might want to get a course of antibiotics, too, just to be—"

"Zombie?"

Greyson jerked the blanket away from her and peeled off her wet T-shirt, leaving her clad only in her bra and panties. Some dim part of her knew she should be embarrassed, but she couldn't bring herself to care.

"Yes, a zombie. You're just learning new things every minute, aren't you?"

"But, am I going to, I mean . . . turn into one?"

The fabric of the fresh, dry T-shirt obscured his expression while he yanked the top over her head. "This isn't *Dawn of the Dead*," he said. His hands brushed her breasts as he helped her get her arms through the sleeves. "These are similar to voodoo zombies. Powered by demons. Somebody put a contract out on you. They were sent to fulfill it."

"Art?"

Greyson tried to help her put on her jeans, but she smacked his hand away. Shocked and horrified she may be, but she could get herself into her own jeans. At least, she could after she'd slipped on some dry panties.

His voice followed her into the bedroom, but he stayed physically where he was while she finished dressing. "I don't know for sure. I suppose it's possible, but I don't think Art has the connections."

"Is he a demon? You didn't answer me before."

"I don't know what he is, but he's not something you want to get involved with."

She wanted to ask more, but the insistent ring of the doorbell made her jump, almost falling into the doorframe as she left the bedroom.

Greyson cursed. He reached into the leather briefcase he'd brought in with him when the cops arrived and pulled out a sleek little black gun.

"I don't like having guns in my house, Dante—"

"Tough."

Moving on silent bare feet, he walked down the hall, holding the gun upright like a cop in a movie. Megan watched him peer out the peephole. His shoulders sagged. "It's Brian. Just a minute!"

He tucked the gun into the waistband of his pajama bottoms. "Not a word," he said to her. "Stick to the same story we told the cops."

Not waiting for her nod, he opened the door. Brian rushed in. "Megan!" He grabbed her, pressing her to his warm, broad chest. He smelled of soap and laundry detergent. "You're all right. I was worried—"

"Why?" Megan heard a click behind her. Dante must have stowed the gun back in his case.

"I have a police-band radio . . . lots of journalists do . . . and when I heard your address—" His arms relaxed, letting Megan go. She sat back on the couch in time to see Brian take a long, hard look at Dante in his pajama bottoms and T-shirt. At Megan with her jeans still unbuttoned. The conclusion he came to was obvious.

"I called Greyson," Megan said. "When I heard the sirens. I thought I might need a—counselor." Behind her, Dante made a face.

"Right."

"Oh, hell, Brian. Greyson isn't a counselor."

"I know. I googled him right after we met. That's something else I knew you lied about."

"Sorry."

He shrugged. "Now you know why—"

"Why don't you two discuss this on the way to the hospital?" Dante suggested. He held out a set of keys. "Megan, I had your car brought back while you were sleeping. Brian can drive."

"I don't know—"

"I do. You should go now. I'll clean everything up here."

LUCKILY, THE NEAREST HOSPITAL was not the same one Megan had visited Monday after blacking out. Coming back so quickly as a crime victim might have raised more than a few eyebrows.

It was almost five in the morning by the time they got back to her house. Megan, stuffed with antibiotics and holding a bottle of painkillers, hobbled her way up to the front door with Brian's warm and reassuring hand on her elbow.

Every light in the house was on and she was grateful for it. Greyson's way of telling her the house was clean and clear, she imagined. Or maybe he just didn't give a damn about her electricity bill. At that moment, neither did she. The lights were reassuring for now, but she had no idea if she would ever feel truly safe there again.

The unfairness of it all, the sick, miserable unfairness, hit her as they entered the house and walked down the hall. In three days, her life had gone from being neat, orderly, and relatively happy to messy, dangerous, and horrible. There were demons after her. They'd sent zombies to her house to eat her or whatever zombies did. There was nothing she could do about it and the one man who knew what was going on was as enigmatic as the goddamned Mona Lisa.

Said man was lying on her couch eating chips and watching infomercials when they entered the living room. "Back so soon?"

"We were gone for almost three hours," Megan said as Brian helped her into her chair. Dante hadn't lied about cleaning. The room was spotless. He'd even vacuumed.

He caught her looking. "Everything's taken care of," he said. "I boarded up your windows and I have a friend who installs glass. He'll be here tomorrow while you're gone."

Shit. The photo shoot.

"We can reschedule the pictures if you're not feeling up to it," Brian said, seeing her face. "We can do it Thursday or Friday."

She shook her head. "We'll see how I feel, okay?"

"Okay. Do you want me to stay?"

"I just want to sleep. You might as well go home."

He glanced at Dante, then patted her on the shoulder. "Try to get some sleep."

"You, too."

"Good night," Dante as the reporter turned to go. Brian mumbled something Megan couldn't quite make out before he closed the door behind him. Dante got up to lock it.

"Well, that was fun. Interesting how your reporter friend managed to get here so quickly, don't you think?"

Megan did think, but she wasn't about to give him the satisfaction. She glared at him. He looked as bright and cheerful as if he'd been out for a brisk jog, sitting on the couch with his chips. "What did you do with the bodies? Did you find out anything?"

"The bodies are gone," he said. "No need to worry."

"What if they're traced back to me?"

"They won't be."

"How do you know?"

"Because I incinerated them."

Megan glanced towards her back yard. "There's ashes and stuff in my shed?"

"I cleaned everything up, okay?" Dante leaned back. "It's done. Why don't we worry about what's important, instead of these minor issues?"

"Dead bodies in my yard are not minor issues," Megan said. "They're big issues. Felonious issues."

"I didn't come all the way over here in the middle of the night to get you sent to jail."

"No, you didn't, did you, Mr. I-didn't-say-I-was-an-attorney?"

He shrugged. "I didn't."

"You are, though."

"Among other things."

"Like what? A housekeeper? You must have worked like a demon—" She bit her lip.

Dante's mouth twisted, but he didn't reply. The whole thing suddenly struck Megan as funny, and she started to giggle.

He watched while her giggles turned to laughter, and by the time the laughter turned to tears he was next to her, pulling her close to him, letting her rest her head on his broad chest while she sobbed.

It didn't last long, and his muscles were stiff and careful as he held her, but he didn't pull away and she was grateful for it. He let her break the embrace when she was ready, and handed her a handkerchief that she had no idea where he'd kept.

He looked at the heavy silver watch on his wrist. "It's very late, Megan. I suggest you go to bed and try to sleep. Did I hear you have a photo shoot later?"

She nodded. She didn't want to go to bed. The thought of being alone in her bedroom again, even with the sun rising outside the windows, made her nervous. With the room boarded up . . .

Dante glanced towards the bedroom, too. "I'll be right here," he said. "Unless you've changed your mind about—"

"I haven't."

He stretched out on the couch and folded beneath his arms beneath his head. His T-shirt rode up, exposing a thin slice of tanned skin. "I'll be here if you do," he said in a falsetto, batting his eyelashes.

Megan grinned, grateful for the change of mood. "I won't."

Chapter Nine

"Is she sleeping?"

Smack. "Whad'ya think? *Is she sleeping,* 'e says. Don't she look like she's sleeping?"

"Yeh."

"That is a sleeping woman, if ever I saw a sleeping woman," the second voice continued.

Megan opened her eyes.

The three men standing next to her bed jumped back, their expressions ranging from terror to curiosity.

"She's awake!" said the one closest to her. She recognized his voice as the second speaker, the one with the strongest cockney accent.

"You just said she was sleepin', Lif," said the next one. He was the tallest, with a large nose and scarred, gin-blossomed skin.

They were all big, broad men with small eyes and stubbled chins. They were all dressed in hitman casual: black trousers, black turtlenecks, black rubber-soled shoes, black windbreakers, black knit caps. Gold rings and watches completed the look.

Megan caught only a glimpse of these things before she seized the lamp on her bedside table and held it over her head. The cord refused to come out of the wall. She yanked at it with her left hand, aware not only that she looked silly, but that the men in her room had ample time to attack her while she sorted out her weapon. Their restraint from doing so provided her some comfort, but her heart still pounded in her chest.

"Who are you?" she demanded. Her voice squeaked.

The men glanced at each other, chagrined. The tall one spoke. "M'lady, didn't—"

"Good morning, gentlemen." Greyson entered the room, clad in a black suit with creases so sharp Megan imagined he could cut himself on them if he wasn't careful. He was freshly showered and shaved, and smelled like vanilla and smoke. "Good morning, Megan. Just barely. Doing a little redecorating?"

Megan glanced at the lamp in her hand, glared at him, then looked at the clock. It was 11:30. "Shit!" She set the lamp on the edge of the table and pushed the covers back, ready to leap out of bed.

"Sit down," Greyson said, holding out his hand. "I called Brian already to make sure you didn't have to be up for a while yet. The shoot's not until two."

"Who exactly are these men and what are they doing in my bedroom?"

"Ah." Greyson looked at the three, who stood a little straighter under his gaze. "Megan Chase, may I present your bodyguards: Malleus, Maleficarum, and Spud."

"My what?"

"Your bodyguards. The one on the left is Malleus, the tall one is Maleficarum, and that one is Spud. I've assigned them to you."

Megan glanced at the three men, still standing against the wall like they were in a police line-up. She got out of bed and grabbed Dante's arm. "I need to talk to you."

"Excuse us," Greyson said, as she led him out into the living room and closed the bedroom door.

"Who are they? What the hell do you mean, scaring me like that? How do you think I felt waking up with strange men in my room after last night?"

"I told you who they are. They're your bodyguards. You need someone with you at all times, and I can't do it." He leaned in a little closer. "They wouldn't have been in there watching you sleep if you'd let me stay, you know. Care to change your mind for the future?"

"No." Megan was suddenly aware that she only wore a T-shirt. He'd seen her in her bra last night, but somehow that was different. She grabbed the blanket from last night off the couch and wrapped it around her. It wasn't great, but it was better. "Look, Greyson, don't think I don't appreciate your help. I do. And I—I'd like it if you'd keep helping me, because I don't want to die. But those men . . . I can't have those men follow me around. They look like they're going to kill someone."

"Only if that someone tries to get in their way," Greyson said. "Or yours. Besides, they're not men. They're demons."

"Of course. I should have known."

"Yes, you should have. Painkillers getting to you? Come with me." Without waiting for an answer, he handed her a cup of coffee, then led her through the French doors to the patio. Her little black cast-iron table and chair set beckoned, the blue and white mosaic tile tabletop looking as peaceful and cheerful as ever. The patio was her favorite place.

The sun had warmed the seats and warmed her skin, too, as she sat down. She sighed, relaxing, but then she caught sight of the shed. Everything came back, the rotting faces, the smell, the screams . . . she set down her mug and pulled the blanket more tightly around her shoulders.

Dante was silent for a minute. "I thought you might be more comfortable out here. Would you rather go back in?"

"No. No, I'm all right." The coffee was hot and strong, almost burning her tongue, but she forced herself to drink deeply. The cobwebs in her head didn't want to go away, and she needed to be on her toes. Which still hurt.

"You're in a lot of pain?"

"No more than I expected." She lied, it was a lot more. On waking she'd thought it wasn't too bad, but as she moved around she realized how badly her muscles hurt, how tender her skin felt.

"I might be able to help you with that."

"Sensual massage?" The minute the words were out of her mouth she regretted them. She'd meant it as a joke, but it sounded like an invitation. The forced laugh made it even worse.

Dante didn't reply, but he stood up and came closer to her. She raised her hand. "I was kidding about the massage, okay? Bad joke, I know, but—"

"Hush." He stood behind her, close enough for her to feel the warmth of his body, but not touching. She sensed his hands in the air over her head. He started speaking, muttering something under his breath.

Energy flowed down through Megan's head into her body, rich and thick, soothing her aching shoulders and arms, relaxing the muscles of her back. She tried to lean away, but he pulled her back, holding her in place while his power washed over her. Her fingers tingled and flexed involuntarily as the energy kept pouring down, until every part of her body felt alight.

It only lasted for a couple of minutes at the most, but when he was done Megan felt better than she had in days. She raised her arms experimentally. No pain. "How did you do that?"

"Fire demons learn healing skills pretty early." He cleared his throat. "Is that better?"

"Yes."

"Good." He sat back down and picked up his mug with trembling hands. Catching her look, he said, "Sometimes it takes a bit out of me. I'll be fine. We have more important things to worry about."

Damn, she'd been feeling so much better too. A cool breeze swept across the patio, sending the first fallen leaves of the season skittering over the concrete. "I don't even want to think about it."

"Too bad. You have to think about it, Megan, or you—"

"Look," she said through gritted teeth, "I get it. I'll die. Will you stop saying it? You make me feel like you're looking forward to it."

He shrugged.

"Thanks. Thanks a lot."

"What am I supposed to say? No, I'm not? I think that should be obvious. I wouldn't be here giving you three of the best bodyguards my family—or rather, my company—has, if I wanted you to die." He slammed his coffee cup back down on the table. "Hell, Megan, I could have killed you myself quite a few times by now if that was what I wanted to do. This isn't a horror film. I'm not waiting for the planets to align or for you to sign your soul over to me. I'm helping you purely out of the goodness of my heart."

He looked sincere, but Megan didn't believe it for a second. He definitely wanted something. She just didn't know what.

At the moment it seemed he wanted an apology, so she gave him one. "Sorry."

He nodded. "As for the brothers, I think if you give them a chance you might like them."

"Do I have a choice?"

"No."

"Are they armed?"

"No. They don't need to be."

"But you do."

He shrugged. "I'm not a guard demon. They are."

For a minute Megan considered telling him to fuck off and leave her alone. To take his demon bodyguards and go, then run away herself. It was a sweet minute, full of promise.

But she couldn't deny the reality of the night before. She didn't want to trust him, but she didn't see she had a choice. If he was offering to help her in order to put her in danger later, there wasn't much she could do about it. If he was behind everything that had happened, he wasn't going to stop just because she told him she didn't trust him. This was her life, and she was going to keep it.

He took her silence as assent. "Good," he said. "I have to go."

"Wait a minute. You need to tell me the rest of what's going on. You never told me who the personal demons are, or what their plan is, or what your plan is, or anything I need to know."

"All you need to know right now is to stay with the boys. They'll keep you safe. Oh, and I've ordered them not to touch you or bother you. If they do, let me know."

"You had to tell them not to—"

"We'll talk more later."

He left without saying goodbye.

THE "BOYS" WERE still standing exactly where she'd left them.

"Ah, hi guys," she said. "How are you?" It was kind of a stupid thing to say, but what was she supposed to say? What did one say to one's demon bodyguards?

The tall one—Maleficarum?—bowed, scooping off his hat to reveal two small but unmistakable horns on his head. So some of them did have horns. "At your service, m'lady," he said. "I 'ope my brothers and I will please you."

The other two followed suit. Six tiny horns pointed to the ceiling from three shiny bald heads.

"Thank you." She didn't know whether to laugh or cry. "I appreciate you being here."

"No need to thank us, m'lady," Malleus said. "Mr. Dante told us we was needed, and here we are. Ready to guard you. With our lives, you know."

"Yeh," said Spud.

"Well, that's fine. But I wonder if you could go wait in the living room, please, while I shower and change?"

"Sorry," said Malleus. "But Mr. Dante said we was to guard you. Every minute, 'e said. So we can't let you out of our sight."

"I'm sure he didn't mean when I'm—" she didn't want to say "naked" in front of them, so she substituted "—undressed. I wouldn't feel comfortable with that. I'm sure you understand."

"Mr. Dante said every minute, and that's what we're gonna do."

"I don't think he wanted us to watch the lady when she's all undressed," Maleficarum said. "She don't want you starin' at her naked."

"'e said every minute, Lif." Malleus folded his arms across his beefy chest. "You wanna be the one wot tells him we didn't do what he said? You wanna tell 'im we let her get done over or somefing? 'Cos I don't. He'll 'ave our heads, he will."

"I think he'll be angrier if 'e finds out we been lookin' at her naked," Maleficarum said. "I think she's 'is."

That was enough for Megan. "I am not 'his'," she said, drawing herself up to her full five feet two inches, "and you are not watching me shower. You may inspect the bathroom before I enter it. That is all."

Maleficarum narrowed his eyes. "And you'll tell Mr. Dante you made us take our eyes off you?"

Megan nodded. "Yes."

Malleus turned to Maleficarum and whispered something in his ear. Maleficarum turned back to Megan. "Could you put that in writin', m'lady?"

She glared at him.

Malleus looked down. "C'mon, guys. Let's check the bog."

The three of them trooped off into her bathroom, presumably to look inside the toilet and down the drains. Megan had to admit, the three demons seemed dedicated to their jobs.

And to Greyson Dante. Who exactly was he?

They emerged while she was still thinking. "Sound as a pound," Malleus said, giving her what he obviously hoped was a reassuring smile. In his squat face it looked more like a leer. "You go ahead. We'll wait 'ere."

She sighed. "Fine."

The bathroom, like every other room, showed no signs at all of what had transpired the night before, save for the boarded-up window.

Water spurted in jerky bursts from the dented shower head as she hurried through her ablutions. She'd have to get a new one.

The familiar walls started to close in on her too soon. *Don't cry. Let it go. Breathe through it. Let it go.*

She pressed her hands against the wall over the taps, letting the water hit her back. Her legs shook. *Let it go. Let it go.*

She was sixteen again, standing in the shower. Over the spray of water she heard the voice. "*Megan . . . Megan . . . don't forget . . . you promised, don't forget what you promised, DON'T FORGET WHAT YOU PROMISED . . .*"

Megan bit back a scream. She didn't want to remember it, didn't want to remember anything that had happened that winter. Damn Brian and his anonymous emailer, damn that article still sitting around in archives. Damn them all.

The hot steamy air felt good in her lungs. She took a couple of deep, cleansing breaths and turned off the faucet. She would have to face that memory, she knew, just as she knew it had something to do with why this was happening, just like she knew somehow there was a reason why she was not collapsing into a heap and checking herself into a hospital for believing that demons were real. Because somewhere deep down, she'd known it all along.

She pushed the shower curtain aside and screamed.

Stumbling backwards in the tub, she yanked the curtain around her body. It clung to her, wet and vaguely slimy. "What the hell are you doing in here?"

"We're not looking, m'lady," Malleus said. Indeed, all three of them had their backs turned to her. Not that it made a difference.

"You said you'd wait outside."

"We did. We waited 'till you was in the shower so we wasn't watching you shower, but we was still in the room. We didn't see nuffin' through the curtain, m'lady. We promise. We kept our backs turned. But Mr. Dante tol' us—"

"I know what he told you." Her heart still had not started beating normally. She'd have to talk to Dante about this. "Will you wait outside now? I want to get dressed."

"Our backs are turned."

"I don't care." She took another deep breath. "Wait outside. Now."

HER TEETH WERE BRUSHED, her hair was dry, and her plain black suit and stockings were on before forty minutes had passed. She didn't bother with makeup. Brian told her not to when she called to finalize everything.

"I'm glad you're doing the shoot, anyway," he said. "Maybe after we can have dinner?"

"Sounds great." They said their goodbyes and hung up.

The brothers were waiting for her right outside the bedroom. She almost walked into them when she opened the door.

"Guys," she said, "I don't think Mr. Dante meant for you to watch me quite this closely."

"Oh, he did, m'lady," Malleus said. "You believe me, he did. He told us you was very important, and you need to be kept safe. Nobody'll keep you safer than us."

"That's a promise," Maleficarum said.

"Yeh."

In the pale greens and tans of her living room, they looked like crows in a field. Large, black, vaguely threatening. She could only imagine what it was going to be like having them with her all day. All day, every day, for the time being. Never had she imagined her life would be spent followed by three cockney demons in black cashmere.

"Um . . . you don't have to call me that." She sat down on the couch. The car *Hot Spot* was sending would be there in about fifteen minutes.

"What?"

"You don't have to call me 'milady'. It's a bit . . . well, I think people might think it's odd."

"What should we call you by, then? Your first name?" Malleus started to chuckle. The others joined in, as if the idea of calling her by her name was too amusing to be believed.

"You could," Megan said. "That would be fine."

They stopped laughing. Expressions ranging from horrified to scandalized crossed their wizened faces. "We couldn't! That wouldn't be right!" Malleus crossed his beefy arms across his chest. His cap had slipped to one side, giving him the rakish air of a cut-rate pirate.

"It's like touching you in your unmentionables," Maleficarum said. "We never could, m'lady, not ever. Mr. Dante wouldn't like it."

Spud said nothing, but he shook his head with conviction.

Megan sighed. "How about 'Miss Chase', then? At least in public?"

"Ain't you a doctor or somefing? Mr. Dante said you was."

"I'm a PhD, not an MD. I don't use the title socially."

The brothers looked at each other. "Miss Chase," Malleus whispered. Maleficarum followed suit. "Miss Chase." They tasted the words for several minutes, while Megan watched, holding her breath. Such a little thing, but their fascination made her feel like she was watching an alien learn about modern culture.

Which in a way she guessed she was.

Finally they nodded. "We can do that," Maleficarum announced. "We'll call you "Miss Chase" when there's other folks about what might hear us. 'Slong as you tell Mr. Dante it was you wot made us. We don't want 'im thinking we was taking liberties."

"I'll tell him," Megan said. "And . . ." She had no idea how to broach the subject of their names. Malleus, Maleficarum, and Spud might be perfectly reasonable names for demons, but they were bound to draw stares from anyone who heard them. Probably best just to do it, she decided. "I'm sorry, gentlemen, but I think we might need something else to call you by when people are around, too. They might think, well, your names are lovely, but they're a bit unusual."

Maleficarum nodded. "'S no problem, m'lady. You call us 'Mr. Brown' when you fink we oughter keep our names secret. We've used that one before."

Malleus and Spud snickered and prodded each other in the ribs.

"Mr. Brown? But how do you know which of you I'm speaking to?"

Maleficarum's eyebrows went up. "Don't matter. You say Mr. Brown, and one of us'll be there. We swear it."

THE STUDIO LOOKED very different, filled with people and camera equipment. The dark blue carpet was littered with boxes and crisscrossed with duct tape, the walls hidden behind lights and reflective umbrellas. Megan couldn't believe she'd been here just a few days before to start her show, when her biggest worry was publicity and not her life.

Richard started towards her, a broad smile on his face and his arms outstretched. Megan started to smile in reply, but Malleus leapt in front of her.

"Oi, mate," he said, jabbing his thick index finger square in the center of Richard's chest. "No need to get grabby, is there?"

"It's okay, Ma—Mr. Brown," Megan said, catching the look—half terror, half outrage—on Richard's face. Gently, she took Malleus's hand and removed it from Richard's sternum. "This is my boss, Richard Randall."

Malleus stepped back, but the suspicion on his face didn't change. He gave a curt nod.

Richard glanced at the demons, then back at her. "Megan," he said, regaining some of his dignity. "How brave of you to come! Brian called us this morning. We're all glad you're okay. How are you feeling? You look great. Like you got some sleep. It's great."

Were the demons making him that nervous?

"Thanks, Richard," she said. "I'm fine."

"Great! Excellent!" He glanced sideways. Megan followed.

"Good afternoon, Megan," said Don Tremblay. "Nice to see you again."

Megan nodded. At least now she knew why he was nervous. Don must have told him about their conversation at the restaurant.

Or maybe Richard somehow picked up on the changes in Don's energy. Looking at him sent cold chills through her body. What was he doing here, anyway? Had Richard invited him? The two men were friends after all.

Malleus glanced back at her. "All right, Miss Chase?" He grinned and winked, delighted to be pulling off "Miss Chase" with such aplomb.

"Yes, thank you, Mr. Brown." All three of them guffawed. Megan turned to Richard. "Richard, these are . . . the Misters Brown. They're friends of a friend. Guys, this is my station manager, Richard Randall . . . and Don Tremblay, a colleague."

The brothers nodded, but they folded their arms across their chests and did not shake hands.

"Megan?" A blond woman in a loose smock top advanced on her, smiling. "I'm Dana Cross. Nice to meet you. I'll be doing your make-up."

She reached for Megan, only to end up almost grabbing Spud, who did not move out of her way. "Excuse me," she said, her smile turning uncertain on her wide, friendly face. Spud still did not move.

Too late, Megan realized she needed to say something. "Mr. Brown, could you move, please? I need to go get my make-up done."

All three of them looked at her with varying degrees of disapproval.

"I mean it," she said.

They moved away, every stiff muscle in their big bodies letting her know what a mistake they thought she was making. Megan sat in the chair Dana indicated, yelping when someone swooped down on her with hot rollers and started twisting them into her hair. The brothers stood against the wall to her left, scowling at the hairdresser, but obediently making no move to intervene.

"They seem very . . . nice," Dana said, smoothing a cotton ball soaked in something that smelled like plastic over Megan's face. It left cold, tingling wet trails on her skin. She resisted the urge to scratch at them.

She had to resist the urge to scratch her entire body, in fact. For some reason she was restless. Dana's soothing chatter as she did Megan's make-up was irritating rather than fun, and for all her reservations Megan had expected to have fun. What woman in the world hadn't dreamed at some point of being a model? Of having people fawn over her and bring her bottles of water before making her look beautiful forever, preserved in a perfect moment on film?

For Megan the dream hadn't lasted much longer than it took her to realize she would never be tall enough to be a model, even if she was pretty enough, which she wasn't. Pretty enough for everyday life, sure. Pretty enough for the cover of *Vogue*? No way.

Maybe that was why this made her uncomfortable, and not just because Hot Roller Man was now gouging into her scalp with a comb. The memory of young Megan realizing that in a world full of attractive girls, she was just one of the crowd? Or maybe it was leftover anxiety from the night before?

She wanted to turn around. Something or someone was behind her, weren't they? Her skin was prickling, as if someone was watching her. As if someone was reading her.

She spun around, half-expecting to see Dante standing there grinning, but there were only the photographer and his assistant, her boss Richard and Don Tremblay. None of them were even looking at her.

Perhaps Don was the problem. His aggression, his anger and hatred, were charging the air around her.

She returned to the mirror, only to jump in her seat when something crashed behind her. She turned to see Malleus, Maleficarum, and Spud giggling, while one of the photographer's assistants lay in a heap on the floor, surrounded by equipment.

"I tripped," he said to the photographer. Megan caught Malleus's eye. She frowned and shook her head. He looked down. The hairdresser grabbed her head in both hands and positioned it firmly, then gave her a final yank, patted her shoulder, and disappeared in a cloud of Aqua-Net. He had not spoken a word to her through the entire process.

"Close your eyes." Dana picked up a pot of greenish brown eye shadow and a brush. Megan gave the shadow a doubtful glance but obeyed. The woman did this professionally.

With her eyes closed, the voices and activity in the room reduced themselves to a low hum. The strong clay-like smell of the panstick makeup Dana had applied to her skin mingled with the various colognes and soaps and something else, something sterile and cold that was the room with its generic furnishings.

Six hours of sleep was more than enough to get an old insomniac like herself moving, but leaning back in the comfy chair, with Dana's soft fingertips patting her skin, made Megan start to tune out the room. She had the sensation of her mind climbing beneath soft white sheets, burrowing down into the silent blackness of sleep.

"Megan."

The voice was right in her ear. Megan's eyes flew open. The quality of sound in the room had changed, and it took her a few seconds to realize what was different. The brothers were no longer talking.

She turned to look at them, only to have Dana's fingers on her chin gently bring her back. "I'll be done in a minute."

Swallowing her panic, Megan opened up and gave Dana's mind a quick scan. There was nothing distressing there, no indication Dana should be feared. Just the normal worries of a single woman in the city: an ex-boyfriend who was trying to come back into her life, a job that didn't pay enough.

Why were Malleus, Maleficarum and Spud not chatting? And why had that voice in her ear made every hair on her body stand on end?

A hand touched her shoulder. "You stay calm, Miss Chase," said Malleus.

"About what?" Her gaze sought the small mirror Dana had propped on the desk. The black plastic frame wasn't centered in front of Megan, so she could only see a small slice of the room.

It was enough. A horrible, grinning face filled the glass, just long enough for Megan to get an impression of greenish skin and sharp teeth before it disappeared. She gasped.

"Are you peeking?" Dana laughed. "You know, everyone does. Nobody trusts me to make them look good."

It took a minute for Megan to find her voice. "I'm sure you'll make me look great."

"It's not hard with you, hon," Dana replied, with the easy familiarity of a woman preoccupied. She reached over and grabbed the mirror, handing it to Megan. "See?"

Megan barely glanced at her reflection. She had a fleeting glimpse of her own eyes, looking impossibly wide from either shock or Dana's skilful makeup, before she started tilting the mirror, trying to find the thing again.

She couldn't. The room looked just as it had when they arrived. Megan turned to Malleus, still standing right at her side. "What do you think, Mr. Brown?"

He glanced at her, but he wasn't paying attention. Instead he, too, scanned the room. Maleficarum and Spud were no longer standing by the wall. "Lovely, Miss Chase. Don't you worry."

"Is there something I should worry about?" she whispered. The uneasy feeling from earlier was starting to spread into a full-blown panic.

"Not while we're here." He wouldn't look at her.

"I think everyone is ready, Megan." Brian appeared at her other side. Megan jumped. "Don't be nervous. You look very pretty, and I'm sure the pictures will be great."

Megan plastered what she hoped looked like a smile across her face and stood up. On shaking legs she made her way to the desk, surrounded by umbrella'd lights like an urban oasis.

"I'm Gene," the photographer said. "Just relax."

Did she look that bad? Probably. Her skin was cold. She still couldn't see Maleficarum or Spud. Malleus stood next to the desk, just out of her direct field of vision.

"Okay, Megan, let's lean forward towards the mic," Gene said. "And smile. Look happy. Look welcoming. A lot of people will see this picture, so let's have some fun."

Like telling her the world was watching would help her relax. Megan leaned forward anyway, folding her arms on the polished wood in front of her.

Something scuttled across the floor at the back of the room, something dull mud-brown with clawed feet and a bald head. She just caught a glimpse of it, like a huge scaly rat. More than one of those things lurked in the studio today, then.

Megan jumped, her eyes wide. The first flash of the camera preserved her look of terror.

Chapter Ten

Megan jumped back from the desk at the same time Malleus reached for her.

"Is something wrong?" Gene faked concern well, but Megan could feel his impatience. He had a date after this job. She ignored him.

"We know about them, m'lady," Malleus muttered. "The boys is keeping an eye out, and I'm 'ere, so they won't get to you, okay? You just smile pretty, cuz nobody sees 'em but you an' us."

"Poor girl," Don Tremblay muttered to Brian. "She's always been like this, you know. High-strung. Nervous. I hear it's been worse lately. I think the pressure is getting to her. Such a shame."

Brian, damn him, got out his recorder.

"Dr. Chase, we do need you at the desk."

Richard came over and took her arm, shooting Malleus a look. "Megan, what's the problem? Are you going to do this or what?" A gnarled hand with long, filthy nails curling over the fingertips waved at her from behind his head.

Megan swallowed the bile that rose in her throat. "I'm fine," she croaked. "I just, ah, need a drink."

Malleus pressed a bottle of water into her hand.

Richard glared at both of them. "Get your drink and get back there. We don't have the studio all day, you know."

The water, cool and delicious, soothed her parched mouth. "I know, Richard," she said when she was done swallowing. "I'm ready."

Smiling while listening to the rumble of Tremblay's voice telling tales about her was not easy. Smiling while lies were being spread and an occasional nasty little face or hand or foot appeared in her line of vision was next to impossible.

"Megan, what's wrong?" Richard folded his arms across his chest and leaned back. If she lowered her shield his irritation would snake itself around her and squeeze.

"Fine, Richard." Her stomach fluttered and twisted in knots. Little beads of sweat ran down her forehead.

"Megan . . . Megan . . . Megan . . ." It was a chant, whispered at first, but getting louder.

Maleficarum and Spud appeared, stationing themselves around the desk, far enough away to make their movements unobtrusive but close enough for Megan to take comfort in their presence. Malleus stayed in his position in the corner to her right.

Still the chant continued. Megan could hardly hear Gene's directions over the voices.

Her face felt like it was going to break. She leaned forward, she touched the microphone, she unbuttoned the top button of her blouse just as she was asked to do, all the while feeling like she was someone else, somewhere else, watching another woman in her body act happy and personable while inside she wanted to scream.

A giggle made her turn towards Brian and Don Tremblay. Some sort of . . . gremlin . . . sat on Don's shoulder.

Obscenely naked, it turned and grinned at her, the same face she'd seen in the mirror earlier. Dark green skin stretched over sharp bones as its lips opened, revealing row after row of pointed teeth. It waved, its fingers long and thin with bulbous joints.

It had no ears to speak of, just indents in the sides of its head, and as she watched its tiny eyes started glowing red.

"Hello, Megan," it cooed, and giggled again.

More giggles sounded. Megan tore her gaze from Don and the thing on his shoulder to see more of them. One stuck its tongue out at her from its perch on Dana's shoulder while she smiled and nodded at Megan, her face innocent and open. Richard had one, a dark blue one who leapt about in the air by his head. Brian's was red, Gene's orange.

She clenched her jaw so tight it hurt. She might be about to break a tooth but she could not let up the pressure. If she opened her mouth she would scream. If she started screaming she wouldn't stop.

Everyone in the room had one of those things on their shoulder. Seven or eight danced around on the floor by Don's feet. To whom did they belong? Every one watched her and grinned, or made jokes or faces.

Did she? What did hers look like? Was hers as horrible, as disgusting, as the rest?

Slowly she turned her head . . . and saw nothing but her own reflection staring back at her from the glass window of the studio.

"WHAT THE HELL was all that about?" Richard grabbed her arm. The crew had cleared out, taking their horrible little creatures with them. Megan assumed they were the personal demons Greyson had mentioned. She shuddered. If those were the things that were after her—

They had stayed away, though. At least the presence of Malleus, Maleficarum and Spud had done that much for her, even if the looks Richard gave the three demons told her no one else was impressed with them.

"What do you mean?"

"You know exactly what I mean, Megan. You show up with these three . . . men, who look like they stepped off the set of some British gangster film. You proceed to act strangely, to ignore people when they speak to you, and to behave as though having your picture taken is a fate worse than death." His fingers hurt her arm. She glanced down at them. He let go. "Look, I know you didn't want to do this. But you agreed. It's in your—"

"Contract. I know, Richard." What was she supposed to say? 'Richard, you have a horrible thing living on your shoulder?'

She knew it was still there, even though it had thankfully hidden itself again. She could still feel its presence, dark and disturbing, insinuating itself into her consciousness.

"I gave you this job because I thought you were a professional. If you're not going to act like one, I'll fire you and find somebody else who will."

It was on the tip of her tongue to tell him to go ahead and fire her. She'd agreed to do the damn show to try and help people. Now she was stuck in some nightmare world of demons and zombies and fear, and all she wanted to do was curl up into a ball and pull the covers over her head.

She didn't, though. Aside from the public humiliation and the very real chance that the attendant bad publicity could spell the end of her practice—if the partners didn't put an end to it first, which reminded her she had some calls to make—the chances that the demons would just give up were slim to none. Greyson said it was a challenge to them. She'd picked a fight, however inadvertently. She wouldn't be allowed to just walk away.

Not to mention the callers. People like Regina, who needed help and didn't know where else to get it.

Richard stared at her, waiting for her answer.

"I guess I'm still a little shell-shocked from last night," she said. "I should have rescheduled, but I . . . well, I was excited about the photo shoot and thought it would cheer me up."

Richard softened a little. "I guess you have had a lot to deal with," he said. "Okay, I'm sorry. Gene thinks he still got some pretty good pictures, so we'll just forget it ever happened." He glanced at Brian, who waited by the door, ostentatiously not listening. "And you have more talking to do, I see. You go ahead. I'll speak to you tomorrow."

Megan left, with Brian and the three brothers trailing behind her. She'd forgotten she'd agreed to have dinner with Brian. For a minute she thought about canceling, but she couldn't. Not after the very clear reminder that failure to cooperate meant the loss of her job.

She was stuck with him.

ONCE AGAIN the parking garage gave Megan chills. It was worse this time than it had been Sunday night with Richard. The ceilings seemed lower, the shadows deeper. Maybe it was time to start finding another place to park—or at least parking on the roof.

One of the shadows moved, twisted, and somehow became Art Bellingham.

Megan blinked. Was that a trick of the light? Had he just been hiding back against the wall?

Brian stopped walking and looked back at her. "Megan?"

Two hands grabbed Megan's arms. She jumped and opened her mouth to scream before realizing it was only the brothers, flanking her, guarding her.

Art insinuated himself across the garage, grinning. His movements made the air around her vibrate. How had she not felt this before, his power? It mingled with the wind whirling through the open walls of the building, lifting her hair from her shoulders, pressing her clothes to her body.

Brian's skin was an odd shade of yellowy-pale, washed out by the bug lights in the garage. "Are you okay?" His voice echoed off the cold cement.

She tried to reply but couldn't. Not when the black, oily-feeling energy of Art Bellingham was coming closer and closer to her. Maleficarum took a step forward, ready to shove Art away, but Megan stopped him. Not with Brian watching, not unless it became absolutely necessary.

"Megan." He stood so close to her she stepped back. Her foot landed on something softer than floor, and Spud's faint gasp behind her told her she'd stepped on his toes.

"Hi, Art." The words felt like marbles she was trying to spit out.

"Lovely to see you again." He reached for her hand. She snatched it away and almost stumbled.

"You too. But we're just leaving."

"Oh, no. I wanted to talk to you about when you're coming back to Fearbusters."

"I'm not."

"Of course you are. You know it, and I know it. Why fight it?"

All of the anger and fear and pain she'd experienced over the last few days suddenly crystallized in her breast. Who the hell did he think he was, anyway?

He thinks he's some supernatural being a hell of a lot more powerful than you are, Megan, and he's right about that, please just let it go and don't do anything stupid, you know your temper—

Too late. "I'll tell you why," she said. "Because I don't know who or what you are, but I want nothing to do with you or any of your evil little buddies. Just leave me the hell alone and tell your friends to do the same, okay?"

She spun around, catching a glimpse of Brian's shocked face before she managed to turn her triumphant exit into a farce by walking directly into Spud.

"Oh, Megan," Art said behind her. There was laughter in his voice. "I think if you're worried about evil, you ought to be more careful about the company you're keeping. Or have you not figured out yet who your Greyson Dante is?"

Malleus growled and stepped forward. Megan grabbed him. "Never mind." Tears ran down her cheeks.

It's not smart to make me angry, Megan. Art's voice in her head. Somehow he'd managed to get past her shields, so easily she didn't even feel him. *Little girls who make big speeches often find out they aren't half as strong as they think they are.*

Something flared over her entire body, a choking, squeezing sensation that made bursts of light dance behind her eyes. Art laughed in her head.

She fled to her car, more certain than ever she'd just made a huge mistake.

"YOU KNOW, you can trust me, Megan. How many times do I have to say it?" Brian shattered the silence as he stood up from the bench to throw his food wrapper in the garbage can a few feet away. They were on the riverwalk, a wide sidewalk dotted with benches and trees planted in circles of earth set in the cement. Another part of the millennium project, but one Megan liked a lot more than the fashionable strip.

After leaving the parking garage she didn't want to be inside, didn't want to be anywhere with a lot of people.

She needed air. They'd stopped off at a burger stand and sat down to eat.

"It's not personal." It was all well and good for Brian to say she could trust him. It was even tempting to do so, until the thought of RADIO COUNSELOR BELIEVES DEMONS WALK AMONG US made her close her mouth. "I'm just not comfortable with any of this."

"Then I'm not doing my job."

"Or I'm just being difficult."

He smiled. "Maybe a little bit of both?"

"Sure." At least he wasn't asking what the scene at the station was all about, though she knew he was dying to.

"Tell me about the Misters Brown," he said, glancing at the bench next to them where the three brothers sat surrounded by piled-high hamburger wrappers. Between them they'd polished off at least three dozen. She had no idea how she was going to keep them fed for the next—week? Month? How long would she be living like this?

"Not much to tell. Friends of a friend."

"Of Greyson Dante's?"

"What if they are?" Megan focused her attention on the river. The last rays of sunlight shone across its surface, making it look like molten gold moving slowly by. Picturesque, certainly, but Megan thought of riptides and underwater predators lurking in the depths. Once or twice a year somebody would try to swim across it. Few survived.

"They look like bodyguards to me. Are they?"

Megan shrugged. "Maybe after last night I felt like I needed some help to feel safe."

"So you asked Greyson to help you."

"What makes you think they have anything to do with Greyson?"

"Don't they?"

The breeze blew light strands of her pale hair across her face to tickle her nose and lips. Irritated, she tucked them behind her ear. "Why do you care? Maybe Greyson did help me find them. Friends help each other. They do favors for each other. Isn't that the way the world works?"

"It's how the mob works, if that's what you mean."

"Stop trying to make this look sinister."

"It isn't hard to make them look sinister." Brian glanced at the brothers, who were scanning the sidewalk and surrounding area with their arms folded. "Look, Megan, I wasn't going to say anything, but I think you ought to know."

"Know what?"

"About Dante. About his . . . connections."

"Connections? As in, who he knows?"

"Connections, as in he's connected." He leaned towards her and whispered. "Megan, your buddy is in the Mafia. Those guys are probably hit men or something."

The residual nerves from the encounter with Art had faded. Now they came back with a vengeance. "If that's the case, isn't it awfully dangerous for you to be discussing it?"

"Not as dangerous as it is for you to be involved. I don't think it would be good for your career if people knew you had friends like that."

Was he blackmailing her? RADIO COUNSELOR REVEALED AS MAFIA PRINCESS. "What are you saying?"

He shook his head. "I'm not saying anything. Just that you should be careful, is all."

This was ridiculous. Why sit here listening to Brian's double-speak when she could just read him? She hadn't done it before because she'd been a little scared to use her abilities. This felt too important to let fear stand in her way. She lowered her shields very carefully and reached over with her mind.

It only took a second to realize it. Another second to try to pull back, quickly, before he caught her.

Brian Stone was psychic.

His eyes widened. "You—"

"What?" She kept her eyes down. *Maybe he'll think he was mistaken, maybe he'll let it go . . .*

She knew he wouldn't. She was right.

"Megan." He grabbed her hand. Something leapt from his fingers into hers, his anger transmitting itself. Her face went hot, and she knew he saw it.

They sat in silence for a minute that seemed like eternity. "I see," he said finally, removing his hand. "The psychic psychological counselor. Makes sense."

Just like the psychic reporter, she thought. He had some fucking nerve getting funny with her about her use of her abilities. How many people's minds had he invaded to get good interviews? In fact, had he . . . he'd been the one reading her at the restaurant the other night, hadn't he? And she'd been too distracted to realize it was him. Only fear of what might happen if he included her abilities in his article held her back from starting an argument.

"I'm a real counselor."

"I know." He leaned away from her onto the end of the bench, dangling one arm over the back, and studied her. "But I guess you're just that little bit better at the job, huh?"

"I help people."

"I'm sure you do. Why don't you tell me what's going on?"

"What?"

"Oh, come on. I'm not a fool, Megan. You just happened to have a break-in, you just happen to be good enough friends with one of the city's most powerful, dangerous organized criminals to have him at your place in the middle of the night wearing pajamas, you just happen to suddenly take a break from your regular practice. Spill it. What is going on, and how is Greyson Dante mixed up in all of this?"

She sucked her cheeks in. If he hadn't been quite so cold, so cruel, she might tell him everything. He might even be able to help. She needed all the help she could get.

But he'd mentioned Dante. Why was Brian so interested in the man? Or demon, or whatever—she still wasn't entirely certain how she should think of him.

She shrugged. "I don't know what you're talking about. I'm having trouble with my practice because of the publicity around the radio show—publicity and problems you contributed to, when you hung around the office interviewing people. Greyson was in his pajamas because he rushed over to help me, and I don't know anything about hit men or mobsters, only that he's an attorney I know vaguely through a friend. The break-in was a coincidence."

"And you didn't read the intruders to see if you could identify them."

"I didn't think of it." Shit, he'd caught her with that one. How could she tell him her attackers were simply dead bodies powered by evil?

"It's usually an instinct. Or do you use your powers for other things?"

"What is that supposed to mean?"

"It means I wonder who you're working for, is all. I can imagine a lot of shady businessmen would love to have someone with our abilities playing for their team."

"This is absurd." Megan ignored the fear tracing an icy path up her spine. "Are you accusing me of criminal acts?"

"No."

She relaxed a little.

"I'm accusing you of being an accessory to criminal acts. You're letting a murderer hang around with you and provide you with bodyguards who look ready to pull the heads of people just for stepping into your path. You're not totally naive, you must have read them all and checked them out. Either you aren't very good, which I know isn't true because I just felt your power, or you don't care. Which is it?"

Megan buried her face in her hands. If she told Brian she couldn't read Dante he'd want to know why and she'd either have to admit he was a demon—which she was not about to do, no matter what—or tell him she'd never tried, which made her look stupid.

Stupid was the better option. "I never tried to read him," she said. "I try not to read people outside my office. I didn't try to read you until just now, right? Besides, if you're that interested, why don't you read him yourself?"

"I tried," Brian admitted. "He blocked me."

"Why would you assume he didn't block me?"

"I figured he had. I was fishing anyway, just in case."

Megan slammed her hands down onto the wood bench. The brothers jumped. So did Brian. "That is it," she said, standing. "I am tired of this. I don't need to be interrogated like I've done something wrong, I don't need to be your guinea pig while you use cheap reverse psychology to try and dig up information. If you have something to say, say it."

"Hey, Megan, I'm sorry. I just thought maybe you could help me with—"

"Say it."

He met her glare for a minute, then looked away. "I want to do a story on organized crime in the city," he said. "I thought you might be willing to help. If you're not part of it, of course. You have nothing to lose, right?"

Chapter Eleven

"**I** think it's pretty self-explanatory," Greyson said, handing her a fresh drink. They sat in a corner booth at one of the hip downtown nightspots Megan generally avoided. Tonight, though . . . she wanted people around her, a crowd of loud, sweaty, half-drunk people, despite the inner shivers she got whenever she thought about what rested on each of their shoulders.

What rested on her shoulder? For the fifth or sixth—or twentieth, or fiftieth—time that day, she folded her hands together to keep from feeling around in the air by her head. Whatever sat there, she didn't want to touch. She didn't want to know. She'd seen enough for one day.

"Humor me." She leaned towards him. To any casual onlooker, they probably looked like—Megan swallowed—lovers. Or, at least, a couple on their third or fourth date. The casually territorial way Greyson's arm rested along the back of the booth would certainly give that impression. The heat of his body caressed her through both of their clothing, the warm scent of his skin assailing her and making her breathe a little more deeply than necessary.

He was so close that if she leaned forward another couple of inches, tilted her head to one side . . . they would be kissing.

He cocked an eyebrow, as if noticing the same thing. "Humor you how?"

She jumped back. "Explain it to me exactly as if I didn't know demons existed until a day or two ago, and I'm a complete novice at this sort of thing, okay?"

He nodded. "The personal demons—the *Yezer Ha-Ra*, as the ancient Hebrews called them, the ones who are after you—are small. They rest on the right shoulders of humans. Everyone has one—well, almost everyone—and they're responsible for most of the mischief and misery mankind causes itself."

"Like when someone cuts in front of you in line at the store kind of mischief, or killing people kind of mischief?"

"Both." He sipped his drink, his eyes scanning the room over the rim of his glass. He looked back at her. "It depends on how many of them there are."

"You said everyone has one."

"No, I said *almost* everyone has one. Try to pay attention. This is important."

Megan swallowed her nasty reply along with a mouthful of gin and said, "Fine, *almost* everyone has one. Some people don't have them?"

"Some people have more than one. Sometimes a personal demon does an excellent job with their human. They manage to send that particular person farther down the spiral of whatever misery they're causing—making them more and more violent, or sneaky, or drunk, for example. The human grows more vulnerable, the demon more powerful. Soon it's powerful enough to call another demon to its command. They both gang up on the person, sucking out the energy and life-force and using that power to attract more demons, who steal more life . . . eventually leaving nothing but a shell, if they aren't stopped."

Megan shivered. "How do you stop them?"

"It's different for everyone. Some people go into counseling or join twelve-step programs or something to help them hold on to the force they have left. In time they can even rebuild it. Others . . ." he shrugged. "They kill themselves. Or other people. Sometimes both."

A drunken woman in a dress so low-cut Megan thought her breasts would pop out at any second stumbled and fell onto the table, jostling both of their drinks and spilling them all over what little there was of her dress.

"What the—" Megan started, but then she snapped her mouth shut.

Greyson looked at Megan oddly,

The woman struggled back to vertical. "Oh, sorry." Her too-large mouth hung open as if she had something else to say, but had forgotten it.

Greyson rose, grabbed the woman by her elbow and whispered something in her ear. The drunk's eyes widened. She glared at someone across the room, then lurched away.

Greyson turned back to Megan. "What was that all about?"

"I could ask you the same thing. What did you say to her?"

"I told her that guy over there was checking her out and his girlfriend called her a whore."

Megan looked. Their drunken friend was already arguing with a blond woman. "Was it true?"

"No. Just fun. Back to you. You went pale, and stopped talking. Why?"

"I just stopped, is all." Her date liked to start fights between total strangers. Then again, what did she expect from a demon? She tore her gaze away from the now-screaming women.

"Megan, getting angry isn't like an engraved invitation to be overrun by personal demons. You're not going to make things worse by being pissed at some drunken idiot."

"Maybe not. But I seriously doubt it's going to make things better, either."

"I don't know. Maybe you need to let off a little steam."

"Are you in the Mafia?"

She'd expected a reaction—anything to make him stop staring at her like that—but she hadn't expected him to practically choke on his drink. "What? What the hell kind of question is that?"

"One I'd like answered, please." She'd never seen him on the defensive before, if that's what this was. It was a rather heady feeling to make him as disconcerted as he made her.

He rubbed his forehead. "Let me guess—Brian Stone told you that?"

"What if he did?"

"Nothing. I could tell you a few things about him, too. Things he may not want to spread around."

"Like what?"

"Oh, no. *Some* of us are honorable."

It was such a ridiculous statement, and he looked so self-righteous making it, that Megan laughed. "If you mean that Brian is psychic, I already know."

"Yes, but do you know because he told you, or because you tried to read him and found out that way?"

"I—" She closed her mouth. Greyson nodded, his eyes gleaming in the reflected neon lights from the bar.

"He didn't tell you. Instead he told you a bunch of crap about me, probably intended to—well, never mind. The point is, old Stone isn't exactly squeaky-clean himself.

Don't you wonder how many people he's read without their knowing it to get a better story?"

Even as she nodded, she was aware of two things—one, that he was deliberately distracting her from the question she'd asked him, and two, that she'd done the same thing, and Dante knew it. "Is this your clever way of telling me I'm unethical with my patients?"

"No, I don't think it's the same thing at all. Your patients pay you to make them feel better. The people Brian deals with aren't paying him for anything, and he's sure not helping them, either."

She considered this for a minute, then nodded. "Are you in the Mafia or not?"

She'd refused to help Brian with his story. She didn't even want to entertain the idea. At least, not until she knew the truth.

"Keep your voice down. Ugh, we can't talk in here. Let's go." He slid out of the booth and stood, slipping on his jacket and nodding to Malleus, Maleficarum, and Spud, who sat in the booth next to theirs downing oceans of beer.

Was he going to fit her with some cement boots? "Maybe I don't want to go."

"Yes, you do. You hate these places."

Damn it, was she that obvious? "Maybe tonight I like them."

"Are you afraid I'm going to—I believe the term is—'whack' you?"

"Should I not be?"

He leaned back into the booth and grabbed her arm, pulling her out of her seat to stand in front of him. "Stop acting like a child."

"Hold on a minute." She wrenched her arm from his grasp. How dare he say she was being childish? Even if she was. Especially if she was. "Why do we need to leave all of the sudden? You wanted to be here twenty minutes ago, now you want to leave, and it's all about what you want and not about me. What about what I want?"

"Fine. What do you want, Megan?"

At that moment, she wanted nothing more in the world than to slap him right across that sharp-boned face of his. Instead she folded her arms across her chest. "I want another drink."

She'd grown so used to reading men's minds she'd never paid much attention to their body language, for all she'd studied it in school. Now she had a chance. His fists clenched and opened, his weight shifted on his feet. The roll of emotions across his face fascinated her; his mouth tightened, his eyes narrowed.

"Fine," he said finally. "Does it have to be here?"

Megan paused. She'd won the battle. Was it worth torturing herself in order to get back at him?

Yes. Yes, it was. "I want to stay here," she repeated, smiling sweetly. "It's fun here."

His glare told her he knew exactly what she was doing. "I'll go get us more drinks."

"You do that," she said. "I'll be waiting. Oh, and Greyson?"

He stopped but did not turn back around.

"Thanks for being so sweet to me."

She grinned as he strode away.

"Hurry up." She unlocked her front door and ushered them all, sweaty and rumpled, inside. "We can talk about it in the living room."

"Thanks, m'lady." Malleus held the bloody handkerchief to his nose as he passed her, followed by Maleficarum, Spud, and Greyson, all of whom were nursing various wounds.

Last to enter was the blond woman in an immaculate black suit whom Megan still hadn't been introduced to, but who'd helped them escape from the club. Why the woman had followed them back here, Megan wasn't sure, but Greyson knew her.

She closed the front door on the cloudless night and locked it. Had she once thought she spent too much time alone at home? Facing a living room full of demons and one woman who looked like she'd stepped off the pages of *Better Than You In Every Way* magazine made her yearn for the days when it was just herself, a few snacks, and bad Lifetime movies.

Greyson was already pouring drinks. "That was fun," he said, his furrowed brow and the swelling of his left eye belying his words. "Thanks for your help, Tera."

The woman glanced at Megan before sitting down. "No problem." Her tone made Megan certain it was a problem. The woman and Greyson seemed to be pretending they didn't know each other very well, but liked each other; felt more like they didn't particularly trust each other and would both rather they'd not met up.

Why was the woman here?

Greyson handed Megan her drink. "Megan, this is Asterope Green," he said, in an oddly graceless manner.

"Call me Tera."

Malleus pulled the sodden handkerchief away from his face. "I fink it's stopped now," he said. He glanced over at Tera. "You're not gonna write me a fine, are you, luv?"

Tera smiled. "I wouldn't worry about it tonight. It looked like a regular bar fight, and nobody seemed the wiser, so I think we can let it go."

She looked like she expected them to thank her. Instead they just looked irritated.

"Nobody the wiser!" Maleficarum folded his arms across his chest. "They'd have to be pretty stupid not to know we wasn't human, wouldn't they? After the way we cleaned that place up. Teach them to come near our lady, that will. 'Oo'd that man fink he was, anyways, walkin' right up to 'er and trying to talk? Like it weren't obvious she was already—"

"I think that's enough," Greyson said. Even the swelling of his left eye couldn't hide the bags under it and he kept glancing over at Tera as if she made him very nervous. "You men did what you thought was right and I'm sure Miss Chase appreciates it."

Megan nodded. It seemed like the right thing to do. "Of course."

"What exactly are the men doing?" Tera asked.

"They're just here visiting," Greyson said. "Just out for a drink with me and my—date."

Tera looked from the brothers, who were covered with blood and bruises, to Greyson in his torn and wrinkled shirt, to Megan, who managed to close her mouth a second before the blond woman's glance fell upon her. "I see."

Greyson clapped his hands in front of his chest. "I guess that's it then. Thanks again for your help, but I assure you, we can discipline the boys on our own. There's no need to worry about a repeat of this happening."

"'Oo's gonna discipline—" Maleficarum started, but Malleus grabbed him by the arm before he could finish the sentence.

Tera smiled. "Of course. I'm sure your boss will handle the matter just fine."

"Great." He started to take her arm to lead her to the door, but she didn't move.

"Just one thing, though. If I'm not mistaken—and I probably am—aren't you obligated to inform us when you're giving outsiders information on our world?" She shrugged. "Just checking. I mean, I'm sure you know more about demon regulations than I do, right? Being an attorney and all."

"This is a special case, Tera . . ."

"Oh, I'm sure it is," she replied, waving her right hand in an I-clearly-don't-believe-you manner. "I know you would never, ever do something against the rules."

"Excuse me," Megan said. "I'd appreciate not being spoken of like I'm not here, especially since this is my house. Mr. Dante has been helping me, there's—"

"Never mind." Dante downed his drink and eyed the bottle for a second before pouring another. "Tera, I assume you'll want to speak to me in your office tomorrow. I'll be there around ten, okay?"

"I have time now," Tera said. "I have to meet Lexie in an hour or so, but I can stay until then. Unless you'd like me to invite her over?"

Greyson's eyes widened. "No. No, no need for that."

"Then you'd better tell me now what's happening, before it's time for me to meet her."

"Tera works for Vergadering, Megan." Dante must have seen the confusion on Megan's face.

"We're sort of like supernatural law enforcement. But not," Tera added.

"Ah." Megan had no idea how to respond to that, which was surely the least helpful explanation she'd ever been given, including Dante's snippets of demon information.

"They make sure we stay secret," Greyson said, as he handed Tera her drink. "They're all witches."

"Ah." Her contributions to the conversation were dazzling so far. Why not continue with the same theme?

"Are you going to keep exposing us right in front of me? Is this how bad it's gotten, Grey? Give me one good reason not to cast a forgetfulness—"

Greyson glanced from Megan to Tera and back. "Maybe there is a good reason, Tera. Maybe you can help us with something."

Tera laughed. "Oh, no. You know I don't get involved with demons. Unlike my sister."

Greyson cleared his throat. "But you do get involved with witches, don't you?" He nodded towards Megan. "She needs help."

Tera looked at Megan with new interest. "She's a witch? No. She's too bland to be a witch. Look at that frizzy hair."

"I'm not a witch," Megan said. She wanted to say something about her hair, too, but decided to keep silent. Not only was it a side issue, it was true. Her hair *did* frizz.

"You're a psychic," Greyson said. "It's almost the same thing."

They all stared at her. Megan suppressed the urge to run into her bedroom and close the door.

"A psychic? Really? I didn't even feel it."

"She's got pretty strong shields," Greyson said.

Tera stood up. "I guess so." She looked Megan up and down, her hazel eyes bright and curious. "Why does she need help?"

"She just needs to find a way to—"

"Excuse me," Megan said. "Do I get a say in this?"

"No. She needs to learn to focus her power, Tera. Think you can teach her?"

Tera didn't take her eyes off Megan. "I'm not going to help you build your family a nice little psychic weapon, Grey. I can't believe you'd even ask."

"It's not for us." Megan could see him fighting with himself over something, before he sighed and said, "She does that radio show. The demon slaying one. The personal demons heard it and—"

"They believe it?"

He nodded.

"Of all the—can't you just tell them it isn't real?"

He made a face.

Tera sighed. "You won't even tell me if that's possible, will you? I don't understand all this damn secrecy among you demons, it's like you—"

"Don't trust the Vergadering? I can't imagine why that would be, can you?"

"That was a long time ago."

"And we still don't have a representative."

"Maybe because none of you will be honest with us and follow the damned rules."

Megan cleared her throat. "Guys? Can we get back on the subject? If you're going to treat me like a piece of meat, I'd at least appreciate not being a forgettable piece, please."

"Witches and demons have a . . . history." Tera glanced at her. "Anyway. If you need help, I guess I'll help you. But you need to be committed. I'm not going to waste my time."

Feeling put on the spot, Megan nodded.

Tera turned to Greyson. "If I find out she's working for you, in any capacity, I'll have you all locked in the cellars. And you owe me a favor for this, right? That's how you guys do things?"

Greyson smiled without showing his teeth.

Tera set down her glass and picked up her purse. "Good. I'm off then," she said. "Megan, I'll call you tomorrow to set up our first lesson."

Her heels clicked along the floor as she let herself out, leaving Megan and the demons alone in her living room.

Greyson shook his head. "I hope you appreciate this, Megan," he said, "because I've just sold my soul, such as it is, to one of the Green sisters, and the last time I tangled with one of them I got—what's wrong?"

Megan shook her head. Her ears were ringing. "I don't know," she said. "I just feel . . . kind of dizzy . . ."

Laughter filled her ears. Art Bellingham's laughter. *Just stopping by to pay you a visit,* he said, the words echoing in her skull and drowning out her every conscious thought. *Good night, little Megan . . . sweet dreams . . .*

A vision flashed before her eyes. A room, the one she'd seen in Kevin's mind, in his dream, when he'd described it to her in his office . . . the room with all the little doors in walls that stretched to the ceiling . . . .

But now the doors were opening.

Megan screamed as Art's laughter echoed in her head.

Chapter Twelve

The wind made her eyes water, but she didn't care. The cool, damp air felt wonderful against her heated skin.

"Just relax . . . just be still and relax." Greyson's voice seemed to come from very far away, though he stood right next to her with his hands hard on her upper arms. "Deep breaths . . . deep breaths . . ."

"He was in my mind," she whispered. "He invaded my mind."

"I know."

"I had my shields up, I don't know how he managed to do that, why is he able to do that, I don't—"

"Come on." Greyson released her arms and took her left hand in his, leading her off her little patio and out into the yard. The stiff grass whispered under her shoes. September had changed from Indian summer to autumn in a day, and winter's approach was fragrant in the air. She shivered.

From inside the house came the low voices of Malleus, Maleficarum, and Spud as they watched television. Apparently they were big fans of the evening soaps. That normalcy only a few dozen feet away helped calm her, as did the motion of walking and the presence of someone at her side.

Megan and Greyson stopped just before the small patch of trees—nowhere near large enough to be called a forest or even a wood—that separated her property from the next neighborhood over. The trees, and the privacy they afforded, had been one of the things that most attracted Megan to the house when she'd bought it late the year before. Now she wished she'd bought a condo somewhere instead, in one of those horrible gated communities with a pool always surrounded by sullen teenagers and retirees, barely tolerating each other on the patio.

To her right, at the opposite corner, was the shed. Where Greyson had burned the zombies.

Greyson followed her gaze. "There's nothing over there," he said. "I swear."

"I believe you."

She hugged herself more closely and looked up at the dusky clouds in the dark sky overhead. What she wanted to do was cry. To curl up under the covers and make everything disappear.

She wanted to go home, but there was no home to go to. It had been made clear to Megan years ago that the only place in the world for her was a place she made herself. Now even that didn't feel safe anymore.

"You know, Meg," he said. "It's okay to be scared about all of this."

"What?" Her fingernails dug into her upper arms she was gripping them so tightly in an effort not to slap him. "What? Was that supposed to be helpful? Do you really think I'm standing here all worried that you might think I'm scared?"

Even as she said the words, she realized that was exactly what she was worried about, that no matter how scared she felt, she didn't want to admit it to him. The knowledge made her even angrier.

"No, I just thought maybe—"

"Maybe what? Maybe you can get me so worried about being afraid that I won't notice you haven't answered any of my questions? You still haven't even told me everything about the personal demons. Did you think I wouldn't notice?" Her shouts roused some birds in one of the nearby trees; they took off in a flurry of wings, sending leaves dancing down to the earth behind them.

"Lower your voice—"

"Not to mention what you hope to get out of this. I'm not stupid; I know there must be something you expect to accomplish. Are you going to explain that?"

"I've been trying—"

"Don't give me trying, you haven't been trying, you've just been smirking and acting superior and enjoying all of this, haven't you?"

"If you would—"

"I don't have to do anything, I'm not going to be all meek and let you—"

His lips stopped her words, warm and firm on hers as he pulled her to him.

The first thing she noticed was how hot his hands were on her face, how hard his body felt pressed against her. The second thing was how he tasted faintly of Scotch and smelled like vanilla and wood smoke.

There was no third thing. She was lost, lost in the sensations his lips evoked from every nerve ending, the way her entire body caught fire just as if he'd set her ablaze with a snap of his fingers.

He pulled her closer, pressing his left hand into the small of her back, switching his hold on her so his right hand tangled in her hair.

Her arms were around him without her realizing she'd put them there, her fingertips brushing against the tips of the *sgaegas* between his shoulder blades.

His tongue darted between her teeth and she met it with her own, surprised at the surge of power that flooded through her when they touched. It sizzled through her veins, white-hot, filling her body with light and pooling between her legs. She wouldn't have been surprised to see them both glowing, to see the trees around them lit up like daytime if she opened her eyes.

Which she did, as soon as Dante pulled away from her.

"May I speak now?" His voice was normal, but his breathing wasn't.

Megan straightened her spine and lifted her chin. "I'm not stopping you."

He stood there for a minute, watching her.

"I'm listening."

"Yes, yes, I'm just—just trying to think of where to start." He shoved his hands into his pockets again and started pacing. Without the heat of his body, she was cold again. The breeze swirled around her, finding the tiny holes in the weave of the clothing and caressing her rapidly cooling skin.

He sighed. "Okay. Here's the thing. Demons . . . we're not like humans."

"Oh, gee, you don't say."

"Don't be sarcastic. I've never had to explain this before—well, I've never been allowed to explain this before. You heard Tera earlier. This is the kind of thing that could get me in big trouble with a number of people."

"Like the verga—vergera—"

"Vergadering. Yes. They're the ruling body for supernatural beings and they don't like it when they catch us telling tales. Neither do my employers. Or any other demons, or witches, or the Fae—although they have nothing to do with this and they're not under Vergadering rules—or the weres, the vampires, or anyone else."

"Weres and vampires? You're telling me vampires are real?"

He stopped short. "Demons and witches you'll believe, but vampires I'm making up?"

"Point taken."

"The Vergadering aren't too crazy about demons. They're all wizards and witches and they view us as secondary beings, beneath them. They attempted to erase us from the planet a few hundred years ago—you heard me mention it with Tera just now—"

"You guys were arguing about something that happened that long ago? You made it sound like it was last month."

"Do you want me to explain this or not?"

"Yes."

"Then be quiet. Time moves a little slower for us and, anyway, it isn't like you people don't carry prejudices from your own history. The point is, since the Vergadering is intent on keeping demons and our activities firmly under their fat little magical thumbs, we've built our own set of rules and standards. Ways to get around things a little. Back in the early nineteenth century, by your reckoning, the *Meegras* came into being. The Families."

"Then you *are* like the Mafia."

"No, no, no." He shook his head. "It's not . . . well, okay. Yes. It's kind of like that. But it's not a criminal enterprise per se. It's just a way to keep track of things and to police ourselves so the Vergadering will stay as far away as possible.

"Are you cold?" It took her a second to catch the question and realize he expected an answer. She nodded.

He made a scooping motion with his hands. Flames rolled off his fingers, flaring orange in the darkness, and hovered a few inches above the ground.

Another move of his hand and the flames leapt higher. It was like a real campfire—only without logs—and warmth caressed her legs.

They sat down. The icy ground froze her skin, but the heat from Greyson's little fire more than made up for it. Megan felt like they were sitting around a campfire telling ghost stories and the dancing flames soothed her. Something deep inside her relaxed as Megan peacefully watched the shapes and colors change. Even the shadows the fire cast on the trees nearby weren't as threatening as they might once have been.

Megan understood now why her prehistoric ancestors had been eager to harness fire. Fire was safety. A precarious safety, yes, for it was still dangerous, still terrifying. But the act of sitting by a small, controlled fire such as this made one feel as though the element had been conquered, even if only for a short while.

She looked at Dante with something akin to awe. Not just because of the way he'd kissed her earlier—her stomach gave a distinct flip at the memory—but because he could do something no human had ever managed to do. He could command an element, bend energy to his will. It hadn't struck her with the same force in her cheery, well-lit house. Out here . . . out here fire was life.

"You're staring at me." His voice sounded as if it were made of smoke itself, husky and low. She wondered if he could see her interest, her attraction, as plainly as she could see the flames reflected in his eyes. Somehow she thought he could.

"Sorry." She looked away.

He paused, but when she didn't speak he continued. "So we have our Meegras. And yes, we do fight for power, but it's not the way you think of power. Remember when you asked me yesterday about gods and souls?"

She nodded.

"Money is important and skills are important. But we all, well, collect souls too. Not the way you're thinking, but we do like to . . . control people. At least, our power as a Meegra tends to be measured by how many humans we have."

"Have?" The cold was back. Did he view people as . . . as creatures, as things put on earth to do his bidding?

"Say you're the head of a large company. Your worth is judged not only by how much money you make, but how large your empire is, all over the world, right? It's the same thing. And if we can manage to make humans' lives a little less, ah, boring, we get some credit for it. Some power. Respect . . . Don't look at me like that. Megan. What did you expect demons to do, teach baking classes and have sewing circles? Fucking with humans is our purpose in life."

She shook her head. "I try to help them, and you try to harm them."

"Our side is much more fun."

"Why are you helping me, then?"

He paused. "Because you've gotten yourself involved in something you shouldn't be involved in and I don't think you should get further involved."

"That's it?" There had to be more. He'd just finished explaining that demons collected people, hadn't he? Tera had called her a weapon. Greyson said someone with her abilities would be seen as a threat. Could he be trying to recruit her?

"Plus you gave your word to us in the beginning, remember? You promised not to accept other offers. We have a vested interest in making sure you don't end up with Bellingham. It would make us look bad."

"But I won't end up with Bellingham."

"We need it to look like you're with us. Part of my job is to make sure it looks that way."

She'd been pulling blades of grass up as he spoke, shredding the thin dying leaves between her fingers. Now her fingertips touched bare, hard earth. She fisted her hands and crossed her arms instead. "I see." This was just business, demon business. Fine. Lots of people kissed their business acquaintances so hard their bodies throbbed. "Am I going to owe you a favor? What if I say no?"

"Maybe you will. Maybe it will be something you want to do."

"I won't join your family or become a demon, you know."

"I don't remember asking you to." The firelight danced over his scowl.

An awkward silence settled between them. No, he hadn't asked her to join his family. He hadn't even asked her on a real date and here she was refusing to marry him. And she wondered sometimes why she was still alone.

"I have a question," she said, hoping to change the subject. "What does mine look like?"

"What?"

"My demon."

Now it was his turn to pick at the grass. "Didn't I tell you?" The studied casualness of his voice might have fooled her two days ago. Not now.

"No, you didn't tell me."

"I thought I had."

"Stop dawdling. What are you hiding?"

"You don't have one."

"Excuse me?"

"You don't have one. You're the only person in the world without one. Strange. We're not sure how it happened. But there it is. You're without a personal demon."

"But I—" She almost bit her tongue. "I don't believe you."

"One thing I'm not," he said, in a voice cold enough to make her shiver, "is a liar."

She stared at him. He relented. "Not about stuff like this, anyway."

"But you didn't tell me this before."

"You didn't ask before."

"That's a lie by omission."

"Megan," he said. "What difference does it make?"

"You should have told me." She stood up, not wanting to be with him anymore, not even wanting to look at him. Away from his fire the cold wind cut through her again. "You shouldn't have waited for me to ask."

"I hoped you wouldn't ask."

He reached for her, but she pulled away. "Is this why you can't tell them I'm not a threat to them? Because they don't have any connection with me?"

He nodded. "It makes you pretty powerful. Anything rare becomes valuable, doesn't it?"

"And I'm rare enough to be valuable to you?"

He opened his mouth, closed it again. This time he managed to grip her shoulders before she tore herself away and headed back towards the house. Whatever he had to say, or whatever he wanted to do, she wasn't ready.

WHEN SHE WAS in college she'd hidden another girl's class notes as a joke. The girl had been mean to her, but without her notes she'd almost failed. Nobody made Megan do that. She'd done it herself.

Once, while shopping, she had seen another woman take the last copy of a DVD Megan wanted off the rack and place it in her cart. When the woman turned her back, Megan grabbed the DVD and rushed to the counter to buy it herself. Her own choice.

Just like all the other petty meannesses and minor transgressions of day-to-day life. The parking spaces taken, the five dollar bills found on the ground and pocketed instead of being turned in, the dirty looks given to people driving too slow.

Most of these choices hadn't bothered her more than the occasional twinge of conscience. Now . . . now she knew everyone else had a demon who ordered or encouraged them to do those things. Was everyone else good, and only she truly bad? Was that why she didn't have a personal demon?

Greyson, damn him, seemed to know the track of her thoughts. He caught up with her, stopped her with his hand on her arm. "You're not a bad person, Meg."

"How the hell do you know?" She wanted to believe him so badly it hurt, but she couldn't. He'd lied to her, he hadn't told her about this, and she felt like she was swimming in the middle of a lake too large and deep for her to ever reach the shore. "How would you know anything about people? And why would your good opinion mean anything, anyway? You're a demon. You do evil shit for fun, for a living. You use people up and throw them out, you just admitted it. How are you qualified to judge me in any way?"

The moment the words left her mouth she regretted them, but she couldn't seem to find her tongue to apologize. They just stood there, the wind blowing between them like an invisible, angry barrier.

Finally he spoke. "Do you want me to take the boys with me when I go?"

"No."

He raised his eyebrows.

"I'm independent, not stupid. Obviously I need some physical protection." Although why, she couldn't be sure. Was a petty, mean-minded soul like hers even worth saving?

Well, yes, it was. No matter how she felt, she didn't want to die. She would just have to make more of an effort. She'd have to be better, nicer.

She sighed. "Look, I'm sorry. I guess I overreacted a little bit. This is stressful, you know, and I'm not sure how I should be responding to it all."

"Sure."

They stood awkwardly for another minute, the voices of the brothers singing a rousing rendition of "Knees Up, Mother Brown" forming a surreal soundtrack to their isolation. "Do you want to have another drink? Might warm us up," she said.

He shook his head. "I should get going. I have to meet with Tera tomorrow morning and I'm pretty tired after last night."

"Sure."

His goodbyes to Malleus, Maleficarum, and Spud were just as smooth as ever, but Megan noticed their curious looks. She decided to ignore them. Screw Greyson Dante. She didn't particularly like him anyway, cool bastard of a demon that he was.

He wasn't even human. What had she been thinking? Just because his appearance rang every bell she had and his kiss made her feel like she'd found something long lost did not mean they were suited for each other or that she was interested in him. Well, interested in him in a way that didn't begin and end in bed. She *was* human, after all, and it had been some time since she'd . . . been with someone.

Not that he deserved the pleasure, but she did. Either way, it wasn't going to happen. Not now, not ever, and next time he decided to plant an arrogant kiss on her she'd be ready with her fists clenched. Or, at least, prepared to pull away and say "no."

Malleus, Maleficarum, and Spud were watching her, and she realized she was staring at the closed front door as if she could will it to open again. She shook her head and turned to them. "Where do you guys want to sleep? I can make up the bed in the guest room, I think two of you can fit there if you don't mind sharing, and . . ." She'd never had this many guests before. Come to think of it, she'd never had any guests before. "I can make up the couch, too."

"No need, m'lady," Malleus replied. "On'y one of us sleeps at a time. The guest bed's all we needs. T'other two'll be on duty, right?"

Visions of them hovering over her bed watching her sleep danced in Megan's head like beer-filled sugarplums. "On duty where?"

"One of us in 'ere, one in your room. We'll take turns."

How to put this delicately? "I get a little, ah, nervous at the thought of people watching me sleep."

Surprise was not a flattering emotion on their crinkly, pug-nosed faces. "We can't let you sleep alone, m'lady," Maleficarum said. "Mr. Dante wouldn' like that at all."

"Maybe I could just leave the door open?" Even as she suggested that, she knew it was no good. Her shoulders sagged. "Okay, but please let me at least use the bathroom and change by myself."

They relented and, after searching the rooms, allowed her to brush her teeth. She put on her oldest, most modest nightgown, a flannel monstrosity with a high collar and a hem that almost reached her ankles. The last time she'd let anyone see it was her last boyfriend; he'd thought it was hysterical and had insisted on calling her "Miss Eyre" every time she put it on, which wasn't often . . .

Even covered as she was, the boys averted their eyes until she finally threw on her bathrobe, too. It wasn't cold enough yet for such clothing, and she was sweating by the time she'd finally had enough bland late-night television and gone to bed.

Sleep refused to come. One of the demons moved around in the room and she pulled the sweltering covers closer around her sweaty head. She had no doubt he was being as respectful as possible and not staring at her, but it was still disconcerting.

All things considered, though, what was one more discomfort? In the past few days she'd made her radio debut, been attacked by zombies, met several demons and a witch, seen quite a few more demons, been suspended, and had her psychic defenses breached by someone—or something—who felt like pure, cold evil crawling up her spine.

She'd just been informed that the entire rest of the human population had something that she didn't and her head ached every time she tried to figure out what that meant about her.

Worst of all was the email Brian Stone received. After all these years . . . she'd thought she would never hear the name Harlan Trooper again, would never have to see his face or hear his voice in her mind. Even now some part of her brain refused to let her remember what had happened. It was a blur, just as it had been for years before she'd finally managed to banish the memory completely. The prospect of telling it again, of dredging it all back up, made her chest hollow and cold.

And what about Brian? Was he friend or foe? She had no idea. Even less did she know for sure which side Greyson Dante fell on. All she knew about him was that her lips still tingled.

Chapter Thirteen

"No, it's not for my home! It's for my office. I don't see why you need my home—" Megan broke off while the man on the other end of the line, obviously a native speaker of English but one who behaved as if he didn't understand a word, interrupted her with yet another request for her address.

"Give me the phone."

Megan jumped. One of the boys must have let Greyson in, she hadn't even heard him knock. If he had knocked. He might have called them on one of the sleek black cellphones they all carried. The brothers found her lack of cell intensely amusing.

She glared at him and turned her back. "Look, if you can just have someone meet me later today, I'll show them exactly where we need the soundproofing and what—no! Why aren't you listening to me?"

"Give me the phone."

Fine. If Greyson wanted to play Mr. Hero, he could. She put the receiver in his hand.

He hung it up.

"Hey! I was on hold there for—"

"I don't know why you're bothering with all of this. We can take care of it for you."

"Take care of what?" She tried not to envision the partners dancing on strings like vacant, demonically-possessed puppets.

He raised an eyebrow. "We'll have your co-workers killed, of course. What did you think I meant? The Meegra has all sorts of employees. I'll send one of our people over to do the soundproofing. I can find you a receptionist, too."

It was tempting. So tempting Megan had to bite her tongue to keep from thanking him. The problem was . . . well, she wasn't exactly sure what the problem was. She just knew she didn't want Greyson and his demon family taking charge of too much of her life.

She didn't want to be in his debt.

As much as she would have loved to hand this tedious business over to someone who had the juice to fix it with a wave of his aristocratic hand, she couldn't do it. Who knew what he might expect in return?

She snatched the phone back from the cradle, turned her back on him, and started dialing the number of the next company listed in the Yellow Pages.

They seemed to at least understand what she needed and agreed to meet her at her office on Friday. With a sigh, Megan agreed. Better than nothing.

"You let us replace your windows," Greyson said when she hung up.

"That was different."

"Oh? In what way?"

"Because my windows were—oh, never mind. It just is. I had to have the windows right away. The soundproofing can wait a few days."

"Suit yourself."

"I will." She gave him a tentative smile, hoping maybe he'd decided, as she had, to let bygones be bygones.

He returned it. "I can't stay. I just wanted to stop by and see how you got on last night."

The words made her feel even worse, or at least they would have if she'd believed them. Something told her he wasn't being completely honest and it wasn't her psychic abilities because he was impossible to read.

If he wouldn't come out with it, she'd find a way to dig it out. "How did your meeting go this morning?"

"With Tera? Fine. I owe her a couple of favors, it seems, which is always a pleasure." He scowled. "She'd like to meet with you as soon as possible. I think, and she agrees, that we don't have much time. We'd both like you to have as much training as we can stuff into you."

"What do you mean, not much time? I—"

"I can't stay," he repeated. "We'll discuss it later. Tera will be by at about four, and I'll take you to dinner afterwards. Maybe we can elude Stone for a couple of hours?"

"I'm cooking, anyway. I promised the boys I would make them a steak pie."

"You haven't offered to cook for me."

"You haven't re-grouted my tub, washed my car, and shampooed my upholstery while I slept. I figured it was the least I could do."

"I cleaned up while you were at the hospital."

"True, and you did a fantastic job, but you also drank quite a bit of my Scotch."

"Now, now," he said. His voice was serious but his smile was still genuine. "Polite hostesses don't berate their guests in such a manner."

"Polite guests don't complain that they're not being given enough."

"Hmmm." He stepped closer to her, close enough that she could smell the wonderful cologne he wore. His dark eyes gave off sparks when they met her blue ones. "I won't complain, but there's certainly something else I'd like to have."

Her stomach did a flip, but she stepped back. "You're welcome to come to dinner with us if you want."

The gleam in his eyes told her he wasn't fooled. He'd seen her reaction and knew what it meant.

He let her get away with it. "Sure. Just tell me what time to be here."

"Around seven-thirty, I guess." She ignored the pang of disappointment in her chest that he hadn't pressed the issue. She didn't want to kiss him again. She didn't want things to go any further than they had. She didn't trust him, pointblank, right?

"See you then," he said, and was off to talk to the boys before she'd finished reminding herself that she wasn't interested.

BRIAN SWITCHED ON his little tape recorder and set it between them on the park bench. She'd refused to meet him at a restaurant, finding that taking meals in public, while imagining or even seeing, if they chose to show themselves, the demons sitting on the shoulders of the other diners was no longer appealing. And who knew what the chefs' personal demons were convincing them to do to the food? She shuddered. Bad enough thinking of Brian's demon, without worrying about everyone else's.

"I know you don't want to talk about this," Brian said, noting her distaste but mistaking the reason. "But we agreed on this the other night. You're the only one who can tell me what happened."

Megan nodded. "I know."

The strained atmosphere between them set her teeth on edge. Where was the cheerful, interesting Brian, the one with whom she'd had such fun at lunch just a few days before?

Now a stranger sat beside her on the bench. He'd apologized—they both had—but Megan still doubted they would find themselves chatting easily again. Disappointing. It would have been nice to have a friend who knew her secret and understood.

"Look, Megan. I'm sorry about yesterday. But you have to look at my side. I'm trying to give you every benefit of the doubt because—well, because I think you're a good person."

"I appreciate that."

"But I've been wrong before. I have to be a reporter here, you know? It's my job."

"Sure."

"You still sound kind of cold."

The weakening autumn sunlight fell on his light brown hair, bleaching it the color of ripe wheat. It made him look somehow innocent, noble, like a man with a child's idealism.

She shook her head. However apologetic he might be, however honorable he might act, he was still a reporter, a man who was essentially blackmailing her into talking about the worst thing that had ever happened to her, and a man whose presence in her life she decidedly did not need. She'd spent the entire morning terrified he would start questioning Malleus, Maleficarum, and Spud—or worse, wanting to know more about Art Bellingham.

Oddly, Brian hadn't asked her about Bellingham. Why? She thought after the parking garage incident that he would, but he hadn't. He'd googled Dante, done some serious digging about him and rushed to tell her about it. Why hadn't he done the same with Art?

Did he already know the reason Art had been there?

If she asked him and he was innocent, it would call attention to the incident. Damn.

"And now you're not speaking to me at all." Brian sighed and slapped his hands down on his jean-clad thighs. "Megan, I—"

"Sorry." She smiled. It felt like her face was going to break. "I was just . . . woolgathering. I can't help being a little distant, Brian. You know how I feel about all of this, you know it isn't necessarily something I want to be doing. I'm trying and I know it isn't your fault, but—"

A flash of color in the copse of trees in the center of the park caught her eye. The deep, murky red disappeared behind the trees too quickly for her to see what it was, but something about it bothered her.

Brian followed her gaze. "What?"

"I just . . . thought I saw something. Probably nothing." She turned back towards him, only to turn away again when the thing moved in her peripheral vision. What the hell was it?

Brian shifted his weight, making the old wood of the bench creak and move slightly beneath them. It echoed in her nervous ears like a ship in a storm. "What's over there?"

"I don't know." She glanced over at Malleus, standing just outside listening distance. Maleficarum and Spud were "patrolling". Malleus looked unconcerned, though, so she shrugged. "I guess it isn't important."

"And this is. I need to know what happened. Just tell me the story and I can make it right."

If he was trying to seem more trustworthy, it wasn't working. Why was he so eager to hear this story? Why was it important?

She took a deep breath, looked down to make sure the tape recorder was running, and said, "I was sixteen."

He nodded.

"All the kids knew him—Harlan Trooper, I mean, that was his name." She glanced at him. "He'd worked as an ice cream man for a while, until he started really drinking, but that wasn't the only reason we knew him. He was a—nice man, Harlan. You know, some drunks get mean. Harlan didn't. He'd just apologize when he fell on you, or when he 'borrowed' money to buy more cheap vodka or Mad Dog, or when you caught him ripping open your garbage bags to look for food." She winced at the memory. The sad look in his eyes, the scraggly beard hiding the pale, wasted wreckage of what had once been a handsome face . . . she hadn't thought this was going to be so hard, fifteen years later.

"Anyway, we all knew him. Most of the adults in town did, too. But it wasn't the kind of place where people really supported people like him trying to get help, or maybe he'd never bothered to try, I don't know. There were probably enough people who'd offer him booze just for the fun of it. My father used to get out his air pistol when he saw Harlan in our yard."

Brian made a small sound next to her. She looked at him. "I know. But my dad, well . . . it isn't important, I guess. He thought Harlan was the way he was because he'd been coddled or something. I don't know. We never talked about it."

Malleus moved around behind her. She heard him talking to the others in low tones, but didn't bother to try making out the words. The story lived in her head, filling her throat with words she couldn't get out fast enough, as if by speaking them she could erase the memories from her mind for good this time. Surprise and amazement at how easily the words came made her speak even faster, afraid it would disappear.

"One night I was downtown. I'd snuck out. I couldn't sleep, I guess. I don't know. Harlan was sleeping on a bench, at least, I thought he was sleeping, but when I got closer to him I realized he looked . . . wrong. Pale, and still."

She didn't want to sit on the bench anymore. Didn't want to feel the wooden slats beneath her and remember the slats stained with Harlan's blood, remember the way he sat up and opened his eyes and something that wasn't Harlan had stared out at her from them . . . oh God . . . what had it been?

She screwed up her eyes, trying to force the image from them. The Harlan-thing opened its mouth, revealing teeth dripping with blood, and said—

Something grabbed her, throwing her off the bench and onto the ground. She landed with a thud that nearly knocked the breath from her body. Spud was on top of her.

"What the—" she managed, but the words died when Brian started yelling. She looked away from Spud's anxious face to see Maleficarum and Malleus on the grass between the bench and the copse of trees, fighting with something that made every hair on her body stand on end.

Megan couldn't make out much detail, they were all moving so quickly. All she could see was the dull, mottled color of its skin, like a blood bruise covering its entire body. She caught a glimpse of long, sharp white teeth when the thing opened its mouth. Megan screamed as the deadly incisors closed on Maleficarum's arm.

The park that only minutes before had felt peaceful and safe turned into a nightmare landscape as Megan watched the two demons fighting the thing, rolling on the grass, their shouts and the high-pitched shrieking of the fiend combining with Brian's shouts of surprise and the growling that came from low in Spud's throat as he held her down, covering her body with his.

She struggled, wanting to be free, to somehow help Malleus and Maleficarum. Her muscles started to burn as she tried to push Spud off.

He didn't even look at her. His muscles were rigid, his face turned to watch his brothers.

"What is it, Spud, oh my god, what is it? Let me go, I need to help them, what is that thing?"

The thing's jaws were still clamped on Maleficarum's arm, blood pouring from the wound. Malleus kicked the monster, slamming his boot into its head so hard Megan heard the heel connect with its skull, but it did not waver, clinging even harder, shaking its head slowly like a dog prying meat from a bone.

"What the hell is going on?"

She didn't know how to answer Brian's question. All she could do was watch Maleficarum's arm flop uselessly in the air.

Malleus stopped kicking its head and started slamming his meaty fists into the thing's stomach. The thing finally let go of Maleficarum. Megan watched blood spurt into the air in an arc, red and terrible against the blue sky.

Malleus took his chance and kicked the thing in the stomach again, toppling it off his brother and onto the ground.

Before she could even start to breathe a sigh of relief, it sprang up from the grass like a jack-in-the-box and turned towards her, standing still for a moment that felt like forever and staring at her. Her insides turned to liquid.

Spud tensed even further and shifted position on top of her. He was vibrating like a high-tension wire, ready to leap to attack if the thing came close.

It was at least seven feet tall, with scaly red skin and horrible, glowing white eyes. Shaggy hair covered its head and its impossibly broad shoulders gleamed in the sunlight. Its arms hung to its knees, but there was nothing of a lumbering ape about the creature; it was wiry and cunning. Its power stretched across the grass to her as it opened its mouth and rippled its muscles, displaying long, sharp, close-set teeth stained with Maleficarum's blood.

It shrieked again, its ear-bursting howl echoed through the trees and in Megan's head. Without realizing she screamed back, terror ripping the sound from her soul.

"Megan? What's happening?" Megan looked over at Brian, still frozen on the bench. "What's happened to your friend?"

Malleus leapt at the creature a second too late. The thing started running, impossibly fast, its hair streaming out behind it.

Spud pulled her up, yanking her from the grass and lifting her in his arms.

"What is he doing? Megan, are you—"

"Brian, run!" she screamed.

The thing was close to them now. Brian stood up and stepped towards her, right into its path. He wasn't looking at it. He was focused on Megan, frightened and concerned, but in that instant she realized he didn't see it, didn't know the creature was about to slam into—

It passed *through* him. Megan caught only a glimpse of the two bodies entangled before she was airborne. Spud threw her. She landed with a painful thud several feet away, and turned to see Spud slamming his knee into the creature's hairless crotch.

Brian's howls of pain and terror echoed through the park as the creature's body somehow disentangled itself from his. He collapsed to his knees, falling silent in the wake of the thing just as Malleus reached the creature and leapt on it. Maleficarum had picked himself up and was half-running, half-limping towards them, his right hand clutching his injured left arm.

Malleus, Spud, and the fiend moved so quickly it was hard to see who was doing what. Since their faces and bodies were coated with Maleficarum's blood and their own, it was just as hard to tell who was who. The thing's screeching was continuous now as it fought, swiping with claws and snapping with teeth.

They tumbled over, landing on the ground not far from where Brian lay as if unconscious. The thing broke free and sat up, turning once again to Megan, its glowing eyes fastening on hers. Ice ran through her veins. It was trying to insinuate itself into her mind, trying to worm its way into her head the way a snake slithers into a bird's nest to steal its young. She tried to blink, tried to look away, but could not. Instead she felt herself taking a step backwards, moving away from the creature and into the trees behind her, her breath echoing in her ears. She did not want to walk away, did not want to be dragged from her protection, but her feet defied her will and kept moving.

The thing only held her eyes for a second or two before Maleficarum managed to grab it from behind, twisting its head to the side, trying to break its neck. Instead the thing reached behind itself, over its head, its huge hairy hands grabbing the bodyguard's arm and squeezing. Maleficarum screamed.

Whatever the creature had placed in her mind kept Megan in thrall and walking backwards, leaving the smell of the fiend and the sweat and blood of the fight and into the cool, fresh pine-scented air of the rest of the park. Inside she screamed and fought, but her body carried her further and further away with each step, until she stood in the trees around the small mechanical boat pond.

No boats whirred placidly along the smooth surface this day. No sound could be heard but the shouts of the brothers and sound of skin slapping against skin until the crunch of dead leaves made her turn to her right, the spell that had held her broken.

Still she did not move. Don Tremblay stood in front of her, holding a gun.

Chapter Fourteen

"Just relax, Megan," he said, his mouth stretched in a Cheshire-cat grin. "It won't hurt, I promise."

Without moving her head Megan glanced to the left. The fight seemed to be slowing down. Maleficarum lay on the grass, unmoving, but Spud and Malleus were both on the thing, their fists blurring in the air. There was no sign of Brian. She tried to move into a better position to see and be seen, between the trees, where she hoped one of the brothers would spot her light brown sweater against the darkness of the trees and water.

"I guess they're pretty busy." Don cocked his head to one side, as if he was listening to something only he could hear. "They're not very good bodyguards, are they?" The whites of his eyes gleamed against his sallow, dirty skin.

Even a few feet away she could smell the acrid, animal odor of sweat and fear, mixed with a healthy dose of cheap malt liquor. A five o'clock shadow flecked with gray covered his jaw and crept up his cheeks like fungus. She'd seen him the day before and he'd looked fine.

"Don, what's happening to you?"

His hand twitched. Megan yelped and tried to step backwards, but she'd maneuvered herself so there was a tree directly behind her. She'd have to duck to the side and go around it, if she wanted to get away.

Panic left her shaking and dizzy. She'd never seen a hole as gaping and wide as the end of the gun's barrel.

"Nothing's happening to me," he said, but his voice shook. Did his eyes plead with her to help him?

"Don." She tried to keep her voice calm and matter-of-fact, just as if he wasn't holding a gun on her. "Don, you're not this kind of person. You're a good person, you know that. People like you, you're a strong man, you don't need to do this."

For a moment she thought she had him. His eyes had lost a little of their dazed look and his hands had steadied and started to lower the gun. But the words she'd hoped would appease him had the opposite effect. His eyes blazed and he targeted her again with the gun.

"Don't tell me what I do or do not need to do," he said. "I know what I need to do! I don't have a choice, do you understand? I don't have a choice."

She held her hands up. Out of the corner of her eye she still saw movement. When would it end? When would the brothers defeat that thing and come find her? Where the hell was Brian?

"Of course you do, Don." Her voice shook. She tried to swallow, but her mouth was too dry. "You're a good therapist, you know things always get better. There's no need to—"

"Shut up!" he screamed. Tears flowed down his face, leaving tracks on his grayish, sweat-covered skin. "You don't know what you're talking about. They said you'd try this, they said . . ." Again, he cocked his head as if listening to something only he could hear. Megan didn't have to think hard to realize he was hearing a voice and she knew whose.

Her pulse throbbed in her head. She could hardly breathe. Slowly, carefully, she started to edge her way to the left. If she could duck behind the tree and run from there, she might be able to stay out of the path of a bullet long enough to get to . . . where? There was no building to hide in, no people to save her. Nowhere to run.

At this range Don would be able to blow her heart out of her chest without even aiming.

"I'm sorry, Megan." His voice shook but his hands were steady as he braced the gun.

Megan dove forward, hitting Don's legs and knocking him down at the same moment the gun went off. The report echoed through the trees, through her head: the loudest, most terrifying sound she'd ever heard. Her ears rang and she could barely make out renewed, frantic shouting coming from where she'd left the brothers.

She raised herself up on one arm, balling her free hand into a fist and slamming it into Don's face as hard as she could. Pain thundered up her arm from her knuckles as bone connected with bone. She screamed. Beneath her, Don twisted. He brought the gun up sideways, trying to smash the side of her head.

Megan leaned into it, managing to deflect the blow with her shoulder. She threw herself sideways and landed on both hand and gun, pinning them to the earth.

Don yanked his arm out from under her just as she grabbed his shoulders and aped Spud's earlier move, slamming her knee into his balls with all the force she could muster.

He shouted and pulled the trigger. The bullet shot off into the trees above his head. Megan scrambled to stand but he grabbed her leg. He was curled into a semi-fetal position on the ground but still managed to flip himself onto his stomach and start dragging her back towards him.

She kicked wildly with her feet, trying to detach him. He held on, but her foot connected with his face again. He grunted.

She spun around and grabbed the hand holding the gun, unsure if it was a very smart or very stupid move but certain there were no other options. Blood poured from Don's nose and down his face, staining his clothes and pooling on the packed brown earth beneath them.

She slammed his hand down onto the ground, digging her fingernails into the thin skin on the back of it. The skin broke. Blood oozed from the wounds, hot on her fingers. He tried to pull his hand away but she held on.

With his free hand, he tried to yank her fingers backwards. She scratched him again and planted her foot on his wrist. It was an awkward position but it put more weight on him.

He lifted onto his elbow and shoved his shoulder into Megan's leg, knocking her back down. Her head hit the ground hard enough to make stars appear in front of her eyes, then he was standing over her with the gun pointed right at her face.

"Megan," he gasped, forcing the words out between sobs. "They won't leave me alone—"

A large body flew from the trees and pounded into Don, knocking him to the ground. The gun went off. The tree behind Megan exploded, bits of bark and wood flying everywhere. She rolled away, only to hit a pair of heavy, blood-soaked legs.

Malleus lifted her up, carrying her as easily as he would a child, and ran away from the trees. His clothes were soaking wet. When Megan lifted her hand from his chest it was red with blood, but his breathing sounded untroubled and normal.

He set her down by the body of the creature lying broken in the blood-soaked grass. Brian sat on the bench next to a slightly paler-than-usual Maleficarum, who was, thank goodness, no longer bleeding. At least, not that she could see.

A moment later, Spud ran out of the trees carrying the gun in one hand and the limp body of Don Tremblay in the other.

"Is he . . . dead?" Megan asked. She wasn't sure if she wanted the answer to be yes or no, but she was relieved when Spud shook his head.

"'E's alive, m'lady, don't you fret none," Maleficarum said, giving Don an appraising look. "You just sit down now an' let us worry 'bout 'im. And 'im," he added, nodding at the red beast on the ground.

Her vision started to go black as she realized it was over. The fight was over, she was alive . . . they were all alive, even Don, and she was glad.

She was also going to be sick. She tried to turn away, but didn't quite make it. Malleus patted her back. "Better out than in, eh, m'lady?" he said, sounding awfully cheerful for a man who'd just been almost killed by a seven-foot, red-skinned hellbeast. Then again, he'd been awfully happy after his scrap last night. Perhaps this was just a fun challenge for him.

"Megan?" It was Brian, his light eyes huge in his pale face. "What the hell just happened?"

Shit.

MEGAN DROPPED CHUNKS of stew meat into the searing hot pan, taking pleasure in the simple prosaic sizzling sound and the fresh, beefy fragrance rising. When she flipped the pieces with her stainless-steel spatula, the sides that hit the pan were already dark brown.

Maleficarum, sitting at the table eating an enormous sandwich made with just about everything in her fridge, sniffed the air and smiled. "Reminds me of me mum's kitchen, that does."

"Oh? She used to make steak pies for you?"

He nodded. "Aye, well, it weren't exactly steak, y'know. It were meat, but not that kind."

Megan dropped the subject.

All three of the brothers had healed amazingly well. That was what guard demons did, apparently. They weren't perfect, but they could certainly move without severe pain and their wounds had already healed.

Megan shuddered and inhaled deeply. Four steak pies was a tall order, and it was one the brothers hadn't expected her to fill after the scene at the park. She'd insisted on it. She was going to cook, damn it, cook a nice hearty meal for her guests. Just as she'd planned.

She'd forced them to take her to the grocery store after the police finally let them leave the park. The body of the fiend hadn't been a problem, because nobody could see it but her and the brothers. Don Tremblay hadn't been much of a problem either. He'd readily admitted to what he'd tried to do, crying and begging for forgiveness, and she'd granted it before they put him in the back of the police car called to take him first to the station, then to the hospital.

At least he would get some help, she thought as she lifted the first batch of meat out of the pot and started dropping in the next. More fragrant steam rose from the pot. Now if only someone would help her figure out what to do about Brian's brush with the demons.

He hadn't seen the creature, either, but he'd felt it. She'd insisted he go to the hospital, too. His reactions were slow enough to make her worried for his health, and he'd barely spoken the whole time the police were there. Kind of a blessing, that was, because she didn't have to try and convince him to go with the cover story they'd concocted on the phone with Greyson in the frantic few minutes before the police arrived.

Putting off the inevitable was all well and good, but they couldn't do it forever. What had he felt when that demon ran through him? What had it done to him?

And what were they going to do about it now?

The voices of the brothers behind her made an oddly homey accompaniment to the sizzling meat. It struck Megan how strange all of this was. She, who'd never had many friends, had never had that "urban family" people talked about, now had three demons sitting in her kitchen sniffing the air with smiles on their faces and chatting about sports.

She put in the last batch of meat and started seasoning it, adding the scents of rosemary and onion to the comforting fog in the air. Her stomach growled.

She'd been right to insist on this. Making this meal was just what she needed, what they all needed, to bring a sense of normalcy back to . . . well, okay, it was just what she needed. The day had been just another day for Malleus, Maleficarum, and Spud.

She sprinkled a good pinch of sea salt on the meat and added it all back together in the pan, stirring it, heating it back up, then opened three bottles of Murphy's Irish Stout and poured them in, scraping the bottom of the pan gently with her spatula. The repetitive motion soothed her tired mind.

She didn't need to hear their voices quiet to know to hand the remaining bottles to the demons. They opened them with gusto.

"I've got more of those," she said, covering the pan and lowering the heat. "There's plenty."

"You're too kind, m'lady," Maleficarum said, and something in his voice made her stop and look at him.

"We don't deserve it, none of it." He sniffled. "We almost let you get kilt today. You may forgive us, but Mr. Dante . . . he's not gonna be too pleased wif us."

"No, he isn't."

They all turned as if they'd been caught doing something they shouldn't, to find Greyson standing in the doorway of the kitchen. He must have left work early; the sleeves of his pristine white shirt were rolled up, the top buttons undone and his tie hanging loose around his neck. He looked like a stockbroker after a satisfying day of bankrupting his enemies—except for the fury pouring off him and filling the room. His body was tense, unmoving, but his rage swept over them like a flooded river washing away everything in its path.

She hadn't felt him like this before. Not for the first time, she wondered how much of that power he held back from her. She didn't have any of her own, but she felt it from others. Some people just had more . . . energy, or strength, or charisma. Whatever you wanted to call it, Megan usually felt it, but she'd never experienced anything like this.

But then, she'd never been around an angry demon before.

"How did you get in here?" She meant the words to come out strong and sure, but it was more like a whisper.

He held up a stylish silver key ring in the shape of a padlock, but kept his eyes focused on the demons. "I made a copy of your key."

"What? I—" She stopped herself. This was not the time to discuss his key-cutting habits, not when he looked as if he would kill the brothers with his bare hands.

They sat very still at the table as he spoke to them. "I need to talk to the three of you."

They hesitated, glancing at Megan as if she could save them.

"Now." He almost didn't sound like himself. All the pleasantness was gone from his voice. It was pure cold fury. Megan shivered.

The demons stood up and filed reluctantly out of the kitchen. "In the spare room," Greyson said. He turned to follow them.

Megan took a step towards him. "Greyson?"

He stopped.

"You won't . . . hurt them or anything, will you?"

He spun around, so fast she almost couldn't track the movement. "What do you think I should do?" he demanded. "Give them a fucking medal for almost letting you get killed today? Twice?"

"No, I—"

"What do you think would have happened if you hadn't been lucky enough or strong enough to beat Don Tremblay? Do you think they deserve some kind of reward for letting a cheap distraction like that *yaksas* today work? Letting Tremblay get to you?"

"No, but—"

"They're here," he said, standing so close now that she could smell his cologne, "to protect you. Their job, what they get paid for, is to protect you. Do you think they deserve to get paid for today?"

"They couldn't have known—"

"It's their job to know. It's their fucking job to keep their eyes open and their fat little mouths shut, and to save your life. What if you'd died today, Megan? What do you think would be a fit punishment for them letting you—"

This time she pulled him to her, this time it was she who cut off his words with the pressure of her lips.

He hesitated just long enough for Megan to wonder if she was doing the right thing at all. Part of her knew she wasn't.

Then his arms went around her, crushing her to him, and all thoughts of reasons and consequences flew from her mind in a blast of pure heat.

Perhaps because his emotions were already stronger than they'd been the night before so, too, was the passion of his kiss. His lips plundered hers, angry, needy, forcing her head back. She tasted blood and wondered if it was hers or his. It didn't matter.

She was caught between the smooth edge of the countertop and Greyson's hard body. He bent her almost backwards over the counter. She lifted her legs to wrap around him, encouraged by his hands supporting her thighs.

The movement brought the already buzzing space between her legs into direct contact with the hard ridge of his erection. She gasped against his mouth, and he responded by pressing himself more firmly into her, letting her feel the entire length of him as he propped her on the countertop.

His hands curled into her hair, tugging her head further back so he could explore her throat and neck with his lips. She blazed everywhere he kissed, every time his teeth scraped against her delicate skin.

This was more than it she'd meant it to be, more than it had been the night before. Megan was drowning in him, in the sensation of every nerve ending in her body springing to hot, instant life.

She clutched at his shoulders, his back, as if she would fly spinning off the earth if he weren't there to hold her to it. Her legs tightened around his waist, pressing him still closer. His hand invaded the small space between their bodies to caress her breast with heat, and she arched her back as he lowered his mouth further to kiss down the open neckline of her shirt.

She didn't know what might have happened if Tera Green hadn't chosen that moment to walk into the kitchen.

Megan wouldn't have noticed if she hadn't opened her eyes to yank Dante's tie out from under his collar. Tera watched them, her arms crossed and a look of intense interest on her face.

Megan gasped and pulled away at the same time Dante spun around, almost dropping her. As carefully as she could, she loosened her legs. They barely held her up when her feet hit the floor.

"The door was unlocked," Tera said. "I knocked, but I guess you didn't hear me."

"Um . . . the meat was cooking pretty loudly." Megan had no idea what to do. Laugh it off? Be offended? Tera shouldn't have walked right in, but Tera didn't seem the type to worry much about social niceties.

"Right. The meat." Tera looked them both up and down. "Is there anything to drink?"

"Yes, um, beer, wine, Coke, water?"

Tera accepted a beer. "I'll wait in the living room, Megan. I don't have all night, either."

Megan didn't breathe again until the other woman's back disappeared around the corner. How must this look, how must she look? Like some stupid teenager, some preposterous woman who couldn't control herself?

Greyson reached for her, but at the first touch of his hand on her arm she cringed. What had she been thinking?

He dropped his hand. "I need to go talk to the boys."

She watched him walk out. Her body still throbbed and ached. Only the conviction that this was the wrong time, the wrong thing, kept her from leaping back into his arms.

At least, she thought that was all it was.

Chapter Fifteen

"**O**kay." Tera stepped back about ten paces, leaving an expanse of browning grass between herself and Megan. In the center stood a plastic cup. "Try again."

Megan glanced over at the house. Greyson was in the living room making some phone calls, and the boys . . . she didn't know what they were doing.

Greyson's voice had echoed through the house, yelling in the demon tongue. She hadn't heard such lengthy speeches in that language before. It sounded like some sort of supernatural Esperanto.

"Don't look for Grey," Tera said. "Try to move the cup."

"I'm not looking for him."

"I do have eyes, Megan." She folded her arms across her chest, covered now by a soft blue sweater and matching jacket. Even her casual clothes looked tailored for her. "Look, I don't expect you to be able to move the cup. You're not a witch. It's just a focusing exercise, to teach you how to focus your power."

"I don't have any power," Megan said, not for the first time.

"Yes, you do. It simply manifests itself as the ability to see into people's heads. You need to teach it to work for you in a better, stronger way. How do you think you build your shields?"

"I don't know. I just know they're there."

"Don't you picture them as anything? See them in your head?"

Megan thought about it for a minute. Her shields . . . they were clear. She saw them, though, transparent walls around her head. "I guess so."

"Okay. How do you focus energy to them?"

"I don't. I keep telling you, I don't know how I do any of this, and—"

"Look." Tera pointed down. The cup had moved.

"How did I do that? Did I do that?" She'd long since come to terms with her abilities, but this—she had to admit, her heart beat a little faster at the thought that she might have actually moved an object with her mind.

"I'm pretty sure you did. See, you got mad. I've noticed that about you. You don't get hurt, you don't shut down, you get mad. I wonder why that is?"

"I don't know. I don't think I'm a very angry person."

"Hmmm." Tera's bright eyes watched her. "If you say so. The point is, your emotions tend to manifest as anger or, at least, anger is the only emotion that manifests itself as power. What you need to do is harness that anger and don't let it get away from you."

"Are you saying I have to be angry in order to accomplish anything?"

"No, I'm saying you're a bit of an odd duck, but if you pay attention you can do this." Tera smiled at Megan's frown. "You're letting me distract you. Stop that. I'm just making observations. Deal with your rage issues on your own time."

The cup flew another foot.

Tera's grin widened. "Almost as effective as telling me to go fuck myself and much more ladylike."

"But I don't know how I did it."

"Think about it. You got mad at me, and . . . what?"

Megan's brow furrowed. She had been mad, mad at Tera for analyzing her so easily and mad at herself for being transparent. The comments about "rage issues" set her teeth on edge. After all the time Megan had spent teaching herself to stay calm, not to let her feelings show, to find out now that she wasn't nearly as good at it as she thought hurt . . .

But the hurt felt more like anger and it had broken through the shield . . . no . . . *over the top* of the shield . . . and reached for something harmless. The cup.

"It was like a wave," she said, staring at the ground. "In my head. I wanted to hit you with it."

"Okay, good." None of this seemed to bother Tera in the slightest. The woman was as emotionless as a lizard. "Now you know how your power manifests, and you have some idea how it works. Try it again. Try to move the cup on purpose this time."

Megan focused, staring at the cup. Tera took her hand.

"Don't look at the cup. Or rather, don't focus on the cup to the extent you aren't looking inside yourself, too. Somewhere inside there's a place where you keep your power, where your strength comes from. Find that place, that door, and open it. See your power hit the cup."

The cup didn't move. Megan searched inside herself and found nothing. She lowered her shields all the way and tried to force her energy to the cup, but it stayed in its spot on the grass as if glued there. She was trying to read it, not move it, she realized. "I can't."

"Damn it. Yes, you can. You're not paying attention." The frustration in Tera's voice sent an echoing shimmer of the same emotion through Megan's body. With her shields down, she was picking up little things like that from the other woman. Not much, not enough to read her—if that was possible—but enough to catch some of her feelings.

"Oh, no," Tera said. "Don't think you can get around this by sneaking into my head. I'm not as impervious as the demons."

"I'm not trying to sneak anywhere. You're projecting. You made me lower my shields, I can't help it if yours aren't strong enough."

Tera inhaled, then blew air out through her nostrils. "Okay. Don't focus on the cup. Focus on your energy and the cup and try to turn your power into something. Something that can make the cup move. A stick or a blade or a flyswatter, even. Anything you can use."

Megan tried again.

The cup blurred in her vision. Damn it, why couldn't she do this? It was so irritating, so annoying . . . and there it was. A peak of something, a brush of energy. She grabbed it as it flared and, in her head, saw it as a stick, a long skinny tree branch. The cup and the stick merged somehow, in her head, and the cup moved, rolling a few inches across the grass.

"I'm surprised. You might not be a total failure at this after all." Tera stepped back and looked at her watch. So much for congratulations on a job well done. "What time do you need to get back into the kitchen?"

"About fifteen minutes. Do you want to just go in now?" *No! I want to play some more!*

"No. Let's try pulling energy from around you. This will be hard for you, because you're not a witch. We do it automatically, but you'll have to focus hard—unless someone's feeding you energy, in which case it's easy to get overwhelmed. My sister Lexie would probably be better at teaching you this part than me, but since Grey doesn't want her around, I'll do my best."

Megan refused to ask. "I'm sure you'll be fine."

Tera's mouth quirked. "Thanks. There's energy all around you, right? You can feel it, like when the wind blows, but you don't know how to access it. It goes around you, not through you. You have to learn to open up to it, so you can keep it stored inside you for when you need it."

"I don't see what good any of this will do," Megan said. "I can't beat them."

Tera glanced towards the house. "You can, with enough power . . . and practice. Let's get to work."

"WE NEED TO TALK." Greyson pulled her into the small hallway leading to her spare room.

"I have to get the food—"

"It can wait a minute." He glanced towards the living room, where Tera settled herself on one of the couches to watch television. "We have to decide what to tell Brian and we have to decide now."

She'd been trying not to think about this. Sooner or later, probably sooner, Brian was going to show up, and he would want to know what happened in the park. "Can't we hypnotize him or something?"

"Not with Tera here."

"After she leaves?"

"I keep forgetting you haven't spent much time with witches. As long as there's free food or drinks, she won't leave. She'll probably want to take your bed tonight just because she's too tired to go home, and as enjoyable as time in your bed must undoubtedly be, I don't think Tera would get the full benefit from it." His hands ran up her arms, transmitting heat along her skin.

"I would have thought having Tera and me both in my bed would be right up your alley."

"How dull. I'm not a spectator, Megan, and I don't share. When I'm in your bed, you won't—"

"Why not just tell him the truth?" She wished her body would stop reacting whenever he made his suggestive little comments. It was hard enough standing this close to him in the darkened hallway without him fondling her arms like that. "Tell him there's little demons after me, and they sent that thing in the park today to kill me, and they made Don Tremblay come after me with a gun?"

"It was a yaksas—a Nepalese mountain demon—by the way. I suppose we could tell him the truth."

"I don't think we have much choice."

"There are always choices."

"Not for me."

He shook his head. "How cynical of you. Faced with what you've seen in the last few days, you still refuse to accept possibilities." His fingers cradled her jaw for a moment, as if tilting her face up to kiss.

"And you refuse to stop patronizing me and listen," she said, but she couldn't put any sting in the words. "I'm having a hard enough time keeping all of this from Brian as it is, what with the whole Harlan Trooper thing, and—"

"What? Who?" He let go of her.

"Harlan Trooper. He was a homeless man who lived in my town when I was in high school. It's a long story."

She expected him to change the subject back to Brian, but he didn't. "Tell me."

"He died. They thought I'd killed him."

"He didn't just die, he was murdered. You saw it?"

"I . . . I think so. I don't remember much. Can we get back to the subject at hand, please?"

"When did he die?"

"I was sixteen. Please, can we not discuss it? We need to decide what to do about Brian, not rehash some old personal stuff of mine."

"Hmmm? Oh, Brian. I thought we'd decided."

"Okay, then. So, we'll just start at the beginning? Do we tell him about you?"

"Do you remember anything about that guy dying? Or what your life was like at the time?"

Megan shook her head. "The oven timer's about to go off, Greyson, so I need to get back in the kitchen. Why don't I decide exactly what to tell Brian and you follow my lead?"

"Why don't I decide and you follow my lead?"

Megan bit her lip to hide her smile. She knew that would get him. "Fine," she said. "You decide. I have to go roll pastry."

It wasn't until she got in the kitchen that she realized he hadn't tried to kiss her or flirt with her once after she'd mentioned Harlan Trooper.

"DID YOU MAKE THAT from scratch?" Tera stood next to her and poked at the pastry with one long red fingernail.

"No. I buy it pre-made. And get your germy hands out of it, please."

Tera pulled her hand back. "My hand isn't germy. And you're going to bake it anyway, right?"

Megan glared at her.

Tera glared right back. "I don't know why you're being rude to me. I'm on your side. I haven't done anything to you."

"I don't mean to be rude, I'm just not used to—"

Tera ignored her and popped a raw baby carrot into her mouth. "My sister slept with him, you know," she said between crunches. "A year or so ago. She said it was pretty memorable. And that's saying a lot, because she's slept with everybody."

Megan opened a beer.

"It wasn't much more than a one-night stand, really." Crunch, crunch, crunch. "I mean, they tried to date, but Lexie isn't exactly the relationship type and Greyson isn't the relationship type at all, so—"

"I can hear you." Dante's voice floated in from the living room, where Megan told him to stay.

"I know," Tera said. "Anyway, they had some weird kind of fight and Lexie hexed his car. I think it almost killed him." She grinned and took another carrot. "It was pretty funny."

Megan stared at her.

"Eh?" Crunch, crunch, crunch. "It *was* funny."

"If you say so." She couldn't help smiling back, though. Standing here in her kitchen, cooking an enormous meal, listening to Tera's rather macabre gossip, felt normal. It felt good. It struck Megan then, as it hadn't before, that Tera was trying, in her own way, to be her friend.

She cleared her throat. "Hey, Tera, I appreciate your help with everything."

Tera smiled. "No problem. You're doing better than I thought you would."

Megan finished fitting the pastry into the pie plates and put them in the oven to bake. "It doesn't feel like I—"

Someone was pounding on her front door. She had a sickening feeling she knew who that someone was.

Greyson appeared in the hall. "Do you want me to answer it?"

"Who is it?" Tera asked. "Is it one of the bad guys?"

"Yes," Greyson said at the same time Megan said, "No."

Megan sighed. "It's a reporter named Brian Stone. He's been doing an article on me and he witnessed the attack in the park today—"

"What attack?"

"We'll tell you later, Tera. I think Brian's about to break the door down."

Tera sniffed. "I don't know why he doesn't just open it. It's not locked."

Megan headed for the door as Greyson said, "Some people don't just wander into other people's homes."

"You always have to say something, don't you, Grey."

The door vibrated and bounced with the force of Brian's fists. Megan hesitated for a minute, taking a deep breath, then jumped back as she flung the door open . . . just as Malleus, Maleficarum, and Spud roared out of her spare room and leapt through the doorway and onto Brian.

It only took her a second to realize what the boys, in their zeal, had forgotten.

They weren't wearing their hats.

Chapter Sixteen

"I'm fine, damn it." Brian swatted her hand away she tried to give him a fresh ice pack. "Just give me a minute and I'll leave."

"You don't have to go. You can stay and have dinner."

He made a sound almost like a laugh. "You think I want to stay here and eat with you? After what you and your—pet demons, or whatever—did to me today?"

Megan's "be honest" plan had not worked out well. As soon as Brian heard the word "demons" he'd jumped to the absolute worst conclusion possible. Megan guessed she didn't blame him. If she'd met someone, then learned they'd been accused of an occult murder, then been attacked by invisible beasts before getting an explanation, she'd probably have thought they were lying about their innocence, too.

"Brian, I know it's hard to accept, but if you'd just let me finish—"

"Let you finish? Why, so you can set me up again?"

"I didn't set you up."

"Oh? If something's after you—and that's a big if—and you made me meet you in the park today, that sounds like a set up to me. You set me up and had your demon friends there put on a little show. You know, Megan, I thought there had to be a reasonable explanation for the whole Harlan Trooper thing. Now I see there was. You're insane. And whatever evil you've gotten yourself involved in, keep it away from me. I know I have the same abilities you have, but that doesn't mean I've gone down the same road."

"Brian, I—what the hell is that supposed to mean? What evil road have I gone down?"

"Calling demons? Blood sacrifice? You think I don't know about that stuff? I saw Harlan Trooper's autopsy reports, Megan, I know about the carvings left on his skin and the organs missing."

"I think that's enough." Greyson spoke up from the corner. Megan jumped. She'd forgotten he was there, he was so still and silent. "Megan, can I talk to you privately?"

"Go ahead," Brian said when she glanced at him. "I'm sure your demon master has some tasks for you to do. I warn you, though, I'm well protected."

Greyson's eyebrows raised. Megan, torn between yelling at him for not contradicting Brian, at Brian for saying such a thing to begin with, and at herself for thinking honesty was the best policy, stood up with a sigh. "I'll be right back, Brian. Because maybe you could use a minute alone, not because my—nobody is my master."

She swept past Greyson into the living room, hoping he wouldn't try to touch her. All Brian needed was to see that.

He didn't, but when she saw the look on Tera's face she almost wished he had.

"What are you two doing? You're not allowed to do any of this. You need to cover it up, now."

"Tera," Megan said, "I'm sure you—"

"There's no 'you're sure' about any of this, Megan. You don't know our rules. Your situation is unique; you need to know things to stay alive. That guy in the kitchen doesn't." She turned to Greyson. "Why wasn't I notified immediately of what happened today? Can you imagine the trouble I'll be in when the rest of Vergadering hears that not only was there a yaksas attack, and not only did a regular witness it, but that a demon then decided to tell that regular everything about us?"

"Tera, listen." Greyson took a step forward. "Just let me explain a couple of things, and I think you'll see—"

"No. No more explaining. I've gone along with all of this because I thought you were right. And despite what you think, not all of us are prejudiced against demons. But to tell that guy in there what you've told him, without even clearing it with me . . . no. He needs to forget it all and he needs to forget it now."

"What?" Megan glanced from Tera to Greyson and back. "Tera, you're not going to do something to him, are you?"

Tera was already walking into the kitchen. "Somebody has to."

"Greyson, does she know Brian is psychic?"

"No."

"You have to stop her. Won't it be a lot harder for her to—"

Amusement glittered in his eyes. "Oh, yes. Probably won't work at all, with him being so emotionally wrought at the moment."

From the kitchen came the low hum of Tera's voice. Megan turned to go, but Greyson grabbed her back.

"Let her go. Might be fun to see."

"But Brian's going to have a fit."

"And our Miss Tera will take the brunt of it." Greyson lowered himself to the couch and pulled her down with him so she sat cuddled into his side. "While we wait and let her."

For once, his body next to hers didn't distract Megan. Her nerves were ready to snap.

"Stop fidgeting," he said. "She wouldn't listen to us—ah."

"What the fuck are you doing?" Brian's roar brought the demons running from the spare room again.

"No, boys, stay here." The brothers stopped at the sound of Greyson's voice, but they wore identical expressions of unease as the yelling in the kitchen continued.

"Are you trying to brainwash me? Who do you think you are?"

Something fell with a clatter, and Brian appeared in the entrance to the living room. "Did you ask her to do that?"

Megan struggled off the couch. "No, Brian, no. Just please listen to me. I can explain everything."

"Yeah, I bet you can."

Greyson remained seated. "Come on, Brian, the least you can do is give Megan a chance."

"No. The least I can do is get the hell out of here before you people decide to get really nasty with me. Megan, I have to keep speaking to you, because it's my job. But I don't have to keep speaking to you now."

The oven timer went off. The pies were done.

"Please stay and eat, Brian." Even as she asked she knew how lame it sounded. He'd refused once already. Now he'd probably rather pluck out his own eyeballs with a fork than sit at the table with Megan, four demons, and a witch who'd just tried to magically alter his memory.

He stared at her. "I'll call you tomorrow. I'd rather not—I don't want to be stuck with you any longer—but somebody has to expose you, and I don't trust you, any of you, not to bewitch one of my colleagues."

They stood and watched him leave.

"Where are we going?" she asked again.

"It's a surprise."

"I don't like surprises."

"Everybody likes surprises." Greyson made another turn, this time onto a narrow dirt road. Signs posted at the entrance warned that Trespassers Would Be Prosecuted.

"You just don't like the anticipation of the surprise. Besides, we're here."

"This is the surprise? Being shot at for trespassing?"

"That would be fun, but no." He braked in front of a heavy stone wall topped with barbed-wire spirals. Dante got out of the car without another word.

The headlights bleached color from his skin as he waved his hand over the gate. His lips moved. The gate opened.

"I don't think this is a good idea," she said as he got back in the car.

"Okay." He drove through the gate. Megan twisted in her seat to watch it close behind them, then disappear as the taillights left it behind.

Trees stood in twisted columns along the sides of the leaf-strewn path as they rolled forward, the car rumbling and jostling over bumps and dips. Megan thought of the town they'd just left. Even closed and dark, it was evidence of civilization. Here none could be seen, like Greyson had somehow driven them back in time. She generally avoided the woods for that reason. Her blood pumped a little faster.

"Here we go," he said, bringing their rolling, shaking progress to a halt.

Megan looked around. They were in a clearing. That was it. She saw nothing special about this particular clearing. It looked like her back yard. She could have gone to her back yard anytime.

Outside the warmth of the car, she shivered. She'd only worn a light jacket and it was after midnight. The wind whistled through the trees and stirred up leaves on the ground. With the car headlights off, the moon and stars provided the only illumination.

It was spectacular. This far out of the city the sky was a tapestry of sparkles, with the moon glowing at its zenith in the south. Her breath caught.

"Pretty, isn't it?" His voice was low and soft in her ear as he stood behind her, wrapping his coat around her so she was pressed against him.

She nodded, feeling very small. The immensity of the glittering sky was unimaginable. How long had it been since she'd even looked at it, really paid attention? She noticed the moon if it was full and she was out at night, most of the time. Every once in a while she'd see the Big Dipper or Orion's Belt and be proud she could find them. But she hadn't looked at the sky, focused on it, in years. The thought made her vaguely ashamed.

"Look," he said, in the same quiet voice, turning them both to the left. The lights of the city glimmered and shone across the dark expanse between its limits and where they stood. It looked like gold spread across the hills. So many people, so many lives being lived all on top of each other. And here she stood with Greyson, alone in the woods, not part of any of it. It was so beautiful, but standing in the middle of it all meant she couldn't see.

Heat radiated from his body through her thin jacket to her back. "Puts things in perspective, doesn't it?"

She wiped her wet cheeks. "Is this why you brought me here?"

"Partly."

She tensed. The memory of his lips on hers flooded back. They were alone, in the woods . . . no. She didn't doubt for a minute he would have been game if she'd suggested it, but she did doubt that he'd planned to seduce her in the backseat of his car. It simply wasn't his style.

"What's the rest of it, then?" Her voice came out as a whisper.

His chest moved against her back as he shrugged. "I wanted to get out for a while. I thought you might enjoy this. I like it here."

"And that's all?"

He stepped away from her. "Have a seat," he said, lighting a fire on the ground and sitting in front of it, tilted so he could look at the city.

She sat. "Greyson?"

"Hmm?"

"Is it hard to do that?"

"What? Oh, the fires? No. It takes a little energy, but it's just the same as your abilities. It just happens, like making a fist."

"Do you think it's because of . . . I mean, do you think if I wasn't psychic, this wouldn't be happening to me? Like maybe I don't have a personal demon because of my abilities? Or would it happen no matter what, because of the show?"

He sat perfectly still for a minute, his profile glowing with reflected fire. The intensity of the light made his eyes look like pure shadow with gleaming gold irises, flaming holes set in the fine bones of his face. "I think everything we do in life has an influence on what happens next," he said. "The decisions we make have ramifications beyond what we see, but we make them anyway, without thinking of it, because we have to make them."

He glanced at her. "Our gifts and talents are part of that. You can't blame yourself or your gift any more than you can blame yourself for breathing. We are who and what we are, Meg, and there's no point wasting time wondering how it might be if things were different."

"That's easy for you to say. You were raised with demons. You were never different from everyone around you."

"Don't make assumptions. You should know better."

"Sorry." He was right, and worse, Megan hadn't even thought of it. Without being able to read him, she didn't know anything about what went on under his skin other than what he told her and what she learned by observation. "You're so self-assured. Most people with your confidence had very nurturing upbringings. Overcompensators read more like arrogance. But you—"

"I'm not one of your patients. Please don't analyze me."

"I'm sorry," she said again. His withdrawal upset her more than she would have thought. Sometimes it was hard to remember that just because she couldn't read someone didn't mean they didn't have depths, or secrets to keep.

He was silent for so long she wondered if he heard her. "Greyson, I—"

"It's forgotten." He leaned back on his hands and stretched his long legs out in front of him. His white shirt gaped open at the neck. "Why do you do it?"

"What?"

He jerked his chin towards the city. "Help them. Use your energy and power to make them feel good, when all they want is to make others feel bad. Are they worth it?"

It took her a moment to find her voice. "Of course they are."

"After everything they've done to you, everything they do to each other?"

"I—I don't think they're bad, Greyson. They're just human, I'm just human. We can't help being the way we are."

"But you don't admit it, either. The things people want, the things they think. You know. You hear those thoughts and you still want to help."

Something odd laced his voice, almost like vulnerability or loneliness. It echoed in her chest.

"I have heard them, yes. I know what they think. I know what they do. But I guess . . . I know how much they hurt, and I think if I can help someone hurt less, maybe they'll hurt others less. As for power, I didn't really think I had that much."

He nodded. "That's what I thought you would say."

"You don't agree?"

He shook his head. "They amuse me at times, but in general I could do without them. I don't give a damn how they feel."

"Good thing you don't have my job, then."

"Yes." He took a deep breath. "I found out who Art Bellingham is. What he is."

She waited, but he did not continue.

"Maybe we should go back to my house," she said, glancing over her shoulder. The woods seemed to loom over her, full of rustlings and creatures with sharp teeth.

"My Meegra owns this land. He can't get to us here."

"You didn't tell me."

"I thought you'd enjoy it more if you thought we were doing something wrong."

She forced a smile. "And now you're avoiding the topic."

He nodded. "Yeah, I am. Okay. Bellingham is . . . he's the Accuser." He glanced at her, but she didn't know how to respond.

"We thought he was a myth. He's older and more powerful than you can imagine, Meg. I don't know why he's interested in you, or what he's doing with the Yezer Ha-Ra, but there's some connection and I have a feeling we're going to find out what it is."

"But what does this—Accuser—do?"

"Same thing any of us do. He feeds. He lives. He gains power. He used to be a bigwig down in Hell. Everyone just assumed he'd disappeared when the old order changed."

"You said Hell didn't exist." The lights in the city below didn't look as brave or cheery as they had a few minutes before. Now every one spoke of isolation, a life lived alone in a little box.

"It doesn't anymore. It used to. I don't know what happened. It's not information they give out. Only the Ancient Ones know." He looked like he was going to continue, but stopped. "There you go. Art Bellingham is the Accuser. You sure know how to pick your enemies."

"And that's how he . . . got into my head? Because he's so old and powerful."

"Not exactly. But I think I can fix that, at least temporarily. Trust me?"

She raised her eyebrows.

"I can hypnotize you. He's getting through because no matter how powerful you are—and you are powerful—you can't match him on your own. You can't match any demon. I can add a little demon protection to yours. That should keep him out."

She huddled deeper in her thin jacket. "I'm not sure I like the sound of that."

"Suit yourself."

"None of this suits me."

"Then let me help you."

"How do I know you won't plant some weird suggestion in my head—make me give you a lap dance or bark like a dog?"

"You don't. That's what makes it exciting." His smile faded. "You know because I give you my word, Meg."

She stared into his eyes for a long minute. She'd never dealt with a man whose word meant so much to him, but she knew his did. Demon rules of engagement. Honor among thieves. Either way, his expression made her shiver, and not just because she was about to allow him into her head. "Okay."

"Good. Comfortable?" He arranged her in front of the fire, his hands brisk and sure. Prickles of apprehension crawled up her spine. She ignored them. "Just relax. Look into the flames." His breath tickled her ear, and she jumped. "Hey!"

"Sorry. Got carried away there. Anyway. There's a door in the flames. See it? Watch it open. You can walk right through it . . ."

He kept talking, his voice turning into a soft, seductive drone, mingling with the breeze through the branches. Her eyes started to drift closed. She could listen to him all night, just snuggle up here in front of the fire and let his words wash over her . . .

She blinked. "What?"

"We're done. Good job. You shouldn't have any more trouble. At least, as long as you don't try to leave your body and wander on the astral plane, or some such foolishness. He won't be able to locate you easily and he shouldn't be able to break into your head at all."

"It seems too easy."

"Some of the best things are," he said. His voice didn't soothe now. A strange undertone roughened it.

"Is something—"

"No, nothing's wrong."

"I see. Do you—"

"How do you think your date with Stone will go tomorrow night?"

Fine. He wanted to talk, they would talk. "Ha ha. If it even does go. He'll probably call me in the morning to cancel."

"I'll take you. If he cancels."

"Thanks."

A companionable silence followed, as they both watched the flames dance.

"Funny," Megan said. "All this time I was just one of those little people out there, with no idea what was hidden beneath the lights. I feel like I spent my life standing on something I thought was solid, but it wasn't."

"It's as solid as it ever was. It's just deeper than you thought."

"That doesn't make much sense as analogies go."

"I do the best I can."

"I'm sure you do." They were back on the old teasing footing again. It made Megan smile. "So, I don't have a demon and the Accuser is after me. Does that mean something? Am I, like, the chosen one?"

"Oh, absolutely. When you were born the angels sang. You humans are obsessed with that concept. You haven't been chosen for anything. You're simply an anomaly and we're still trying to resolve it without any problems. We're not sending you off to Mordor just yet."

"You read *Lord of the Rings*?"

"All demons read *Lord of the Rings*. It's the perfect example of what not to do. Armies of mutant bad guys, shrieking entities on bloodied horses . . . Sauron could have done much better for himself if he'd spent more time persuading and letting nature take its course, less time posturing and trying to look scary."

"Is that what you do?" She knew he was trying to change the subject, but couldn't resist.

"Of course. It's all about leading people down the path to darkness while making them think it's their own idea." He checked his watch. "We should go."

She let him help her up and watched while he extinguished the fire. "Thanks," she said. "For helping me shield, and bringing me here. It was . . . thanks."

"Always happy to help."

"My hero."

His fingertips brushed her cheek, so softly she would have doubted the touch if she hadn't seen his hand move. "I'm not interested in being a hero," he said.

Chapter Seventeen

"Naw, naw, m'lady. Not that color."

Megan paused with the lipstick halfway to her mouth. "What's wrong with it?"

Getting ready for this stupid party was hard enough without Malleus, Maleficarum, and Spud standing behind her watching. She wished they wouldn't. The long, thick sleeves of her heavy robe kept catching on things as she tried to apply her make-up, but the brothers would not budge. After what Megan thought of as The Park Incident, they refused to let her out of their sight, or even more than a few feet out of reach. She'd had to call Dante to get them to leave her alone when she used the bathroom.

"It's all wrong, it is," insisted Maleficarum. "Makes you look sallow."

"Yeh." Spud shuffled his feet.

"I don't have any other colors."

"I can't believe this," Malleus muttered. "A beautiful girl like you, and you don't even know 'ow to do your own face."

Megan blushed, from the compliment or the insult she wasn't sure. "Fine." She picked up her makeup bag and handed it over. "You pick something."

Maleficarum took it. "Roight. And Spud'll do your 'air."

"Wait a minute. I was joking."

"Aw, no. We're gonna make you look pretty tonight, m'lady, don't you fret none. Sit down." He pushed her onto the edge of the tub.

Megan had barely arranged her robe over her thighs when Maleficarum came at her again with a brush tinged violet with eyeshadow. "Not that one," she started. "It's too—"

"Trust me." His fingers were warm and rough on her chin as he lifted it. She closed her eyes while the brush whispered over her eyelids. It was just like being at the photo shoot earlier in the week, except instead of a professional make-up artist, she had a guard demon applying her makeup.

She was the luckiest girl in the world.

She did feel fairly lucky, though, all things considered. She was slowly getting better at moving things with her mind, although the sensation still bothered her and she tired quickly.

She'd used Friday to meet with the soundproofers, who promised to have the work done at the Serenity Partners office by the end of the following week. She'd be able to go back to work soon. Luckily the extra money the radio show brought in meant her lack of salary for the month wouldn't be such a bite. It had been good to be back in the office, that was for sure. She'd been able to pretend, even if only for a few minutes, that she wasn't being chased by an army of tiny demons and one of the Legions of Hell disguised as a mild-mannered group therapy counselor.

Tera had helped too, oddly enough. They'd only spent an hour working on strengthening Megan's shields and trying to direct her energy out instead of in, but Tera said she'd done a good job. Even Dante had commended her.

Of course, then he'd tried to get her into bed, so she wasn't sure how honest he'd been. "You stink at this" wasn't exactly a line guaranteed to make any girl slip between the sheets.

And Dante certainly knew what to say to get a girl between those sheets. She didn't know how much longer she would be able to resist. She didn't think she wanted to.

Maleficarum plucked her eyebrows so savagely she winced, but that wasn't as bad as when he insisted on applying false eyelashes. They were heavy on her lids, and sticky when she blinked.

"Just leave your eyes closed," he said. "Let the glue dry."

"Where did you get those things?"

"They were in your bag."

"I don't have any—oh, no. These aren't the ones in the pink package, are they?"

"Aye."

"Those were for Halloween, they're like three inches long. I can't wear these." She reached up to peel them off, but Maleficarum's hand stopped her.

"I'm telling you, let me finish."

She bit back a sigh and waited while he dabbed powder over her lips, used a brush to color them in twice, then dabbed at them with a tissue. "I'm just going to lose the lipstick on glasses and stuff anyway," she said.

"You mean you'll chew it off," Malleus chuckled. "We seen your nervous habits, m'lady."

Megan opened her eyes to glare at him, only to have her chin jerked back by Maleficarum. "Keep your eyes closed," he ordered.

A fingertip ran over her lips, so softly she wasn't sure at first it was there. The skin beneath it tingled as it continued its journey, until her mouth was a ring of pins-and-needles tickles. "What are you doing?" It was difficult to form the words.

"Just setting it."

"Can I open my eyes?"

Another tingly dab on each eyelid. "Aye. But no fair looking till your hair's done. Spud, you want 'er on the loo?"

"Yeh."

Megan sat on the toilet lid while Spud jerked and twisted at her head for what felt like an hour. Pins scraped her scalp and the smell of burning hair filled the room as he plied the curling iron.

Being Spud, he didn't speak, but Malleus and Maleficarum carried on a running commentary. "Ooh, tha's good, there." "Aye, curl it t'other way round, so it falls to the left."

Spud jammed something else into the hair at her crown and stepped back from her.

"There you go," Malleus said with satisfaction. "'ave a butcher's at that, then."

Megan, her face feeling rubbery and as covered in paint as a prostitute's, lifted her now-stiff muscles off the toilet seat and looked in the mirror.

She'd never looked more beautiful in her life. It took a few seconds to convince herself she wasn't looking at a picture they'd stuck in the mirror frame to fool her.

Spud had curled and teased and twisted her usually frizzy, dirty blond hair into a high crown of smooth, shining gold. Hair wrapped around the base of a ponytail held it into itself, and a few curls escaped the bonds, making it look as though she'd just piled her hair on top of her head casually. Sparks of light twinkled from beneath it; he'd stuck a comb into her crown, at the base of the updo. It wasn't one of hers. She couldn't imagine where he'd gotten it.

Soft bangs swept to the side and fell over her eyes, startlingly blue and deep under the soft, cool colors on her lids. It wasn't just violet, it was green and silvery, too, and it all shone with iridescence like a butterfly's wing. The false lashes framed her eyes, a thick black fringe that made her look innocent and sexy all at once, and her lips looked impossibly soft and lush, tinged with brick red.

"How did you guys learn to do this?"

"We been around a long time, m'lady," Malleus said. "You picks things up, when you're as old as us."

"How old are you?"

They shrugged in unison. "Five hundred years, maybe?" Malleus said. "We ain't exactly sure."

Spud wiped a tear from his eye. Maleficarum patted his arm. "She does look pretty," he murmured. "You did a good job, you daft old sow."

Spud blushed and ducked his head.

Megan wanted to throw her arms around each of them, but refrained. They wouldn't be comfortable with that, especially since she was still undressed. She didn't want to spoil the moment. They watched her like three proud, horned papas seeing their daughter about to be married. Tears started in her eyes. No one had ever looked at her like that before.

She blinked them back before they could damage Maleficarum's careful make-up. "You did a lovely job. Thank you." They nodded and grinned.

"Let's get me dressed, then," she said. "If you gentlemen would turn around for a minute . . . ?"

They followed her into the bedroom and placed themselves one at each door and Spud at the window, all looking out. Megan opened her lingerie drawer and pulled out her garter belt and stockings. Were they too sexy?

She was going to this thing with Brian, after all, who at this moment liked her maybe a little less than he liked barium enemas. It wasn't as if—well, it wasn't as if someone else was her date.

But it wasn't as if she had any clean pantyhose, either. They would have to do.

She took her new taupe dress out of the closet and stepped into it, slipping her arms into the elbow-length sleeves. It was a plain, safe kind of dress. Calf-length, slim skirt, darted high-cut bodice. "Zip me up?"

Malleus turned around. His wrinkled face fell. "Is that the dress you bought?"

"Yes, why?"

"Nothin', no reason." He came over and zipped her up. Maleficarum picked up his phone and started muttering as she looked down at herself.

She'd lost a couple of pounds this past week, it seemed, and no wonder. She'd been nervous enough to power a small country with her energy, and there hadn't been much time or inclination to try and eat.

The dress had been large on her to begin with, though. Now she looked a little like a girl in her mother's gown.

She sighed. It would have to do. Nobody ever said she was the most stylish woman on the planet. In fact, if someone had said it, she would have laughed at them. Megan would have loved to recognize designer clothing at a glance and buy very expensive shoes and perfectly tailored outfits, but she had to live in the real world and support herself on a real salary, and there was no point looking at pictures of what she couldn't have so she avoided fashion magazines, too.

She looked good enough to attend a work-related function with a reporter who thought she was trying to brainwash him, anyway.

As she dug around in the mess at the bottom of her closet to find her shoes, Maleficarum said, "M'lady, Mr.

Dante's coming by. 'E says, he'll be 'ere in ten minutes, so you sit and wait."

"Great," Megan muttered. One shoe dangled from her hand. The other continued to elude her. A visit from Greyson was perfect with Brian on his way.

SHE SAT PRIMLY ON THE COUCH when he arrived, recalcitrant shoes finally located and firmly on her feet. With him he brought a breath of the cold air outside, fresh and tinged with the smoky scent of fall. Formal wear suited his tall, lean frame; he wore it comfortably and well. Megan had to fight to keep from stroking his lapels to make sure he was real.

"Stand up," he said.

"Nice to see you, too."

He rolled his eyes. "Stand up. Your date will be here in a few minutes, won't he? I don't think either of you will be happy if he finds me here."

"My goodness," Megan said. "I didn't know you were scared of him."

He glared at her, his lips thinning they way they did when he was particularly annoyed. "Just stand up."

She obeyed, irritated at herself for doing so but not seeing the point in doing otherwise. So she could argue for another ten minutes and still end up doing it? No, thanks.

He shook his head and made a face. "Ugh. The boys were right." He headed back to the door. "Wait here."

Ugh? She'd never looked prettier, and she was in a new dress, and he said ugh? Arrogant son of a—

"Here." He held a large white box out to her. "Put it on."

"Excuse me?"

He waved the box. "It's a dress. Put it on. Quickly, I have to go."

"I don't want to put it on."

"Would you rather spend the evening looking like somebody's grandmother's couch?"

"Hey! It's not that bad."

"Yes it is. Now go change. Burn that thing."

Megan took the box and set it on the couch, determined to pooh-pooh whatever was inside. The notion flew from her head when the lid came off, though, and crystal beads twinkled at her from a nest of black chiffon. A gasp of pure feminine pleasure escaped her painted lips as she lifted the gown from its bed of tissue.

The strapless bodice glittered with jet and crystal, and the flowing layers of the skirt hung in graceful lines from the fitted waist. She'd never owned anything like it.

"I can't," she said, tearing her gaze away. "Thanks, Greyson, but I have a dress."

"It's ugly."

"How nice of you to say."

"Look, Megan. It doesn't matter to me if you want to look like the frump that ate Manhattan, but there will be press people there tonight. Not to mention my boss, who'll be expecting to meet you, and several other high-ranking members of my Meegra. Demons are very . . . let's just say some of us judge books by their cover. So try to look pretty, won't you? You do want their help."

"Are you saying they won't help me if I don't look pretty enough?"

He grinned. His teeth were very white. "I'm saying it won't hurt your cause to look like a sweet, attractive woman, and not the prickly, fussy ball of nerves you actually are."

Megan eyed the dress with exaggerated distaste. She wanted to put it on more than anything. She just didn't want him to know that, so she nodded and walked into the bedroom holding the dress at arm's length, as if it was a piece of particularly nasty garbage she was forced to touch.

It fit perfectly, adhering to her small breasts and making them look larger while making her waist look smaller, and swirling gracefully to the floor. Her pale skin glowed against the black chiffon. After one long, pleased moment, she fixed her face in a frown and left the bedroom.

"Fine, I'll wear it, because I need your Meegra's help. But I'm giving it back tomorrow, and that's that."

Greyson's lips twitched. "Of course. Just because you need help."

A knock at the door made her jump. Greyson sighed. "That'll be your date. I'll see you there."

Before she could reply, he leaned forward and planted a quick, soft kiss on her lips.

"Hey," she said, but he'd already slipped out the patio doors, fading like a vampire into the night.

Chapter Eighteen

Megan pulled her fake-fur wrap tighter around her shoulders. She shouldn't have been cold in the car. The heater was on. But the waves of disapproval rolling from Brian's stiff frame made her want to hide under a pile of blankets.

"This is fun," she said. "Oh so much fun."

"Sorry, I guess I'm not as interesting as your mobster boyfriend."

"He's not my boyfriend."

"He's not your fucking babysitter, either. You know what, Megan? I didn't give a shit what your relationship was with him, until the two of you set up that attack or whatever in the park and decided to try to mess with my head because of it. But you did. Whatever little game you're playing, you better be careful. Because I'm going to find out. And once I do, so will the rest of this city."

"Or at least the ten or fifteen people who read *Hot Spot*." She'd wanted the words to be cold, uncaring, but her voice broke on "Hot."

"We have a lot more readers than that. And besides, once I break this story, I won't be working for them anymore. I'll be at a real paper, maybe even in a bigger city."

"I'll tell them what you do. How you cheat."

"And they won't give a damn even if they believe you."

Damn it, her makeup would run if she let those tears fall. She dug a tissue out of her sparkly little evening bag and dabbed at her lower lids.

Brian must have seen the movement. Some of the chilliness faded.

After a minute, he said, "I won't apologize. But I don't want to go down this road, Megan."

"Why? You certainly seem happy to."

He sighed. "I thought you were a good person. When we met I thought you were a good, nice person."

"And now?" Why she cared she couldn't say. Who was Brian anyway? A reporter assigned to do a puff piece on her. Not someone she would ever see again. Not a friend. Barely an acquaintance.

It just hurt to have someone, anyone, think so badly of her. Someone not from her hometown, at least. They still thought of her as a "murderer" there.

"Now . . . I think you're just someone who can't help being what you are. I don't think you deliberately try to deceive anyone. It doesn't make it right, what you're doing and what you did—but I don't think it was malicious. You just don't think. Or care, or whatever. It's sad. I don't understand it."

"But I'm not like that," she said. Behind her, one of the brothers shifted position, leaning forward and resting his meaty hand on the back of her seat. She must sound more upset than she thought.

"I wish I could believe that," he said. They finally reached the valet. Cool air swirled into the interior of the car as the doors opened, and Megan stepped up onto the curb with her wrap still clutched around her shoulders.

Brian handed over the keys and stood next to her. "Ready?"

"What? No. No, I'm not ready. I don't want to spend my evening knowing you think I'm some kind of murdering, cheating mind-rapist."

"Keep your voice down." He moved to take her arm, but Spud's hand grabbed him before he could. Megan glanced back. Spud frowned and shook his head.

"'E's right, m—Miss Chase," Malleus muttered. "This ain't the place to be speaking too loud."

Megan looked around. People passing by were indeed looking at them strangely, though how much of that was their conversation and how much was the three stocky men in tuxedos and faded newsboy caps she couldn't say. "Fine." She reached out and took Brian's hand. "Come here."

"You're dragging me into the bushes alone?"

"Yes."

"M'lady—Miss Chase, I don't fink this is such a good idea, I don't fink Mr. Dante would like—"

"Be quiet, Mr. Brown."

Her heels sank into the sharp-smelling mulch as she led Brian back into the pine trees next to the building. Curious partygoers turned to watch them go. *Great. Now everyone will think I couldn't wait to seduce Brian up against a wall.*

But this couldn't wait. She needed him to read her and tell her honestly if she was a bad person or not. If all those choices she'd made, all those decisions to steal that parking spot, or close the elevator door on someone carrying heavy packages, or make sarcastic comments—decisions she'd made on her own—qualified her to be just the kind of person he thought she was.

Or if there was hope for her after all.

"What are we—"

"Shut up and read me." She squeezed his hand and lowered her shields. Completely.

For a second she felt nothing at all, then the impact of the thoughts of the crowds around her, of Brian's mind entering hers, slammed into her body and knocked her over.

She felt the brothers' hands rough on her bare skin as they picked her up, but she didn't register it. They touched her body, that was all, and she was not fully in her body at the moment. Instead she was in the air, while someone else invaded her mind.

Thoughts replayed themselves for her as he rummaged through them, coldly, without mercy. Harlan Trooper's face loomed in front of her, replaced by Art Bellingham. Regina, her radio caller. Her mother, fear in her eyes. Trooper again, his face green and covered with saliva as his mouth opened to reveal row upon row of silvery teeth. The kids in her school, laughing at her, tripping her in the halls or teasing her to tears in class. Greyson Dante, his arms tight around her, pulling his face away from hers in the back yard . . .

No! The part of her that could still think tried to pull away, but it was too late. Dante's back, while her hand slid up the little knobs of his spine. Then another image, a guy she'd dated in college, sprawled naked on the sun-dappled bed of his dorm room while she straddled him.

"No!" This time she screamed it, her body twisting and shaking as she tried to pull away from Brian. Strong hands closed over his, over hers, hands that were all the more welcome for not transmitting anything at all. The demons.

Brian tried to pull back, but something tangled between them and held fast. Before she could get her shields back up she was assaulted. Crowds of people were just on the other side of that wall, were lined up in cars or standing around outside. Their thoughts hit her, engulfed her, their emotions swelling inside her until she thought she would explode.

"I wonder what time he'll have his service call with an 'emergency'. Some emergency, her new lingerie."

"Ooh! This is exciting!"

"Okay, five to eight. Drew will be waiting for us in two hours. Don't forget to throw that damn watch in the garbage before you call the police."

She twisted, thrown from her body, flying somewhere in the sky, still assaulted by thoughts and emotions. Hate. Envy. The grinning, toothsome faces of personal demons filled her mind, dancing around her. She screamed again, screamed at the knowledge in their eyes. Screamed because behind them was the shadowy face of Art Bellingham, and as she tried desperately to escape and go back to her body she heard his voice.

"Watching you, Megan . . . you can't block me forever . . ."

His laughter echoed around her, as if she was floating on it, swimming in it. She caught a glimpse of Brian's terrified face before something slammed into the air between them, cutting off Art's laughter and the leering demon faces. Something that burned her like fire, but it was a fire she could stand, a heat that gave her strength. It roared in her ears, flames in her vision.

"Help me," she heard Greyson gasp and the flames wavered for a second then grew stronger, their tips rimmed with blue-white. She came back to her body, thudding into reality and finding herself clasped in Greyson's arms, almost horizontal. Malleus, Maleficarum, and Spud all had their hands on her, her shoulders, her legs. She had a brief second to be embarrassed before they let go. Greyson set her unsteadily on her feet with his arm tight around her waist, pressing her against the safety and strength of his body.

"What the hell happened here?"

"Mr. Dante, she insisted we—"

"She said it'ud be fine, she said she just wanted to—"

"Jesus, I don't know." That last was Brian, his voice shaking. Megan pulled her face away from the solid warmth of Greyson's torso to look at him, pale and shivering against the ivory stucco of the building.

"I let Brian read me," she said. Her voice didn't sound like her own. "He didn't believe me . . . and I thought, I just wanted to . . ."

"Shit." Greyson's grip on her tightened. "Got more than you bargained for, Stone?"

Brian leaned against the wall and reached into the breast pocket of his tux, producing a slightly crumpled pack of cigarettes. She'd had no idea he was a smoker.

"I'm not," he said, answering the question she knew must be on her face. "I keep them with me in case people I interview want one." He shook one cigarette out and put it between his lips, then flicked a cheap plastic lighter.

Greyson snatched the cigarette away. "You're about to light the filter," he said. He turned it around, gave it back, then took another cigarette for himself. "I don't, either," he said to Megan. His eyes looked larger in the pallor of his face.

The boys did. Megan, feeling left out and more than a little irritated that smoking had suddenly become more important to all of them than what just happened, grumbled and grabbed one for herself. Dante lit it for her. She noticed that while he still held Brian's lighter, he didn't use it. He gave her shoulder a light caress as he withdrew his hand.

The smoke burned her throat and her chest, but she managed not to cough, although her eyes stung.

"Great," Brian said finally. "Now that we're all smoking buddies, can someone tell me what just happened?"

Dante exhaled a thin stream of grayish smoke. It hung in the still, cool air, wreathing his face with haze. "Power transfer," he said. "It's my guess, anyway. Nothing else feels like that."

"Power transfer? Really?" Brian leaned forward, his eyes bright. "I've never done it before. That was intense."

Megan's hands finally stopped trembling. "Transfer?"

Dante nodded. "Trust me, every damn sensitive in the place felt that. Megan, you lowered your shields all the way, right?"

"I didn't want him to think I was hiding anything."

"She didn't hide anything," Brian said. "I'm sorry, Megan."

She knew the apology was for what he'd seen as much as anything he'd said. She gave him a half-smile, more relived than she thought she would be. He didn't think she was an awful person. A weight she'd barely been aware of lifted from her chest. Someone knew her secrets and still thought she was okay.

Someone human, not demon.

"Okay, but when she lowered her shields all the way you weren't expecting it, right? You were pushing with everything you have. You went all the way into her head, into her power. You took it from her without meaning to, and her psyche or *ka* or whatever you want to call it reacted by stealing yours right back and locking the two of you together. I guess she couldn't get her shields back up and the thoughts of everyone in here leapt into her head."

Brian nodded. "I heard it was a pretty dangerous thing to do. My old teacher told me once."

"It's usually not a good idea, no. You could have been bound together permanently, or you could have stolen all of her power and not been able to give it back. It's rare, but it's best not to do transfers unless there's no other option." Greyson looked at them both. "You both seem fine, though, and I'm a little worried that people are going to come looking for us soon. We'd better finish these up and head inside."

Megan had forgotten about her cigarette, now just a long tube of ash hanging from her fingers. The men had smoked theirs down to the filters.

"Here." Brian held out his hand, and Megan handed the butt to him. He stubbed it out in the dirt and pocketed it. "Wouldn't do to leave any evidence of our little social crime, would it?" He smiled, but Megan hardly noticed.

"Don't forget to throw that damn watch in the garbage . . ."

She clutched Greyson's arm. "I heard something."

"Hmm?" He glanced around. "Like what?"

"No. I mean, when I was . . . when I was reading everyone. Someone is planning to kill his wife, or have her killed. He was thinking it. I heard it."

"Don't we have more important things to worry about right now?" His eyebrows raised and he glanced at Brian.

Right. He must have felt Art Bellingham, or known Bellingham had been there in her head. The thought made her queasy.

"Is there something more important than the possible murder of a woman tonight?"

"Yes. You don't even know who she is."

Every time she started thinking of him as a man, something happened to make her remember. Not a man. A demon. The death of most humans affected him about as much as the death of a fly bothered her, which wasn't much.

Not for the first time, she wondered why he seemed interested in her. Not for the first time, she wondered if she wanted to know.

"It doesn't matter," she said. "No, I don't know who she is, but I'm going to find out and we're going to save her. You know why? Because that's the right thing to do."

He looked peeved, but he nodded. "Fine. We'll try to figure out who it is. But to do that, we need to go inside, so may I suggest . . . ?"

They wandered back out of the trees and onto the sidewalk, ignoring the curious glances from the dwindling crowd outside. Megan's hand flew to her hair. "Shit! I'm sorry, guys. My hair, my make-up, you did such a beautiful job and it's probably ruined."

"You look fine. Not a hair out of place," Greyson said.

"We used, er, fixative on it. So it won't fade or nuffing."

They stopped just outside the doors. Brian took her arm. "Megan," he said, pulling her slightly to face him. "I truly am sorry."

"That's okay. If we can save this woman, it will have been worth it."

She gave them all a brief rundown of what she'd heard and what sort of man she thought it had come from. She'd only received a flash and it was muddled, but it felt like a younger man, mid-thirties, wealthy. The wife was older, or at least the man perceived her that way.

"So, basically, he's a gigolo and she's old and rich?"

Trust Greyson to get right to the point. She couldn't dispute it, though.

Brian sighed. "That describes half the couples in here."

"Then we'll just have to read them all, won't we?" She knew she should wait for Brian, since technically he was her date, but she couldn't resist sailing in ahead of them all and letting them watch.

Chapter Nineteen

Of course, she'd forgotten how dedicated Malleus, Maleficarum, and Spud were to their jobs. They ploughed through the crowd and caught up with her before she'd gotten five feet.

She'd also forgotten that she didn't have the tickets. Brian did. He smiled faintly at her as he handed them over and she checked her wrap.

"Very dramatic," Greyson whispered in her ear. She shivered as his lips brushed against her lobe. "It would have been quite spectacular if it had worked."

She turned to make a face at him, but he hadn't moved at all. Her movement brought her lips within an inch or so of his.

Their eyes caught, held. His left hand came up to rest on her left shoulder, half of a loose embrace. "If I find this guy," he said in a low voice, "will you come home with me?"

She wanted to say something flippant and sexy. She couldn't think of anything, though. Instead she shrugged and turned away with her chin held high, hoping he would read something clever into it.

He squeezed her shoulder, then his hand and the heat of him against her back disappeared as he made his way into the ballroom.

"Megan?"

She turned to see Brian watching her, a sort of half-smile on his face, and realized she'd been staring after Greyson like a lovesick teenager. She tried to rearrange her features into a pleasant blank. "What?"

"I asked if you wanted a drink once we get in."

"Absolutely."

He offered his arm and she took it, grateful that the fabric of his tux kept that jolt of energy away.

She wasn't sure quite what she'd expected. Probably something like a cafeteria filled with flowers—in fact, probably something like the high school prom she'd only seen pictures of. But the Femmel benefactors had gone all out. Twinkling lights hung from the ceiling and white fabric hid the walls. The polished wood floor was clear in a wide semi-circle in front of the stage, where a long table was set up. For the charity board and a few of the most generous donors, she guessed. Not far from that an orchestra was just starting to play "It Had to be You."

She was glad she decided to wear Dante's dress. Her plain tan one would have been very out of place here, where most of the women were in ball gowns and glittering diamonds.

Brian didn't stop to gawk, taking her straight to the bar and ordering her a gin and tonic without asking. Megan didn't care. He had the same and they stood warily eyeing each other and sipping.

"So," he said. "Power transfer."

She nodded, her eyes scanning the room. Someone in this beautiful building was planning a very ugly crime. She'd never dealt with anything like this before, she thought, then stifled a laugh. So far this week she'd dealt with demons, zombies, fiends, and witches. Now a spot of good old-fashioned murder was making her nervous?

"What was Art Bellingham doing there?"

At least she knew Brian wasn't involved with him. She hadn't gotten much of Brian's thoughts or feelings, but she'd gotten enough to know that. "He's . . . he's powerful, somehow. And he's been harassing me."

"I guess that's why he's been calling me, too."

"Is that why you asked about him?"

Brian nodded. "I'm a curious guy. Why, did you think I worked for him?"

"I wondered."

"I guess I can't blame you," he said. "But I don't work for anyone but Tremple Media, Inc."

"Good." She wanted to ask him more about it, but she didn't want to draw more attention to Bellingham, either. She changed the subject entirely. "See any candidates?"

"Did you get anything more from the guy? You said young, did you feel how young? Or anything about her at all?"

Megan shook her head. "Although . . . he was thinking very specifically about her watch. Maybe it has some significance?"

"I don't know. I don't think people wear wristwatches to balls."

She looked down. "You are."

"Yes, but I'm just a reporter who doesn't know what's appropriate."

"Anyway. That's all I have. We should start looking. He's waiting for someone named Drew, or someone named Drew is going to help him. You might see if maybe you overhear that name, if you can't read someone for whatever reason."

Brian nodded. "This wasn't how I planned to spend the evening."

"Me neither." Megan finished her drink and set it on the bar. "But at least it's something to do."

She turned and set off into the crowd, with Malleus, Maleficarum, and Spud trailing after her.

"MEGAN, MEGAN! Come over here. I've got some people I want you to meet." Richard Randall, looking natty as ever in his tux, waved at her from near the stage.

"Megan Chase, this is Charles Dunne, the head of the station." He kissed her cheek, and she knew he was hoping to schmooze Charles into giving him a raise tonight. "Charles, this is our little demon slayer."

Megan ignored her twinge of irritation and pasted a smile on her face as she offered her hand. "Lovely to meet you."

Charles Dunne was wondering if the hair below her belt was the same color as the hair on her head. Scumbag.

"It's a real pleasure for me, Megan," he said. He glanced back at Malleus, Maleficarum, and Spud, obviously dying to ask about them, but Megan pretended they weren't there. "We're all very excited about your show, and the ratings forecasts look great. Everyone's talking about you."

Yeah, I know. "I'm glad the station is pleased." Who was that man standing behind him? The young man holding the arm of a woman whose face was stretched beyond humanity by plastic surgery?

"In fact, since you're already doing the *Hot Spot* story, we've gained some national interest. How do you feel about television?"

"Um . . . I own one." The man and his date walked back towards the bar. Megan searched the crowd as unobtrusively as possible for Brian or Greyson, anyone who knew what to look for.

Richard and Charles were both chuckling, but Richard's eyes bulged slightly. Right. Not so flippant.

"To be honest, I feel like the radio show is enough for right now, especially since I'm not giving up my practice."

"Why? Why bother with the tedium of seeing patients when you can go on the radio once a week, go on TV once a week, and make twice the money?" He named a figure that made Megan's own eyes bulge.

"Just for going on TV once a week?" *No! I'm not interested!*

"You'd be bringing the demon slayer to our local news station, doing call-ins there and also giving your opinion on current events. You know, what demons drive the president, for example, or why you think this or that Hollywood marriage won't work out."

Ah. Never mind. "It sounds interesting," she lied, "but I don't think—"

"You don't have to answer now. Just think about it. Talk it over with Richard. How's your interview going this week, anyway? We're very excited about seeing you in *Hot Spot!*"

RADIO COUNSELOR: MURDERER, FRIEND OF DEMONS. "It's going great." She stretched her lips into a smile. "The reporter is a very nice man." *Who invaded my head forty-five minutes ago and saw me having sex.*

"Excellent. You know, when Richard came to me with this idea, I wasn't too enthused, but he was right. You're a lovely little spokesgirl for us, a pretty fresh face to bring our image up-to-date."

She didn't need Richard's warning look, but she wasn't going to stand there any longer and be patronized, either. *Think of the contract you signed, the iron-clad contract.* "I'm glad I can be of service."

The man and his date appeared near where Greyson stood deep in conversation with two other men. If she hurried, she could head them off.

"If you'll excuse me, though? I think I see—someone I need to talk to. Nice meeting you, Charles."

Richard didn't look happy, but Megan ignored him and sped away, her skirts swirling around her feet. The brothers followed her like the shark in *Jaws*, cutting through the crowd.

"Greyson." She stared at the man and woman. "Nice to see you again."

If the demon was surprised, he didn't show it, instead taking her hand and leaning over to give her a kiss on the cheek.

Or rather, to scrape her earlobe softly with his teeth. She shivered. His breath puffed against her cheek as he chuckled. "Nice to see you, too," he said. "Have you met Hunter Kyle and his lovely mother, Julia?"

"No, I haven't." Megan shook hands, her heart falling into her stomach. She read them both, just to be sure, but this was not her killer and his planned victim. This was a very nice divorced man whose socialite mother could afford both being on the charity board and remaking her face out of rubbery space-age polymers.

They chatted for a few minutes. Megan tried not to be rude but her nerves wouldn't allow her to stand still for long.

Greyson squeezed her shoulder. "Let's dance."

"I don't think—" she started, but he'd already taken her hand and was leading her out onto the floor, where quite a few couples already took advantage of the orchestra.

He spun her towards him, his arm going around her waist and pressing her close. She rested her hand on his shoulder, more because it was expected than anything else. "I don't want to dance right now."

"Then you haven't been paying attention. Look around us."

Almost every couple dancing consisted of an older woman and a younger man.

"Gigolos," Greyson murmured in her ear. This close, the scent of his skin overwhelmed her. Her nipples hardened. She hoped he wouldn't notice it, but she knew he would. "Kept men. Young trophy husbands. If you were going to kill your wife, would you spend the evening ignoring her, or would you make sure everyone saw you showing her a good time, dancing and laughing?"

She couldn't believe she hadn't thought of it before. "I guess I'm not very good at this," she said, as he edged her closer to one of the couples.

"I'm sure you'll get better. Oh, terribly sorry!"

He'd bumped into one couple, just long enough for Megan to get a quick read on them both. Nope. Not him.

"I don't need to touch them," she said. "And if you try to touch them all, people will leave the floor awfully fast to get away from the klutz."

"I know you don't need to touch them, but touching makes it easier, doesn't it? So you aren't using as much energy, you aren't lowering your shields very far. That way it won't be as noticeable."

"Noticeable to whom?"

"I told you, my boss is here tonight. So are a lot of other . . . people, for lack of a better term. I'd rather they not know about this little rescue mission of yours."

"Could it be one of them?"

"No. You can't read them."

"But when we did the power transfer—"

He shook his head. His dark eyes were just a few inches above hers, serious and deep. "You still couldn't read me, or the brothers. We should definitely be looking for a human."

"Okay, I'll touch instead of reaching with my mind, but you better be the one who looks stupid, not me."

"Oh, of course." He danced her off to the left. Megan managed to brush against a few more people. No. No. No. She giggled.

"What?"

"That man is wondering if the reason his wife likes to dance so much is because she enjoys stepping on his feet," she whispered.

Greyson smiled. "Get ready for a spin." He flung her out to his right. Megan stretched her arm out, grinning as if she was doing nothing more than dancing rather foolishly, and managed to touch another man, who was cheating on his wife with one of the men who ran the charity. Sleazy, but not a killer. She shook her head as Greyson spun her back into his arms.

"I don't understand it," she said. "I know what I heard. I know what he was planning to do."

"Maybe they left already."

"No. He said two hours. We should have at least another half hour before they go." She started to let go of him, but his hands did not loosen their grip on her waist. "Come on," she said, refusing to struggle. "I need to try to touch everyone else in the room."

The music stopped.

"This is important to you, isn't it? You need to do this."

She nodded. Of course it was. How could she just let someone die?

"Go ahead," Greyson said. "Just open up and see what you can get."

"What about everyone knowing what I'm doing?"

He smiled and leaned forward. His lips barely brushed hers. "Read," he said, and kissed her.

Megan lowered her shields, aiming behind towards the rest of the dancers and the back wall where people were standing, but she only managed to get a few jumbled impressions before she lost herself in Greyson's kiss.

Both his arms encircled her, pressing her to him. Some vague part of her mind remembered they were in the middle of a ballroom where her employers and his could see them. The rest of her didn't give a damn where they were or what was happening, because her lips parted and his tongue dove in to caress hers, sending sparks of pure heat along her every nerve ending. With his tongue came the odd sensation of him in her head, then a rush of power. He didn't seem to be reading her, but enveloping her, pressing himself into her mind and imprinting his energy on hers. His mouth caught her soft moan of surprise and pleasure. Her body hummed with his flames, flowing through her, pure and intense, free of thoughts.

His fingers curled into the soft fabric of her dress just at the juncture of skirt and bodice. His erection pressed against her, and all she could think, not too coherently, was how badly she wanted him. How the normally insensate space between her legs was on fire with need. How if it wouldn't mean career suicide and more press than she could imagine, she would let him lift her skirt and take her right here on the dance floor.

Somehow her arms were around his neck, her fingers entwining in his hair as he kissed her harder. This had never happened to her before. She'd never been with someone she couldn't read, someone who forced her to leave her head and focus on her body. And, oh god, her body felt good. *His* body felt even better.

He pulled away, his breath ragged. His left hand cradled her cheek, his thumb hard under her chin. "Let me take you home, Megan," he said. "Let me make love to you." His lips traveled up the side of her neck to her ear, where his tongue darted out to lick at her earlobe. "I've waited, god I've waited, don't make me beg."

The words sent a sharp thrill straight through her chest and down still lower. "It's only been a week," she murmured, trying to keep her thoughts straight. It wasn't easy, especially when he pulled her earlobe between his teeth and sucked it gently.

"It feels like forever," he said. "Megan . . . please." He shivered slightly, as if it was an effort to say the word. Maybe it was. All she knew was his shiver sent an answering one through her own body.

"We haven't stopped the killer," she said.

"Brian can do it."

"Brian thinks you're a dick."

"I don't care. Don't change the subject." Then, in a different voice, "Hi, Brian."

Megan jumped back and almost stumbled. Greyson caught her. "How did you manage to live as long as you have without losing a limb? You're the clumsiest woman I've ever met."

"Flatterer." Things were back to normal, it seemed, but she knew this was different. The urgency of his voice, the feel of his hands on her skin . . . there was no going back and he knew it as well as she did. A new possessiveness transmitted itself in the way his hands rested on her waist as he pulled her to stand in front of him, the way he pressed her to him. Something had changed in that kiss. She'd given in, though she hadn't spoken the words. Maybe she never would. The outcome would be the same.

Brian had the grace to color slightly. "I'm sorry to interrupt, but I think I've found the guy."

"That's great!" she said, a little louder and more enthusiastic than she'd meant to. "Where?"

"Over there, in the corner," Greyson said. "The blond guy."

Megan did a double take. "How do you know?"

"I read him. Through you."

"What? I thought you could only force thoughts on people, but can't read them."

Brian stepped closer. "Yeah, what?"

"I'm not psychic," Greyson said. "You and Megan are. If I make close physical contact, I can use your skills with my power behind it. I read the whole room."

Megan pulled away and glared at him. "You could have done that right from the start." She glanced at Brian, who looked as though he'd like nothing more than to put his hands around Greyson's throat. "You made us spend the last hour frantically reading the entire crowd, tiring ourselves out, when all it took was physical contact with one of us?"

"Close physical contact," he said, stepping nimbly to the left as a dancing couple threatened to mow him down. "Would you rather I'd kissed Brian? You weren't exactly in the mood earlier."

"I'm not in the mood now," she snapped, pulling away. It was a complete lie. Her body still throbbed.

He cocked an eyebrow. Damn him. Could he read her? Being in the dark like that made her twitch. It was unsettling.

Then again, everything lately was unsettling. What was one more thing on top of it?

Chapter Twenty

"What do we do now?" Brian asked. "I mean, we can't exactly go to the police, right?"

Greyson gestured over to the near wall, where Malleus, Maleficarum, and Spud lounged, looking like vaguely threatening grandpas.

"Wait a minute." Megan stepped away to look Greyson in the face. "Why not hypnotize him?"

"I'm sorry?"

She glanced at Brian, trying to gauge his reaction. This didn't seem like the type of plan he would be in favor of, but she couldn't think of anything else—save Greyson having the brothers kill the man, which she thought he might be planning but which she wanted to avoid.

"Can't you—I mean, especially if Brian and I help— get into his head? Make him cancel the plan?"

"I'm not so sure that's a good idea," Brian said, taking a step back.

Megan caught his sleeve. "What do you want to do, Brian, let somebody die? Isn't this the lesser of two evils?"

"I'm just worried about what would happen if we accidentally do another power transfer, Megan."

"Oh." Nothing like running into the field with all guns blazing, only to find the enemy wanted to negotiate instead.

Greyson shook his head. "I'd rather not, Megan. It's one thing to use my power through you the way I did it, but if I do this here—"

"If you do this here, what? Someone's life is saved?"

"Why don't we just have the boys beat the shit out of him?"

"I should have known," she said, turning away.

He grabbed her arm and pulled her a couple of steps away. "What's that supposed to mean?"

"It means, you don't give a damn if this woman lives or dies, you don't give a damn what I want. I'm asking you to do one thing for me, Greyson, one little thing." She knew this wasn't fair—he'd done plenty for her, whether by choice or by order of his boss or some other reason she didn't know yet, but she owed him her life. "Why won't you do it? Why should I do something for you, something with you, if you don't even care enough about me to save someone's life?"

He stared at her, then shook his head. "Okay," he said, glancing over to his right. Megan looked, but didn't see anyone she recognized. "Okay, I'll do it. For you."

"Thanks." She smiled at him.

He nodded, but did not return the smile. "Let's go, then."

He took her hand in a warm, firm grip and led her off the dance floor. Just as well, since she'd caught a few annoyed looks from people trying to actually dance.

"You guys wait by the—ah." He stopped. They all stopped, like a halted army.

A tall, heavy-set man stood in front of them, a wide white grin on his tanned face. Power rested easily on his broad shoulders, but Megan felt no particular vibrations from it at all. Which meant he was probably Greyson's boss.

He shook Greyson's hand, covering it with both of his. The diamond pinky ring on his left hand glinted at Megan.

"Grey." Wrinkles formed at the outside corners of his eyes as he smiled. He was older than he'd originally appeared; Megan looked closer and saw gray sprinkled through his jet-black hair, and patches of skin showing through the hair at his forehead. "I was looking for you."

"Megan," Greyson said, not taking his eyes off the older man as they released hands, "may I present my boss, Templeton Black? Temp, this is Megan Chase."

Megan smiled and offered her hand. Templeton Black's skin was warm and very dry. She longed to offer him some lotion.

"Such a pleasure, Miss Chase. I've been looking forward to meet you."

"Well, now you have," Megan said. What did one say to that, anyway?

Templeton laughed. "Grey said you were smart. Wonderful. He's told me quite a bit about you."

"Oh?" She knew he was waiting for it, so she gave him the cliché. "Don't believe a word he tells you. I don't."

"Oh, no. I've always found him to be a most truthful sort of employee. At least, he's never given me any reason to doubt his loyalty to me. Have you, Grey?"

Greyson's smile didn't reach his eyes. "Of course not. You know our goals are the same."

Templeton eyed him. For a second his features seemed to rearrange themselves into something Megan didn't find half as pleasant as he'd looked a moment ago, but it was over before she could even be certain she'd seen it. "I believe they are the same," he said softly. "I never did before."

Megan looked at Greyson. He was still as an archer just before the bowstring is released.

Templeton clasped his hands together, ending the moment. "I take it Malleus, Maleficarum, and Spud are working out for you? I wanted to send you the best, you know."

"Thank you." So Greyson hadn't been lying when he said his boss was protecting her.

"You're welcome. Unfortunately, dinner is about to start, and I must get to my table. Perhaps Grey can bring you to my house tomorrow for a late lunch? Say, three o'clock? Wonderful. See you then."

Megan waited until he was out of earshot. "Am I crazy? Did I answer him without realizing it?"

Greyson smiled, but his lips were tight. "That's just the way he is."

"What's wrong? What was that 'we're on the same side' stuff about, anyway?"

"What? Nothing. I'm just thinking about what I'll say to our murderous friend over there. Wait here for me, won't you? Thanks."

Then he, too, was gone without waiting for a reply. Megan turned to Brian, standing just behind her, and said, "Is this some man thing I don't know about, just walking away like that?"

"Maybe it's a demon thing." Megan tensed, but he continued. "Or maybe they're just busy. I don't want to fight with you anymore, Megan."

Megan bit her lip. "I'm glad."

A passing waiter produced flutes of champagne, and she and Brian sat down. Megan kept one eye on Greyson, who was now leading the blond man out of the room and down a hall towards what she guessed was the restroom.

"So you didn't kill that guy, Trooper," Brian said. "But you don't know who did, either."

Megan took a long sip of her drink. "I was hoping maybe you'd know." Her voice shook, and she cleared her throat. "I mean, maybe you saw something I don't remember, or maybe it made more sense to you as an outsider . . ." Brian's face didn't change. "I guess I'll never know."

"Maybe it will come back to you one of these days. Sometimes memories work like that. Something could trigger it, and before you know it the whole story is there in your head."

"What about your story? What will you write about it?"

"I'll bury it," he said. "A local homeless man died. You found the body. That's it. Nobody needs to know about the court or his name even. If you could give me a quote about how that was what made you want to be a counselor, that would be great, too."

"I can definitely do that. Thanks, Brian. Hey . . . how are you doing, anyway? I mean, with all of this?"

"As well as I can, I guess. Not like you."

"Me?"

"Does any of this even affect you? You seem just like you did the first day we met. Like there's all this stuff going on around you, but it doesn't touch you at all. How do you do that? How do you keep yourself so locked up inside, that it seems like you don't even have feelings sometimes? You fall down, you pick yourself up, you move on, and if somebody mentions your fall you look surprised. Just like you look now."

"I-I deal with people's feelings all the time, Brian. I had to learn to shut myself off."

"Yeah, but you're shutting yourself off from your own life."

"No, I'm not."

He folded his arms and stared at her.

"I'm not. Of course I'm scared, and freaked out, and of course all of this bothers me. But I can't just curl up in a ball under the covers and hope it all goes away. I still have to live my life."

"But you seem to be enjoying this life. I mean, your boyfriend there—don't try to tell me he's not, maybe he wasn't, but he certainly is now—is a *demon*." He whispered the last word. "And you let him touch you. And if you don't like it, you sure are a good actress. I don't think you understand the reality of demons here. Greyson's not just some guy who's a little different, like maybe he's a different religion or grew up in another country. He's not human."

"People might say we're not quite human." Her glass was empty. She looked for a waiter, drumming her fingers on the tabletop until she caught one's eye and lifted her glass at him.

"It's not the same thing and you know it. And you can anesthetize yourself with drink all you want, but that doesn't change the fact."

"I do not—"

"No, you aren't an alcoholic or anything, but give yourself time."

"That's a shitty thing to say."

"Yeah, well, the truth is shitty sometimes." He glanced over at the hallway Greyson and his victim had disappeared down.

Megan looked, too. It had only been a few minutes, but she tingled with anxiety. The air in the room hung close around her, charged with something she didn't understand.

"You're letting him have you, you know," Brian said. "You're letting him take your soul without even a fight."

"They don't take souls." The waiter brought her drink, but she refused to even take a sip after what Brian said. "What do you care, anyway?"

"I just don't like to see the bad guys win. That's why I became a reporter."

"And who's the bad guy here? The guy trying to save my life, who is right now saving another woman's life, or the one who can't look beyond *what* he is, and see *who* he is?"

"They're the same," Brian said. "A demon's a demon."

"Who told you that?"

"Father McElory. My priest."

"You told a—you have a priest?"

Brian nodded. "I've been going to Saint Michael's since I was a kid. Altar boy, the whole works. I'm trying to keep an open mind, but it goes against everything I believe, everything I've been taught. So I have to ask myself, who's right here, a girl I've known for a few days or two thousand years of teachings? Demons seduce, Megan. They convince. They'll do anything to win. How do you know this isn't all a set-up, just to get you to their side?"

Megan shook her head, tears blurring her eyes. "I have to go with what I feel. And what I believe. Fact is, nobody's ever tried to save me until now. Set-up or not, and I don't believe it is, I'm making my own choices based on what I know."

Greyson chose that moment to appear. He looked like a man who'd just won the lottery. Megan's brows knitted. She'd been sitting out here panicking and defending her personality and choices to Brian, and he was trotting jauntily over to the table? He could have at least looked like he'd been exerting himself in some way.

"Done," he said, sitting down next to her and scooting his chair close enough to place one hand on her chiffon-covered thigh, just over the lace of her stockings. He straightened his bowtie with the other. "Did I miss the food?"

"Yes."

Brian cleared his throat. "How did it go?"

"Oh, fine. Just fine. He's going to get a divorce then get out of town, no harm to the lady. He was a bit resistant at first, but we reached an understanding."

His fingers swirled in lazy circles on the top of Megan's thigh. Her mouth watered. How was it possible to be both furious and liquid with desire at once?

"That's it, then," Brian said. "You found the guy, you took care of it, and the rest of us just get to sit around and congratulate you?"

"Sorry there isn't even a story in it for you."

Megan looked from one of them to the other. Did Greyson know why Brian was hostile? Did he care? Did *she* care? It was hard to think about anything when Greyson's fingers were now moving so close to where she ached for him that she had to fight to keep her legs together.

She bit her lip and tried to act normal, while Greyson caressed her thigh and Brian scowled.

"There's lots of stories out there," he said. It took Megan a second to recall why he was saying it. "Don't worry about me, Dante. I'm sure I'll find something."

Megan wondered exactly what Brian was threatening Greyson with, but Greyson didn't seem concerned at all. "Good luck with that," he said, and finished Megan's drink.

"WE ALREADY DANCED."

"That wasn't dancing. It was investigating. Come."

He didn't wait for her reply this time, pulling her to the crowded floor and sweeping her into his arms. "There." His voice was low in her ear, mixing with the strains of 'That Old Black Magic'. How appropriate. She giggled.

"Don't laugh. How am I supposed to seduce you properly if you're snickering at me?"

"Is that what you're trying to do?"

"You know damn well it is." His hand left her waist to touch her head, encouraging her to rest it against him. "You're not very good at this, are you?"

"Insults aren't very seductive."

"It isn't an insult, it's a question. You kiss like you know what you're doing, but all the trappings seem completely lost on you. I wonder why."

"Most men don't bother with seduction anymore," she said. "They just buy you a few drinks and leap on you."

His laughter came out in soft puffs of air stirring her hair. "I can do that, if you prefer."

"No, thanks."

"Good. It's not my style."

The music switched, something slower, softer, that Megan wasn't familiar with. She sighed and closed her eyes as Greyson slowed their movements around the floor, aware that she was sinking into him like melting ice cream into cake and not caring at all.

"When thou sigh'st, thou sigh'st not wind, But sigh'st my soul away," he said, startling her.

"What?"

"For godsake hold thy tongue, and let me love."

"Is this part of your seduction?"

"Yes. Be quiet. 'She is neither white nor brown, but as the heavens fair; There is none hath her form divine In the earth or in the air.'"

"Who wrote that one?"

"Sir Walter Raleigh. I haven't gotten to the good stuff yet, this is just a warm-up."

"Does this usually work?"

"Yes. Don't you like it?"

"I didn't say that." In fact, she did. No one had ever quoted poetry to her before. "I just wonder where you picked those lines up."

"I went to college. I have a degree in English literature. Did you picture me at home, poring over anthologies in order to lure women into my bed?"

"Actually, yes."

"How little you think of me. I enjoy the poems. I don't need them."

"Oh?"

"No." Before she knew what he was doing, he'd stopped and taken her face in his hands. "If you prefer a more direct route, I'm happy to oblige."

Even expecting it as she did, the kiss still made her legs weak. She fell forward, into him, clinging to his shoulder like the only steady thing in a world that swayed and tilted and rapidly became nothing more than a vague, unimportant buzz in her ears.

He rested his forehead against hers. "Now come on."

She liked that he didn't wait for her reply. She liked that he led her off the floor with his warm hand enveloping hers. It made her feel, for the first time in a long time . . . safe. Wanted.

She knew he could be thinking the same things most of the other men she'd taken to her bed had been thinking. "I hope she goes down." "I hope she doesn't want to spend the night."

There was every chance in the world that Greyson was thinking those things. But this time, she didn't know about it. She didn't feel his rejection in her mind before it had even happened. For the first time she could remember, she felt hope. Nervous excitement. The feelings she imagined every other woman in the world felt when a man took them home to bed.

Brian was deep in conversation with an attractive brunette and barely noticed when she told him Greyson was giving her a ride. Her boss Richard had already left.

Dante led her over to where Malleus, Maleficarum, and Spud chatted over a table full of empty glasses. "Take the rest of the night off," he said. "Miss Chase will be with me."

Chapter Twenty-One

Greyson ushered her into his apartment and followed, closing the door behind him. Megan caught only a glimpse of light through tall windows on the wall opposite before he grabbed her and pulled her to him, his lips hot and hard on hers.

His hands slid up her waist, under the wrap draped over her shoulders, pushing the fabric off onto the floor as they tumbled sideways into the wall. The wrap lay in a puddle under Megan's feet. She didn't care. Didn't care about anything but the hands now skimming her collarbones, her shoulders, and down her arms. She reached into his open coat, intending to remove it, but she got lost in feeling his chest through his shirt. Under her palms he felt so broad, solid. Like she could rest herself against him and never, ever fall.

He yanked his coat off, leaving her skin cold without the touch of his hands. She reached for his tie, her fingers fumbling until he swatted them away and undid the tie in one quick, smooth movement. Her fingers were drugged, clumsy, while the rest of her body felt lithe and weightless, an electric wire humming with power. His power. Her power. It didn't matter.

Together they struggled with his buttons hidden under a panel on his tuxedo shirt, their fingers twining together and getting in the way, until Greyson finally growled and ripped the shirt open. He seemed to be moving on air, so lightly, as he scooped her up and carried her into the darkness with his shirt sleeves still around his arms, his mouth still devouring hers.

His power slid into her, feeding the energy. The room outside her closed eyelids lightened and when she opened them she discovered tiny flames dancing in the air, like fairy lights under the high ceiling of his bedroom. They cast smudged shadows into the corners and made her think of cathedrals, of silent places that no longer existed in the hard, bright modern world.

Their wavering light emphasized the sharp bones of Greyson's face. He looked outlined in gold as he set her down, her feet sinking into soft carpet. His eyes were opaque, black, save for the reddish glow from the reflected flames.

Or was that reflection? She peered at him, only to have him blink and lower his face. "My eyes . . . demon's eyes . . . they go red sometimes," he said. More than the intense throbbing of her entire body, more than the burning desire to see him naked, that insecurity in a voice that had only ever been confident made her melt.

She raised her hand to his jaw and pulled him back to her, answering his unspoken question.

He made a sound low in his throat and found the zipper of her dress, pulling it down, sliding his hands across her bare back as the dress fell to her ankles.

". . . the liquefaction of her clothes," he murmured. Megan smiled. She knew that line. She opened her mouth to tell him so, but his fingers stroked along the top of her strapless bra cups, raising goose bumps on her skin and stealing her breath.

He kissed a line down her throat from her ear to her collarbone while he opened the row of hooks down the back of the bra and let it fall. Another gasp escaped her lips when her hard nipples pressed against his chest, when he ran his hands firmly down the bare skin of her back to cup her bottom and press her closer to him. His insistent hardness beneath the slightly rough fabric of his trousers made her moan.

"Garters," he said, his voice muffled by her skin. "I suppose the trappings aren't lost on you, after all." His nimble fingers slid under the back of her panties and unfastened the belt. "Let's take these off."

He eased her back onto the bed. Her own skin glowed before her eyes, soft and smooth in the flickering light. She'd never seen herself like this before, as if through the heat and desire he felt. Approval and desire were plain on his face as he untwisted his cufflinks, dropping them, removing his shirt all the way.

Her panties disappeared in one quick, smooth movement. The garter belt followed, the stockings leaving her legs with a whisper of silk. Megan had thought he would want her to leave them on. His preference for her bare skin made her flush with pleasure.

"*Re ngarla*," he whispered, running his hands up her thighs, his thumbs stopping just short of the soft curls covering her mound. He loomed over her, eyes glowing, before slipping his hands up to her waist and bending his head, taking first her right nipple, then her left, into the heat of his mouth.

She arched her back, air hissing through her teeth. His bare chest pressed against her stomach, his hands held her fast. The scent of his shampoo, the smoky smell of his skin, filled her nostrils. She lost herself in it, in him. There was nothing in the world but Greyson's bed, no person in the world but Greyson as he suckled her so slowly and softly she almost sobbed with the need to have him. She burned, she ached, her body twisting beneath the solid heat of his chest.

She couldn't watch as he moved lower, his teeth scraping the sensitive flesh over her ribs, over her hipbones. Occasionally his tongue darted out, tasting her skin. Nothing of his thoughts came through to her. Only the ragged hoarseness of his breathing told her what he felt, what he was thinking. His hands slid over her bare skin to her thighs, lifting them, and nothing but heat and desire transmitted itself. It was like hovering on the edge of a void, a place of darkness and silence and a deeper peace than she'd ever felt. When his lips brushed against the wet, tingling flesh between her legs she threw herself into the void with a soft cry.

Everything she'd imagined about the gentle fork in his tongue was true and he knew how to use it. He nestled the hard little bundle of nerves hiding in her folds between the twin tips and shifted it, rolled it. Megan danced for him, helpless to stop. He was so hot, his hands gripping her thighs, sneaking up her stomach to caress her breasts. His breath on her tender, swollen skin, his tongue delving into her secrets and pulling from her everything she'd ever hidden from anyone. Slowly he moved, then faster, then slowed again, until she trembled, balanced on the wire between sanity and abandon.

He slipped his tongue into her, exploring her. Her hands in his hair tugged and pulled without her conscious knowledge. Greyson shifted his grip, resting her heels on his broad shoulders, then sucked her swollen little bud into his mouth.

That was enough for Megan. Her back arched off the bed. Her heels dug into his shoulders, but she didn't know it, wasn't aware of anything but the climax ripping through her body and leaving her lost, crying his name, her eyes open but sightless. For what felt like hours she floated, lost in unbelievable pleasure, her body thrumming and howling as if her soul could escape it in one glorious burst.

He pulled away, kissing her trembling thighs, the muscles of her stomach heaving with her every gasping breath, her incredibly sensitive nipples, her throat, until his face hovered over hers again. His trousers rubbed against her skin, and she forgot any last vestiges of shyness she might have had as she reached down to tug at the button and zipper keeping them on, keeping his bare skin from her.

Without looking away he reached down to undo them, peeling them off his lean thighs. Megan looked down to see all of him, and found nothing in his nakedness to displease her. Quite the opposite. The perfection promised by the hard muscles of his upper body continued all the way down. Greyson Dante might have been a demon, but he had truly been blessed.

"I can't get you pregnant," he said, his voice low and hoarse. "I can't catch human diseases, or give them. But if you want me to wear something, I will."

"No. But thanks."

His response was to climb onto the bed, sliding her across the enormous silk-covered mattress until his body rested completely on hers. He kissed her throat, her forehead, her shoulder, one hand stealing under her back to grip her neck from behind. The other caught her right leg in the crook of his arm, holding her thighs far enough apart for the blunt, heavy head of his cock to find her entrance.

One smooth, hard thrust brought the entire length and width of him into her, stretching her walls, filling her. Not only with the hard heat of his flesh, but with his power, driving through her torso into her head, so strong it made her scream. Pleasure beyond pleasure, pleasure bordering on pain. She shook with it, already desperate for release. Nothing in her life had ever prepared her for this, nothing could. She wrapped her arms around his neck and let him swallow her cries as he started to move inside her.

His fingers curled into her neck, holding her still as he shifted his weight to delve more deeply. She matched the slow, steady circles of his hips as he moved, his lips still exploring her throat and chest, dipping down to capture her nipples while she watched the top of his dark, sleek head. The pressure in her pelvis already threatened to explode when he gave something, did something, and more power slid into her body.

She was made of fire, the same flickering fire hovering near the ceiling of the room, the same quick fire that consumed buildings and forests and everything in its path. She opened her mouth and hot smoke escaped with her cries of ecstasy. His right hand held her hip, but she did not need his encouragement to quicken her movements as she was consumed by him, made whole by him, as she lost herself completely in the sensation of his body meshed with hers. The delicate friction of his skin rubbing against hers inside and out as he shifted and thrust made her bite her lips, bite his lips. They writhed together on his black satin sheets while pale gold poured over their skin from Greyson's flames, now growing larger as the power between them built.

His skin was alive under her fingertips, his mouth so hot on hers. She stroked his back, digging her fingernails in just enough for him to feel it, then losing control and digging still harder. He growled and thrust into her with more force, pressing forward until her knee touched her upper arm.

Megan hadn't realized he'd been speaking almost the entire time, bits of poetry, snippets of the demon tongue, mixed in with English and what sounded like French. Now she heard it, both soothing and arousing. He said her name a few times like a mantra, a spell cast into the shadows of the holy place his room had become.

The flames flared higher. Her skin was sweaty, they were both sweaty, as they strained and reached for the pinnacle just out of their grasp. His hands moved, holding her face on both sides so their gazes could meet. She wanted to blink and look away but he dragged her back, forcing her to stay with him, to look at him, and it was in the red-black depths of his eyes that she found her own presence, the well of her soul. As he increased his pace she fell into it, his name on her lips, and when her body started to shake she climbed out, covered in the sweetness of him, and screamed as she shuddered around his swollen length.

He thrust again once, twice, gasping, groaning, before he swelled inside her. She felt him jerk and throb just as she throbbed around him, her arms struggling in vain to hold him even closer. His lips claimed hers in one final searing kiss and the muscles in his back shuddered under her palms. It was her turn to swallow his cries as flames filled her mind and Greyson came, claiming her as his own deep in her core and deep in her head.

She woke up in the darkness some time later, her feet freezing without covers but the rest of her body warm where Greyson wrapped around her. The flames were gone, and only the faint light coming through the window illuminated the room. The reflective surfaces of the picture frames on the wall and the clock by the bed turned blank faces at her in the gloom.

Her mouth was dry. She started to slide sideways off the bed, hoping she'd find the kitchen, or at least the bathroom, to get some water.

"Megan." The dreamy quality in his voice sent shivers down her spine.

"Just getting a drink," she whispered, hoping he would stay in bed. Butterflies danced in the pit of her stomach, and she wanted to be alone, to try and figure out why without the distraction of his bare skin against hers.

"Kitchen's to the left," he mumbled. "Don't be long."

She padded her way across the soft, thick carpeting on the floor, scooping up his discarded tuxedo shirt and sliding her arms into it. Half the buttons were gone, and she blushed as she fastened the few that remained.

Once out of the bedroom, the light brightened. Here windows lined the walls, floor-to-ceiling. Greyson lived on the seventeenth floor. The only view she had from where she stood was smudgy charcoal sky, the lights from the city below keeping the stars hidden.

The cavernous room lay silent before her, revealing nothing of its owner's secrets. Megan couldn't even make out the colors, but she was reluctant to turn on a light. She'd be too exposed if she did.

Now why would she think such a thing? She couldn't think of a safer place in the city for her to be and in the next room slept a man who'd gladly kill to protect her. Not necessarily because of his feelings for her, but just because killing things didn't matter to him.

To her left she saw the kitchen and headed towards it, but something stopped her, turning her back towards the windows. The open shirt flapped around her thighs like limp, ghostly wings as she crossed the room, her heart pounding.

Greyson's name formed on her tongue but she refused to call him. No matter how good he'd made her feel, no matter how amazing it had been, she wasn't ready yet to hand herself over to him. She didn't even know if he wanted her to. *"Greyson isn't the relationship type at all,"* Tera said again in her head. So turning him into her knight in shining armor probably wasn't the best idea. Hadn't he said he wasn't interested in being a hero, anyway?

The curtains in her hands were made of thick velvet, soft and slightly prickly against her palms as she bunched them up and yanked them open all the way. The sheers were next, whispering across the curtain rod.

Cool air seeped in through the tiny spaces around the edge of the window, but that wasn't what made Megan cold. Her eyes widened, dilating, her muscles freezing as she looked across the street below to the roof of the building opposite.

There was no point in wondering how they came to be there and she already knew why. The moonlight glanced off their bald heads, emphasizing the hollows of their eyes, the elven caverns of their mouths as they stood motionless on the rooftop opposite. Staring at Greyson's windows, staring at her.

She didn't know how long she stood, ridiculous in the too-big, open shirt, her bare skin turning to ice in front of the window and her hands still tangled in the sheers on either side. Watching them as they watched her, not even daring to blink.

You won't beat me, she thought, raising her chin in a defiant gesture she didn't think they could see. You won't beat me.

She stared them down until the sky started to lighten and they disappeared one by one, until the roof was bare and Greyson's sleepy voice came from the bedroom asking where she was.

Chapter Twenty-Two

The car pulled up to the curb and Megan took a step towards it. Greyson grabbed her hand and pulled her back for a kiss.

"Megan, I need you to know something."

She nodded. The smile on her face faded as she looked into his dark, serious eyes.

"Whatever happens today, whatever happens at this little lunch meeting . . . I made the decision. And I knew what would happen when I made it."

"What? I don't—"

"Shh." He opened the back door, ready to help her in. "Just remember. Don't talk." He glanced at the driver.

Megan nodded, but her blood ran icy. What did he think was going to happen? Or rather, what *was* going to happen, because he wouldn't warn her about something if he thought it was unnecessary.

At least he was telling her. She suppressed a twinge of guilt. She hadn't mentioned the demons watching his apartment last night. There hadn't been a good time. It wasn't that important.

The truth was, she'd been afraid to mention it. She didn't want to ruin an amazing morning, starting with mimosas and French toast and ending with a steamy shower *à deux* in which Megan learned that some fires were waterproof.

Now her feet were cold in the black, spike-heeled boots Maleficarum brought over for her. How he'd found them shoved in the back of her closet she didn't even want to think—she'd never worn them, they were a bit *too* black and spike-heeled—but find them he had. Along with a houndstooth skirt she thought she'd thrown away, a black turtleneck, and a red jacket; though, she had to admit she looked good. The outfit would never have occurred to her on her own.

The boys weren't riding with them. Megan twisted around in her seat to watch them following in her little Ford. At least they would be there, whatever happened, but Greyson's words sent a chill of foreboding down her spine that wouldn't go away, no matter how calmly he sipped a glass of wine from the basket on the seat of the car.

The driver had barely dropped them off before she turned to him.

"What are you talking about? What's going to happen?"

He took her hand. "There's no point in discussing it, Meg. It might not happen. Just remember what I said."

"But—"

"Greyson! Miss Chase! Nice to see you both."

"Hi, Temp. Megan, you remember Templeton Black."

Megan nodded and smiled, her hands numb as she shook with Templeton Black and let the men lead her into the white mansion where Black lived.

If she hadn't been so nervous, the interior would have impressed her. Pure white walls rose high to the mosaic ceiling, the design of which Megan couldn't quite place. Something swirling, moving . . . just when she thought she had it, it disappeared, like one of those infuriating "Magic Eye" images. Megan could never really see whatever she was supposed to see in those pictures.

"It's a dragon," Greyson said, leaning over. "The symbol of our Meegra."

"Fire."

He nodded.

"It's beautiful."

"The whole house is beautiful," he replied. "It's called *Iureanlier Sorithell,* the House of Flying Fire, and it belongs to the *Gretneg* of the Meegra. Right now that's Templeton. When he's gone . . . who knows?"

Something in the way he said it made Megan's skin prickle. What exactly was going on here? Greyson thought something horrible might happen, yet he still planned, or hoped, to become head of his family?

Then again, why would he not want to become head, if he could live in this place. Their footsteps clattered across the marble floors as they followed Templeton into a dining room the size of Megan's entire house. Here the walls were covered with ivory damask paper and oil paintings of what Megan guessed were former Gretnegs, frowning imperiously at her from their ornate frames.

Megan expected they would stop, but they did not, continuing instead to another room, green and gold, with soft leather chairs and a wide mahogany desk. Templeton motioned them to sit.

"Drink?"

She nodded as she sank into her chair, feeling like a little girl in a palace. Without asking what she preferred, Templeton brought her a gin and tonic. She glanced at Greyson.

"I noticed last night at the ball," Templeton said. "You weren't far from me when you and that reporter ordered your drinks. I assume it's satisfactory? I have wine, if you prefer."

"It's fine," Megan said, taking a careful sip. Something told her it was best to stretch this one out.

Templeton handed Greyson Scotch and sat down with what looked like the same for himself. He cleared his throat.

"It's such a pleasure to have you in my home," he said. Megan wished she could read him. "As I said last night, Greyson's told me so much about you. I suppose when it comes to you, he can't stop talking." He chuckled.

Greyson didn't move, didn't react in any way, but Megan knew something was wrong. This was not a friendly brunch and Templeton Black had plans she didn't want anything to do with.

And she was trapped here. Malleus, Maleficarum, and Spud, standing in the corner, were Templeton's employees. They couldn't help her, even if she begged them to.

"He hasn't told me much about you at all," Megan said, widening her eyes. "Perhaps he talks about me, but I can't get anything out of him."

Templeton's eyes narrowed. Just as it had the night before, a shadow of something passed over his broad, handsome features. Something Megan didn't like at all.

"I seriously doubt that, my dear," he said, smiling as if nothing had happened. "But I hear you're quite close-mouthed yourself. Certainly I'm informed that reporter isn't having a lot of luck with you."

"I think he's getting a good enough story," Megan said, smiling as though she thought this was simply a little chat. How did he know what Brian was or was not getting? Her heart pounded loud enough for her to hear it, though, and she was worried they could to. How good was demon hearing? She'd never asked.

All she wanted at that moment was to be back home, alone under the covers with a book. She shivered.

"Cold?" Templeton waved his hand at the fireplace. Immediately a fire started burning merrily. "Better?

Good. As for the reporter, I'm told he has some rather interesting abilities himself. Oh, Miss Chase—may I call you Megan? And you must call me Templeton—don't look like that. Surely you must have guessed I know all about your gift."

"I—"

"Megan doesn't like to discuss the subject, Temp," Greyson said.

"But there are some subjects she will have to discuss, aren't there? Some truths, hidden in the depths of time, that must come to light if we are to truly know how to proceed against the Accuser. Perhaps we could work out some sort of trade, do you think, Megan?" He said her name, but he was looking at Greyson. "You know that's how we do things, with our equals. Trade. Favors."

"I appreciate the vote of confidence, Templeton," Megan said. "But I'm not a demon. So I don't know that I can participate in a trade."

Templeton started to laugh. "Oh, I'm glad you've come to dine. Which reminds me, our meal should be served. As much as I'm enjoying myself, we do have more pressing matters, do we not?" He set his glass down with a thud.

Greyson's fingers were cool in hers as they walked back into the dining room. She'd never felt his skin anything but warm, almost to the point of hot. She opened her mouth to ask what was wrong, but he stopped her with a warning glance.

"Remember what I said earlier," he whispered as he ushered her into her chair.

Megan's forehead and underarms were damp despite the comfortable temperature in the room. Greyson hadn't wanted to do this to begin with. Now vague threats hung in the air and he knew what they were about but wouldn't tell her. Malleus, Maleficarum, and Spud wouldn't meet her eyes. She felt like Alice in Wonderland at the Red Queen's court. This was definitely curiouser and curiouser, but she didn't think she'd be able to drink a potion and go back home. Or whatever it was Alice had done to get out of the rabbit-hole. She couldn't remember.

Servants in black and white with red caps brought heavy silver trays into the room, setting them on the wide marble-topped table, opening the lids with a flourish. Had Megan been hungry, the sight of all the food—roast pork and beef, roast potatoes, lobster salad, heaps of wonderful-smelling bread so fresh the steam still rose from its pale, spongy surface—would have thrilled her. Two pasta dishes, one Alfredo, one tomato, sat next to a bowl of black olives. There was broccoli, green beans, asparagus, and at the far end rested what looked like caviar. She'd never seen such a spread before.

As it was, she could only focus on their uniforms. Black, white, and red. The same colors she wore, the outfit picked by the brothers. She didn't think it was a coincidence.

The staff busied themselves serving everyone, but even when two heaping plates sat in front of Megan the table still groaned under the weight of the feast in the middle.

Politeness forced her to eat, though she could barely taste the food.

Maybe she was being foolish. Greyson ate with relish, and the brothers did too. Templeton polished off three plates full, all the while chatting to Megan about the ball the night before, about the food, about her practice. He asked excellent questions. If she hadn't been terrified she would have enjoyed the conversation. But Greyson wasn't speaking much and she'd never known him to be so silent.

Finally Templeton leaned back and dropped his napkin next to his last plate. "Well," he said, nodding to the servants, who flew into action clearing plates, "I suppose it's time for us to discuss some business."

The servants left. The table was still covered with food.

"We have a few more guests coming," Templeton said. "They may want to eat. Greyson, perhaps you would like to go greet them?"

Megan's nerve endings crackled in the stiff silence. Finally Greyson nodded, catching Megan's eye. The brightest fire in the world couldn't have kept her from shivering as she read the warning.

"If you have other guests," she said, using her calm radio voice, "perhaps we shouldn't stay. Greyson can take me home, and you can call me later."

"But they're eager to meet you. And we still have much to discuss."

Greyson hadn't even waited for this reply. The door closed behind him. Megan watched it, her eyes stinging. *I want to go home, I want to go home . . .*

"So, my dear." Templeton leaned back in his chair with a happy sigh. "I have much to tell you. To teach you. I can be of great help to you, if you'll let me."

He sounded so much like the devil offering to buy her soul Megan had to bite her lip to keep from breaking into nervous laughter. "I appreciate the offer. But I think I'm okay on my own."

"Oh? Do you think you can handle the Yezer Ha-Ra by yourself? Or the Accuser?" He leaned forward now, peering at her. She looked away. "Do you even know who the Accuser is, my dear? Or anything about him? I know Grey told you quite a bit about us and how we operate, but even he doesn't know anything about what you're up against."

"Perhaps you could put it in a letter for me," Megan said, stilling the restlessness in her legs by standing. "I really must go now."

"Sit down." The command in his formerly lazy voice was so strong her legs gave out beneath her before she realized it. "You may be able to play this clever little game with Greyson—he's always had a weakness for a pretty face—but it won't work with me. I know you're hiding some answers in that lovely blond head and I intend to get them. Do you understand?"

"I don't know anything—"

"Then we'll have to jog your memory." He stood up and strode to a sideboard at the far end of the room, returning a moment later with a cigar and lighting it from the palm of his hand. "I'm sorry, do you mind if I smoke?"

The genuine concern in his eyes was such a contrast to the anger of a moment ago that Megan blinked. She shook her head.

"Thank you. I apologize for not asking before. It's been a while since I've had a visitor who doesn't indulge." He gave her a little bow before continuing to speak. "As I said, Megan, I believe the memories we need, the information we need, is still there, in your head. But perhaps we need to resort to some more extreme measures in order to extract it."

What sort of weapon did one use to fight a fire demon? Flour? She had no idea what would hurt them, even if she had access to anything more dangerous than a dessert spoon. She doubted seriously that would do any damage at all.

"Greyson could hypnotize me," she said. Tears stung the backs of her eyes. "He said he probably could."

"Hypnosis isn't a good idea." Smoke puffed around Templeton's face. "We don't want you to relive the experience and we don't want to damage your subconscious. No, it's far better if we simply work with you to get at the memories, isn't it?"

Her head pounded. "You want to know about Harlan Trooper, don't you? That's the information you need, the memories you need. Because it was the Accuser in Trooper that night and somehow I called him."

She didn't need his slow nod to tell her she was right. "Very good, Megan. See? I told you, you know more than you think. All it takes is a sense of urgency, a sense of need, to find out what we want to know. We won't be interrupted by a fiend this time, or some unhinged loser with a gun."

How did he know about that day in the park? Had Greyson told him? But Greyson didn't know what she'd been discussing with Brian, did he?

Templeton picked up the silver bell on the table and rang it. "Now." He smiled. "Once our guests are seated and served, we can begin."

"Who are the guests?" Her drink beckoned to her, but she refused. Gin was not what she needed. She wanted coffee, or a Coke, something with caffeine and sugar.

Especially if the room was about to fill with personal demons, as she suspected it would. This was it. She was being handed over to them. What else could Templeton mean by "guests"?

"Calm yourself, you're white as a ghost. The other guests are simply the heads of a few other Meegras. I was given the responsibility, you see, of solving this little mystery. I invited them over to watch me do it."

"What if I can't remember anything?" she asked, as the doors opened and people started filing in.

There were only six new guests, five men and one woman whose beauty made Megan gasp. The woman smiled and waggled her fingers in greeting. They were topped by three-inch red fingernails, filed into impossibly sharp points.

The men were no less attractive, each in their own way. Megan remembered what Dante had said to her about demons and beauty the night before. Here it was in practice. Seven impossibly gorgeous demons, looking at her, watching her for signs of weakness like hyenas studying a kitten. She made sure her shields were as tight and strong as she could make them and gave her blankest smile.

"I think you will remember," Templeton said. "Because we're going to help you."

The door opened one more time and Greyson entered.

He was shirtless, wearing only a loose towel, almost a kilt, from the waist down. Megan tried to meet his eyes, but he would not look at her, staring instead at Templeton and each of the other demons in turn. Two sets of dull black shackles bound his wrists, but they were not chained together.

He said something in the demon tongue and the others laughed. Megan wished she knew if it was a joke. He still wouldn't look at her.

"Megan," Templeton said, and he was looking at her. "Greyson will help us jog your memory today."

"It's not necessary." Two servants were busy behind her, but Megan kept her eyes focused on Greyson. She had a horrible suspicion she knew what they were doing, what was going to happen. Her fingers ached from gripping her thighs under the table.

Templeton nodded. "Perhaps it isn't, but Greyson must pay for what he's done, anyway. This seemed like a good way to accomplish both his punishment and your interview."

"Punishment?" *I made the decision, okay? And I knew what would happen when I made it.* Now she understood. The bastard! Why hadn't he just told her, why were they even here?

Her vision blurred and she looked down at her legs, refusing to let the others see, but it didn't matter.

"She's crying." One of the other demons, one of the Meegra heads. "I smell the salt."

Still she refused to look at them. Greyson swept past her in a faint whiff of smoke, and chains rattled behind her as they fastened him to whatever it was they were fastening him to. She didn't want to look. She wouldn't look.

"Megan, surely you didn't think Greyson could do all he's done for you and go unpunished, did you? I thought he'd told you everything about how we operate. He told a member of the Vergadering about the Accuser. He told her about the Yezer Ha-Ra and their pursuit of you. He used his powers at the ball last night to change human events—for the *better*, to *save a life*. He knew what the consequences would be, even if you were so naïve as to think there wouldn't be any. And worst—"

"He did it to help me!" Megan looked up now, staring at Templeton Black. "He did it because I asked him to."

"And now you can do what I ask you to and tell me what I need to know. Once you've given me what I need, Greyson can go home with you. Until then . . ." he made a gesture to his right. Something rattled against the marble floor. "He will be punished. The power is in your hands, my dear."

"You can't do this," she whispered.

"I'm a demon, my dear child. I can do whatever I want."

The unmistakable sound of a whip slicing the air echoed in her ears.

Chapter Twenty-Three

One thin line of blood ran down Greyson's back, soaking into the pale fabric of the skirt-thing he wore. Beneath it she could barely see the pad on which he knelt. At least Templeton had done that. He might order Greyson whipped with an iron-tipped whip, but he wasn't barbaric about it. He'd provided some padding to protect his victim's knees. Bile was sour in her throat.

Greyson's head bowed forward, his arms lifted in a V and bound by the wrists to a metal frame. Megan closed her eyes but the image wouldn't disappear. Once she'd seen his back in her dreams. Now it would forever be part of her nightmares and she knew the worst was yet to come.

"Please don't." She turned panicked eyes to Templeton. "Please, I'll try to remember. I tried before, with Brian, and I almost did. Just give me a minute to—"

"No."

Megan yelped as the impassive servant standing a few feet away raised the whip again and brought it down. Greyson's muscles twitched as another line of blood joined the first, but he made no sound.

"Templeton, you're hurting him, I can't think—"

Tension laced Greyson's voice. "Not helping, Meg."

"Remember, Megan." Templeton puffed his cigar. "Greyson must be punished. We're just giving you a chance to mitigate his pain."

Another lash. Another twitch. Megan shrank back into her chair, her mind racing. The demons watched her. She hated them. Hated them so much she wanted to leap from her chair and scratch out their eyes, to rip them apart, to bite and kick and—

The face of the doctor. She scratched and bit, until blood ran from his cheek, and laughed as he stumbled away from her. Too bad she hadn't laughed sooner. Her arms were bound, her legs tied at the ankles. Bound the way Greyson was bound now, but she was in bed, and someone else watched her from the corner, someone she couldn't see but who spoke in her head.

The Accuser.

"That's good, Megan," he said.

Was he there in the room with the teenage Megan in her room, or was he here, now, in her head? He shouldn't have been able to find her here, but she didn't remember him being there, that summer. There in her room when the doctor came.

She shook her head.

"Remembering something?" Templeton's voice interrupted her thoughts.

"I don't . . . I don't know."

Another lash. She couldn't look at him. Greyson was still quiet, but how long would he be able to stay so? Ten lashes? Twenty? Sooner or later even he wouldn't be able to hold it in, right?

Think, Megan, think. What happened in the bedroom? Why was the doctor there? The memory was a white space in her head, a cloud of oblivion she couldn't seem to wade through no matter how hard she tried.

Another lash. This time she looked, forcing herself to face what was happening because of her reluctant brain. The blood seemed to form a pattern against the smooth tawny skin of his back. A pattern, random like rain on a window but with its own design anyway, just like—

The blood criss-crossing Harlan Trooper's face as the invisible thing attacked him.

He'd tried to save her.

She'd been sixteen, coming home to an empty house. How exciting! The Ouija board was waiting. Megan had always wanted to see what it would be like to communicate with spirits. Maybe they would tell her something special about herself. Maybe they knew why she always felt different from the other kids.

She'd always suspected she had special abilities in that direction. Sometimes she just knew things. What people were thinking, what they'd done. Like when she was going to sell Girl Scout cookies and just knew not to go to old Mr. Urster's house. Mr. Urster turned out to be a bad man and the police came to get him.

Clearly she was a witch or something. And witches used Ouija boards and Tarot cards, but Megan had no way to get Tarot cards so this was the next best thing. She ran up to her room and pulled the box out from under her bed . . .

The whip hissed through the air. Megan jumped, a tiny shriek escaping her lips. Greyson still made no sound, but his ragged breathing filled her ears. The muscles in his arms were corded and veined where he strained against the cuffs. The blood-soaked waist of his kilt clung to his lean hips.

"I'd be happy to stop his punishment, Megan, anytime. Normally this would continue for hours, but the information you can give us is important enough to cut it short. Anything yet?"

She shook her head, unable to look away from Greyson's bowed head. How soft and smooth his hair had felt in her hand. How his forehead pressed against hers as he slid into her body. His back . . . so smooth under her fingertips . . . the way his muscles moved when they were in bed together.

She forced herself to stop recalling it, to move further back, back to that day in her room. It became harder to breathe as she pushed her way through the fog in her head, great choking clouds that threatened to kill her before she could reach the memories she needed. Damn it!

There had to be something, a word, a sound, something that would bring it back, the way the blood pattern had given her a flash just moment ago. She thought of a Ouija board, of the ornate lettering on the tan box she'd bought at a garage sale . . . and something opened a crack, just enough for her to force herself inside.

She put the Ouija board back under the bed, disappointed. Why didn't it work? She'd been up here for an hour now, her fingers as light on the planchette as she could make them, and nothing happened. Her parents would be home soon and she hadn't done any of her chores, either. It hadn't even been worth it . . . there was nothing special about her.

Megan didn't bother to fight the tears. Nothing special at all. The kids at school were right, the way they talked about her, the looks they gave her. She was dirt, less than dirt. A loser, a freak . . .

"But a freak with potential," said a voice. Megan, curled under the bedcovers, sat up so fast her head swam.

"What?"

"You have potential, little one. You're not wrong about that. And I can help you reach it."

The voice seemed to be coming from inside the room, but Megan was alone. Now she was imagining things. Great. One more thing to make her the butt of everyone's jokes. She pulled the covers back over her head.

"Don't try to hide from me, Megan. I know you hear me. I have a deal to make with you."

"You're not really here," Megan said.

"No, I'm not. But I am real and you can help me come back. I'll help you in return."

"How?" Not that she would say *yes*. But it never hurt to ask.

"I can strengthen your abilities. You'll know everything, Megan. One look at someone, one touch, and you'll know what they're thinking, what they're doing . . . you're not a bad psychic, now. But you could be great. You won't need a Ouija board to talk to spirits."

Somewhere in the back of her mind Megan knew this wasn't the best idea. A disembodied voice offered to give her—no, *strengthen* her—psychic abilities. She should say *no*.

But she didn't want to say no. Imagine the looks on their faces, those jerks at school, when she laughed at them for what she knew they were thinking, their reactions when she could gossip about all of them and always be right. Then they would know how it felt to be laughed at. The way their laughter echoed in her ears every day, every night. If she listened hard she could still hear them . . .

Another lash. Greyson's hands fisted and straightened, fisted and straightened, covered in blue-white flames.

The demons around her ate and chatted quietly, watching Greyson's skin being sliced open with the whip as if it were a mildly entertaining film. The smell of the food made her sick. Her stomach roiled, twisting, until she was certain she was going to throw up—

All over the floor, all over the bed, until there was nothing left in her stomach and still she could not stop it. The thing in her head spun and whirled. Spots danced in front of her eyes, the colors so bright they shrieked. Even when she forced her lids down they didn't stop.

Sweat poured off her forehead. Her clothes were drenched with it, but her teeth chattered and her fingers were so stiff she couldn't pull the disgusting comforter back over her body. She was going to die. She knew it, just as surely as she'd ever known anything. This was the end.

Her throat, already raw from the force of her sickness, burned as she screamed. Another voice mixed with hers, deep and male, turning the scream from terror to triumph and Megan's sickness into ecstasy.

She stood up, her hands running along the smooth lines of her young body. Her own fingers felt her skin, but someone else felt it, too, through her, and it liked what it felt. She couldn't hear him in her head anymore but she knew he was there, waiting.

Waiting for what?

"He invaded my head," she gasped, squeezing her arms as tightly around herself as they would go. The room swam, like a double image, her childhood bedroom superimposed on the demons eating dinner.

"Stop." Templeton held a hand out to the figure holding the whip. For a moment only Greyson's tortured breath broke the silence.

"What do you mean, he invaded your head? The Accuser?"

She nodded. Her lips refused to form the words themselves.

"How did he do that? Did you invite him?"

Again she nodded. "He said he had a deal for me. I took it." She looked up at him and was shocked to see sympathy on his broad face. "I was only sixteen, I thought—"

"Why her?" asked one of the male demons. "What was so special about her, that he could use her to get back in?"

"Power." She barely recognized Greyson's voice. Only her fear of what they would do to him kept her from running to him.

"But I wasn't powerful, I couldn't even get a Ouija board to work. I only had hunches, feelings. Nothing like what I have now. He gave me this power."

Greyson cleared his throat. "You had it. Without him."

"But—"

"We can discuss it later," Templeton said. "Grey needs to save his breath. How did he do it, Megan? How did he invade your head?"

"He made me say something." The words were there, in her head, just out of reach.

"Don't repeat it." Something like fear colored Templeton's words. "Don't even think it."

"I can't remember anyway."

The demons exchanged glances, but didn't speak.

"What happened next?"

She bit her lip. "Just give me a minute, okay? Just wait a minute, let me—"

The whip cracked again. Greyson grunted.

"I'm telling you! I'm telling you what I know! Leave him alone!"

"But this seems to be working so well to jog your memory." He nodded at the man holding the whip. Another line of blood. Another soft grunt. The flames in Greyson's hands leapt.

"What did he want, Megan? What did he want you to do?"

"He . . . he wanted me to find . . ."

The hospital. The one in their town had what was still called, even in those days, a mental ward. At least, that's what the hospital called it. The citizens of the town had worse names, names that used to hurt Megan when she heard them.

The people living there were less than human in the eyes of her neighbors, her teachers. They laughed and made jokes, especially when the nurses would take their patients out for the day. Megan hated that. She'd see them, these people just like her—better than her, at least these people seemed to like each other—smiling as they bought themselves a Coke or a movie ticket, and she'd remember the jokes and taunts. Her eyes would fill and she had to look away.

The thing in her head—the Accuser—made her go there. Every night. They would stand outside the hospital. Megan hated it. The Accuser was always eager to go. It made her skin crawl, feeling his longing, his desire. Afterwards his satisfaction would come through to her too, the sensation of fullness.

She stopped eating. She barely slept. She'd go to bed in the middle of the night and wake up a few hours later, exhausted but full of queer, swimming energy. She didn't shower, she didn't brush her teeth. Now she saw how she gave up, how she'd screamed deep inside at the horror of her guest, but then . . . she was too happy. The kids were scared of her, genuinely scared, and she swallowed their fear and their secrets, feeling like the most powerful girl on the planet.

The doctor came and she attacked him, while the voice in her head cheered her on and praised her.

Then they sent her to the hospital. To the mental ward. And the Accuser took over.

"He fed on despair," she muttered. "Their unhappiness, their confusion and anger . . . it's what he needed. It's why he came to me. Not just power. Sadness."

"We're so close, Megan," Templeton said. "I think we almost have what we need."

The whip struck again. Greyson's ruined back was covered in blood, red as a nightmare, red as a child's finger-painting.

Red as Harlan Trooper's face as something sliced at him, as he sat up from the bench where he'd died to curse her. More than the invisible foe he battled, the thing Megan had never seen, the sight of the blood made her sick. The sight of his body destroyed on the bench and the tiny figures flitting around just out of her conscious vision, the personal demons that in her demon-possessed state she'd been able to see, racked her body with cold, nauseating chills. The hospital food she'd eaten just before her escape came up, both from the horrible faces staring at her and the sight and smell of the blood. He'd died to save her, to help her. He'd asked her if he could help and the thing had leapt from her to kill him, so full of power was it.

"It feeds on despair," she gasped, swallowing hard as Greyson screamed. The tortured sound echoed through the room. One of the other Meegra heads smiled and licked his lips, and if Megan hadn't been so sick and miserable and terrified she would have leapt across the table to scratch his piercing blue eyes out.

"What?"

"Despair." She folded her upper body over her legs, staring down at her feet. Her stomach felt better pressed into her thighs this way, and she could control the shivering better. "It's what he feeds on. It's where he gets his power. Despair and fear. He needs them." He'd certainly picked the perfect job. Through the haze of sweat, blood, and tears, Megan thought of the poor people at Fearbusters. How much of their energy had Art stolen so far?

And the personal demons worked for him. They created the despair he needed to live . . .

Templeton nodded. "You believe the Accuser is controlling the Yezer Ha-Ra? An interesting idea, Megan. Greyson was right to say you're smart."

"Isn't that enough? Can't you stop hurting him?"

"Almost." Templeton checked his watch. The bastard. "I have another appointment in an hour or so."

How he thought Greyson could take this for another hour she had no idea, unless he intended Greyson to die. Which was entirely possible, wasn't it?

She couldn't let that happen. Greyson's back looked like so much meat when she dared to glance at it, the kilt soaked red all the way down his thighs.

"But I don't know anything else," she managed. "I don't know how I got him out of me. We were in the park and I wanted him to go, to leave me alone, and Harlan Trooper was there, and I saw them, the personal demons I guess, and . . . I was so angry, and I don't know how it happened but I kicked him out. And he killed Harlan, and he was in Harlan's body, and he wanted back into mine but I . . ."

Something flashed in front of her eyes, something tall and dark and covered with blood, a face that wouldn't come into focus. Its mouth opened, and she fell into it, and all she saw was blackness as its teeth closed around her.

Chapter Twenty-Four

The room was so dark that for a moment Megan thought she was still in the horrible mouth, and she sat up with a smothered half-scream. As her eyes adjusted, though, she realized light came through heavy-curtained windows, and beneath her the sheets were soft and smelled of lavender. Not the mouth, not home, and not at Greyson's place either. So where—

Ah. She must still be at Templeton's house, at Iureanlier Sorithell. She crawled out from under the covers, ignoring the pain in her head, and crept over to the window.

The moon hovered cold overhead, its glow lost in the floodlights illuminating the house and grounds. It looked as if Templeton was preparing for an enemy invasion.

Or like he thought the enemy was already within his walls and he was lighting the prison yard to prevent their escape.

She had no idea where Greyson was or if he was even alive. She assumed so. She had a vague memory of hearing his voice again after she'd passed out.

Someone walked across the lawn below. Megan shrank back behind the curtains to watch, but she didn't recognize that face. A guard, probably. She was right. It would be almost impossible for her to get out of the house without being seen.

She had to try, though, didn't she? She couldn't stay here and let Templeton force her to finish the story, to fill in the gaps. He had the highlights. She hoped he choked on them.

Not wanting to turn on a light, she used the bathroom, then hunted for her shoes. Those damn boots the brothers picked were not appropriate for sneaking out of a fortress, but if she got out and back onto the street she would need them.

There was no phone in the room, of course. No phone, no matches or candles, no weapons of any kind, not even a heavy vase. Except for the little pepper-spray can she didn't carry anything weapon-like in her purse, either. She didn't even have a cell phone like everyone else in the world. Why bother? Nobody ever called her.

She picked the purse up and swung it over her shoulder, then tried the door of the room. It opened with a faint click. They hadn't locked her in. Should she be pleased or worried by that? She was worried enough already—her muscles refused to relax—so she decided to take it as luck and keep moving.

The hall was dark. Worse, Megan had no idea where in the house she stood. Looking out the window had told her she was upstairs and in the back, but how did she get to the front? Did she dare try the front door anyway?

There had to be servants' quarters of some kind somewhere. Maybe a back staircase, or even a servant's entrance. She'd keep an eye out for it.

She headed off to her left, her feet silent on the carpeted floor. She could barely see, so she pressed her shoulder against the wall and tiptoed along.

Voices echoed behind her, and a light switched on. Someone was coming up the stairs.

Megan grabbed the nearest door handle. It opened, and she flung herself into the room, pulling the door shut as quietly as she could. If someone slept in here . . . well, she would be caught anyway.

The room had the unused feel of a guest bedroom. The dim light through the windows outlined a bed, a desk, a table with a lamp. Generic furniture. The voices outside grew louder, and she tensed, crouching to the floor with her side hugging the wall. If they opened the door they wouldn't see her right away.

They didn't, though. They continued walking. She recognized Templeton Black's voice, but not the other. He'd mentioned an appointment, was this his guest? Or simply one of his employees?

To her left stood another door. A bathroom? Still clutching her purse and boots, she sneaked over and opened it.

No bathroom. Just another bedroom. Megan wondered if it was possible to get to the end of the hall without ever venturing into it. Worth a try, anyway.

She listened carefully at each door, but her luck ran out just the same. The last room was occupied, and the figure huddled under the covers on the bed saw her before she could close the door. This room did have a bathroom; the light coming from it seemed brighter than it should have to her dilated eyes.

"Meg?" His voice was gravelly, either from sleep or from earlier, but it still sounded wonderful.

"Greyson."

He struggled to sit, his chest wrapped in bandages. "Come to kiss me better?"

She didn't know whether to laugh, cry, or hit him. "Do you honestly think it would help?"

"It might. Let's try."

His skin was still too cool, and it was awkward to kiss him without touching his back, but that didn't stop her from thoroughly enjoying herself. He pulled away too soon.

"Hmmm," he said. "Why don't you come up here on the bed with me? I have a few other places you could kiss. I'm sure that's all I need to be back on the road to perfect health."

"I think you should save your energy," she replied with a shaky laugh.

"Oh, no. I've been in bed all evening. I have plenty of energy, see?" He pulled her onto the bed and grabbed her hand, sliding it along his bare skin under the sheets so she could feel his arousal. His kiss cut off her protest.

The need to escape warred with the needs of her body as he stroked her thigh, his hand rising a little higher each time.

"Take off these stockings," he murmured. "And everything else. We've time before they'll want us again. *I* want you now."

It took her a minute to register his words through the thick syrupy lust making her body heavy and warm, but when she did, she pulled back so fast she almost fell off the bed. "What? What do you mean, before they want us again?"

"They haven't finished questioning you. Or punishing me."

"Oh, god." She reached for the light, then thought better of it. "You mean . . . they're going to do that to you again?"

"Probably for days, off and on. So it's even more important that you get those clothes off. You don't want to send me back down there without some lovely new memories, do you?"

The tone was teasing, but Megan couldn't focus on it. The thought of watching that disgusting performance again . . . she shuddered.

"I can't," she whispered. "I can't go through that again."

"No offence, *bryaela*, but I think my part is a bit more difficult than yours, don't you? Come help me build up my strength."

"You are the most single-minded man I've ever met."

"It's going to happen, whether we like it or not, so there's no point worrying about it."

"I can't help worrying about it."

"Then let me distract you." His hand slid back up her thigh, all the way up to press between her legs. Her eyes closed.

"See," he said, moving his fingers slightly, "there are much nicer things to think about, aren't there? Let's take off these clothes, and I'll tell you a lovely story about exactly what I'm going to do to you, and how much you're going to enjoy it. It has a very satisfying ending, I promise."

"Doesn't your back hurt?"

"It's not too bad. They basically healed me up before they brought me in here, the bandages are just to keep the ointment on. They don't want to kill me, just hurt me." His thumb zeroed in on the spot he knew would be the most effective. "You could make me feel even better."

She shivered. If she didn't put a stop to this now, she never would, and they'd still be here when Templeton came back for them later. "Greyson, I want to escape, I want us to get out of here, not sink ourselves in."

"Meg . . . there's no way out of here. Every exit is guarded. The gates are guarded. The fence is patrolled. I've been here more times than I can remember since childhood and nobody has ever left without permission from the Gretneg. Not ever."

"Then we can be the first."

He removed his hands from her body and sat still for a minute. "Where do you plan to go?"

She hadn't thought of that, and she guessed it was plain on her face.

"Uh-huh. You can't escape here and go home, they'll be waiting. We can't go back to my place, they'll watch there, too. In fact, I can't think of a single place in this city or in the state where they won't be watching."

"Then we'll leave the state."

"I didn't think running away was quite your style."

"I can't do it again. I just can't."

"Sooner or later you're going to have to, you know."

"What, watch you get whipped?"

"No." He slid an arm around her shoulders and she leaned over, snuggling into his chest. The bandages were soft under her cheek, and beneath them his heart thumped reassuringly. "You're going to have to remember the Accuser. How you got rid of him. How you got rid of your personal demons. You know that."

"I don't want to."

"If we all only did what we wanted to do, the world would be a very inefficient and scary place. I thought you were braver than this. Don't tell me my faith was unfounded."

She pulled away, wanting to argue with him, but she couldn't find the words. Not because there were none to speak, but because he was right. And he knew it.

"Okay," she said finally, with a sigh that seemed to come from the depths of her soul. "Okay. But please . . . please don't ask me to remember it here, while they beat you. Let's go, let's get out of here, and—we'll go to Tera. The Vergadering can keep us safe, right?"

"They might," he said. "But for how long? And what would they want from you in exchange?"

"It can't be worse."

"You don't know that."

"Look, I know you guys have a lot of problems with them, but that doesn't mean—"

The knock at the door interrupted her. Megan hopped off the bed, looking desperately for a place to hide, but Greyson grabbed her wrist. "Come in."

She didn't recognize the man standing in the doorway. "Mr. Dante, is Miss Chase—oh. You're both wanted in the dining room in fifteen minutes."

"Thank you." Greyson turned to her. "Why did you leap off the bed like that?"

"I didn't think I was supposed to be in here."

"They left your door unlocked, *bryaela*. Oh." His lips twitched. "You thought you'd done something daring, didn't you?"

She snatched her hand away. "Don't make fun of me," she said.

"Sorry. An honest mistake."

"What does that mean, anyway? *Bryaela*?"

He checked the clock by the bed. "Just a casual endearment. You'd better go get ready. I need to get dressed myself."

"Do you need help?"

"Not unless you want to help me with something else first." He raised his eyebrows.

"I don't."

"You're no fun at all sometimes. Go get dressed, then, and I'll be at your room shortly. And Meg?"

"Yes?"

"Don't be scared."

HE MUST HAVE KEPT some clothes at the house, because the suit he wore when he arrived at her room was not the same one he'd worn earlier. She, of course, had to make do with the same outfit, one she was rapidly beginning to loathe. The colors had to be significant, and she couldn't help thinking Greyson was keeping something from her.

Candles burned in metal sconces all along the hall, their glow warming her. Fire was Greyson now, his quick smile and the confident tone of his voice, the smoky scent of his skin and his strong arms around her. She wondered if she'd ever be able to see it another way, and drew strength from the flames as they walked past them to the wide staircase.

Her boots clicked on the wide marble stairs as they descended into the empty cavern of the main hall. Greyson must have felt her tense, because he squeezed her hand.

"It will all be over soon," he said.

"That's comforting."

"Take it as you will."

"How can you be so calm?"

He stopped. Megan would have stumbled if his grip on her hadn't been so tight. "I'm calm because I have to be," he said. "I'm calm because I've done everything I can do."

She stood on the step beside him. Now he stepped down one, so their faces were level. "You won't fail me." His dark eyes stared into hers, stripping her bare. "I know you won't."

"That's gre—"

His power poured over her as their lips met, filling her, but there was nowhere for it to go, no release she could find. So she just let it grow and throb within her as his hands tangled her hair and his tongue slipped into her mouth. They were both gasping when he pulled away. "Time for the fun to start."

She hadn't thought it possible to enter the dining room in a good mood, but her apprehension had definitely faded, or perhaps she was too buzzed on power to feel scared. Greyson's energy roared through her body, searching for a place to escape, and she shut it up as tightly as she could with the strongest shield she could muster. He hadn't given her this much energy without a reason. She'd hold on to it until the time came.

Maybe he planned to bust them out of there, or maybe he simply wanted her to go into the night with more confidence. Either way, the cheery, slightly euphoric feeling lasted until she walked into the dining room and saw Art Bellingham sitting at the table.

Chapter Twenty-Five

"Megan," he said, rising from his seat. "Always a pleasure."

Her dry throat clicked when she tried to swallow. "Art." Automatically she turned to look for Malleus, Maleficarum, and Spud, but they were nowhere to be found. She was completely alone.

Greyson, the bastard, didn't even have the grace to pretend to be surprised. He practically whistled as he headed for his chair.

"Megan, please sit down," Templeton said. "We'll be eating soon."

Megan turned to stare at him while wheels turned in her head and facts clicked into place. She wanted to pick up one of the bone china plates on the table and smash it over his head.

Templeton had made a deal with the Accuser. He was handing her over. All the interrogation earlier, the torture . . . just some demon game, a bit of fun on a dull Saturday afternoon.

And Greyson had known. What's more, he wanted her to know he knew.

He'd kept her here. She'd wanted to escape, and he'd . . . he'd kissed her and petted her, and refused to help. Perhaps he'd even lied about their chances. There would be time later—she hoped—to think about how his lies made her feel. She'd trusted him. She'd liked him. Had he felt anything for her at all? She shot him a look of pure loathing.

He caught it. His eyes widened and he looked away.

"I'm tired of this," she said. "If you have something to say, say it please."

She spoke to Greyson, but it was Art Bellingham who answered. "Let's have pleasure before business, for once. There's plenty of time. Besides, I'd rather you not weaken yourself. I've waited a long time for this, and it wouldn't be sporting if you weren't in good shape."

"I'd hate to spoil your fun."

"It's not fun," Templeton said. "It wouldn't be honorable for the Accuser to engage you in battle before you've eaten."

"Oh yes, honor. I forgot it's such a big deal for you guys. How honorable is it for you to trade me to him for— what do you get in return, exactly? I'm a guest in your home. This isn't very hospitable."

Templeton's face darkened. His anger crackled in the air. "I've kept you alive for the last week. My demons. My bodyguards."

"Why? Why not just hand me over several days ago? Or did you . . . oh. You just made this deal, right? When was it, you shithead? Last night? I'm surprised it took you as long as that." Why could she feel his anger?

But then, she'd felt Greyson's as well, hadn't she, a few days ago in her kitchen? She couldn't read demons, but somehow she could pick this up. She hadn't thought about it then. So much had been going on it hadn't even occurred to her. Now . . . she didn't want to look at Greyson, but she felt his gaze on her.

Which pissed her off. Which made Templeton's anger seem to grow around her. If she opened up to it, she could probably suck it in, direct it back at him. What had Tera taught her about pulling energy in from outside sources?

"Oh, Megan," Art said. "You'll spoil your digestion if you let negative emotions fester within you, you know. You don't want your last memory on earth to be of stomach cramps, do you?"

"Go to hell."

Art laughed. "How ineffectual."

The servants brought in the food, another feast Megan could hardly stand to touch. When had she last enjoyed a meal?

Other than this morning's French toast, which she didn't want to even think about thinking about, it was the pie she'd made for the brothers. Now she would never see them again, their crinkled faces smiling proudly at her . . . she pressed her palm against her forehead, trying to push the memory away, and elbowed her plate out of her line of vision.

Greyson didn't seem to be very hungry, either. Whenever she dared to peek at him, he was looking down, or playing with his fork, or checking his watch. Odd that he'd worn a watch. He hadn't at the ball, and she had the feeling he would regard this dinner as formal enough to leave it off.

In fact . . . that wasn't his watch. It had a leather band. Greyson's watch was silver. She'd seen it on his wrist a few times, shiny and expensive. Why was he wearing a watch not his own?

He caught her looking and scowled, pulling his sleeve over the watch and dropping his hand to his lap. She scowled back. Jerk. He was an asshole, and she was an idiot for believing him. What was wrong with her? Why had she trusted him, even for a second? He was a demon. What in the world had made her think one night was worth this, was worth anything?

To think she'd been upset when they tortured him, to think she'd almost given in to him up there in his room. Good thing she hadn't, the creep. She didn't need his friendship or his affection. His body? Well . . . he didn't do anything a good vibrator couldn't do.

Except make her feel beautiful.

Fuck him.

Conversation died down while everyone ate. Now, as silverware started to clink against empty china, talk picked up again.

Megan's stomach fluttered and tightened. It was all very easy for Greyson to say he was calm because there was nothing he could do, but Megan didn't feel that way at all. She felt as if her skin was about to crawl away, as if her heart would leap out of her chest and take her brain with it. She felt like she was about to die. Which made sense, since she probably was. And they all just sat and ate like nothing out of the ordinary or particularly interesting was about to take place.

She couldn't beat the Accuser. She hadn't succeeded when she was sixteen or he wouldn't be back here again. She'd only managed to send him away for a little while and erase the entire thing from her mind. She couldn't do that again, either. She didn't think she wanted to go on living, knowing she would have to do this again in another fifteen years. What kind of future was that to have? Watching the days and months tick past, every minute gone a minute of freedom lost?

These thoughts seemed to take a long time to go through her head, but only a few seconds had passed when Templeton cleared his throat.

"Well," he said, addressing the entire table. "We have a few more guests waiting outside and then we're going to have cause to celebrate. As you all know, I've been waiting for years for the opportunity to set Meegra Sorithell apart, to broaden our power. It is the dream of every Gretneg to conquer the other families. Tonight, we will succeed.

"I am sure you all know by now who our guest is." He nodded at Art, who smiled back. Sweat ran down Megan's temple. "Some say he is only legend . . . certainly the Vergadering believed it and the other Meegras believe it. Even now they doubt. They have no idea what awaits them when he stands behind us, when he inhabits a body wearing our colors and his power is ours to use. My *rubendas*, tonight we will make that happen."

The cage Greyson had earlier been chained to descended from the ceiling again. *A body wearing our colors* . . . Art Bellingham would invade her body again. She had a feeling this time he wouldn't let her stay in there, too.

Well, fine. If this was going to happen, let it happen. She'd fight as best she could, but if she didn't win, she didn't win. At least she went down trying.

What had Tera said about pulling in power? So many memories leapt through her panicked mind, it was hard to pick one out. Megan tried to calm down, to stop thinking and remember. Remember what Tera said, remember what she knew about the Accuser.

He feeds on despair. She'd been pretty upset that day she met him, hadn't she? Despairing. That made it easier for him. If she was convinced he would win . . . he would win, wouldn't he?

The opposite of despair was hope. Determination. Would that defeat him?

The servants opened the wide double doors. Templeton smiled. "Ah. Our guests."

Megan didn't expect to see the other Meegra heads—they obviously didn't know what Templeton was up to.

But she absolutely did not expect to see the people who entered now, gazing around themselves in awe.

The Fearbusters clients. All of them. Grant the psychic teenager. Hanna, the lonely woman in another faded-looking dress. Tall, angry Bob. Joe, who looked even more nervous than he had when she'd met him. And Kevin, Kevin who'd started it all.

The atmosphere in the room changed when they walked in, projecting so strongly that for a minute Megan felt as if she was them, each of them. But instead of the images she'd received at Fearbusters, the mundane pictures of their lives, this time she saw the same thing in all of them. The Accuser. His face hovered over them, his energy pervaded theirs. Their personal demons overshadowed them and the Accuser overshadowed the demons, so completely Megan couldn't imagine how these people still lived. They were empty shells.

Had they been this bad at Fearbusters? Or had Art somehow kept her from seeing it then?

"Megan, you remember my clients? And I'm sure you all remember Megan Chase. Megan has agreed to help me tonight, when you all graduate."

Megan's fingernails dug into her palms. What the hell was he planning, why were these people here?

"Hi, Dr. Chase," they all mumbled. Grant was uneasy, probably because of his abilities. He could feel something was wrong here, even though the others couldn't.

"Why don't you all sit down here," Art said, indicating the floor by his feet. "We'll dim the lights, and you can start your special graduation affirmation as soon as you feel comfortable."

"Mr. Art, I'm a little nervous," Grant said, sitting close to Hanna. "I don't feel ready."

"Don't you worry, Grant. I say you're ready. Soon, everything will be very different for you, I promise."

Megan wanted to scream. To warn them, to do something. She opened her mouth and started to stand, only to be shoved back down by Templeton Black.

"Don't try anything. If you cooperate, he'll let them live. If you don't . . ."

"Well done, Temp," Greyson said. Megan's head snapped up to look at him. He looked cool and calm as man holding four aces. "She's a little slow, our Megan. Best to spell everything out so her sad human brain can understand."

"It's a bit better than human," Templeton replied.

Greyson shrugged. Megan stared at him, waiting for him to wink, to do something, anything to show her he didn't mean this, that this was part of some plan she didn't understand yet. He didn't. Instead he said, "Not really. Her abilities are somewhat better than average, but she's mediocre everywhere else." He leaned forward a little, and now he did look at her. "*Everywhere* else."

"No more than you deserve," Templeton said. "How you thought you could convince her to help you overthrow me, I'll never know. All you did was buy punishment for yourself and death for her."

Greyson shrugged. "Worth a shot. Spending time with her was dull, but it would have paid off if I'd succeeded."

The only way to keep from bursting into tears was to get angry. Megan did, letting her fury build, letting herself picture what she'd like to do to him if she ever had the chance and a nice array of weapons. She read a particularly effective torture scene once involving a seatless chair and a carpet beater wielded from below. Now she pictured Greyson sitting in it and her own hand holding the beater. It made her almost smile.

Something flickered in Greyson's eyes. He looked quickly away. He was scared, was he? Scared of her anger? She'd show him anger. The bit of power he'd given her earlier still buzzed around in her head, in her body. In a flash she remembered how he hypnotized her that night, watching the city lights. He'd done something, put some sort of demon protection in her . . . had he planted something, some link to the Accuser that would be activated by his energy? He'd given her his word . . . but despite all their talk of honor, she'd seen now exactly what a demon's word meant. She assumed they'd promised snowballs in Hell there was no danger of melting, too.

She should unleash that power. She could open it up, open herself up, and let all that anger spill out over all of them. If she could read theirs, maybe they could feel hers. Maybe she could even hurt them with it. Maybe there would be a chance, a moment, while the Accuser entered her, when she could fight back.

The opposite of despair was hope. Now Megan had some. The hope that she would live to get her revenge on them all. Especially Greyson.

The lights dimmed. The chanting started.

At first the words sounded much like the ones she'd heard at Fearbusters, but after the first minute Megan realized they were different. Still familiar, but not . . .

No. They were familiar. They were the words she'd spoken in her bedroom at sixteen, the words that allowed the Accuser to enter her body. Now they were being spoken by the Fearbusters clients, and the power in them rose and swirled around Megan. It was all she could do to block them, all her anger and plans forgotten as she focused on putting every bit of energy she had into keeping herself safe.

Hands grabbed her and lifted her from her seat. She felt herself being carried to the cage, felt the metal close around her wrists, but she didn't struggle. She couldn't spare the strength for her body. She needed it for her head.

Blackness rose in a seductive cloud, dancing and swirling, filling the space. She could hardly see anyone in the room, or anything, just the twisting darkness growing and spreading like a stain. Despite her focus she shrank back from it, convinced she would scream if it touched her.

Over the chant and the whispering sound of the cloud rose Bellingham's voice. Not out loud, inside her head. "Are you ready, Megan?" he said. "Repeat the chant, and it will all be over."

"No."

"Yes. Or I'll start killing the clients. I think I'll start with Hanna. Poor Hanna. You identified with her, didn't you? A woman, all alone in the world, no man, no friends . . . a woman just like you. But a much better person, Megan. Hanna's demons have made her do many things she didn't want to do. But she always felt bad about it. Not like you. You haven't had a demon for a long time, but you still haven't been a very good person, have you?"

"Shut up."

"All the terrible things you've done . . . all your own choice. Such a selfish woman you are, so cold, for all that your job is in one of the so-called caring professions. You don't care and you never have."

"That's not true." Was it? The woman with the DVD, the girl with the notes, parking spaces, people she hadn't held the door for or cut off in traffic . . . she wasn't a terrible person, was she?

"Then prove it. Say the words, Megan. Let me in, and save these people's lives. They can be good people, happy people. It's all up to you."

"You son of a bitch!" she shouted, but over the anger, over the power, her sadness and despair seeped in.

Was she going to give up? Just let him in?

Did she have a choice? She couldn't let him kill those people. If she could prevent that, it would be worth it. Payment, maybe, for the things she'd done in her life she wasn't proud of. Payment for Harlan Trooper, a man who gave his life to try and help her.

She started to speak, the words coming as readily to her lips as her own name. She was barely three words in when she felt him invade, ripping into her. Her back arched; the words were interrupted by a scream. He was reading her, taking everything from her, her thoughts, her memories.

It seemed as if everyone she'd ever known flew through her mind again. Her stomach squirmed and shifted inside her body. Hot tears flowed down her cheeks. She'd never felt pain like this before, not even the last time, because this time the Accuser was rifling carelessly through her mind and discarding her soul, taking what he thought he might use and letting the rest fall away.

She waited for the oblivion of death. Any hell had to be better than the cold dread of the Accuser. Any hell would be better than seeing the failure of her life again, seeing even the events of the last week and the first time she'd ever felt like she might belong anywhere disappearing in Greyson's cruelty at the table.

She tried to focus on the anger which had been so strong a moment ago, to grab it and be ready in case an opportunity to fight presented itself, but it was fading. Fading like the last vestiges of light in the room, leaving her broken and alone, and as she opened her mouth to choke out the final words of the chant she felt the last bit of Greyson's energy flare with rage in her body, a spark that could not ignite.

———————

THE LIGHT HURT her eyes, so bright and pure it burned. Megan squinted against it and sat up, trying to clear her head.

She'd been . . . oh. She'd been chained up. She wasn't now. Her arms and legs were free, her body aching but intact.

What happened? Why hadn't it worked?

As her eyes adjusted she realized it had. Wherever she was now, it wasn't the Solithell.

She lay on the floor of a room with a ceiling so high she couldn't see it well. Shapes and colors shifted up there, but the pattern eluded her.

The hardwood floor shone. Megan stood up on shaking legs and tried to ignore the pain in her head. Did dead people get headaches? Was she dead? Or simply in some other dimension?

Or was this heaven?

It looked familiar enough that if she'd been religious, she would have believed it. Her soul, before birth, had lived in this silent place, and now she returned, and perhaps through the large door at the end sat god on a golden throne . . .

But Megan didn't think such things waited for her. Perhaps through that door was Hell, or something worse. Greyson never had fully explained everything about the demon world, or even most of it. Greyson. Why had he betrayed her so cruelly? For fun? Was she another power notch on his slim leather belt?

Her footsteps echoed in the still air as she started across the wide, clean expanse of floor. The door at the end looked so far away. It could take days to reach it, or minutes. Her depth perception didn't seem to work properly here. She didn't care. It was enough to be here at all, to be thinking and feeling instead floating in space. Instead of being nothing but extinguished.

A faint creaking sound interrupted her thoughts. She spun around, her breath catching in her throat, but the room still stood empty, its secrets hidden.

Except . . . was that a faint line of light, on the wall? It hadn't been there before. Now it looked almost as if a door had been opened in the wall, a cupboard.

A cupboard . . . she had seen this room before. She'd been here in Kevin's dream, in the vision that sent her to the hospital. The Accuser had sent Kevin to her, had sent that room to her.

She was in the home of the personal demons and, as the realization hit and her heart started pounding, more doors in the walls opened.

Chapter Twenty-Six

Megan's throat worked convulsively as she attempted to scream, even though she knew screaming wouldn't do her any good.

The demons poured from their cupboards, crawling along the walls, swarming across the ceiling and down. The walls were alive and moving, a sight made all the more impossible by the almost near-silence of their movements. Their dry little hands and feet rustled along the wood, whispering things she could not understand, but none of them spoke. They didn't chant her name, they didn't laugh or sing. They were like roaches under a log when the log was turned to the sun, scattering and moving, their horrible bodies scabrous in the bright light.

Megan started to run, but even as she turned she knew it was too late. Had been too late the minute she arrived here, the minute she went to dinner. The minute she sat down in that radio station. What would everyone think happened to her? Or would . . . would the Accuser use her body, pose as her, to do her show? Of course he would. He'd take over her practice, her show, her life. She could easily picture him on television analyzing Hollywood marriages and the inner pain of government leaders.

Sparks of anger flashed through her. Her reputation, the life she'd worked so hard to build after she left home for college and her parents actively encouraged her not to come back. She hadn't spoken to them in years. She wondered if she regretted that and decided she didn't.

But she didn't slow down as she ran for the door. It was impossible to tell how far away it was and the floor rumbled under her feet as the first demons reached the slick wood and came after her. She might have gone down the way Art Bellingham wanted, to save the Fearbusters people, but there was no way she was bending over for these fucking little demons, these miserable beasts who did nothing but make people unhappy and laugh as they did it.

She skidded to a halt, almost falling as those damned boots skidded on the polished floor. Why was she running? She couldn't escape them. They were coming for her, and they would get her, and she would face them head on.

Now she understood what Greyson said earlier about being calm because he'd done everything he could do. As she turned to face the demons, her breathing slowed, her eyes focused. She'd take out as many of those little bastards as she could before they killed her.

The demons stopped, too. One minute they were running, the next they were still and silent in front of her. A Mexican stand-off without the guns. Megan felt vaguely like Dorothy in Munchkin land, an odd feeling for a woman only a couple of inches over five feet tall.

Up close they were no less terrifying than they'd been before, an army of bald creatures with large, loose-lipped mouths and pinkish eyes, but Megan's calm didn't leave her. "What do you want?"

They didn't reply, but a shuffling movement among them made Megan think they weren't expecting the question.

"If you don't even know what you want from me, why don't you leave me the hell alone?" Her voice echoed against the high ceiling, the words continuing long after she'd closed her mouth again.

She expected a reply, but not the kind she got. They didn't speak, they didn't attack. Not physically. Instead they sent a wave of choking power, anger and despair, frustration. Above it all was the feeling of being trapped. Unable to move or breathe. She wanted to get up but couldn't, she was so heavily weighted with the force of their frustration.

She screamed and fell back, pain shooting up her wrist as she used her hands to break her fall. Her shout turned into a choking gasp. She couldn't breathe, couldn't move. They'd captured her, enslaved her, using only their energy.

"No," she managed. "No!" Somewhere deep inside her was a door, the door Tera had tried to teach her to open. Now she found it, her desperation making her mental fingers shake, and pulled.

Every muscle in her body tensed and vibrated, an orgasm without the pleasure. Instead pain ripped through her, rendering her insensible for a moment that could have been forever. Flames roared through her head, obscuring her vision. Agony ripped her body apart. Her hands scrabbled claw-like at the floor, her feet kicked at nothing.

Somewhere in the middle of it, Megan's mind still fought. She gathered all the force together, everything terrible that had crouched behind that door, and turned it into a sword in her head. Her body disappeared. She couldn't feel it anymore and, in that second of blessed relief, she turned the sword outward and flung it through the air, severing the connection between the demons and herself, pushing them away with all the force she could muster.

The demons screamed, their voices rising as one, drowning out Megan's own cries. She opened her eyes and found them all on their knees, their horrible little faces contorted with pain, but also with something that looked like . . . triumph. As if she'd pleased them. Had she done the wrong thing, had she given them all of her energy and left none for herself?

A voice. "She can do it."

"What?"

The demons hadn't moved, didn't move even as Megan pulled herself to her feet. She swayed on her heels and wanted to take them off, but didn't dare. She couldn't show any weakness now, not when they looked at her with wide, respectful eyes. She'd scared them.

One demon, slightly bigger than the others, stepped towards her. He bowed slightly.

"Will you help us?"

"Okay, let me get this straight." Megan sank back in the soft leather chair and rubbed her eyes. "I bound you to the Accuser?"

The little demon—Rocturnus, his name was—nodded. "Have some more water. And try one of those cookies. We got them just for you." He nodded towards the little table next to her, on which sat a silver tray covered with chocolate cookies. Across from her a small fire burned merrily in a brick fireplace. The room behind Rocturnus's little cupboard door was larger than she'd imagined and very comfortable. Like a gentleman's study, instead of a demon's lair. She liked the room, and in spite of herself she liked Rocturnus. She even managed not to shiver when she saw the rest of the Yezer Ha-Ra watching through the open doorway.

For a week now she'd imagined the horrors the personal demons would visit upon her when they finally caught her. Not once had she supposed they would give her tea and cookies, and settle her in an easy chair for a nice chat.

"Thank you. How did I manage that?"

"We don't know for sure. But for the last fifteen years of your time, he's been using us. All of our power, he took. Everything we feed on, he took. So we branched out. We took more and more, just to survive. You understand."

Megan nodded. The personal demons had been faced with a choice—get meaner, or die. They'd chosen meaner. She couldn't say for sure she blamed them.

"Normally we don't like to gang up in such numbers," Rocturnus continued. Like the room, he was strangely elegant for a naked three-foot-tall demon with lurid green skin. Megan kept expecting him to smoke a pipe or play concert piano. "It dilutes our power. When we have to share, when we're forced to gang up on people who don't have the strength to give, it deadens everyone. Our victims aren't as strong to begin with, their friends and family aren't as shocked and upset when—well. I'm sure you know to what conclusion we normally take our humans."

Megan nodded.

"But he took that choice away from us. You took that choice away from us, Megan, and we'd like our freedom back—at least as much as we can have it back. We want you to undo it."

"I don't know how."

"You do. You just don't remember that you know. But somewhere in there, you know how you did it and how you can fix it. You beat us, just now. That takes tremendous power."

She shook her head. "I don't understand. If it was so easy for me to beat you, and you just wanted my help, why did you scare me? Why all the business with the photo shoot, and the restaurant? What about sending Don Tremblay after me and my radio show?"

"We thought your show was a threat to us, a message for us. We wanted to see how powerful you really were. And we were his personal army." The venom in Rocturnus's voice hit Megan almost like a physical blow. "When we're not here, in our home, we must do what he says. The show gave him a convenient excuse. But we made sure Tremblay missed that day in the park, you have to give us that."

"Thanks. But why did he send me here? That doesn't make any sense."

Rocturnus sipped his tea. "He didn't. We don't know how you ended up here. Certainly we wanted you. That may have been enough. Now we can go after the Accuser."

"But I don't know how I did that. It just sort of happened. I mean, I knew what I was trying to do, but I don't know how it worked. And I can't remember how I did it."

"The Accuser does. And we have a connection to him, just like you. All we must do is go back to where he is. You'll find what you need."

"You'll take me back to him?" It came out as a whisper.

"No. We can only come when called. You'll take us back."

"Won't you have to obey him if I do?"

Rocturnus smiled. She tried not to look at his teeth. "We can rebel a little, if we concentrate, but not for long. You'll need to defeat him quickly."

"But I can't. I can't go back. He kicked me out. I don't have a body anymore, he's in it."

"Not completely." Rocturnus dropped out of his chair in a smooth slide and held out his hand. Megan hesitated, then took it. His skin was cool and dry, his fingers like long animated sticks in her palm.

"Someone left a line for you," he said. "All you have to do is follow it back."

"A line? I don't—"

She saw it then, a faint red scar pulsing in the air, leading from her chest up into the ether.

The personal demons stood up en masse and lifted their arms. Rocturnus said something in the demon tongue, one word. They repeated it.

Their power slammed into Megan again, but this time she did not scream. This time she opened that door she'd found, and sucked it all in. Their demon power, her own power, mingled in the furnace in her soul and she grabbed hold of the thin scarlet streak and pulled.

The room disappeared. Colors flashed and swirled around her. There was a tremendous thump. Megan opened her eyes and found herself back in the Solithell, lying on the floor beside a slathering horned beast with three eyes who she knew immediately was the Accuser in his true form.

THE ACCUSER ROARED, his huge black body shaking as he raised his fists into the air. Megan screamed, too, not just out of fear or anger but because being in his presence made the energy inside her body flare to a point where she didn't think she could control it. Behind her the personal demons shrieked, their voices echoing through her.

How long had it been? It felt like hours, but the position of the people in the room made her think only minutes had passed, at the most.

The black smog no longer filled the room. She couldn't see the Fearbusters clients, but Dante still sat at the table, visibly tense even at a distance. Her eyes watered when she spotted Malleus, Maleficarum, and Spud, huddled on the other side of the room around something she had a sneaking suspicion belonged to her. Templeton Black shouted in the demon tongue, his voice hoarse with terror as he faced the Accuser. He hadn't seen her yet. She didn't know if he could, if any of them could. Could they?

A quick glance down told her no. She could see through herself, as if she was some sort of faded reflection. For a moment the world spun and she stumbled before righting herself. No time. She'd already died or agreed to die. This was her chance to live and if it meant spending a little time in Casper form here in the Solithell she would do it.

She shook her head and stood up.

"Hey!"

The Accuser stopped. His eyes glowed red as he turned in her direction, his pig-like nostrils flaring. Blood ran down his bulging arms and matted the hair on his body. If Megan hadn't been ethereal, she thought she would have peed her pants.

"You didn't get rid of me after all," she said, her voice squeaking, "and I've brought some friends to see you, too."

The Accuser looked at her, then turned away, back towards Templeton. The temptation to hide from him, to run around the room, find her body, and steal it back, was almost unbearable.

Then Megan looked behind her and saw the little demons watching her, hope shining in their bulgy eyes. Funny, they were almost kind of cute in a horrible way, once you got used to them. It was her fault they'd been enslaved for fifteen years and her responsibility to rescue them.

She took a deep breath, and attacked the Accuser.

He'd been about to pick Templeton Black up in one ham-like fist. Megan's energy hit him with enough force to make Megan stumble, but the Accuser merely stopped what he was doing. He looked at her, puzzled, as if she was an insect, then gave an almost human shrug.

Megan didn't think anything had happened until she found herself flying across the room, slamming into the wall and falling to the floor. The Accuser had hit back, without even looking as if he was trying to. The little demons hissed.

She stood up, reaching for her head. She wasn't injured. She had no body to injure.

He couldn't harm her any more than he had. She could stay as she was, or she could get her body back, but she couldn't be hurt any worse than she was already hurting.

With a scream, she ran towards him, lowering the shields she still carried and sucking energy from the little demons, shaping it into a ball of fire in her head. A ball so large and hot she would have been sweating if she'd had a body to sweat. She held it in her hands, let it envelop her, until she was flame and she was Megan, and they were both the same.

She laughed, a delighted sound that echoed across the shouts and chaos of the room. She floated above it all, running across the floor on feet that wanted to dance, pulling energy as she ran. Templeton's, and the other demons' and the brothers', and then with a final giggle, Greyson's, fiery red in her hands and her mind.

She ran with it all, flying with it, across the marble floor, and when she got to the Accuser she didn't hesitate. She kept running, right into him, his flesh collapsing around her with a sickening squelch.

Her own memories flooded back, bending her backwards with the pain of them. Her disappointments, the things she'd seen and done, the loneliness . . . and then something else, something clean and pure that was love, and happiness, and pride in her accomplishments. The soft blue of Tera's new friendship, the green of Brian's respect, even the blazing black-edged orange of Greyson's desire and companionship. They wiped away the shame and sadness, not erasing it completely but making it manageable. She shouted in triumph, dug her fingers into the slime-covered flesh around her, and *read*.

Chapter Twenty-Seven

He was older than humans, older than time. She saw dinosaurs and crawling, filthy slug-things. She saw Cro-Magnons and prehistoric animals, chanting Druids, people growing and changing. Occasionally they challenged him, but they never won. He slaughtered and licked them clean of blood, danced in the flames as their bodies burned, and cried out in triumphant glee. Their despair filled him, went to his head like fine wine. Megan tasted it with him, *was* him, and threw her head back in delight.

The images changed, grew. Something slithered through Megan's mind, a feeling more than a vision. She grabbed it before it got away, saw what it held, and turned it on him.

That was it. That was how she'd done it. And she could do it again.

In the very center of his body, by the foul beating mass of his heart, was the psychic strand binding him to the personal demons. She'd put it there. When Harlan Trooper died, when the Accuser turned back to her, she'd found Harlan's demons and her own demon and used them as shields, flinging them in his path, but it had backfired. He'd sucked them into himself, absorbed them, and in desperation she'd found something to use against him, something she hadn't realized she had.

Her power, swirling and spinning in the air around her, created that cord. It was sixteen-year-old Megan bound in there, Megan and the Yezer Ha-Ra, and she grabbed hold of it with her mind and pulled. The bit of her younger self trapped in the Accuser's innards screamed, holding on to his heart. All of her anger, her fear and alienation, washed over Megan.

Tears stung her eyes. All that pain . . . how unhappy she'd been. It hadn't disappeared. It had changed, turned inward, locked itself behind the door. But it never left and all the Accuser kept was an echo.

Her raw throat burned as she gave a final mighty wrench of the cord. The last piece of her young self disappeared, her cries lost in the Accuser's roar as Megan grabbed his heart in her transparent hands and squeezed, feeling it squelch and explode in her fingers.

The cord wrapped itself around her, pulling her out of the shell of the Accuser's body as it collapsed. Megan stumbled and fell, her skin slick with blood.

The brothers knelt on the floor about twenty feet away. Megan hauled herself to her feet and ran towards them, her blood-soaked feet gliding across the marble floor with a grace her physical form never seemed to manage, knowing without being sure how that without the Accuser there to power it she would die.

She pushed between Malleus and Spud and knelt beside her still-warm body, patting it, trying to move it somehow. Trying to ignore the very strange sensation of looking at herself in this manner.

Maleficarum's voice soared over her terror, over the whole room, raised in song. It was beautiful but she barely heard it. How would she get back in? Was she dead, or traveling astrally, or what? Tears of panic ran down her cheeks. She tried touching her own hand, placing her head on her chest. It didn't work. "Come on!" she screamed, pounding her chest with her fists.

Whether it was her scream, the pounding, or even Maleficarum's song she didn't know, but the thin red line that brought her back into the room reappeared, blazed, and engulfed her. The last thing she saw before everything went red was Brian Stone running into the room, followed by Tera Green and an army of figures swathed in black robes.

SOMETHING SLAMMED into her, deep inside her chest. Megan gasped and arched her back, it hurt, oh whatever it was hurt, she pushed against it but it burned, and she wanted to pull away but she couldn't . . .

"Do it again!"

Through the panicky haze of receding pain, she heard someone yelling. It sounded so familiar. She knew that voice.

"I don't think this is working!"

"God damn it, Brian, do it again or I will rip your fucking head off with my bare goddamn hands, do you—"

More pain. Megan screamed. She pushed again, pushed against whatever it was grabbing her and yanking her swirling into dark agony, and suddenly she was in her body again, moving, rolling away. Her eyes opened. The walls of the Solithell's dining room swam into her vision. Sweet air filled her lungs, and she gulped it down. Her muscles ached. Pain shrieked from her left hand, but she was alive. Fully, completely, solidly alive.

She only had a second to enjoy it before someone grabbed her, lifting her upper body from the floor and pressing her into a broad, flat, warm surface with crushing strength. She didn't need to catch a glimpse of his white face to know it was Greyson holding her.

His heart pounded beneath the solid muscle of his chest. It sounded wonderful.

Wait a minute. No, it didn't. Who did he think he was? He'd used her to try and overthrow Templeton Black. Why did he even care that someone as *mediocre* as herself was still alive?

"Is she okay?" Tera's voice, calm but with an undertone of fear.

"I think so." Greyson pulled away from her, his hands trembling on her shoulders. "Are you okay? Meg, I have to tell you—"

Megan smiled. "I'm fine." She raised her right hand and slapped him across the face with all the strength she had.

The sound of skin against skin echoed in the silence. Megan forced herself to a stand, a rather difficult maneuver without the use of her throbbing left hand, and brushed her right palm on her dirty skirt. "Now," she said, looking at the destruction surrounding them, "what happened? Why are you guys here?"

Brian blinked. "You don't know?"

"If I knew, I wouldn't have asked." *Did* she feel okay?

She felt as if she'd been given a shot of adrenaline. Shaky and weak, but buzzing and confident, too. Even the sight of Art Bellingham's crumpled, discarded body in the corner didn't shake her as much as she would have imagined it would.

"M'lady! M'lady!" The brothers' faces, wet with tears, shone like beacons in the dimly lit room. Malleus grabbed her hand and squeezed. A little too hard; she had to tighten her lips to avoid a grimace. "We was so worried, we thought sure you weren't comin' back, and we was so—"

"Mr. Black, he locked us up, we couldn't get out in time to help you—"

"Yeh, yeh."

"And when we got up here, an' we saw—"

"Okay, okay." She reached out with her free hand to pat each of them on the shoulder. "It's okay, guys. Thank you. You helped me find my body, that's what I really needed. You let me know somebody cared."

"Well of course we cared, of course we do. And we're sorry we had to spy on you an' tell Mr. Black what you was sayin' in the park and all. We din't have no choice, y'see, he were—"

"It's okay, guys. Thanks." She looked at Brian, not wanting to upset the brothers but eager to hear his story. "What happened, please?"

"Dante set it up. Last night, at the ball. He made me promise to come. And to call Tera before I did."

"He told me about it on Thursday," Tera said. "And I told them." She gestured towards the black robes, two of whom now had a firm grip on Templeton Black.

They didn't need to hold him very tightly. He was bound at the wrists and ankles with shiny black rope.

"Why is he tied up?"

"He's being arrested. He tried to sacrifice a human to bring the Accuser back. It's a pretty big no-no."

"Why try it, then?" Megan turned away from Black as the black robes led him away. Her skin prickled under his furious gaze, but she ignored it. So Greyson had his way after all. Black was gone. He'd managed to use her and get rid of her in one smooth move.

"Once it was done, nobody could prove it." Tera shrugged. "And it would have been done, if—"

"If Megan hadn't managed to somehow overpower the Accuser," Greyson interrupted. He stood up and shoved his hands into his pockets. "I assume, Megan, those little ones had something to do with your victory?"

Megan turned around. The personal demons lined the walls, watching. She nodded. "They helped me. Gave me some of their power, and brought me back here."

"We didn't bring you back." Rocturnus stepped forward. "You had a line. We just helped you use it."

"I couldn't have done it without you." She smiled at the gnarled little demon. "Thank you."

Greyson scowled. "If we're all done with the mutual admiration, can we wrap this up? I'm rather tired."

He did look tired. Deep circles shadowed his dark eyes, and the clothes covering his lean body were rumpled and smudged.

"I'm sorry," Megan said. "Are we bothering you?"

"Not at all. I'm just going to sit down. Let me know when you're done."

"You do that." She refused to watch him walk away, turning instead back to Brian and Tera, staring at her with identical furrowed brows.

"Maybe we should all sit down," Tera suggested. "And have something to eat or a drink or something."

"The servants are all asleep," Greyson said from the table.

"Then I suppose we'll just have to serve ourselves." Tera took Megan's hand and started to lead her toward the table, but Spud stepped in the way and, before Megan could stop him, scooped her up and carried her to a seat next to Greyson. Megan shook her head and pointed opposite. She did not want to be so close to him. Tera busied herself with glasses and bottles and Brian sat next to Megan. Greyson stayed where he was with his arms folded across his chest and an empty glass in front of him.

Tera brought back drinks and handed them out. "Everybody gets wine," she said. "I don't know what your preferences are."

The red was fruity and spicy on her tongue, and warmth spread through her body as she swallowed. "Thank you." She turned in Greyson's direction but didn't meet his eyes. "Where are the Fearbusters people?"

"We sent them home." He didn't look at her, either, which was just as well. Megan didn't think she could stand to see his eyes again. "As soon as you were gone."

"They're okay?"

He nodded.

"Good. I was worried about them. What happened?"

Greyson cleared his throat. "Temp made a deal. He thought if he handed you to the Accuser, he'd be able to control him. He was wrong. The Accuser had what he wanted—you—and he planned to use you. For what, I'm not sure, but I think we can bet it wouldn't have been pleasant.

"They argued for a few minutes. Then the Accuser got angry. He left your body and changed to his pure physical form, which you saw. He was about to kill Temp when you came back and did whatever it was you did to defeat him."

"I used the personal demons' power."

Rocturnus, sitting on the floor a few feet away under the watchful gaze of Malleus, Maleficarum, and Spud, cleared his throat. "It's your power now, Megan."

"Excuse me?"

"Our power. It became yours, when you bound us to you."

Megan finally broke the silence. "Say that again?"

"You bound us to you. When you released us from the Accuser. You held the string. We pulled you out of him, but you didn't let go. It was still wrapped around you when you re-entered your body and that man—" he pointed at

Brian— "did the power transfer to bring you back to life. Besides, you promised us back when you bound us to the Accuser that one day you'd save us. Now we're yours."

"But—but you can't be," Megan said, spluttering. *Don't forget what you promised* ran through her head. That day in the shower, after the zombie attack. She'd been trying to remember it all. She just hadn't put the pieces together. "You're, I mean, you've been very nice to me and all, but you're demons. I'm human. And I'm a psychological counselor. My job is to fight you, to help people get rid of you."

"You're not entirely human," Greyson mumbled.

"What?"

He leaned back, looking at his hand holding the stem of his wineglass as if the words he was about to speak were written on it. "You're not entirely human. The Accuser left some demon in you the first time you met him. And you kind of . . . grew over it, I guess is the best description. You're not demon, but you *have* demon, if that makes sense. That's why you could bind them to you."

"Okay, either I haven't had enough to drink or you've had way too much," Megan said. "Or is this another fun little game of yours? Another round of 'let's laugh at Megan'?"

"Are you going to use your head and listen to me, or are you going to keep up with this petty revenge?"

"You mean my mediocre mind?"

"Fucking—fuck!" Greyson stood up and threw his glass across the room. It shattered on the wall in an explosion of crystal shards, leaving a purplish stain on the damask wallpaper as the wine ran down. The others gasped. He glared at them, his face dull red.

"It's your vocabulary that impresses me most," Megan said.

Greyson shot her a dirty look and strode out of the room, slamming the heavy door behind him.

"Megan, don't you think you're being a bit hard on him?" Tera asked.

"I don't think I'm being hard enough," Megan snapped. "After what he did to me—"

"What, save your life?" Brian leaned forward in his chair, resting his elbows on the table. He still looked pale. "Megan, you do know he saved your life, don't you? You felt his energy bring you back?"

Greyson's energy. Greyson's line.

He'd kissed her before they entered the room, shoved his power into her body. Not to give her a boost, but to bind her to him somehow. To create the line.

She'd seen the flames. She'd seen the sparks die out right before she appeared in the personal demon's hall.

His energy sent her there, his line brought her back. She swallowed. "Brian. What did he tell you about tonight? How did he get you to come?"

"He told me you'd probably die if I didn't show up. He took my watch. I could focus on it, because it was mine. It's one of the ways my abilities work. With him wearing it, and me focused on it, he could let me know when I needed to be here. As soon as you guys finished eating he said it was time. I called Tera. And we came so I could do the power transfer."

"*You* came to do the power transfer," Tera said. "*I* came—with the other Vergadering—because Greyson told me at our meeting Thursday morning what he thought Templeton had planned and to be ready. When Brian called, I was expecting it, and so were they."

Of course. She'd known that watch Greyson wore wasn't his. She just hadn't been able to recall where she'd seen it before—on Brian's wrist, at the ball.

"That still doesn't excuse what he said to me," she mumbled.

"Megan, the man was fighting for both your lives," Tera said. "If Templeton found out what he'd done, he would have been killed, and so would you. You made it obvious how you felt. He had to do something to make Templeton think he didn't care about you. And to get you angry, since your power flares when you get mad. As you know."

"He used me. He seduced me to use my power to overthrow Templeton Black. He just wanted to take over the Meegra."

She smiled faintly for a moment. "He's going to have an awfully hard time taking over, after ratting Templeton out to us. He did that for you."

Megan couldn't remember ever feeling this bad about anything. "And I slapped him," she said.

"That was a pretty good slap, too," Brian said, looking very satisfied. "I didn't think you had it in you."

"You thought I might have killed somebody once," she said, but her mind wasn't on the argument.

"And you thought I was probably working for Bellingham and would write all sorts of horrible rumors about you in the magazine."

The smile came to her lips unbidden, but once it was there Megan discovered it felt good. She liked Brian, despite the differences they'd had, the differences they still had.

He smiled, too. "Call it even?"

She nodded, and he leaned over to plant a small kiss on her cheek. "It'll be a great article," he said.

"Oh. I'd forgotten about that."

"What? Oh, yeah, your profile. That will be great, but I'm thinking of the article I'll write about this.

Art Bellingham, forcing the Fearbusters clients to perform dark occult rituals, almost killing them in the process . . . and Megan Chase, Dr. Demon Slayer, rushing in to the rescue. With a little help from—" he glanced at Tera, who shook her head slightly. "A little help from me, and nobody who is supernatural in any way," he finished.

Tera smiled. "Sounds great, Brian. I hope you'll send me a copy when it's done."

"I'll be sure to do that, if you promise not to try and hypnotize me ever again."

"Deal."

Brian poured more wine, but Megan picked up her glass and excused herself. She had someone else she needed to talk to.

Chapter Twenty-Eight

He sat on the floor in the hall, his back against the wall and one leg stretched in front of him. The other was bent so he could rest a bottle on his knee. His eyes were closed when she entered the hall, but as she pulled the door shut behind her he opened one, then closed it again.

"Oh, it's you."

Megan stood for a minute, watching him. "You have a right to be angry," she said finally. "But so do I."

"Spare me the counseling speak."

"Oh, spare me the tortured, misunderstood bit," she snapped. "I came out here to apologize. If you don't want to hear it, that's fine with me."

He opened his eyes. "I suppose Tera and Brian have been filling your head with breathtaking tales of my heroic deeds."

"Something like that."

"Pure exaggeration. Like I said, I've never had any interest in being a hero."

She sat down next to him and took the bottle. "So that was all self-preservation. And a plan to take Templeton's place."

He shrugged. "It was a pretty good plan, you have to admit."

Megan almost stood back up and left, but something flickered in his eyes when he glanced at her and she knew she had to try. Yes, maybe he had made her part of his plan. That didn't mean he didn't care. And no, he wasn't the kind of man who committed himself. That was fine. She didn't expect a commitment, not after a week. Nor did she especially want the hassle at this point, either, not with a budding radio career on top of her practice, and especially not with the additional publicity bound to come when Brian's "Fearbusters occult" story broke.

Besides, she was used to having time to herself. She enjoyed being alone. Most of the time.

She raised the bottle to her own lips, drank, and set it deliberately back on the ground.

"Just tell me one thing. Why did you send me to the personal demons? And how did you know it all?"

"That's two things."

Megan raised her eyebrows and waited.

"Because I knew what they wanted," he said, after a pause. "They obviously weren't trying to kill you, or they would have done it before I got involved. They couldn't have created those zombies, either. Something had to be behind it, something with enough power to create multiple fast-moving zombies. Not many creatures have that kind of strength. I already knew you had demon in you; I discovered that back when I kissed you the first time. You knew the Accuser was after you. You just didn't know his connection to the Yezer Ha-Ra."

"And you didn't tell me."

"No."

"Why not?"

He shrugged and looked away, but Megan didn't let him get away with it. She grabbed his hand in her left, and used her right to tilt his face back towards her. "Greyson."

He didn't meet her eyes at first. Megan waited, barely daring to breathe. She hadn't said or done anything to be ashamed of . . . yet. If she was wrong she could just get up and leave.

"Damn it," he whispered, just before his arms went around her and his lips met hers with bruising strength.

His hands caressed her face, then slid back to tangle in her hair, stroking her neck, pulling her closer to him. The angle was awkward but she didn't care. She didn't care about anything at that moment, not even the gang of tiny demons in the other room waiting for her orders.

Together they slid over, Greyson's hand supporting the back of her neck to rest her on the floor. The icy cold of the marble seeped through her clothes to her back, but Greyson's weight like a banked furnace above her countered it nicely. His tongue slid into her mouth and she welcomed it, raising her chin, returning his passion with equal intensity.

It was several breathless minutes before he pulled his mouth away from hers and pressed his cheek to hers, so his lips rested just next to her ear. "I couldn't tell you, *bryaela*. I was sure I knew what Temp had planned, and I knew the Accuser was going to read you when he . . . invaded you. I couldn't take the risk of him knowing and maybe paying more attention to where he sent you. He had to be careless, so I could use your anger to give you to the Yezer Ha-Ra."

"I know," she whispered back. "I know now."

"And I had to make you angry. They were lies, Meg. You know they were. What I said."

She nodded. "It's okay."

For another minute or so he just held her, his slowing breath hot on her neck. Then he pulled away, kissed her hard on the mouth, and helped her sit back up.

"So." He took another swig from the bottle. Megan recognized the action. That speech, made into the hidden shadows at her throat, was all she would get from him. Whatever fear or panic for her safety he'd experienced, whatever his feelings were towards her, she'd have to take the clues she'd just been given.

But then, reading clues to people's emotions in their behavior was her business.

"What do you plan to do with them?"

"Who? Oh. The personal demons." She shook her head. "I have no idea, to be honest. I can't very well tell them not to do what they do. They'll die, and I promised to take care of them. But I can't just give them free rein, either."

"Business could boom. They reel them in, you cure them and send them on their way."

Megan took the bottle from his hand and tried not to laugh. "That's one way to look at it. But I'd rather see if we can't help society and not just line my pockets."

"The Gretneg of a Meegra has to do what's best for her family first."

She hadn't thought of that. "You mean . . . I'm a Gretneg?"

He nodded. "Gretneg of Meegra Io Adflicta. They haven't officially been a Meegra for some time, but I'm sure you can build them back up."

Gretneg of a Meegra. A week ago, she was a lonely counselor with the ability to win every hand at cards if she wanted. Now she had friends. A lover. A . . . family. Granted, her family consisted of small scaly creatures who lived on the unhappiness of humans, but it was better than being alone, wasn't it?

Yes. It was.

"What about you?" she asked. "What happens to your Meegra? Tera said—"

"Ignore Tera. You don't think I would have gone into all this without some contingency plans, do you? Half the Meegra was ready to kill Templeton themselves—he doesn't have any sons to take over anyway—and put me in his place already. I think Malleus, Maleficarum, and

Spud can help me with the other half. They certainly proved their loyalty to you, breaking out of the dungeons to save you. Maybe we'll take them with us."

"Hmm? Where?"

He stood up and grabbed her hand, lifting her to her feet. His eyes met hers, searching her depths, his lips quirked in a dangerous half-smile.

His arm stole around her waist to press her to him. "I was thinking of someplace sunny. Italy? What do you think, *bryaela*? You want to go to Florence for a week or two with me?"

"Maybe. What does that mean? You wouldn't tell me before."

"Come with me and find out."

"What happens after we get back? Aren't our families in competition or something?"

He kissed her forehead. "Let's take it one step at a time, shall we?"

Megan nodded and followed him up the stairs. One step at a time, all the way to his bedroom.

MEGAN LEANED FORWARD in the shadowy studio, smiling as Bill patched the first call of the night through. It was Regina, her caller from last week, the girl being tormented by demons.

Across the room, Rocturnus smiled at her from where he sat on the floor. He held up his hand. Regina was now off-limits. He'd called off her demons that morning, after Megan had finally woken up and gotten herself ready for work.

Bill pointed at her. Megan opened her mouth.

"Hi, Regina," she said. "How can I slay your demons tonight?"

Megan's Meat Pies

  2-3 lbs stew beef or sirloin, cut in chunks
  12 oz dark beer (Guinness or Murphy's)
  2-3 tbsp olive oil
  2-3 tbsp flour
  1 tbsp or so onion powder or ½ onion chopped
  salt & pepper to taste
  2 tsp or so each of parsley, thyme (or whatever herbs you like)
  1 tsp or so of rosemary or to taste
  1/8 tsp or so nutmeg or to taste
  2-3 tbsp Worcestershire
  ½ beef bouillon cube or 1 tsp bouillon paste (like "Better Than Bouillon")
  2 tsp or so gravy powder (optional)
  1-2 pkgs frozen puff pastry (Check to see how much pastry is in a package. A block of pastry will usually give you enough for a top and bottom crust, whereas a roll-out sheet may only be enough for one.)

Heat olive oil in a large frying pan or saucepan with a lid. Cook chopped onions (if using) until they start to brown. (If you're not using onions, add the onion powder just before the beef or at the same time). Add beef, in batches if necessary, and brown. (Pan should be very hot, so the beef sears well). Sprinkle with herbs while cooking. Salt lightly, but do not pepper. (This tends to be a little salty, so go easy on the salt until you've tasted later). The beef will be hard at this point, like tough little nuggets.

When beef is all browned, add it all back to the pan and sprinkle with flour. Stir well. Add Worcestershire and bouillon, stir well. Add pepper and beer and stir well, scraping at the bottom of the pan, until it comes back to a low boil and the foam from the beer is mostly gone. Let it boil a couple of minutes, then cover and simmer 2 ½ hours or so, until tender, stirring very occasionally and checking liquid level.

When done—the meat should be very tender—taste and adjust seasonings. Check the liquid amount. It shouldn't be soupy (if it is, dump some of the excess, but save it in case you need to add it back in.) Make a Beurre blanc with some of the cooking liquid and some flour, then stir that back in to thicken it (or just add a little flour at a time and stir it in well). Set aside to cool once it's reached the consistency you like. It should resemble a slightly thin gravy. (It will thicken a bit as it bakes, so don't worry if it still seems too liquidy.)

While the filling cools, roll out the pastry and shape it for the pan. Line a pie pan (Megan uses a 9-inch deep dish pie pan, but you can even make square pies) with pastry, bake at 400 degrees (or according to package directions) for 15-20 minutes or until puffy and starting to brown. Add filling, cover with second pastry sheet, crimp edges. Be sure to cut a vent in the "lid" so steam can escape.

Bake a further 30-40 minutes until top crust is puffy and brown. Serve with gravy and whatever side dishes you like. This reheats beautifully, too, in the microwave or the oven (350 degrees for 20 minutes or so, and cover the pastry with foil so it doesn't get too brown).

Acknowledgements

W riting a book is hard. Writing a list of people for whose support I'm thankful is . . . well, okay, still hard, but not as bad. We have the usual suspects first: My husband Stephen and our two little girls, who have always been more understanding than I could hope for when I spend hours crouched over the computer ruining my vision. My parents and my brother Ray should, of course be thanked, for putting up with me my whole life. My best friends, Corinne Knell and Anna J. Evans, without whose comments and suggestions this book wouldn't be what it is now. My good friend George Beliard. My favorite girl Ariana Chang. All of my fellow Reluctant Adults: Mark Henry, Anton Strout, Jill Myles, and Ilona Andrews. The wonderful Caitlin Kittredge. Carol Nelson Douglas, and my editor Paula Guran. Briana St. James, Miss Snark and the Snarklings, and her secret boyfriend Evil Editor and the Evil Minions. All of my blog friends and readers, you know who you are, and I continue to be amazed that you actually care what I say or think about anything.

Special thanks go to Heather Massey, for her invaluable information about therapy, psychology, qualifications, practice, and licensing. Any errors are of course mine and not hers.

Excerpt from

Demon Inside by *Stacia Kane*
Coming January 2009 from Juno Books

MEGAN WAS COMPLETING her umpteenth lap of the small holding room when a matron finally came and opened the door. "Megan Chase!" She scanned the room and found her. "Come on, you're free to go."

Trying not to smile at the others who weren't as lucky, Megan brushed past her and out the door. Every fiber of her body screamed to be outside. Only two hours had passed, but it felt like a lifetime. Worrying about going to jail, worrying about her career, worrying about her demons, and as time stretched, worrying about why Greyson Dante hadn't shown up yet.

The worry deepened when she got to the little check-in desk and saw the man standing there holding a briefcase and smiling: Hunter Kyle. Definitely an attorney, but definitely not the one she'd called. They'd met a few months ago at a charity party, and she'd seen him once or twice since, but . . . why was he here?

The officer behind the desk grabbed the manila envelope containing her possessions and handed it to her. "Check to make sure everything's there, please, and sign here."

She did. "What's happening? I mean, did I have to post bond, or . . . ?"

"The owners of the house declined to press charges."
He gave her a tight smile, an unfriendly one. "Lucky you."

"Yeah . . . thanks." Did it bother cops when anyone got
to go, or what? For a moment she contemplated reading
him, but it didn't matter. Who cared what he thought?
She was free! She had to suppress the urge to skip out the
bullet-proof glass door separating the booking area from
the rest of the building. Innocent women didn't skip.

"Are you okay, Megan?" Hunter asked, taking her arm
solicitously. "I got everything started as soon as I could,
but it took some time for the homeowners to agree to drop
charges."

"I'm okay, thanks." They burst through the double doors
into the icy darkness broken only by dim streetlights. The
temperatures had hovered around freezing for weeks before
finally sinking lower two days before. Now her entire face felt
chapped, stretched by the fierce wind. "Where's my car?"

"I had one of the boys drive it to my place." Greyson
Dante emerged from the shadows outside the circles of
light like a villain in a James Bond movie. Megan hadn't
seen him in four days. It was a little embarrassing how
her heart leapt at the sight of him, his dark hair shining,
his strong-boned face twisted in a little half-smile as if he
knew the effect his appearance had on her.

Which he probably did.

He extended his hand to Hunter. "Thanks, Hunt. I owe
you one."

Hunter smiled. Megan didn't think he had any idea
what exactly he was being promised; Hunter wasn't a
demon and so wasn't familiar with the complex system
of favors and promises they used. Greyson was powerful,
more so now than he had been when she'd met him. To be
owed a favor by him . . . a lot of demons would have killed
for that opportunity. Maybe some of them did.

Then again, maybe Greyson said it because he knew Hunter wouldn't realize. Greyson never said or did anything without having more than one reason for it, she knew.

Her suspicion was confirmed when Hunter merely replied, "No trouble at all, I'm happy to help."

Megan stood in the cold and bit her lip while the two men chatted for a minute, until Greyson slipped his arm around her waist and made their good-byes.

His black Jaguar wasn't far away and she was grateful when they reached it. Her toes were numb.

Not so numb, though, Greyson couldn't make them tingle. His lips, like the rest of his body, were blissfully warm, and the kiss he gave her sent flames blazing up her spine—just like the real flames he could create from thin air anytime he wished.

"You okay?" His thumb caressed her cheek while tiny sparks of red showed in his eyes.

She nodded. "A little freaked."

"By being in jail, or by what happened to your demon in that house?"

"I . . ." Shit. She hadn't told him what happened, only that she'd been arrested by mistake. She hadn't told him about the other demons, either. "Both."

He nodded and put her in the car, then got in on his side and started the engine. "When were you going to tell me?"

"I wasn't. How did you—"

"Come on, Meg. Where do you think I've been?"

"What do you mean?"

The parking lot disappeared behind them as he sped down the street, past deserted office buildings with bright strings of Christmas lights draped across the windows. It was not yet eight o'clock, but nobody was in this section of downtown. Even the homeless had deserted the streets and found shelter from the cold.

"I went to convince those people not to press charges. It looked like a fucking abattoir in there."

"I tried to clean up."

"How thoughtful. Why haven't you told me what's going on? I hear this is the third one."

"Why are you so mad at me? You said yourself, how I run my Meegra is my business."

"Yes, how you run it. But when your demons start getting killed, and demons in other Meegras start getting killed, it's not just up to you anymore."

"But I—what do you mean, other demons?"

"I mean, you've lost three. I lost one two days ago. House Concumbia have lost four, House Caedes Fuiltean two, everybody's had at least one loss. I only just found out about it."

"None of the others told you, then, so why—"

"I'm not sleeping with any of the others, either. I would have—*Shit*!"

Something thudded on the rear of the car, like a large rock kicked up from the pavement. Greyson swerved so hard Megan fell against him despite her seatbelt. Cold air flooded the car as he downshifted violently and sped up, jerking the wheel to the right and roaring down a narrow side road.

"What's—"

"Get down, damn it, that was a gunshot!"

Demon Inside
Chapter Two

"What?" Megan jerked up in her seat, instinctively trying to look behind them, but his hand forced her head back down. Her ear pressed hard against the padded console.

Another shot. This time Megan heard it, heard the rear windshield shatter. She screamed, the sound ripped from her throat as Greyson cursed again and spun the wheel. She fumbled with her seatbelt, wanting absurdly to crawl onto the floor and hide like a small child under her bed covers at night.

Orange light filled the car, pulsing, disappearing and coming back as Greyson sent balls of flame into the car behind them.

He cursed. She popped up, unable to resist looking, and saw the flames extinguish, saw the black car behind them still racing along as if nothing had happened. Another tiny explosion happened inside their car. Again it disappeared and they advanced.

What sort of creatures were these, impervious to fire? Were they *vregonis* demons, like Greyson himself?

As if in answer to her question, the Jag filled with smoke, black and foul-smelling. It filled her nostrils, stuck to her skin.

"Stay the fuck *down*! Cover your face!"

She ducked, just as fire filled the car, burning away the smoke. Sweat broke out on her skin from the brief, intense blast of heat. "What was—"

"Open the glove compartment, get the gun."

The car bounced over something, a pothole or speedbump. Megan's arms flailed in the air. She'd tried to reach for the dashboard but the impact sent her back against her seat.

Greyson made a sharp left. The Jag's tires complained loudly about such rough treatment. Megan clutched at the center console to keep from hitting the door.

"Open the glove compartment, Meg, come on!"

"I'm trying!" The engine roared. The interior was bleached white by the headlights of the car behind them, switched on high. Greyson flipped the console lid up and grabbed his sunglasses, snapping them open and sliding them on in an effort to block the glare.

The car bounced again. Another gunshot broke the air, and another. Loud thunks came from the car and it shook with the impact; they were shooting the trunk, the roof, as Greyson swerved back and forth, trying to avoid the shots.

"*Fuck*! My *car*!" For the first time she felt his anger, a breeze colder than the air outside brushing over her skin.

Megan yanked the handle of the glove compartment with clumsy fingers and opened it. Greyson's leather gun case rested on the owner's manual inside.

Light flared behind them. Megan turned and saw flames erupting from under the hood of the pursuing car, as Greyson tried to make the engine explode. Even as she started to breathe a sigh of relief, the flames disappeared and the car lunged at them She could almost see the figures inside, two shapes, pale flashes in the dark exterior. Maybe if she lowered her shields . . .

"Megan!"

"I'm trying to read them."

"You won't get anything. They're not human. Just open the case."

It took her three tries to grasp the slider and pull it down, and another second to force herself to look at what lay inside the case. She knew he carried it, she'd seen it several times. But she'd never really thought about it before, about why he needed it or what he might do with it.

"Take the gun out. Be careful, it's loaded. Take off your seatbelt."

"I can't."

"Do you want to die?"

"No!"

Greyson swerved again, riding up on the curb. They'd turned onto a busier road; horns honked and tires squealed around them. "Then get the fucking gun out *now*!"

Her mouth was so dry she didn't think all the water in the world could help, but tears poured freely from her eyes. The gun sat heavy and cold in her hand, dwarfing her palm. She didn't like guns, had never liked them, and Greyson once told her he didn't particularly care for them either.

She turned around so her chest rested against the seat.

It's them or us, it's them or us...

"Okay. Steady your arms on the back of the seat, and look straight down them. Use your dominant eye and close the other one."

She obeyed. "Okay."

"Good. See those notches at the end of the barrel? Line up what you want to shoot between them. Then squeeze the trigger—don't yank at it, just squeeze it. Be ready, it's going to kick back on you, so don't lock your arms too hard."

This felt unreal. She could do this, she could, she'd destroyed two zombies once with nothing more than a showerhead and some hairspray, she could definitely shoot these fuckers trying to kill her . . .

She took a deep breath and fired.

The Jaguar was going too fast for her to recoil far. Inertia forced her body against the seat like a large hand, but her arm kicked back. The gun's report echoed in her ears, thundering all the way through her body. She couldn't see where the shot had gone.

More black smoke filled the car. This time she acted instinctively, ducking forward while heat flared behind her back.

The car behind them swerved and sped up, its front end only inches from the Jag's rear. Greyson jerked the wheel to the left. Megan fell against the door, her hair blowing wild around her face, obscuring her vision. The Jag bounced and lurched, cutting into the next lane, flying across the center divider and down another side road. Metal crashed against metal behind them.

"Okay, get my phone and hit 1," Greyson said. She couldn't believe how calm his voice was, how through all of this he'd barely yelled at her despite the rage she felt simmering below his surface. Even now his face in profile didn't reflect any anxiety save the slight tightening of his lips and a faint furrow in his brow. Whereas had she looked in a mirror she doubted she would have been able to recognize herself.

She obeyed, the sleek little phone much friendlier in her hand than the gun now resting on her lap. The other end rang once, twice, before a familiar Cockney voice answered.

"Malleus! Malleus, we're being chased, they're shooting—"

"Tell him where we are and that we're heading for the reservoir," Greyson interrupted. "Tell him to meet us at Exit 22."

She'd barely finished repeating his words when Malleus hung up.

"Are they gone?"

Her answer was another gunshot. The aluminium accents on the dash broke with a sharp, loud crack. Megan's hands flew up to cover her face. Greyson said something, but she didn't understand him.

"Shoot them again." Roughness underscored his tone.

"What's wrong?"

"Just shoot!"

She braced her heels against the underside of the dash and raised the gun again, shaking with adrenaline and fear.

"Shoot the grill!"

She did, aiming as best as she could, but just as she squeezed the trigger the car shot forward. Greyson jerked the wheel to the right and Megan fell onto him. His gasp was audible even over the screaming engine and the rushing of blood in her ears.

The world spun dizzyingly around the car; they were turning in a full circle, leaving ink-black tire marks on the street. Before Megan even had a chance to duck they'd sideslipped the black car and passed it, heading back the way they came. Flames leapt up behind them, completely obliterating the road.

They went right, taking the turn wide, almost ramming a truck coming through the intersection. The truck's horn added to the cacophony of sounds around them.

"Did we lose—"

The black car flew around the corner, its tires still burning. Without being told she raised the gun, her fingers working of their own accord as they pulled the trigger. This long smooth stretch of road was the best chance she'd have.

This time she hit something. The black car lurched sideways, the dim shapes inside moving. A ball of blue-white fire came out of nowhere and slammed into the grill, through the grill, flames licking the top of the hood from beneath. Black smoke poured out. Then, as Megan watched, the smoke formed itself into a shape like an arrow aimed at the Jag, only to vanish in another conflagration.

Her eyes burned from the horror and heat. She shot again, not knowing how many bullets were even left in the gun. More smoke, white now, came from the car behind them. Still it burned. Hope blossomed in her breast.

"Hang on," Greyson said, spinning the steering wheel. The Jag slipped up an entry ramp onto the highway, the black car still following but slower now, lurching forward. Its tires exploded in a mass of flames. The car leapt in the air, forced up from the blast, and landed on its side against the retaining wall of the ramp. Megan watched until Greyson merged into traffic, but the car didn't move again.

"Oh my God, oh my God, who were they? Why were—"

Pale grey light from the streetlamps flashed into the car and out, like a slow-motion strobe, highlighting the black splatter of blood on the charcoal dashboard, the gleaming river of it soaking Greyson's sleeve.

"I'M FINE," he said again, just as he had so many times in the last hour as they drove all over the city to make sure they weren't being followed. Megan stopped just inside the dimly lit white entry hall of Iureanlier Sorithell, the mansion on the outskirts of town belonging to the Gretneg of Greyson's Meegra.

Right now, that was Greyson, at least in theory. Since his takeover of the position had involved handing the former Gretneg, Templeton Black, over to the supernatural law enforcement agency known as Vergadering, some members of his Meegra doubted his integrity. The other Gretnegs were still debating whether or not to allow him to have that much power and authority.

It was a battle she knew he was still fighting, but one they didn't discuss. She'd never asked, and she doubted he would give her a straight answer if she did. It was his business, just like the changes she'd been implementing in her Meegra were hers. Although she knew he didn't approve of them, he'd never once told her so, or tried to change her mind when she made a decision.

"You're getting blood all over the floor," she said, following him through the small crowd of rubendas— members of his Meegra—who stood waiting. Clearly the wound wasn't serious, but the sight of it still made her nervous. Uncomfortable.

Especially since something deep inside her, some small part she refused to acknowledge, liked seeing it. Liked the contrast of dark red blood on the white marble floor. Wanted to touch it, to raise fingertips smudged with it to her lips and taste it, spicy and tinged with smoke.

Horrified, she looked away, swallowing hard. Her eyes caught those of one of the rubendas and saw the same yearning reflected there.

Her heels clicked on the floor as she hurried to catch up with Greyson, staring resolutely at his sharp profile. Malleus strode along beside him, carrying the overnight case he'd gone to her house and packed for her. Through the open door of the kitchen she saw Maleficarum and Spud opening a large bag and setting out silvery instruments on white cloths.

Malleus, Maleficarum, and Spud were guard demons, terrifically strong and tough, with self-healing powers accelerated even beyond those of normal demons. She'd seen them lose enough blood to kill a man and do a jig three hours later, but knew they'd spent some time learning medicine as well, especially over the last three months. They were among the few demons Greyson really trusted, so their duties under his rule had increased from simple bodyguards to something more like personal assistants.

"Mr. Dante?"

Megan and Greyson both stopped. Megan turned around to see the *rubenda* who'd caught her eye earlier step cautiously forward and gesture to the droplets on the floor.

"Mr. Dante, can I have your blood?"

Angry mutterings broke out in the small crowd of demons near him. Megan's mouth fell open, but when she looked back at Greyson he stood perfectly calm, as if the other demon had asked him about the weather.

"No," he said, and strode into the kitchen without looking back.

HER FEET SANK into the soft pale carpet under her feet as she paced back and forth, trying to somehow walk the adrenaline out of her system. Whiskey had taken the edge off, but her mind still raced.

From the way Greyson's eyes tracked her movements she knew he was well on his way to being drunk. He slouched in his heavy chair by the wall, shirtless, his bandaged arm resting on pillows beside him. His other hand clutched yet another glass.

"I really don't think painkillers and booze are a great combination, Greyson, why don't you—"

"Why don't you let it go?" he snapped. That, more than anything else, told her how unnerved he'd been by their experience. Greyson almost never lost his temper.

She stared at him for a minute then kept walking. Tension hung in the air between them, weighing Megan down even more fully than she already was. She'd found another of her demons exploded all over some suburban home, she'd been arrested, she'd gone to jail, she'd almost been killed . . . and she'd had the bizarre and unfortunately not unfamiliar desire to lick her boyfriend's blood. A desire shared by at least one demon in the house, if not more.

"Sit down, *bryaela*," Greyson said softly. "You're making me dizzy."

"I can't sit. I'm too nervous."

"We could lie down."

Her laugh sounded slightly hysterical in her ears. "Is this really the time?"

"It's as good a time as any, isn't it?" He stood up and crossed the room to her, capturing her between his hard, warm body and the heavy dresser behind her. "You're here, I'm here . . . I believe you're familiar with the bed . . ."

"We almost got killed tonight. After I went to jail!"

"Mmm, that's so sexy." His lips tickled her ear, then traced a path down the side of her neck, stopping so he could scrape her skin with his teeth. "You bad, bad girl."

She didn't intend to respond, but she did, meeting his lips with a ferocity that stunned her. Her arms slid up under his so her fingertips could run over the tiny sgaegas—dull little spikes—covering his spine. Goose bumps broke out on his skin under her hands.

He gripped her waist with his right hand and pulled her closer, pressing his erection against her belly, while his left hand tangled in her hair. She raised herself on tiptoes, forcing him to kiss her harder, wanting to forget everything and lose herself in him.

Heat exploded in her chest, in her stomach, working its way to points lower. Her fingers yanked at his belt. The entire night, the shame, the terror, her failure to protect her demons, disappeared in a haze of need so strong she thought she might die from it.

She shoved his pants down and grabbed his cock, hot and heavy in her palm. His breath rasped into her mouth, onto her throat, as he pulled away enough to lift her shirt.

One quick move slid it over her head, and another adroit twist unfastened her bra. It slid down her shoulders and he pulled it all the way off, then pressed his chest to hers, forcing her hips harder against the dresser. She caressed his back, down the hard muscles of his behind, forward again to stroke him where she knew he'd appreciate it the most, and all the while her heart beat with fire and fear and the need for oblivion.

He lifted her up, his powerful hands curving under her thighs, and propped her on the edge of the dresser.

"Your arm," she gasped. "Be careful."

"Hush." His mouth caught hers again while he undid the button of her trousers and lowered the zipper. Underneath she wore a tiny scrap of black silk he'd bought her on his last trip to Paris. Greyson liked to give gifts, especially gifts he could remove later.

She started to lower herself from the dresser but he stopped her, bracing her back with one hand while he used the other to peel the panties off and drop them on the floor.

"I thought you wanted the bed," she whispered.

"Changed my mind."

Her head fell back as he thrust into her, gripping her hips with both hands. She clutched the short, soft hair at his nape, twisting it between her fingers and bringing him closer. His mouth hovered not half an inch from hers, his eyes glowing reddish and staring into her, through her.

"Meg . . ."

He dove closer, capturing her lips, invading her mouth with his tongue, and the flames in her body leapt higher.

Their mouths fused together as he thrust, keeping his pace steady, but she felt his arms shaking and the loose urgency of his lips and knew this wouldn't last, couldn't last, that the fear and pain which made her want to escape acted like an aphrodisiac for him.

Her hips left the dresser. She braced herself with her hands on the smooth, cool surface and wrapped her legs around his waist while he held her up, moving her pelvis in slow circles so he hit all the right spots deep inside her. She tensed, her thighs urging him on, begging for more.

His grip shifted, freeing his right hand so he could slide it down between them, and that was all she needed. Her back arched, shoving her hips further forward, and she cried out as her body shuddered and clenched with release.

He joined her moments later, his fingers digging into her skin so hard it hurt, his entire body shaking, her name on his lips.

They stayed like that for a long, lost minute, their foreheads pressed together and their breath slowing in unison, until her arms started to cramp and she lowered her feet to the ground.

He brushed her cheek with his fingers, then bent to retrieve her panties, handing them to her as he pulled his trousers back up.

"How's your arm?"

He shrugged, but the quick smile he gave her warmed her heart just as surely as he'd warmed her entire body moments before. "Hurts like a bitch, but I'll be fine in the morning. Good thing, too. I have to go to New York on Monday and there's a bunch of stuff to organize before that."

"But—I mean, aren't you worried?"

He picked up the half-full glass he'd left on the little table by his chair and drank it off. "Why? Harrel's a good pilot, and—"

"Somebody tried to kill us, Greyson. Aren't you worried about that?" She grabbed one of his T-shirts from his drawer—she didn't have anything else to wear—and yanked it over her head. Exhaustion started sinking into her bones, and the bed had never looked more inviting—almost never, anyway. But although the memory of the car chase and its attendant panic had faded, thinking about it didn't do her nerves any good.

"They weren't trying to kill us, darling. Don't be so dramatic."

"They did a pretty good imitation."

"No." He poured himself another drink, and a shadow crossed his face. "That was just a warning."

"How do you know?"

"Because they were witches. If they'd wanted us dead, we'd probably be dead."

Demon Inside
Chapter Three

"I don't understand."

"There's no way I could have defeated those witches so easily if they'd really wanted to kill us," he said. "Not unless they were just a couple of kids hunting demons for a lark, which we know isn't the case."

"How do we—oh. The jail. They knew I was there."

He nodded. "And they knew I'd come for you. They were too powerful to be kids, too."

"The police said someone called them and told them there was a dead body in that house. Do you think the witches might have called? That they're the ones killing the demons?"

"I don't think so, no. I think our little friends just took advantage of the situation." He emptied his glass again. Worry started creeping up Megan's spine. He looked like he was bracing himself for something, like he was trying to forget. Even with a demon's metabolism, which she knew was pretty good, four Percocet and half a bottle of whiskey couldn't be helping him think faster.

What was bothering him so much?

"Why did they come after us? Why would witches want to ki—warn us?"

"*Me*, not us, if I'm right—and, of course, I am—I'm taking care of it, so don't worry."

If she pressed he would tell her, but now it felt like an invasion of privacy. Which was probably his intent.

"So who is doing it? Killing the demons, I mean?"

He shook his head. "I don't know. Nobody knows."

The chill air swirling around her legs was starting to make her uncomfortable. Greyson kept the room ice-cold, and usually she preferred it that way too because he was so warm all the time. But there was no point standing here shivering. She climbed into bed instead, not realizing until she slid between the heavy silk sheets how hard it was to keep her eyes open. "Rocturnus said they used to be punished this way, with the explosions."

"Did he?"

"Yes. Why?"

"So for the Yezer this is normal?" She could almost see the wheels turning in his head.

"I wouldn't say *normal*, but I guess it's not unheard of. Isn't it the same for the rest of you?"

"Did he say who used to do it? Was it the Accuser, or—"

"Are you going to answer my questions, or what?"

"Only if you answer mine."

"Nooo. Who used to punish them that way?"

"Roc didn't say. Do you all blow up, or what? I mean, should I expect you to explode one of these days?"

"Only if you don't do everything I say, all the time."

Her fist gripped his pillow. His reflexes were a little slower, maybe, from the injury and the chemicals. She might be able to hit him with it if she moved fast enough . . .

His eyes gleamed. Damn it. "Where is Roc, anyway?"

"Checking on the others. I kind of wanted some privacy while I was—"

"Rotting in jail."

She smiled in spite of herself. "You put it so nicely."

He raised an eyebrow, but didn't take the bait. "Do you remember anything else he said?"

"No. Why?"

He glanced at the clock by the bed. "It's past one. You should get some sleep."

"Aren't you coming to bed?"

"Eventually. I have a few things to do first."

She expected him to get up and head back down to his office, but he didn't. He was still sitting in his chair, drinking and watching her, when she drifted off to sleep.

WINGS OF FATIGUE beat behind her eyelids three hours later as they walked into the casino. Her entire body ached. All she wanted to do was go back to bed.

Unfortunately, for reasons she still couldn't seem get straight in her sleep-muddled head, that wasn't possible. Instead she was here, making her way across the floor under scarily white lights and the watchful gazes of at least a dozen demons.

She'd only been to the casino once before, when Greyson was doing some work and called her to meet him for lunch. It had been daytime then, the casino a dark silent room waiting for the crowds.

Now the crowds were here. The floor roared with bells and shouts and the harsh bright rattle of poker chips hitting each other. So much noise in such a small space made her head hurt. She didn't even know how all of these people knew about the place. The demons, yes. But at least half of the shoulders crammed up against the craps and card tables had Yezer Ha-Ra perched on them. It bothered her. She didn't know much about Greyson's various legal enterprises, and even less about the illegal ones, but she'd assumed this one—illegal—was demon-only.

He stopped when she did, and followed her gaze. "You're not the only human who knows demons," he said quietly. "Just the only one who knows what we are."

She tried to smile. "Knew I was special. Where's Gerald?"

He nodded towards the back. "They managed to get him into one of the storerooms. Come on."

His hand in hers was reassuring as he led her through the room, past a roulette wheel and a long, well-lit bar where several pretty young ladies served up drinks. They smiled as Greyson walked past, their big eyes following him. To Megan they gave the barest of nods, not daring to ignore her completely.

Two guards stood outside a nondescript doorway. "Mr. Dante," said the first. "He's inside."

"This is Dr. Chase," Greyson replied. "He asked for her?"

"Yeah, he seemed, I don't know, really off," said the second. Both of them kept their eyes averted, she noticed, and nervously shuffled their feet. "He sounded like he was speaking our language, but . . . not . . ."

"Like some weird dialect," the first added. "Then English again."

Greyson and Megan exchanged glances. One of her clients speaking the demon tongue? She couldn't understand more than a couple of words of it herself. "*Bryaela*," of course, although why anyone but Greyson or John Wayne would call someone "pilgrim" she had no idea. He said it was because she was like a little explorer in a new world, but that wasn't exactly a satisfactory explanation. "*Sheshissma*," she knew, but he only used *that* one when he was feeling particularly amorous.

In fact, now that she thought of it, the only words she knew seemed to be essentially useless outside the bedroom. Maybe he'd agree to give her lessons, or if he wouldn't Rocturnus would.

Speaking of whom, where was he?

"Did he say anything else?" Greyson asked.

The second guard shook his head. "No, sir, he just started crying and asking for Miss Chase. He didn't want to come in here at first, but . . ." he glanced uneasily at Megan. "We, uh, convinced him. He was strong, too."

"Let me in," she said, hating the way he glanced at Greyson and waited for his nod before opening the door. Bad enough she'd managed to get herself involved in this demon underworld of violence and crime. Now innocent people were mixed up in it, people who came to her for help and instead got roughed up in a storeroom.

In a casino—which made no sense. Gerald wasn't a gambler. She'd never read the slightest interest in gaming from him, unless you counted the occasional football pool at his office, and even that was simply him trying to fit in. Which was good because he lost every time.

Still he was a nice man, a good man, and he deserved better than this. A kind, gentle—wait a minute.

"Did you say he was strong? That you had to fight to get him in here?"

The guard nodded. Muscles bulged from every inch of his body. He was like a demon Conan, with a smaller chin. Gerald—the Gerald Megan knew—would have been a snack for him.

She pushed the door open and entered the small, dingy storeroom, half hoping, half expecting to see a stranger in there, someone pretending to be Gerald.

But no, it was Gerald. Cowering in the corner, his bare feet scraped and dirty and a bruise marring his narrow face.

"Megan! Megan!" He scrambled across the floor towards her like a broken-legged crab, his limbs jerking under his clothes. She jumped back. The unnatural movement sent shivers up her spine.

Gerald stopped, glancing up at her. His expression was innocent, fearful, but something in his eyes . . . Megan lowered her shields to read him. Maybe he was on some kind of drug, maybe he'd gotten hold of something . . .

Nothing. No images came, no stray thoughts, no flashes of emotion. Fear chased the last of her sleepiness away. This wasn't right, not at all. She'd always been able to read Gerald, he was a heavy transmitter, and the only times she'd gotten nothing at all from a person was when they weren't actually a person at all, but a demon...

Gerald's eyes glowed. Just for a second, but long enough for Megan to see it. Without thinking she turned the energy she was using to read him into a shield, a weapon, and aimed it at him.

The pressure of the hit reverberated through her entire body, but Gerald only wavered in place. Trying not to let fear overwhelm her, Megan braced herself, certain she was about to be hit back, and hit hard. The place deep inside herself that she saw as a door, the one she'd only opened once before in her life, seemed to throb and glow, wanting her to open it, to reach into it and through it to the personal demons. This is where they connected to her, this was where she knew without thinking that she could harness their power. It would be so easy, so simply to open it up and let the demon inside her take over . . .

But so wrong. So scary. Just the idea of it made her shake. So instead she forced everything she had into shielding herself and ducked down, her knees slamming against the dusty cement floor, the doorjamb against her shoulder.

Screams filled the room, high-pitched squeals of delight that sent shivers up her spine. They reached a crescendo, hurting Megan's ears, making her scrunch herself into a tighter ball, her heart pounding with terror and her entire body braced for the pain she knew was coming any second—but something inside her wanted to scream too, wanted to leap in the air and dance. The desire beat in her chest, so strong and fierce she screamed herself and wrapped her arms around her chest. She couldn't hold on, couldn't keep herself from bursting into flame—

Silence.

Large bodies pushed past her, knocking her into the wall. She was too afraid to open her eyes. Where was Greyson? He didn't usually leave her like this, didn't force her to stand by herself, especially not when she was certain it was obvious that something was very, very wrong with her.

"He's dead." The other guard's voice, the non-Conan one, sounded strangled somehow, confused. "Mr. Dante, he's dead!"

In the space between the male feet crowded around it, she saw one hand on the floor. Gerald's hand, fingers curved up like a dead spider, still and unmoving. The image filled her mind. Even when she closed her eyes it stayed, burned in like a photographic negative, luminous against the blackness of her eyelids. Her client was dead. Her nice, sweet, non-gambling client died on the floor of a storeroom in a demon casino, with his eyes glowing and an unearthly scream—a scream almost like a laugh, she realized now—on his lips, and none of this made any sense and she thought she might faint.

"Get Dr. Chase out of here," she heard Greyson say. "Take her to the car." She wanted to argue but her tongue and lips didn't seem to be under her control. Gerald was dead, and she knew it was her fault. Knew it as surely as she knew her own name, knew it as surely as she knew Greyson wanted her to get in the car not just because he didn't want her to

have to look at that hand on the floor, but because he needed
to get the body out of his casino before anyone noticed it.

SHE WOKE UP with vague, shattered memories still floating
through her mind and the vague bitter taste of pills
Maleficarum gave her when he put her in the car . . . she
and Greyson sleeping squeezed together across the big back
seat . . . Malleus carrying her up to bed. The room was dim
when she opened her eyes, thanks to the heavy blackout
shades on the windows, but there was enough light to see
her stupid cell phone buzzing angrily on the beside table.

She picked it up and fumbled with it, trying to find the
catch to slide it open. Greyson had bought her the damn
thing, and she still couldn't figure out half of the spiffy
tricks it was supposed to perform, much less open it with
a flick of the wrist the way he and the brothers could.

"Hello?" It hurt her throat to talk.

"Hey! I'm running a little late, do you want to meet me
at four instead of three?"

Tera Green sounded chipper and well-rested, the way
she always did, as opposed to Megan who at the moment
probably sounded as wrung out and hungover as she felt.

She pulled the phone away to look at the time. It was
twenty to three in the afternoon. She and Tera had a date to
go shopping and have dinner. She'd totally forgotten.

Rather than admit that, though, she nodded vigorously
until she remembered Tera couldn't see her. "Yeah, of
course," she said, trying to put some enthusiasm in her
voice. "I was just—just getting ready."

"Great. I'll see you at four, then."

Megan echoed the response, although "great" was the
last word she thought it was at the moment, and dragged
herself to a sit.

"Tera?"

He sounded tired, but not as tired as she felt. She looked at him, his hair rumpled with sleep and his eyes still heavy, and nodded. "We're going shopping."

"What fun." He yawned and reached for her, pulling her closer so he could rest his head in her lap. "Why don't you stay here instead? I have some things to do but I'll be free in a few hours."

"And sit by myself in your room all day? No thanks." She didn't move, though. Memories of the night before started coming back; Gerald on the floor, the scream, the pounding in her chest . . . she shivered.

Greyson's arms tightened around her. "It wasn't your fault."

"Yes it was, and you know it. I appreciate your not saying 'I told you so', though." She tried to keep her tone light, but it wasn't working very well.

He paused. "Yes, I worried something like this might happen, but that isn't why I want you to give up your practice. It still isn't why." He sat up and wrapped his arm around her, pulling her down a bit so she could rest her head on his chest. Beneath the smoky scent of his skin she still smelled last night's whiskey, and whatever Spud had put on his wound. She glanced at his arm. The bandage was gone, but a small puckered scar showed where the bullet had penetrated his skin.

"Meg, people die all the time. Would it have been your fault if gentle Gerald's problems had overwhelmed him and he killed himself? If he got hit by a car crossing the street because he was thinking of something you said and forgot to look both ways?"

"A demon possessed him and led him there to die, I think that's a bit dif—"

"No, it isn't different, it's exactly the same. It's too bad the guy's dead if it bothers you, but all of your patients could die and I wouldn't give a damn. The only life I'm interested in saving is yours. And mine, of course."

"Of course." She didn't know if she believed him, didn't know if she really felt less responsible, but the black cloud over her head seemed to lift a little just the same.

"Which is why I want you to take Malleus with you today."

She pulled away. "No, I can't."

"Yes, you can. Tera will just have to deal with it. And don't tell her why."

"She's going to know something's up if she sees him."

"She can think what she wants to think. What did I just say? I want you to stay safe. Malleus can make sure you do."

"I thought they were just after you."

"Call me paranoid."

He looked, sitting on the bed framed by the black satin pillows and sheets, like a medieval king granting favors, but his eyes were tired and serious.

"If I didn't know better I'd think you really cared," she said. It wasn't an unusual joke, or one they'd never made before as they edged carefully around the issue of their feelings, but this time it fell flat. Her face flooded with heat.

He blinked. "Yes, well, I've got you rather a nice Christmas present, I'd hate to see it go to waste." The covers whispered as he shoved them off and got out of bed. "Malleus will be waiting for you when you leave. He brought your car over last night."

"Greyson . . ." But there was nothing to say.

He fastened his pants and came over to her, planting a kiss on her forehead. "I'll try and come by tomorrow night," he said. "I have to leave early Monday, though, so don't wait up."

Without meaning to she reached for him, curling her fingers around his arms, stroking up and down the hard, smooth muscles. Just the feel of him under her palms made her warm.

He kissed her again, on the lips this time, lingering just a moment longer. "Unless you want to cancel out on Tera after all . . ." His hands traveled down her ribs to her waist, where they paused.

She shook her head. Much as she wanted to stay, she was looking forward to going out into the normal world again. As normal as it could be when you were shopping with a witch and had a demon following you, anyway. "She'll be hurt if I cancel."

"Just make sure you have your phone on. And be careful."

He started to move away, but she grabbed him. "What did—what did you do with him?"

"Gerald?"

She nodded.

"Took him back to his place, put him on the bed. Someone will find him."

The cold feeling started creeping back. He sounded so nonchalant, like he moved dead bodies around—or ordered them moved—every day. Which she supposed he might. "Who did this to him? Was it someone from a different Meegra, or . . ."

His knuckles under her chin forced her to look up at him. "We'll figure it out. Meanwhile—"

"I know. Be careful, don't tell Tera anything, and keep Malleus with me."

"See? It's so much better when you just obey me."

He ducked away before she could swat him.